THIS
PASSING
HOUR

Center Point
Large Print

Also by Leslie Gould and available from
Center Point Large Print:

A Faithful Gathering
Piecing It All Together
A Patchwork Past
Threads of Hope
A Brighter Dawn

AMISH MEMORIES
Two

THIS PASSING HOUR

LESLIE GOULD

CENTER POINT LARGE PRINT
THORNDIKE, MAINE

This Center Point Large Print edition
is published in the year 2024 by arrangement with
Bethany House, a division of Baker Publishing Group.

The text of this Large Print edition is unabridged.
In other aspects, this book may vary
from the original edition.
Printed in the United States of America
on permanent paper sourced using
environmentally responsible forcsting methods.
Set in 16-point Times New Roman type

ISBN: 978-1-63808-992-6

The Library of Congress has cataloged this record
under Library of Congress Control Number: 2023946176

To my siblings,
Kathy, Kelvin, and Laurie.
Thank you for your care, love, and friendship
throughout my entire life.

He has made everything beautiful in its time. He has also set eternity in the human heart; yet no one can fathom what God has done from beginning to end.

Ecclesiastes 3:11 NIV

In our changing world nothing changes more than geography.

Pearl S. Buck

1

Brenna Zimmerman

OCTOBER 18, 2017
LANCASTER COUNTY, PENNSYLVANIA

I hated the apartment. The hum of the dishwasher. The smell of the new paint. The scratchy carpet. The straight-back chairs and rickety table in the dining room. My secondhand desk and office chair.

Ivy, my older sister by three years, had convinced me to move out of our Amish grandparents' farmhouse. We didn't have internet on the farm and had to do our coursework at the closest coffee shop, which closed at five. That was a problem for two college students.

I had hoped I was ready to move out.

I wasn't.

"You need to start thinking about more than yourself," Ivy said to me as I stared at my backpack on the table. "It's been over three years."

She didn't say *since Mom and Dad died*. She didn't have to.

"Remember what Chet told us at their service?"

I'd never forget. Chet was the principal of the high school where Dad had taught in Oregon.

9

He'd told my sisters and me, *"I hope, in time, all three of you will follow your parents' footsteps and serve others even more than you already are."* Except I wasn't serving anyone then, unlike my sisters. And I hadn't served anyone since. Also unlike my sisters.

I chomped on my gum.

"You could start by taking Treva to the airport on Friday. That would be a really big help. I can't skip class—and you don't have class. Mammi said you could take off work."

"I hate driving in Philadelphia."

"It's just to the airport. All you have to do is put the address in your phone." Ivy put a hand on her hip. "You're better at geography than any of us."

Just because I have a thing for geography didn't mean I liked driving anywhere near big cities. I didn't like driving at all. I only did it because I had to.

"It's time to step up," Ivy said.

No doubt it was. I grabbed my backpack off the table and slung it over my shoulder. "I need to drop a box of china by the store before class starts." Our paternal grandmother had an antique store where I worked. "Class is from ten to noon. It takes a half hour to get there, but with the stop by the store I need to leave now." It was 8:45. I hated to be late for anything. I started toward the door.

"Brenna!" Ivy stomped after me—or tried to, but she was wearing fuzzy slippers, so her stomps were just little puffs on the carpeted floor. She was five inches shorter than I was, but I always felt as if she towered over me. "Will you take Treva?"

I opened the front door. "I'll think about it." I stepped out into the chilly morning, grateful I'd put tights on under my denim skirt and wore my puffy jacket. I headed toward Mom's van in the parking lot. I'd inherited it when Ivy drove her old clunker Camry out from Oregon the summer before.

I had two goals in life, and serving others, even though it was a foundation of our Mennonite church, wasn't one of them. My goals were to somehow figure out how to create a life for myself and to be a functional adult. I had no expectations of actually being successful at either.

My phone dinged. I stopped at the back of the van and pulled it from the pocket of my jacket. *Johann.* I smiled as I read his message.

At work. I hope your classes go well today!

He was eight hours ahead of us, which would become seven after the time change.

Dyakuyu, I texted back. He was teaching me Ukrainian, which was complicated because it

11

used the Cyrillic alphabet, although one slightly different than Russians used, instead of the Latin alphabet. There was a Ukrainian Latin alphabet, a transliteration. Johann was using that to teach me so I could learn vocabulary and pronunciation. Then we would concentrate on the Cyrillic spellings.

I headed around the side of the van to the driver's door.

"Hey!" a man yelled. "You!"

I opened the door, certain he wasn't talking to me.

"Hey! Girl! With the thing on your head."

Maybe he *was* talking to me. My Mennonite prayer covering might seem like a "thing" to someone who didn't know better.

I stepped to the back of the van and turned toward the voice. It belonged to a man standing next to a pickup. I recognized him. "Rylan Sanders."

He leaned against his cane. "You know my name?"

I nodded, feeling a little creepy. I'd noticed him the first day of class and every class since. He looked the way I'd often felt in the past—anxious. One time the professor accidentally knocked a book off his table, and it made a loud pop as it hit the linoleum floor. I jumped—but Rylan jumped even more. After he realized what had happened, he ducked his head for at least five minutes. I'd also noticed that Rylan was thin and had a noticeable limp. I couldn't help but wonder what happened to his leg. I guessed a car accident or something.

Today, he wore a black down jacket, a beanie over his short hair, and sports pants. "You're in my information security class, right? On Mondays and Wednesdays?"

"Yes. I'm in your Tuesday and Thursday class too. I'm Brenna Zimmerman."

"Got it," he said. "I've noticed you. Probably—" He nodded toward me. "Because of that thing on your head."

"It's a *Kapp*," I said. "A prayer covering."

He shrugged. "So, do you drive that van?"

"Yes."

He gestured toward his pickup with his free hand. "It won't start."

I paused a moment. *Serve others.* Ivy was right. I needed to stop thinking about myself all the time. Here was my chance to help someone else—even though I hated to give people rides. It made me nervous. "I can take you to class, although I only have the one today."

He smiled. "Same."

"Hop in." I winced. That was a stupid thing to say.

"Thank you." He came around the back of the pickup. "I'll get my buddies to look at my truck."

I was relieved to hear that he had buddies. At

least he wasn't without some sort of support. That had made all the difference for me. There were times when my family and community seemed suffocating, but I'd be lost without them.

He turned toward the passenger side of his vehicle and opened the door. Then he leaned his cane against the side and pulled a backpack out of the front seat.

I hit the unlock button on the fob in my hand and started toward the driver's door of the van, taking a few deep breaths. I expected the ride to be awkward—everything I did was awkward. My therapist advised me to embrace the awkwardness and not try to change it. *Just be your awkward self* had become one of my many mantras.

Rylan came around the passenger side of the van, opened the sliding door and swung his backpack onto the floor, and then climbed into the passenger seat, positioning his cane to the right of his legs.

I fastened my seatbelt and turned on the engine. I decided not to go by Mammi's store before class. I'd go after. I didn't want to chance being late.

Before I put the car into drive, I thought through arriving at the college, just as I thought through the details of everything. Every errand. Every class. Every trip. Every workday at Mammi's antique store. Every social event, which were nearly nonexistent.

I would drop Rylan off and then park.

"What are you waiting for?" he asked.

"Your seatbelt."

He didn't move. "Are you a mother or something?"

"Fasten it." I knew what happened when seatbelts *were* fastened. I didn't want to imagine what might happen if one *wasn't*.

"Yes, ma'am." He did as he was told, and I backed out of the space.

Neither of us spoke. After what seemed like an hour but was only a few minutes, I turned west onto Highway 30 and headed toward the city of Lancaster.

Ivy had chosen the apartment in the village of Gap because it was about twenty miles to the community college to the west and fifty miles to her graduate program in Philadelphia to the east. Mammi's store, on Dawdi's farm, was less than ten miles to the northwest.

There was an openness to Lancaster County that I found inspiring. It wasn't like the vast openness of Utah and Wyoming that gave me fits of anxiety on our trip east. That was a sort of gloomy openness. This was an ordered openness of manicured farms and managed spaces. It was different than the foothills of Mount Hood, where I grew up, which were full of gullies and ravines and forests. That was a landscape that was gloomy in its own way with the constant

15

shadows from the trees along the roadways.

Lancaster County was the antidote to that with its patchwork fields. Add the covered bridges, the white rail fences, and the changing leaves of October and the landscape was as much a work of art as an Amish quilt.

Once we were on the highway, Rylan said, "I didn't think Amish people drove."

"I'm Mennonite." I pointed to my head as I kept my eyes on the road and my speed at fifty miles per hour in the fifty-five miles per hour zone. "This is a Mennonite Kapp. The Amish ones are heart shaped." I sometimes wore heart-shaped Kapps at Mammi's store if I was wearing an Amish dress and apron too.

"So Mennonites drive?"

"Most of us do."

"Weird," he said. "Although—" he grinned at me—"you're not as weird as I'd expected."

It seemed he thought I might take it as a compliment. I didn't.

I dropped Rylan off as close to the building as possible.

He climbed out of the van, opened the sliding door, and retrieved his backpack. Then, before closing the door, he said, "I'll save you a seat."

I wished he wouldn't. He'd only prolong my awkwardness.

He slammed the door, stepped to the sidewalk,

16

and then turned and waved. Then he pivoted and started toward the building. I couldn't tell what was wrong with his leg by watching him walk. Perhaps it was a bad break that didn't heal correctly. Or even a bad hip.

When I reached the classroom, Rylan was in his usual place in the middle of the room. He turned, grinned, waved, and then pointed at the chair beside him. My face grew warm, even though it was cold inside. Two girls between Rylan and me turned to see who he was waving at. When they realized it was me, one of them frowned and the other laughed. They both turned around and faced the front of the classroom again.

"Brenna!" Rylan called out. "Down here."

I started toward him, clutching my backpack. He put his hand on the plastic chair next to him as I approached. "Sit here." He grinned.

I froze for a moment. His grin caught me off guard. It seemed so genuine, as if he were truly happy to see me. Not many people were.

I sat down. As I extended my leg, I bumped his foot. "Sorry," I said.

He smiled a little. "I didn't feel it."

My face grew warmer. I wriggled out of my coat, pulled my notebook and textbook from my bag, and then asked Rylan if he was majoring in computer information security.

He nodded. "You?"

"Yes, but I've been taking business classes

too." I paused a moment and said, "I don't remember seeing you last year."

"I finished up a paralegal program a couple of years ago," he said. "Then I started online classes in IS last year. I'll finish this program in the spring."

Two associate degrees. Maybe he could combine them. I was about to ask if he planned to work as a paralegal or just in IS or in both when the instructor arrived, plopped a stack of books and papers on the front table, and then logged into the computer and pulled up his slideshow.

"Good morning." He began the class without any chitchat. He was all business, thankfully.

I took notes. Rylan opened his binder and jotted down the date but didn't write anything else. Maybe he was one of those people who remembered everything. I, on the other hand, had to write everything down—notes were like a map of the class. I'd be lost without them.

When the instructor dismissed us for a fifteen-minute break, I headed down the hall to the restroom. The two girls who'd stared at me earlier peered in the mirror. Both had long, straight hair.

"How do you know Rylan?" the taller one asked.

"I don't." I stepped into the last stall.

When I came out, they were still there.

"I knew him before he went to Afghanistan," the shorter one said. "His girlfriend was friends with my oldest sister."

"Oh." I concentrated on washing my hands. I hadn't thought he might be a soldier—or was. Johann served in the Ukrainian army for eighteen months, and I was grateful every day that he came through it. Johann told me that his fellow Ukrainians were grateful to him for his service, and many went out of their way to show appreciation. Perhaps I could do the same for Rylan.

"It looks like you know him," the other girl said.

I flicked the water from my hands and grabbed a paper towel. "I gave him a ride to class today," I said. "That's all." After I dropped the towel in the garbage can, I spit out my gum and then pushed through the door.

"Not very friendly, is she?" the second girl murmured.

I hesitated a moment but then continued. Gran told me once that what other people thought of me was none of my business, which wasn't really advice I needed.

Ivy always had a bad case of FOMO—fear of missing out. I had a bad case of the opposite—JOMO—joy of missing out. The less I interacted with other people, the better.

After the class ended, I told Rylan I could give him a ride home, but I needed to stop by my grandmother's store first. "Is that all right?" I asked.

"Yeah, that's cool," he said.

"If you need to get home right away, the two girls who are sitting behind us said they know you. They might be able to give you a ride."

He scowled and turned to look at them. "I don't know them."

"The short one said her sister was friends with your girlfriend."

He didn't respond at first. Finally, he said, "I don't remember her. But there's a lot I don't remember."

Ten minutes later, I was driving toward the farm. I slowed for an Amish buggy with several children peering out the back at us. I waved. The children grinned and wildly waved in response.

Rylan laughed and then said, "I get so tired of driving around those buggies."

I didn't answer. I never got tired of seeing Amish families out and about, but my current worst fear was accidentally hitting a buggy. Especially one filled with children. Driving in Amish country was a big responsibility. "Did you grow up in Lancaster County?" I asked Rylan.

"Nah. I grew up in Ohio. But not in Amish country."

"What brought you here?"

"An army buddy." Rylan turned his head and stared out the passenger window for a few minutes, but then he asked, "Why are you always chewing gum?"

I must have been smacking it without realizing it. According to Ivy, I did that a lot. "My mouth gets dry."

"Oh."

I braced myself for more questions, but they didn't come. The antidepressants I took made my mouth dry, but they were worth it. They didn't make me exactly functional, but they did help me to cope with daily life, along with therapy. Although I hadn't gone for the last six months. When I did go, it was to Edenville Behavioral Health, a place that worked with Mennonite and Amish people specifically. Rosene knew about it, and Ivy made my first appointment and drove me the first year we lived in Lancaster County. Soon after that, I got my license and started driving myself.

Rylan and I rode in silence, but I was feeling quite accomplished to be driving a stranger. I was serving someone else. Ivy would be proud.

I turned into the parking lot of Mammi's store, Amish Antiques, built nearly a hundred years ago on the edge of the Zimmerman family farm. It was a wood building with boards that had to be stained every other year and a plank porch that was about a foot off the ground.

"Wait," Rylan said. "You work here?"

I nodded.

"Your grandmother is the Amish lady?"

"Jah." I opened my door as Mammi's buggy

turned into the parking lot. The day had grown warm. I inhaled the earthy scent of hay drying in the field behind the shop. "Stay here. I'll be right back."

"I thought you said you're Mennonite," Rylan said.

"I am. My grandparents are Amish." I gestured toward Mammi and her buggy. "That's my grandmother."

"Weird," he said.

I slammed the door shut and hurried to the back of the van for the china. I picked up the box, balanced it on the back bumper, and pulled the hatch down. As I did, one of the barn cats—a longhaired gray, one of many—slinked around my ankles.

Mammi climbed down from the buggy and tied her horse's reins to the hitching post in front of the shop. "I thought you were going to bring the china earlier."

"I intended to," I said. "Why do you have the buggy?"

"Gabe's van broke down on the way to work, so I needed to make a delivery." Mammi wore her work coat over her cape dress and apron and a black bonnet over her white Kapp. "I'm just dropping off some paperwork before I unhitch the horse." She had a file tucked under her arm.

As she held the door, I followed her into the shop as the collection of clocks all chimed the half hour, feeling as if someone was staring at us. I'm sure Rylan was. And probably the gray cat that had followed me up onto the porch too.

The smell of Mammi's store always calmed me. The wood floor was scrubbed with a special soap that made the whole place smell clean and fresh. She—well, usually me—rubbed the old oak counter with lemon oil every week. Mammi had set up the business like an old-fashioned store, with shelves and drawers behind the counter, quilts on the wall, and a woodstove in the back, surrounded by chairs.

Mammi sold dining room table sets, bureaus and dressers, kerosene lamps and lanterns, old washboards and irons, sets of china and lone dishes, silver and Depression glass, old sewing machines and wringer washers, linens, and quilts. And clocks. Lots of clocks. Cuckoo clocks. Mantel clocks. Grandfather clocks. Mechanical wall clocks. All of them chimed, and the mandate was that they all chimed in unison, which was pretty much impossible to achieve.

A portion of the merchandise came from estate sales and yard sales, although some of the items—including most of the clocks—were new. Each antique that came through the shop was cleaned and refurbished with oil or re-stained or treated or painted however it needed to be. Lots of the people in Lancaster County came to Mammi first with their family items, knowing she'd give the best price possible. Both tourists and locals alike frequented the shop.

Tourists loved it because it was like stepping back in history. Our great-great-grandmother, Monika Kaufman Zimmerman, started the store in the 1920s as a mercantile. She was Mennonite and grew up in Germany. Her oldest daughter, Clare, married an Amishman—Jeremiah Zimmerman—and they inherited the farm and store. Clare ran the store until her daughter-in-law—my Mammi—took it over in the 1970s and turned it into an antique shop. Now, she wanted it to be mine someday. In fact, she was training me to manage it.

I put the box on the counter as Gabe appeared with the feather duster in his hand. He wore trousers, a white shirt, and suspenders. His sandy hair was cut short, but not in a bowl cut. Which gave away that he wasn't really Amish.

Except not to the tourists. Most of them didn't know little details like that. Mammi liked us to dress Plain when we worked in the shop.

Gabe dropped the duster on the counter. "I tried to call you like ten times."

I patted the jacket of my coat for my phone, which I had on silent, and then pulled it out. "Three times," I said. "Not ten."

He rolled his eyes. "I wanted to get the china cleaned up. The customer is stopping by in an hour."

"Well"—I opened the box as I spoke—"you can do it now." Gabe was the younger brother of Ivy's boyfriend, Conrad, which made Gabe like the annoying younger brother I never had. Except he wasn't younger than me. He was two years older. Regardless, he was annoying.

"Who's in the van?" Mammi asked.

"A guy from class." I turned toward the door. "He lives in our apartment building."

Mammi scowled. She'd been absolutely against us getting an apartment. It made no sense to her when there was plenty of room in the farmhouse.

"He's harmless. I'm just helping him out today. That's why I couldn't bring the china earlier." I headed toward the door, and both Mammi and Gabe followed me. As I stepped outside onto the porch, the first thing I noticed was that Rylan wasn't in the van. I looked to my right and then quickly to the left. He was nowhere to be seen.

I yelled, "Rylan? Where are you?"

"Back here." His voice came from behind the building. I jumped off the end of the porch and walked around the side of the building. Mammi and Gabe didn't follow. I guessed they were headed through the store to the back door.

There was a rickety staircase in the back that led to an upper storeroom, where the view of the farm and the surrounding land was fantastic. Several years ago, according to Mammi, a young couple had climbed past the *Do Not Enter* sign and were sitting on the stairs, taking selfies. When Mammi came out the back door, they'd asked her to take a photo of the two of them on the woman's phone. I could only imagine what Mammi said in response.

After that, Dawdi made a bigger sign that read *Private! Do Not Enter!* and bought a bright yellow rope as a barricade. Recently, even though the staircase was roped off, Dawdi realized it had deteriorated more and had ordered lumber to repair it. But it hadn't been delivered yet.

"Rylan?" I called out as I rounded the corner. As I feared, he stood on the first landing of the staircase, about five feet off the ground. The rope was on the ground, and I didn't see the sign anywhere. The gray cat sat on the bottom step.

He turned toward me and leaned his back against the railing as Mammi and Gabe came out the back door.

"Get down!" Mammi barked.

Rylan leaned back some more, probably to get a better view of Gabe, who stood behind Mammi. "Gabe? Gabe Johnson? Why are you wearing those clothes?"

It all happened in slow motion. Rylan put more of his weight against the railing as he tried to stand up straight, turning as he did. But then he fell forward, into the wooden railing, and it snapped in two. As he fell over the edge, his arms flailed and his cane flew. I froze. The cat ran.

He hit the ground with a thud. For a moment, all was silent.

But then a spine-chilling scream brought me to my senses.

2

As I ran around the back porch, I heard Gabe ask, "Is that Rylan Sanders?"

I ignored him as I kneeled beside Rylan. "Are you hurt?"

Rylan rolled from side to side, hugging his arms and gritting his teeth. "I think I broke my leg."

I gasped. There was a gap in the leg of his sports pants—the bottom half of his bad leg wasn't connected to the top. Something was horribly wrong. I yelled, "Gabe, call 9-1-1!"

Rylan grimaced. "I broke my right leg. My prosthesis fell off my stump."

"Oh." I inched forward. "How do you know you broke your right leg?"

"I landed on it. I heard it crack."

I winced and took off my coat and put it on top of Rylan.

"What are you doing?"

"You might go into shock."

He swiped at his sweaty forehead with his hand.

I could hear Gabe on the phone, giving the 9-1-1 dispatcher the address of the shop.

"Pull my prosthesis out of my pants leg, would you?" Rylan asked. "And then knot the bottom of my pants." Noticing my cringe, he said, "Just grab my shoe and pull. It will come out."

I did as he said, tugging on his running shoe. Then I stood and pulled slowly. The prosthetic was sleek and made of a metal rod and a plastic foot inside the shoe.

"Put it on the porch." Rylan spoke with his teeth clenched. "Hitting the ground probably messed it up—I'll need to get it adjusted. Hopefully, I won't need a new one."

I looked around for his cane, grabbed it, stepped up on the porch, and then leaned both the cane and the artificial leg against the building.

"It won't take the firefighters long," Gabe said. "The firehouse is only a mile from here."

Mammi stood by the back door. She hadn't moved.

"What more can we do?" I asked her.

"I don't think anything," she answered. "We shouldn't move him. Go back down and stay beside him. I'm needed in the store—there's a customer in the back looking at a couple of chairs."

I wrinkled my nose. "Can't Gabe help with that?"

Mammi shook her head. "I want him to stay out here with his phone." She patted my arm. "You're handling this well. You'll be fine." She gave me a nudge. "Go."

I followed her directions, and Gabe followed me. We both kneeled beside Rylan.

"Hey, Rylan. It *is* me. Gabe Johnson."

Rylan spoke softly. "No one told me you're Amish."

"I'm not."

"He's Mennonite," I said. "Like me."

"To clarify—" Gabe stood—"I was raised Mennonite."

I turned toward Gabe. He went to the same Mennonite church I did.

He kept his eyes on Rylan. "I work for Priscilla Zimmerman is all."

Rylan lifted his head a little. "Who?"

"Brenna's grandmother. She owns the place."

His face tensed up even more as he said, "Oh."

I could hear a siren, which was steadily growing louder. "The firefighters are here." I stood too.

Rylan turned his head.

"Go tell them we're back here," I said to Gabe as my younger sister, Treva, came running into the backyard of the store. Yesterday, she wore jeans and a sweatshirt. Today, she wore an Amish dress, apron, and Kapp.

"What's going on?" she asked with panic in her voice.

I nodded toward Rylan. "He fell from the staircase and hurt his leg."

"Is he a customer?"

Rylan clenched his teeth and shook his head.

Treva gave me a questioning look.

"He's in one of my classes. And lives in our apartment complex."

Dawdi arrived next. I explained again what happened.

"Where's Priscilla?" Dawdi asked.

"In the store," I answered. "With a customer."

He headed toward the front door. "She needs to be out here."

Gabe, who hadn't done what I asked, followed him and said over his shoulder, "I'll see if I can cover for her."

"No!" I shouted at Gabe. "Go tell the fire-fighters where we are and then come back and stay with Rylan."

Gabe turned around.

Anxiety rose in me. "Please."

"Take a deep breath," Treva said. "It's going to be okay."

I turned toward her. "I'm fine." I wasn't. "But Gabe knows Rylan. I only met him today."

Treva glanced up at Gabe. "I'll go in the shop."

Gabe left and then returned with two fire-fighters, a woman and a man, each carrying a bag.

"Can you tell us what happened?" the woman asked.

"This is Rylan Sanders. He fell off the landing of the staircase." I gestured above us. "And broke his leg."

"Whose prosthesis?" she asked, pointing to where it was propped up against the porch.

"Mine," Rylan said. "I broke my right leg."

"Let's take a look." One firefighter kneeled beside him and began his assessment while the other firefighter stepped away and spoke into her radio.

I took a step backward and began to cry.

"Don't cry, Brenna," Rylan said. "I've been through worse."

No doubt he had. And so had I. But that didn't make any of it easier.

Mammi came out of the shop with Dawdi, saying, "He's the one who went up the back staircase. He must have untied the rope. Who knows what happened to the sign."

Dawdi, his voice low, said, "We need to make sure he's all right—and do all we can to help." As he closed the back door to the store, all of the clocks chimed. It was one o'clock.

A broken leg could be fixed—at least I hoped it could.

The female firefighter said, "An ambulance is on the way."

"I figured," Rylan said. "Hey, Gabe?"

"I'm right here." Gabe stepped forward.

"Could you text Marko and Viktor and let them know I'm headed to the hospital? They were going to fix my truck this afternoon."

"Sure." Gabe took his phone out of his pocket and began texting.

The wail of an ambulance grew closer. The

woman firefighter headed back toward the parking lot.

I surprised myself by asking Rylan, "What can I do to help?"

"Come to the hospital. Bring my prosthesis." Rylan winced and paused. Then he continued, "The last time I fell, it took me forever to recover it."

I took a deep breath and nodded.

"Bring my cane too."

I took a step toward the porch.

"They'll take him to Lancaster General," the male firefighter said, unwrapping a blood pressure cuff from Rylan's arm. "Go to the emergency department."

I looked around, wondering who would go with me. Gabe? My eyes met his, and he shook his head. "I need to take care of the box of china."

I looked around for Treva, but she was still in the store. Mammi and Dawdi wouldn't go with me. I already knew that.

Where was Rosene, our great-great aunt? She was the most empathetic of the adults in my life. Well, Gran was pretty empathetic, but she was back in Oregon. "Where's Rosene?" I asked Dawdi.

"Resting. She didn't sleep well last night." Noticing my alarm, he added. "She's just tired. That happens at her age."

I couldn't bear the thought of losing another

33

family member. Rosene was ninety-one, so it was inevitable that she would pass away sometime. But not soon. At least I hoped not. Her sister in Germany was 101 and still lived in her own house.

The EMTs followed the woman firefighter around the side of the building, hauling a stretcher behind them.

"I'll tell Marko and Viktor to go to the hospital. Just stay until they get there," Gabe said. "You can do this. I'll come as soon as I can."

"Hang the rope," I told Gabe as I glanced at the back door. "So no one else goes up there." The *Private* sign still hung on the door. Maybe the *Do Not Enter* sign had been down for days. Or weeks. Maybe even months. I hadn't noticed. "And see if you can find the sign and put it back too."

I grabbed Rylan's prosthesis and cane and then my coat. After the EMTs transferred him to the stretcher, I headed to the van. I put the leg in the back, climbed into the driver's seat, and put Lancaster General into the navigation app on my phone. Nine miles; twenty-one minutes. I followed the ambulance as it turned west on the highway, toward Lancaster—back the way we'd just come.

I hit start on my phone in case I couldn't keep up with the ambulance, even though it didn't have its lights on, nor was it speeding.

My phone dinged. A text from Treva.

> Why didn't you wait for me? I wanted to
> go with you.

I wouldn't answer her, of course, until I parked the van.

Five minutes later, as we neared the outskirts of Lancaster, my phone dinged again. A text from Ivy.

> Treva called me. What's going on????
> Who is this guy? Do you want me to meet
> you at the hospital? I'm on my way home
> from class.

I'd text her back later too. I kept driving, keeping a good distance behind the ambulance, but not too far. I'd been to Lancaster General over two years ago when I had a panic attack, around the anniversary of Mom and Dad's death. It was the third time I'd had to go to the ER with a panic attack. I'd had a few since but not as bad.

I parked, climbed down from the driver's seat, and then grabbed Rylan's artificial leg but left his cane. I clicked the lock button on the fob and then carefully put it in my purse. When I was anxious, I tended to misplace things. I also tended to rub the scar on my forehead.

I was trying to be more mindful of my actions.

I followed the *Emergency* signs, clutching Rylan's leg with one hand and rubbing the scar on my forehead with the other as I chomped on my gum.

An ambulance took me to the hospital the night our parents died. I was driving. Having no memory of the accident, I thought for months that I'd killed our parents, until Ivy figured out that her ex-boyfriend's cousin had rear-ended us, causing the rollover. To make it worse, her ex-boyfriend, Alec, had helped cover up the accident by hiding the pickup his cousin had been driving. The cousin and Alec ended up pleading guilty to a couple of different charges. Because the cousin was a minor, he served some time in detention, and then they both were put on probation and had to do community service. Ivy and Gran had attended the sentencing for the two, but I had no desire to go.

Even after my memories had started to come back, I did my best not to remember that night. I didn't want to think about it now.

I kept walking.

A few minutes later, I entered the emergency department. Glancing to the left and then the right, I saw Rylan coming in on the stretcher.

"That was fast," he said to me. "You drive so slow, I thought it would take you longer."

"Ha ha." I held the sleeve of my free arm up to my nose. I hated the smell of hospitals. And the sounds. And the sights. I hated everything about hospitals. My scar began to burn, though I knew it was purely psychosomatic. The wound had healed over three years ago.

"Just kidding." He lowered his voice. "Thank you for coming. I really appreciate it."

"You're welcome." It was the least I could do. He'd fallen from the staircase of my grandmother's store. "How's your pain?"

"Better. They gave me something in the ambulance."

"Is there anyone you want me to call?"

"No," he said. "Gabe let the guys know."

"What about your family?"

He shrugged. "I'll let them know sooner or later."

I wanted to ask him what that meant but didn't. I held up his prosthesis. "Do you want me to put this beside you?"

He shook his head. "Last time I was in the hospital, they lost it, and it took a week to locate it. Hold on to it, would you?"

"Okay." I gripped it a little tighter. "Your backpack is in my van."

"Could you bring it to me before you leave? My phone charger is in there." He patted his side. "But I have my ID and phone in my pocket."

A nurse approached Rylan. "We're going to take you into a room." She turned toward me. "Are you with the patient?"

"Yes," I answered.

"Whose prosthesis?"

"His."

She turned toward him. "Worst of luck, huh?"

He nodded, smiled, and rolled his eyes all at the same time. "I had a transfemoral amputation. Afghanistan."

"Bummer," the nurse said to him. Then she said, "Come along," to me and nodded to the EMTs. They helped her transfer Rylan to the hospital bed, and then left with the stretcher.

The nurse took Rylan's vitals. Then she said, "I'll be back in a few minutes."

I sat down in the chair next to the bed, not sure what to do.

"How much do you think a leg weighs—a real one?" Rylan asked.

"Hmm." What percentage of a body's weight was in a head, a torso, each leg, and each arm? If a man weighed two hundred pounds, how much would his leg weigh? "I'm going to guess twenty pounds."

"Nope." He winced. "Less than ten pounds. That's all. For three-quarters of my leg." He reached down and rubbed his stump through his pants. "My leg always hurts—phantom pains."

I'd read about phantom pains and how our brains hold maps of our bodies. When we lose a limb, our brains don't know to delete the missing part. I wondered if it worked the same way for missing loved ones—our brains couldn't fathom erasing them, so we continued to feel them and grieve for them. I still had physical pain from losing Mom and Dad.

"It really hurts when the prosthesis pops off like that." He winced. "Now, for once, my other leg hurts more." He shifted a little. "You know how amputees play basketball and run marathons and climb mountains?"

I nodded, wondering what he was getting at.

"Even though there are wounded warriors who want to summit Mount Everest, I don't," he said. "None of that is me. I was a good soldier, but I didn't do any of that other stuff before I lost my leg. I don't want to do it now."

"There's probably a lot more veterans like you than—"

He cut me off. "Did you know amputees are more likely to die at an earlier age?"

"No."

"There are all sorts of factors that lead into that. Psychological stuff—depression and anxiety."

I was a pro when it came to psychological stuff, but before I could say anything, he continued.

"Then there are the infections. Problems with the prosthesis. The falls due to balance and stability issues. Like today. And I'm more at risk for cardiac events and for deep vein thrombosis." He turned his gaze on me. "There's also a need for more calories because it takes more energy to get around with one leg than two. And right now I'm starving."

"I don't know if they'll let you eat anything now, but I can get you something for later." I stood, glad for an excuse to get out of the room. "What do you want?"

"A turkey sandwich. A sports drink. That sort of thing." He took his wallet from the pocket of his jacket.

"I'll get it," I said.

"I'll pay you back."

After putting the prosthesis in the chair, I said, "I promise I'll come back for it. I'll trade you a sandwich for a leg."

He laughed, despite his pain. "Absolutely."

"I'll get your backpack from the van too."

I did that first, slinging his backpack over my shoulder and then returning to the hospital.

It took me a while to find the cafeteria. As I stood in line to get the sandwich, I quickly texted both Treva and Ivy the same message.

I'm fine. Rylan is waiting to see a doctor.
I'll let you know if I need anything.

Once I had the sandwich and sports drink, I headed back to the emergency department, munching on a protein bar. When I neared Rylan's room, I heard voices. I expected it was the nurse or hopefully a doctor. I stopped at the door, realizing someone was speaking Ukrainian. I was horrible at speaking it, but I was pretty

40

good at comprehending it, thanks to Johann's help.

There were two male voices. One said in Ukrainian, "I can't believe this happened to him."

A deeper one said, "I hope it doesn't set him back again."

The first voice asked, "Do you think he still doesn't know what happened in Afghanistan?" *Afghanistan* was pronounced the way someone speaking English would pronounce it.

"Nah."

My free hand went to my scar, but I caught myself and forced it back down to my side.

"We should have been honest with him," the deeper voice said, still in Ukrainian. "I hate that we've been lying all this time." Thankfully the vocabulary they used was basic and familiar to me.

"Viktor, we haven't lied."

The deeper voice grew soft. "Maybe so, but we haven't told the truth either."

3

I kept walking to the end of the hall, aware I was chomping my gum. I dreaded going back into the room, but I knew I had to. I returned, pretending as if I'd just arrived. I said, "Knock, knock," as I pushed the door open slowly. I smiled at the two men just beyond the door as I stepped inside and then glanced at the bed. Or glanced where it should have been. It wasn't there. Both Rylan and the bed were gone.

"Where is he?" I asked.

"Who are you?" the shorter man with the deep voice demanded.

"Brenna. I know Rylan from school." I smiled again. "I'm guessing you two are Marko and Viktor."

"That's right." The one with the deeper voice again—he was stout with dark hair and brown eyes. He tapped on his chest. "I'm Viktor." He pointed to the other man. "This is Marko."

I smiled again, first at Viktor and then Marko, who was probably close to six feet tall, with a broad chest, sandy hair, and brown eyes. Both were dressed in jeans, blue denim work shirts, and sturdy boots.

"Where's Rylan?" I asked.

Marko answered, "Getting an X-ray."

42

I put the food on the table and then slipped out of Rylan's backpack and put it on the floor. Next, I picked up the artificial leg from the chair and leaned it against the wall. "One of you can sit."

"Oh no," Marko said. "You must sit."

Both men spoke with slight accents, but not as much of an accent as Johann, though he really didn't have much of one either.

I shrugged and sat down. "How do you know Rylan?"

Viktor said, "We served together in the Army Reserve."

Marko nodded. "Now we stick together. We'd do anything for him."

Except tell him the truth apparently, I thought. I internally chided myself. Whatever that was about, it wasn't my business.

Johann had told me how quickly the soldiers he served with became like brothers and sisters. He said he had to trust them—they were all that stood between him and death.

"Do you still serve?" I asked.

"Yes," Marko said. "But we are still close to Rylan. We even moved into the same apartment complex as him."

"Oh," I said. "My sister and I live in the building next to his."

"Then we're neighbors." Marko grinned. "We live in the last building, on the west side of the complex."

That explained why I'd never seen them. Then again, I'd never seen Rylan, and we actually were neighbors.

I wondered if I could leave now that Rylan's buddies had arrived, but the thought of Gabe arriving made me stay. He had Marko and Viktor's numbers. What was his connection to them? And Rylan?

"Do the two of you want sandwiches?" I asked. "I can go get you some."

"I'm hungry," Marko said.

Viktor nudged him. "We can get our own food. Brenna doesn't need to wait on us." He stepped toward the door. "If Rylan returns before we get back, tell him we won't be long."

"Will do." After they left, I leaned my head back against the wall and closed my eyes, thinking through the rest of my week to try to distract myself.

I worked in the morning and then had class tomorrow afternoon. On Friday, it seemed I'd be driving Treva to the airport in Philadelphia. She had graduated from high school a year ago, took a year off to help Dawdi on the farm, and was now going back to Oregon to help Gran with our Christmas tree farm. They had just over a month to get everything ready for the you-cut sales that started the day after Thanksgiving. The workers who cut the trees for shipping would arrive soon.

Gran, our maternal grandmother, was in remission from cancer. She'd spent two of the last three years living in Dawdi and Mammi's *Dawdi Haus* behind the farmhouse while friends ran the Christmas tree farm. A year ago, she moved back to Oregon.

Ivy and I would join Gran and Treva for Christmas, and then Treva would return to Lancaster County and start taking classes at the community college.

I wasn't thrilled about going back to Oregon. Somehow I'd avoided it for the last three years, but I couldn't figure out how to get out of Christmas.

"Wake up, Brenna, wake up!" Rylan's voice startled me.

I opened my eyes, and he grinned. His pain meds must have really kicked in. I sat up straight as a hospital worker wheeled his bed into place. "I brought you a sandwich." I pointed to the table.

"Thank you." Once the bed was secured, he said, "I'll wait to eat it until I talk with the doctor."

A couple of minutes later, Viktor and Marko returned with their sandwiches. Rylan started to introduce us, but Viktor said, "We already met Brenna."

"Did she tell you she knows Gabe?" Rylan asked.

"We go to church together," I explained.

Viktor cocked his head. "Gabe's Amish?"'

"Mennonite." I rubbed the scar on my forehead.

A doctor stepped into the room, putting an end to the conversation. After introducing herself as Dr. Reeves, she said, "It's a bad break, and we may have to put in a plate. We can't do the surgery until the morning, though."

"Should I get transferred to the VA hospital?" Rylan asked. "That's where I've had all of my other surgeries." He patted the upper thigh of his left leg.

"Is your medical insurance through the VA?"

"Yes, ma'am."

"I don't see any reason to move you," she said. "But I'll have someone give them a call. In the meantime, transportation will move you to a room upstairs."

After she left, Rylan ate his sandwich. A few minutes later, transportation showed up. I put on Rylan's backpack and then tried to put his prosthesis on the bed, but he scolded me. "I told you to carry it." I kept the fake leg in my arms as I trailed behind Marko and Viktor.

When we reached the room, I propped the artificial leg against the wall and motioned for Marko and Viktor to sit down. "I should get going," I said, unsure of how much longer it would be until Gabe arrived.

"We should exchange phone numbers," Rylan

said. "You're the only way I'm going to pass my classes."

That was fair enough. I stepped closer to him. "What's your number?" He rattled it off. I saved his and then sent a message to his number so he'd have mine too.

As I turned toward the door to leave, Gabe stepped into the room. He wore jeans and a black hoodie.

"There he is," Viktor said. "The mystery man. You never told us you go to a Mennonite church."

Gabe's face grew red.

Rylan chuckled. "Where's your Amish outfit?"

Marko turned toward me. "I thought you said he was Mennonite."

"He is," I answered. *Or was.* "He works for my grandmother. She's Amish." Without telling Gabe hello, I asked him, "How do you all know one another?"

"Gabe joined our unit a few months ago," Marko said. "He's the new guy. We're not sure if he'll make it or not. I'm thinking he will, but—"

Viktor cut him off. "I know he won't."

Gabe just shrugged and smiled.

"Unit? What's that?"

"Army Reserve unit." Viktor faked a backhand to the side of Gabe's head. "Shouldn't Brenna know that already?"

No doubt Gabe didn't want Mammi to know. I couldn't blame him.

Viktor shook his head. "Are you ashamed of us? You won't make it as one of our brothers if you are."

I didn't understand boys. Men. Whatever they were. Their banter made no sense to me. I could never tell when they were being serious or joking.

Johann served with some of the same soldiers for a year and a half, and yet he didn't know what they did in their civilian lives. Were they students? CEOs? Teachers? Retail workers? Computer programmers? *"We don't talk about that stuff,"* he'd say when I asked.

What did they talk about?

As Gabe tried to think of how to respond—at least that's what I thought he was doing—I said again, "Well, I'd better get going." I tried to keep my tone chill. I didn't want to sound as if I was trying to run away. But the truth was, I'd reached my limit of being around people, in addition to being in a hospital. I turned to Rylan. "Text me if you need anything. If I don't hear from you, I'll text you tomorrow."

A forlorn expression settled on his face. "Are you sure you need to go?"

I nodded. "Do you want me to let our professors know you're in the hospital?"

"Would you do that?" he asked.

"Sure, and I'll let you know what the assignment is from tomorrow's class."

He pointed to the end of the bed. "Would you

hand me my jacket?" When I did, he unzipped a pocket and pulled out his wallet and set of keys. He took an insurance card and his license from the wallet. "Would you lock my wallet in my apartment and hold onto the keys?" He gestured toward his backpack. "Would you get my charger out and then take my backpack too? Put the wallet in the front pocket. And don't forget my prosthesis."

I wrinkled my nose as I looked around at the others. First Viktor and Marko shrugged. And then Gabe. I asked Rylan, "Are you sure you don't want one of your buddies to take your stuff and hold onto your keys?"

"Positive," he said.

Viktor asked, "What about your truck?"

Rylan took another set of keys from his jacket pocket and dangled them. "Here you go, Viktor and Marko. She's all yours." He tossed the keys and Marko caught them. "I think it's probably just the battery. If you could take care of it, that would be great. The sooner the better—although who knows when I'll be able to drive again."

"We'll take care of it," Viktor said.

Rylan raised his bed. Then he said, "Can someone stick around for a while?"

"I can," Gabe said. "I'll just go get something to eat and then I'll be right back." He turned toward me. "I'll walk you out." I was pretty sure that was code for *I need to tell you something.*

I picked up Rylan's backpack, took out his charger and handed it to him, and then put the wallet inside. Then I picked up his prosthesis and gave him a wave. "I'll be in touch."

"Thank you for everything," he said, as polite as could be.

I nodded in acknowledgement and said, "You're welcome." To Marko and Viktor, I said, "Nice to meet you."

"You too," they said in unison.

As Gabe and I left, Marko said, "She seems really nice" as Viktor said, "I hope she and Gabe aren't going out."

I pretended, for Gabe's sake, that I hadn't over-heard either comment. "So, you joined the Army Reserve?" I asked as we neared the elevator.

"About that . . ."

The elevator doors opened, and we stepped inside.

When he didn't say any more, I said, "What about that?"

He shrugged.

"Does Mammi know?"

"I'll tell her."

"Does Conrad know?"

"Not yet."

"Does your mother know?"

He didn't answer. Obviously she didn't. The elevator door opened. He followed me until I stopped in the middle of the lobby.

I shook my head. "I'm not going to keep your secret."

He shrugged again. "I don't expect you to."

"Why did you do it?"

"The GI Bill. I want to finish my education."

"I didn't know you'd even started."

"Not everyone has a trust fund."

"Ouch," I said. Was that how he saw me and my sisters? As trust fund babies? Hardly. Our parents made sure we'd be provided for if they died, but we were hardly wealthy. We had help with tuition and living expenses—that was all.

"You can say whatever you want to whoever you want." He was bluffing. I was the least gossipy person either one of us knew.

"Did you find the *Do Not Enter* sign?"

"No," he said. "I looked all around—under the staircase too."

"See you around," I said. "Like tomorrow morning."

"See you then." He turned, waved, and headed in the direction of the cafeteria.

Joining the military as a Mennonite was a big deal, which was probably why Gabe hadn't told anyone. Everyone would be shocked and concerned for the well-being of his soul. We followed the principal of nonresistance, of Jesus commanding us to love our enemies and overcome evil with good. Joining the military definitely went against those teachings. We weren't to fight against the evils in society. We were to pray for earthly authorities and submit to them when possible, but only if we could do so without disobeying God. Our obedience to God must come first.

As I walked out the front doors of the hospital into the bright sunshine, I squinted and traced my finger over my scar. It was just after three. I didn't want to go back to the apartment, so I decided to stop by the farm. A check-in with Rosene to make sure she was okay was what I needed.

I parked in my usual place by the shed, turned off the engine, and then sat and gripped the steering wheel. I didn't like living in the apartment, but I didn't plan to become Amish.

However, Mammi did want me to take over her antique store in a few years. Maybe I could remodel the storeroom, where the outside staircase led, into an apartment. Taking over the store at least gave me some direction in life.

I became conscious that I was rubbing my scar again. I thought leaving the hospital would alleviate my stress—obviously it hadn't.

I opened the door of the van and climbed down. Then I zipped my coat and started toward the house. I hoped Rosene would be awake. She was calm and empathetic and never made me feel as if I wasn't living up to the ideals of my parents, my sisters, Mammi, and sometimes Dawdi too.

I knew I was different. It seemed perhaps Rosene, who had lived in Germany for the first twelve years of her life and was then adopted by my great-great-grandparents and then nurtured by my great-grandparents, could relate to feeling different. She'd felt that way herself.

As I approached the back door of the house, Rosene, who was not even five feet tall, stepped out onto the porch and tossed a pan of water into the herb garden to the left. As she turned, my presence startled her.

Her free hand flew to her chest. "Brenna, what a surprise. I heard you had some excitement earlier today."

"I did."

"How were things at the hospital?"

"Rylan needs surgery—he'll have it tomorrow."

Rosene clucked her tongue. "Poor thing. That was good of you to help him."

"It's the least I could do. Where is everyone?" I hoped no one was in the house.

"Treva and Arden are milking. Your Mammi is making chocolate chip cookies for your friend."

Confused, I asked, "Who's running the store? Gabe's at the hospital."

"Priscilla closed it early." Rosene lowered her voice. "She's upset by what happened."

"She didn't seem upset. . . ."

Rosene tilted her head toward the door. "She is now. Come on in. She just took the first batch out of the oven."

As I followed Rosene up the steps, I asked, "How are you feeling? Dawdi said you were resting earlier this afternoon."

She smiled. "I rest some most days. Remember, I am ninety-one."

I wished I could forget.

Mammi paused in the middle of placing a spoonful of dough onto a cookie sheet when she saw me. "How is he?"

"He's having surgery tomorrow."

"Goodness," she said. "Is his leg that bad?" Mammi sometimes seemed to think modern doctors exaggerated medical problems.

I answered, "I don't think they would do surgery if it wasn't bad."

She turned her attention back to her cookie sheet.

Rosene poured me a cup of coffee and then put two warm cookies on a plate. "Sit down," she said.

I spit my gum in the garbage and turned toward the table as the back door flew open. I expected Treva, but it was Ivy, followed by Conrad and then Gabe.

I took a bite of the cookie to suppress groaning out loud, wishing instead I'd gone back to the apartment.

"Why didn't you answer my text?" Ivy asked without saying hello.

"I did."

"No, you didn't. Check your phone."

It was in my coat pocket on the back porch. "I believe you," I said. "I must have missed it."

"*It?* I texted you five times. I was starting to get really worried until I texted Gabe and he said you'd left the hospital. When you didn't come home, I figured you were here."

"I came here for some peace and quiet," I said. "Why are you here?"

Mammi said, "Now, girls, no need to bicker."

We weren't bickering. But I didn't say that.

Ivy ignored her too. "I came to find you. Gabe said Rylan is hurt badly. And he's upset."

I answered, "He didn't seem too upset to me."

"That's because he was being nice around you," Gabe said. "Because you helped him. He ordered me to leave once I returned to his room—after he said he was thinking about suing."

Mammi gasped. "What?"

"Jah," Gabe said. "Suing the store. He's a paralegal and used to work for a law firm in Lancaster. He knows about this stuff."

"Oh, that's ridiculous," Mammi said. "He's the one who trespassed up the staircase."

A staircase with a rickety railing. I kept my mouth shut.

Ivy poured a cup of coffee for Conrad and then

poured one for herself. "People say that sort of thing lots of times and never do."

Rosene poured coffee for Gabe and then put cookies on a plate and put them on the table. Everyone sat down.

"We shouldn't think about whether or not he'll sue, not now." Ivy picked up a cookie. "We should think about how we can help him." She looked from me to Gabe and back to me. "What does he need?"

"I'm baking these cookies for him." Mammi stared at the plate on the table. "And we can fix meals for him when he's out of the hospital."

"Good," Ivy said. "What about you, Brenna?"

I shrugged. "I already told him I'd tell our professors about the accident, get his assignments, and help him with our coursework. I can probably give him rides." I thought that was plenty, especially for me.

Ivy smiled. "Good." I hated when she got this way—Miss Social Worker with a take-charge, let's-solve-this-problem-together attitude. She turned toward Gabe. "What do you think Rylan needs?"

"A family."

"What do you mean?"

"According to Viktor and Marko—"

Ivy blinked and shook her head at the same time. "Who?"

"Marko and Viktor. Friends of his."

I added, "They're Ukrainian."

"That's odd," Ivy said.

I rolled my eyes. People were who they were.

"Yeah, a family," Gabe repeated. "According to the guys, he doesn't have one. No one came when he was in the hospital before, after he was injured in Afghanistan."

"What do you mean?" Ivy asked.

"He was in the Army Reserve," Gabe said. "He got most of his left leg blown off. No one in his family came to see him when he was in the hospital."

Ivy's eyes got all big and buggy. "You're kidding."

"About what?" Gabe asked. "That he was in the Army Reserve? Or the bit about his family not coming?"

"Both," she said.

I looked between Gabe and Ivy. Was no one going to ask how Gabe knew all about Rylan's Army Reserve service?

"No," Gabe said, "I'm not kidding about either. But the point is, the guys don't think his family will show up this time either."

"We're a family."

I turned. Treva had come into the kitchen without my hearing her and stood behind me.

"We *are* a family," Ivy said.

I folded my arms and put my head down on the table, feeling like the Eeyore of the family.

We weren't Rylan's family, and to make it even worse, we were an Amish/Mennonite family. I doubted he'd want us to take him under our wing. Probably what he wanted most was for us to stay out of his way.

4

Half an hour later, I managed to slip away with a box of cookies for Rylan, saying I had homework to finish for the next day. But mostly I just needed to be by myself.

Rosene said, "I'll walk you out." She grabbed her coat from a peg on the back porch, which meant she planned to walk me all the way to the van.

"Sorry you didn't find any peace and quiet today," she said. "Can you come by tomorrow?"

"I'll try," I said.

"I have a story to tell you."

I brightened for the first time all day. I loved Rosene's stories. "What's it about?"

"Soldiers here on the farm during World War Two."

"Here?"

She nodded.

"Why were there soldiers here?"

"I'll tell you tomorrow," she said as we reached the van. "I have a scrapbook from that time to show you too. I made it, but it helps tell the story of your great-great-aunt Martha Simons."

"Clare's and your sister, right? I asked about her when you finished Clare's story, and you said you'd tell me about her someday."

"I remember. It's time I tell you Martha's story." Rosene patted my shoulder. "You remind me of her."

I sighed. "Does that mean it's a downer?"

"Not at all," Rosene said. "It does have sad parts, but Martha was a remarkable young woman. It was a difficult time. Her father was ill, there was a labor shortage, and the farm was threatened."

I wrinkled my nose. "Are you worried about what will happen if Rylan sues? Is that what made you think of this story?"

Rosene hesitated. "I thought of the story because of Rylan being a soldier—and a traumatized one, at that. But you're right. That could be another parallel story." She hesitated again and then said, "However, there's no need to borrow trouble. How about if we make a few freezer meals for Rylan while I tell the story tomorrow? And then maybe you can help Treva pack for Oregon."

I crossed my arms. "I'm horrible at packing."

She patted my shoulder again. "I know. But Treva needs help, and it's out of my area of expertise."

"Mine too." I liked organizing ideas, not stuff. Especially not someone else's stuff.

After I told Rosene good-bye, I slowly headed back to the apartment. The driver of a truck behind me honked, and then as he passed, he made some sort of gesture. I wasn't quite sure what and didn't care. I slowed down even more.

When I reached the parking lot of the apartment, the hood of Rylan's truck was up. I parked in my spot and climbed down. Both Marko and Viktor were bent over the engine, speaking in Ukrainian again. This time I couldn't make out what they were saying. Perhaps they were talking about the truck, which involved vocabulary I didn't know.

I grabbed my backpack, shut the door, and yelled, "Hey!"

Marko raised his head. "Oh, hello, Brenna. How are you?"

"All right. How are the two of you doing?"

Viktor raised his head. "Not so well. We're having a hard time figuring out what's wrong with Rylan's truck. It's not the battery."

"I'm sorry." Did I acknowledge they were speaking another language or ignore it? I decided to ask. "Where are you from?"

Marko's face reddened. "Aww, how could you tell?"

"You were speaking another language."

Viktor chuckled. "We do that without realizing it."

"Ukraine," Marko said.

I slung my backpack onto my shoulder. "When did you move here?"

Viktor said, "I was eleven when we came."

Marko rubbed the back of his neck. "And I was nine."

I stepped closer. "Did you two know each other in Ukraine?"

Marko smiled and nodded. Then Viktor said, "We're cousins."

That made sense. They seemed to have a deep connection. "What made the two of you decide to join the Army Reserve?"

Viktor blinked, as if he had something in his eyes. Marko cleared his throat before answering. "Probably the same reason anyone does. A sense of duty to the country you're living in—for us, the country that took in our families. A sense of gratitude." He shrugged. "And the GI Bill. There wasn't any other way we could pay for college."

"So, you've gone to college?"

"We're going—a civil engineering program," Marko said, "at Thaddeus Stevens College, down-town. Our fathers own a construction company that we'll run someday. Currently, we work part-time for them, fitting it in around our classes and Army Reserve drills."

"Nice," I said. "Well, I'll let you keep working on Rylan's truck. See you later." Since they lived in the same complex, perhaps I would.

"Good-bye," they said in unison.

I gave them a wave. Why did Rylan send his prosthesis, backpack, and wallet home with me when his buddies lived nearly as close as I did? I opened the side door of the van, grabbed his things, and then headed toward his ground floor apartment, feeling uncomfortable.

Had I lied to Viktor and Marko by implying I didn't know what language they were speaking?

My uneasy feeling continued as I unlocked Rylan's door. I didn't like the idea of going into his apartment, but I didn't want to keep his backpack and prosthesis in our apartment either. His layout was just like ours, except it only had one bedroom. I flicked the light on as I stepped inside. I'd heard about guys' apartments—beer cans and dirty dishes, clothes strewn all over.

But Rylan's was in perfect order. Too perfect. There were no pictures or even posters on the walls. He had a recliner and a TV in the living room. No couch. No table and chairs in the dining room. There were no dirty dishes in the kitchen—just bare counters.

I put the backpack down by his recliner, leaned his prosthesis and cane against the wall under the TV, and then walked out of the apartment, locking the door behind me. Now I felt uneasy and sick to my stomach. I'd never seen such a bleak living space. What did such starkness say about Rylan? It was as if there were no landmarks in his home—just a vast, open space. Which was surprising. He definitely had landmarks in his life—tragic ones, if nothing else.

• • •

I had a spoonful of peanut butter and an apple for dinner. After I finished, I put my spoon in the dishwasher and retreated to my bedroom. As I logged into my laptop to do my homework for the next day, a message popped up from Johann.

Do you have time to chat?

Chat or talk?

Talk, actually.

I hesitated, my hands resting on the keyboard. Did I have the energy to talk? If it was anyone else, I'd say no. But Johann usually energized me instead of draining me.

Ivy knew Johann from a mission trip she took to Ukraine in 2013. Then, in the summer of 2014, Ivy, Conrad, Gabe, and I traveled to Germany for the Global Gathering, a Mennonite youth event. Rosene traveled with us and stayed with her sister, Lena, in Frankfurt. We all met Johann then. Ever since, he and I had stayed in touch, and even more so after he was discharged from the army.

My computer started buzzing, and I accepted his call. It took a moment for both of our videos to connect, but a couple of seconds later our faces appeared on the screen.

"*Dobryden*," I said. Hello.

"Hello!" Johann said. "How are you doing?"

I blinked several times.

"Brenna, what's wrong?" His blue eyes were full of concern.

I quickly explained about Rylan falling behind Mammi's shop and then ending up in the hospital. I backtracked and explained he was a soldier and had a prosthesis because he lost his leg in Afghanistan.

Johann grimaced. "And now he's injured again?"

"Yes," I said. "He's having surgery tomorrow." I swallowed and said, "Sorry. I shouldn't be upset. He's the one in pain and having surgery. It's just that it's been a long day."

"Of course you should be upset." Johann always knew the right thing to say. "I was just praying for you and felt like I should check in. I'm glad I did."

"So am I."

"What do you plan to do as far as Rylan?"

"Try to help him, if I can. I'll explain our assignments. Share my notes. Give him rides. That sort of thing."

"Expect him to be out of sorts." Johann ran his hand through his short, dark hair. "If he's angry, that's normal. Help as much as you can, but if it gets to be too much, take a break."

I exhaled. "I think I can handle it." Then again,

Rylan told Gabe he planned to sue Mammi. That might be too much.

"He might be triggered by another surgery." Johann spoke English perfectly. He'd studied it for years, and now he worked for a US software firm.

I nodded. "Thankfully, he has army buddies around. I haven't told Ivy or Conrad this yet, because he hasn't told them, but Gabe joined the Army Reserve unit Rylan was in."

Johann's video froze. When it unfroze, I realized he was dumbfounded. "Gabe joined the Army Reserve? Really?"

I nodded.

"I didn't think American Mennonites joined the military."

"They don't, usually," I said. "I think that's why he hasn't told anyone. Not Mammi. Not even his mother."

"Ouch." He turned his head. "Speaking of mothers, Mama wants to say hello. She just got home from a late shift." She worked as a nurse at a care center.

Natasha stepped into the video frame. "Brenna! How are you?"

"Good," I said, "How are you doing?"

She smiled. "I can't complain." She nudged Johann. "Did I say it correctly?"

Johann laughed. "Yes, Mama. You said it perfectly."

She grinned and then said, "Have a good day!"

66

"Night, Mama," Johann said.

She laughed. "Night night."

I loved Natasha. She made me miss Mom, even though the two weren't anything alike.

I called out, "*Davaj*!" Bye.

She held up her hand and waved. "God bless!"

My heart warmed. I was so glad Johann called—and that Natasha wanted to speak to me too. For the moment, I didn't feel lonely.

"How are you doing overall?" Johann asked.

"I think I'm okay. I don't feel as if I'm going to have a panic attack or anything."

"Remember what your therapist told you? About taking care of yourself first?"

"Yeah," I said. "But I think I need to start thinking about serving others too." I didn't want to tell him what Ivy had said about me needing to stop being selfish. "Rylan is a built-in opportunity for me to help someone else."

Johann hesitated and then said, "Just be aware of your needs too."

"I will."

Johann felt like a big brother. Ivy was often critical of me, but Johann only encouraged me. I wasn't sure what I did for him, though. He contributed far more to my well-being than I contributed to his.

"Take it a day at a time," he said. "Message me if I can help."

"I will," I said again. "Thank you." I glanced

at the clock. "You need to get to bed." It was one in the morning in Ukraine. Johann worked from home and tended to stay up late. "Davaj."

After we both logged off, I realized I hadn't told Johann about Marko or Viktor. I think he'd get a kick out of me meeting two Ukrainian refugees in Lancaster County, especially ones who belonged to an Army Reserve unit and had served in Afghanistan.

I sometimes imagined Johann coming to visit, but not enough to actually invite him. What if he said no? What if he thought I had a crush on him? I didn't want to jeopardize the friendship we had by making him think I was asking for more. But I thought he'd enjoy coming for a visit. Besides knowing Ivy and me, he also knew Conrad and Gabe. He would be fascinated by Mammi and Dawdi and the Amish farms and families and buggies and workhorses.

That was the thing about Johann. He wasn't judgmental. New groups of people and ways of life fascinated him. Nothing seemed to faze him, and yet his insight into Rylan's war trauma made me think that Johann's own experience with war had been worse than he let on. At least to me.

I worked for two hours the next morning at Mammi's store, and then went to my one o'clock class. I psyched myself up and approached the professor before class to tell him what happened to Rylan. "I'll share my notes," I said, "and help him with assignments, but I'm not sure how long he'll be in the hospital or how long until he'll be able to come back to class."

"Thanks for letting me know," the professor said. "Tell him to email me with a status update as soon as he can and let me know when he'll be back. If it's not soon, he may need to take an incomplete."

I hoped that wouldn't happen. That class, I took the best notes of my life, which was saying a lot since my notes were always top-notch anyway. When class ended, I drove to the hospital, eating a protein bar on the way.

When I arrived, I headed straight for Rylan's room. I knocked on the door, and a weak voice said, "Come in."

Rylan stirred and opened his eyes when I entered the room. "Brenna? What took you so long?" But then his head sank back into his pillow, and he closed his eyes again.

My heart lurched at how vulnerable he appeared. Pale. Gaunt. Helpless.

I sat down in the chair beside his bed and waited, feeling much less anxious than I had the day before. First, because I was more familiar with the hospital now. But mostly because Rylan had support. He had the cousins. It wouldn't be up to me to take care of him. I needed to help him with school, but that was all.

I leaned my head back against the chair and closed my eyes. I needed Rylan's email address so I could send him my class notes. And—

"Brenna?" Rylan turned his head toward me.

"How are you?"

"Bad."

I waited for him to say more, but he didn't. He just stared at me.

"What, in particular, is bad?"

"Everything. My leg. Legs. My head. My gut. My future. My past. My present. All of it is bad. Nothing's good."

I'd felt that way before. "I'm sorry," I said.

He exhaled. "How was class today?"

"Good. I spoke with the teacher so he knows what's going on. I took copious notes. I just need your email address to send them to."

"Don't bother," he said. "I think I'm going to drop out."

"Drop out?"

"Yeah."

I swallowed hard. It seemed premature to decide that. But maybe he was just talking. Maybe he'd feel better the next day.

"I figure with my disability money and what I get after I sue your family, I'll do okay."

"Are you serious?"

"I used to work for an attorney. One of his specialties was personal injury lawsuits against the Amish. That's one of the reasons I quit—his business model felt predatory. But now I'm not so sure. . . ."

Gabe had been right. I felt ill.

"If I do, will you stop helping me?"

"If you drop out of the classes we have together, there won't be anything I can help you with anyway."

"So you won't be my friend?"

Yesterday, I felt as if we might be able to be friends. Now I wasn't so sure. Was Mammi responsible for his accident? If she was, what was my responsibility to Rylan?

Deciding to change the topic, I asked, "How did the surgery go?"

"I have a plate in my tibia."

"Is it permanent?"

"Seems so," Rylan answered. "The doctor said it will take eight weeks or more to heal."

That would be nearly Christmastime. "Did you let your family know what happened?"

Rylan nodded. "I left a message, but my mom hasn't called back." He grimaced. "It's normal for my family. They're not like yours. Not everyone has a family they can count on."

I wasn't sure how to respond. "When will you be discharged?"

"Maybe tomorrow afternoon."

"Okay." My hand drifted to the scar on my forehead, but I forced it back down.

He closed his eyes again and started snoring

71

softly. I stood and took a step toward the door. When he didn't move, I fled the room. I felt ill. This wasn't Mammi's fault. It was mine. I was the one who'd brought Rylan with me to the store.

Ten minutes later, as I drove out of Lancaster, I headed northeast toward the farm instead of taking Highway 30 toward the apartment. I wanted to hear Rosene's story. I needed to be distracted. I wouldn't bother to tell her that Rylan had also told me that he planned to sue. Hopefully he was only thinking out loud or bluffing or out of it from the meds. Who knew? I certainly didn't.

Hopefully he'd be in his right mind soon.

This time, when I arrived at the farmhouse, I found Rosene in the kitchen, grating mozzarella cheese at the kitchen table. "I'm making lasagna, including one for Rylan. Grab a cup of coffee," she said, "and a brownie. Then I'll start the story."

Once I'd sat down, she said, "This is Martha's story, so I'll be telling it from her point of view. It starts six years after I came home to Lancaster County. I was nineteen, but still—in many ways—a girl. Martha, on the other hand, was twenty-five going on forty. She was tall, smart, and beautiful. Plus, she was a strong and forceful woman. She'd always been an old soul and as capable as could be. I don't know what we would have done without her."

5

Martha Simons

MARCH 7, 1945
LANCASTER COUNTY, PENNSYLVANIA

She wouldn't allow it. How could *Vater* even consider such a thing? Not after what happened last time.

"It's the only way," Vater said. "We need the POWs to help us." Others called the prisoners of war PWs, but Vater always said POW. "The farm is at stake, Martha."

She tied the scarf around her head tighter and then knotted it. "We agreed last fall we wouldn't use them again."

"That was before Jeremiah was called away. There's no other option, except to not get our crops in the ground, which will mean no harvest and no profit. Which will mean . . ." His voice trailed off.

He didn't need to say the rest. *No farm.*

A gust of wind whipped at the legs of Martha's overalls, an old pair of Vater's that Clare had tailored to fit her. They were still too big.

The only help they had now was Zeke and occasionally Rosene when she wasn't helping

Mutter in the store. Or helping Clare with cooking and housekeeping and tending to little Arden, which Rosene would need to be doing more of now that Clare was expecting another little one in August. They were barely keeping up with the milking and chores, let alone plowing the fields, dragging the pastures, and mending the fences. They needed to start the planting soon.

"You can't keep working eighteen-hour days," Vater said. "I'm sorry I've put you in this position."

"You haven't done it on purpose." His blood pressure was high. The doctor said he needed to cut back on his hours of work, which meant she'd needed to increase hers.

"It's been decided." Vater met her gaze. "I've already made the arrangements."

Martha's heart raced. "Without speaking to me?"

He nodded.

The wind picked up even more, stinging Martha's eyes. Or were those tears? "I need to finish the plowing." She turned her back on her father and stepped toward the tractor.

The next gust of wind brought a few drops of rain. Then more fell. Icy drops pelted her face.

"*Nee*, come eat," Vater called out. "The rain won't last long."

Martha turned toward the house. Rosene stood on the back steps, ringing the bell. The sound had nearly been lost in the wind.

"I'll be right in. You go ahead." She didn't want to walk with Vater. She needed to honor him, yes, but first she needed a moment to herself.

As he started toward the house, Martha leaned against the back wheel of the tractor. Last fall, a crew of German PWs had come to help with the harvest. They were mostly city boys. One, when he figured out Rosene was fluent in German, tried his best to converse with her as often as he could. Rosene did her best to avoid him, as she had no interest in the PWs, but he went out of his way to interact with her.

On the other hand, Mutter, who'd grown up in Germany and didn't seem to understand the risks of interacting with the PWs, went out of her way to interact with the soldiers, speaking German with them and even quoting poems and singing songs. Then the PWs started confiding in Mutter about their problems. Mutter said they weren't Nazis, just young men who'd been conscripted. She insisted they were harmless. Obviously, she felt sorry for them.

But Martha wasn't as sure. She worried about the PWs harassing Rosene—and also about Mutter being far too sympathetic toward the German men.

Still, last fall, at first all of them followed Mutter's lead and acted kindly toward the eight PWs assigned to the farm, but soon it was one thing after another. Fights between the PWs.

Then the highest-ranking German, an officer, began taunting Zeke. Soon all the PWs were mocking Jeremiah for being a CO.

Before long, the PWs had everyone on edge. Except Mutter.

Martha had heard plenty of stories about PWs. Some had even escaped. Thankfully, that hadn't happened on the Simonses' farm—she'd be mortified if it had. Regardless of what Mutter said, Martha also worried about the Nazi influence on the PWs. Clearly not all of them were Nazis, but the officers at the camps were, and they influenced the lower-ranking men. Two of the PWs last fall had been officers.

No. She couldn't bear the thought of having the PWs on the farm again. Last fall, Jeremiah—her brother-in-law—had been here. And Vater had been healthier. Now, would it be up to her? She was strong both physically and mentally, but she couldn't oversee a group of German PWs.

The rain fell harder, and she pushed away from the tire. It would do no good to get soaked to the bone just to avoid another conversation with Vater. She took off toward the house, marching as quickly as she could without breaking into a run. She caught up with Vater as he rounded the pond in the pasture. There was no denying he was slowing down.

Surely the war would end soon. Jeremiah would return from where he'd been sent to work as a conscientious objector, a CO, in a mental hospital in Philadelphia. And then the soldiers and all the Amish and Mennonite COs would come home, and Vater would be able to hire more farmhands. He truly could rest more, and Martha could figure out what she wanted to do with her life.

She followed Vater up the steps to the back porch, where she took off her boots and coat, then washed at the utility sink. She stepped into the warm kitchen, heated by the woodstove, and inhaled the scent of slow-cooked beef and fresh bread.

Zeke was already seated, a cup of coffee in his hands, while Rosene finished setting the table. Clare dished up bowls of stew from the Dutch oven on the stove. Baby Arden, who was a year and a half old, sat in the high chair that Jeremiah had made. Arden had dark hair and gray eyes and a mischievous smile. He was the bright spot for all of them, born nine months before D-Day, when no one knew if the war would turn in the Allies' favor. At least now they had hope.

After saying hello to the others, Martha filled the pitcher and began pouring water into the glasses on the table. Her cold skin began to tingle from the heat.

A few minutes later, they were all seated at the table with a bowl of stew in front of them and slices of buttered bread. Except for Mutter. She often joined them late for the noon meal if she

77

had a customer in the store before she closed for the hour.

Vater led them all in prayer, and then as they dug into the stew, he said, "I already told Martha this, but we'll have a crew of POWs coming this spring."

"Vater." Clare handed Arden a piece of bread. "Are you sure that's a good idea?"

"Jah. Zeke, Martha, and I can't do it all, not even with Rosene's help. Besides, she needs to be with you in the house," Vater said. "Or assisting Mutter in the store."

Mutter slipped into the kitchen and sat in her chair as Vater spoke. Her silence made it clear that she and Vater had already talked everything through and agreed.

Rosene passed the bread to Mutter. "We shouldn't let any of them know we speak or understand German this time."

Martha said, "I agree."

Mutter put a piece of bread on her plate. "Oh, I don't think that's necessary."

Rosene glanced at Martha and wrinkled her nose. She shared Martha's worries about Mutter's interaction with the PWs last time.

Vater didn't respond. Instead, he said, "I've requested four POWs."

"Will they send a guard for such a small number?" Zeke asked.

Vater answered, "Yes. Several of the neighbors

will have crews, so a truck will be coming out here anyway. They agreed to it."

"But we'll need to supervise them too." Martha paused, her spoon hovering over her stew. "Especially if we have a couple of different jobs that need to be done all at once."

"We'll make it work," Vater said.

Martha believed he was overly optimistic about supervising the PWs. They needed a strong, constant male presence.

"When will the PWs arrive?" Martha asked.

"Tomorrow."

She couldn't hide the shock in her voice. "Tomorrow?"

Vater nodded.

"When did you make all of these arrangements?"

"A few weeks ago."

Martha shook her head. Why hadn't he consulted her? Instead of responding to him, she brought up a topic she'd been putting off but now saw her opportunity to broach. Vater wasn't the only one holding back information. "I'm going into town this evening for the Red Cross meeting."

Vater simply nodded to acknowledge what she'd said.

Having the PWs' labor at least meant she'd have more time to do what she wanted to do, which was volunteer for the Red Cross and spend time with George Hall.

• • •

That evening, Martha didn't go back out to the fields after supper to plow by the tractor lights. Instead, she bathed, brushed her wavy hair out, and put on a skirt and blouse with a cardigan sweater to go into town. Then she put on a wool pillbox hat instead of a Kapp. She took the back staircase to the kitchen. Vater sat by himself at the table. Without speaking to him, she grabbed the key to the Studebaker off the peg by the back door.

He said, "I didn't want to talk about this in front of the others, but you need to stop this volunteer work."

"They need me," she said.

"*We* need you," he countered.

"I can do both."

"I know you can," he answered. "But you shouldn't. Besides, we don't have the extra gas coupons for trips into town."

"I'll pick up extra coupons tonight to cover it." She wouldn't tell him George would give her the coupons—or that she would even see him. She made the mistake of mentioning him one time, and Vater had quizzed her about him for an hour.

Yes, he was a kind man.

No, he wasn't Plain.

Yes, he went to church. A Methodist one.

No, he wasn't from Lancaster. He grew up in Chicago.

Yes, he was a city person. Didn't you live in Frankfurt, a city, for a year?

Vater had replied, *"That was different. I wasn't a citizen of Frankfurt."*

"Well, now George lives in Lancaster," Martha had said, *"which might seem like a city to us, but it's small compared to Chicago."*

"Does he plan to stay in Lancaster long?" Vater had asked.

"I don't know," Martha had answered, even though she did. At least she knew what he hoped for. He hoped to go to Europe and help refugees get resettled. He said there were millions of displaced people who needed help.

George was a friend, that was all. One who would soon leave Lancaster County far behind. She wanted to spend time with him while she still could.

She opened the back door. "I won't be late." She stepped onto the back porch and put on her good coat.

Thankfully, Vater hadn't said anything about her wearing a skirt and hat instead of a cape dress and Kapp. If they were to be modest in their dress, then why stick out in a group of people from all different religions? Her skirt, blouse, and sweater were as modest as her dress, although she knew plenty of Plain people wouldn't agree with her.

"Martha!" Clare opened the back porch door.

"What do you need?"

Arden sat on Clare's hip. "Can you pick Jeremiah up at the train station tomorrow night?"

It was Jeremiah's first visit home since he was sent to work at Byberry Hospital in Philadelphia. Martha poked her head around the door and asked Vater, "Is that all right with you?"

"Jah. The POWs will leave by five," Vater said. "That will give you enough time."

"I'll do it," Martha said to Clare. "Do you and Arden want to come with me?"

She shook her head, which Arden mimicked. "I'll need to finish supper. Mutter needs Rosene's help tomorrow."

Martha nodded. "See you in the morning."

"Have a good time." Clare smiled. Arden waved, and Martha waved back to him.

Vater smiled too and reached out his hands for the boy.

Martha closed the back porch door. Neither of their parents seemed to think Martha had a private life—or should. But Clare did.

As Martha turned the Studebaker onto the highway, she began to smile too. She hadn't felt free since the last Red Cross meeting she went to, which was over two months ago. If she could do anything she wanted, she would go to Europe to drive with the Red Cross motor pool, but the war would soon end and there would be no need for that.

She loved to drive, whether it was the tractor, the truck, or the car. And she was good at it. The majority of her volunteer work for the Red Cross around Lancaster had been driving. Sometimes it was delivering supplies between local military bases and local hospitals. Or a food box to a family with a soldier overseas. One time it was transporting the ill child of a soldier to the hospital. Last Christmas Eve, she delivered gifts to families of soldiers. That was her favorite day of volunteering.

George Hall had arrived in November of 1943 as the director of the Lancaster Chapter of the Red Cross. He was twenty-eight and would have been in the military except for his heart murmur. He was tall, thin, smart, and handsome. And very much a city boy.

He'd been the administrator of a medical supply company in Chicago, which gave him the experience to manage people, budgets, and inventory. Since he'd been in Lancaster County, he'd done well with the staff and volunteers— so well that Martha had expected him to be transferred to a larger Red Cross chapter. No doubt he would be soon, unless he obtained a job with the Red Cross in Europe first.

If only Martha had the hope of going to Europe to serve too.

6

As Martha reached the city limits, she slowed. Because she was good at farming, people assumed she didn't like being in town. But she did. She liked the lights of the houses so close together and the streetlights and the headlights on the cars and trucks.

Vater had never agreed with her working for the Red Cross, but Mutter, who grew up in Germany where the Red Cross originated, had been pleased that Martha volunteered. *"We need international organizations,"* Mutter had said. *"The Red Cross does good work."*

"But it's associated with the military," Vater said.

"It takes care of soldiers and their families, jah," Mutter had responded. *"Someone must. Don't you believe Jesus would do the same? Don't you believe Martha should, given her gifts?"*

Martha was raised to trust the Lord for her well-being, direction, and future. She agreed with those teachings. And yet, she'd only ever known trusting Him in the safety of Lancaster County, where she'd spent her entire life except for a few trips to Philadelphia. She wanted something more.

Martha reached downtown, where the Red Cross office was, and parked at the end of the block. As she stepped from the car, she shivered. The evening had grown colder and threatened frost. Hopefully it would be one of the last of the season.

As she neared the entrance to the office, George came bounding out, bumping into Martha. As he grabbed her shoulders to steady her, she grabbed his arms to steady him, and then they both laughed.

"You came." He smiled.

She nodded and smiled back.

His brown eyes were bright. "I forgot a notebook at my apartment." He lived a block away. Martha had walked with him to a nearby diner a year ago, and he'd pointed out his building. "I'll be right back," he said. "Go get a cup of coffee and a cookie."

Martha made her way into the office. In the back room, half of the chairs were already filled. She picked up a cup of coffee but skipped the cookies—they were always dry—and sat down in the middle of the room. Many of the other volunteers, both men and women, were middle-aged, but there were younger women in their twenties too. Many of the women were nurses, and several wore white uniforms.

George returned to the room and the conversation between the others stopped.

"I'll get straight to the business at hand," he said. "We need more volunteers to staff the canteen at the depot. Troop movement has slowed some, but it's still significant. Hopefully it won't be long until it increases again, God willing, with troops coming home."

He looked down at his notes. "We'll also have more responsibilities with the German POWs as farm work picks up and then, later, cannery work. And as the war winds down, the POWs need to be prepared to return to their countries, although it won't be for several months, most likely after the harvest is over. Our work with the POWs will increase due to that too, in time."

Martha shivered, but not from the cold. There were PWs in the area from Germany, Italy, Poland, and Ukraine. She knew they needed help, but she didn't want to be the one to help them. Too many—from her experience—seemed manipulative. Mutter was far too trusting. Martha would much rather help refugees in Europe than German PWs in the United States.

"There are currently nearly four hundred thousand German POWs in the US, including thousands in Pennsylvania," George said. "That number will most likely grow before the war is over. How we treat them is strictly mandated by the Geneva Convention, and the Red Cross is determined as an organization to treat them with dignity and care."

The man in front of Martha crossed his arms.

Martha doubted the Germans treated the US POWs in Europe well, regardless of the Geneva Convention, especially after what Clare and Rosene had seen the Nazis do at the beginning of the war to their own citizens. What would they do to citizens of other countries and Allied troops?

George explained, "The Red Cross is responsible for helping to serve the German POWs. We're to see to the complaints from the camps, including the smaller one nearby that was established late last summer. The numbers there will expand to three hundred to provide farmhands and staff for local canneries in a couple of weeks. Last fall, we used the guards as translators, but the Red Cross wants us to use our own translators this year."

The man in front of Martha cleared his throat as if thinking about whether he should speak or not, and then he said, "Why are the Krauts allowed to complain? They're fed better than our own soldiers. They should be made to pay for their crimes, not coddled."

"Mr. Anderson," George said, "I hear your frustration, but as you know, we must comply with the Geneva Convention. Our duties as workers and volunteers for the Red Cross are strictly outlined. One of our tasks is to hear complaints from POWs and determine their validity. I've studied German, but I'm not fluent.

All the translators in the area are now being used in the camps and on worksites, and I don't have anyone to accompany me to hear complaints." He looked around the group. "Can anyone here speak German? Anyone?"

Martha sat back in her chair and slumped a little. She'd never told George she spoke German.

"We desperately need translators," George said. "If you speak German, or know of someone who does, please let me know."

The man in front of her turned. "What about your sisters and mother?"

Martha recognized him as a man who sometimes came into Mutter's store. "I speak German," she said, "although I don't have time to volunteer during the day." Better her than Rosene or Clare. Or Mutter.

George appeared surprised. "I'll talk with you after the meeting."

The next morning, as Martha strode out to the barn wearing Vater's overalls and one of his old coats, she vowed to call George and tell him she couldn't help him after all. What had she been thinking last night? No one was going to come force Rosene or Clare or Mutter to translate for the German PWs.

As much as she tried to deny it, she was attracted to George. That was why she'd made such a ridiculous offer.

But she didn't have time to drive to PW camps and translate German PWs' complaints about the coffee and bread they were served. Second, what if she showed up at a camp where the PWs assigned to the farm were housed? She'd give away that she spoke German. And that she worked for the Red Cross. The less the PWs knew about her—about her entire family—the better.

She entered the barn and then headed toward the door to the pasture. Already the cows were mooing, demanding to be fed and milked.

After Clare had returned from Germany with Rosene, Martha convinced her parents to let her take classes at Franklin & Marshall College in Lancaster. She'd wanted to understand both Mutter and Rosene's backgrounds better, and Vater's and Clare's stays in Germany, although two decades apart. She'd taken two years of German language and turned out to be very good at speaking, writing, and understanding it as she built on what she'd learned from Mutter, Clare, and Rosene. She also took classes in German literature and culture.

She also wanted to understand the German-American groups in the US that sympathized with the Nazis. Her pluralistic country, before it had even become the US, had given her Mennonite ancestors religious freedom when they fled what was now Germany. Why would citizens now want to embrace fascism and the politicization of religion instead? She wanted to refute those groups.

After the US joined the war, Martha had to stop her studies to work more on the farm and help Mutter. She wasn't sure if she'd ever return to college or not.

She opened the barn door for the first of the cows.

"Hallo!" Zeke jogged across the field toward her.

"Good morning," she called back.

As Zeke reached her, he asked, "Is Rosene helping this morning?"

"Jah. She's on her way, but once the PWs arrive, she'll be mostly helping Mutter and Clare."

In the dim light, Martha thought she saw a frown on Zeke's face. She watched as he led the first cow into a milking stall. Was he sweet on Rosene? Rosene had just turned nineteen. Zeke was seventeen. Martha guessed Rosene would eventually join the Amish. She was closest to Clare and had admired her decision to join the Amish before she accepted Jeremiah's marriage proposal.

Presently, they were a half-Mennonite and half-Amish family. Jeremiah and Clare's bishop had given them temporary permission to live in a house with electricity because of the circumstances. But someday Clare and Jeremiah would inherit the property and the Simons Mennonite farm would become the Zimmerman Amish farm.

Although Mutter, Vater, and Martha—and currently Rosene—were Mennonite, they weren't conservative Mennonite, as Vater's parents had been. A choice to send Vater to college and then off to Germany to study for a year had changed the trajectory of the family. He'd returned with a German bride, Mutter, and they soon joined a more liberal church and then bought a car, truck, and finally a tractor. And they had electricity installed in the house. At some point, Jeremiah and Clare would have it uninstalled.

Over the last four years, Vater had also modernized the farm, adding more dairy cows and even vacuum pumps to do the milking, along with a milking room in the barn with sinks, drying racks, and a large strainer. Inspectors from the government could arrive—and did—at any time to inspect the herd, barn, equipment, and milking room.

A truck stopped by twice a day to pick up the milk and deliver it to a plant outside of Lancaster, where it was bottled and distributed to families in town. Because the herd was bigger, more feed had to be grown for the cows. Vater had taken out a loan to enlarge the herd and buy equipment, which meant even more pressure to turn a profit so they could make the payments.

Mutter continued to sell milk, eggs, vegetables, and fruit from the farm in her store on the edge of the property, along with other goods, but the majority of the money they earned now came from the milk production. They had fifteen cows, which meant one hundred and twenty gallons of milk a day.

"Hey, Boss!" Zeke called out, the feed shovel in his hands. "Should I bring in the next cow?"

Martha realized she'd been standing still. "No, I'll do it. Go ahead and get started on the feed."

As she guided the next cow into her stall, Rosene arrived. She wore a long wool coat over her dress.

"You can get started on this one." Martha gestured toward the stall.

The three fed the cows, cleaned udders and teats, fastened the vacuum pumps, carried the milk to the strainer in the milking room, and then released the cows. Vater came out and helped at the very end, cleaning up the manure.

Once the four of them finished, they returned to the kitchen together with a bucket of milk. Martha felt as if it were a last meal before the PWs arrived. The Germans wouldn't eat with them, nor come in the house, but their sense of peace—as much as they could muster with Jeremiah being gone and the war still ongoing—would be gone.

Regardless of the trouble last fall, the extra

labor had made the difference. Crops had been harvested. Milk had been sold. Money had been made. Loan payments had been on time.

Martha admonished herself to trust the Lord. If it meant saving the farm, she had to accept the PWs. If it alleviated Vater's stress, it would be worth it. No matter what it did to hers.

After breakfast, Vater, Martha, and Zeke headed outside. Vater would work on the plowing while Zeke and Martha dragged the field. Several times Martha heard a truck and expected the Germans, but each time it was something else. The milkman to pick up the cans. The mailman. A load of hay being delivered to a neighbor's farm.

Finally, the army truck with the PWs arrived. Vater stopped the tractor, and Martha pulled the workhorses to a stop. "I'll be back in a few minutes," she said to Zeke.

Vater waited for her, and after stopping in the milk room to grab a stack of leather gloves for the PWs, they walked together toward the driveway. The driver of the truck stayed in the cab, but another soldier, carrying a rifle, jumped down.

"Hello!" he called out. "I'm Sergeant Schwarz. I'm the guard for the PWs."

"Ervin Simons," Vater said, extending his hand as he reached the soldier. "And this is my daughter Martha."

Martha nodded toward the sergeant.

"You'll need to translate for us," Vater said to the guard. It seemed he was going along with Rosene's idea.

"I expected so," Sergeant Schwarz said. "Where would you like the PWs to start?"

Vater answered, "I'm plowing pastureland for corn. The rocks need to be pulled out." He handed the stack of leather gloves to the sergeant. "Make sure the POWs wear these."

"Thank you." Sergeant Schwarz took the gloves. "That's work they should be able to do easily. We'll break for lunch at noon."

Vater pointed toward the two picnic tables. "You can eat there. The outhouses are to the north of the house. We'll have a bucket of water with soap and a towel on the picnic table to wash up."

"Thank you." Sergeant Schwarz stepped to the back of the truck and opened it. In German, he called out, "*Folge mir*." Follow me.

A soldier who appeared incredibly young jumped down. He was slight and had sandy hair. Then a man who looked to be in his early twenties with dark hair followed, and then a second man with dark hair. A man who seemed to be older, mid- or late twenties, jumped down. He had a defiant look in his eyes. He brushed his dark blond hair out of his face as he landed on the ground. They all wore blue pants and work shirts with *POW* on the back. The older one carried a jacket and swung it onto his back and then pushed his arms through the sleeves.

In German, Sergeant Schwarz said, "This is Ervin Simons and his daughter. They don't speak German, so any communication will need to go through me."

"She's dressed as a man," the last man said in German, a smirk on his face. "And she looks like a man too."

Martha kept her face slack, not giving away that she understood what he said.

Sergeant Schwarz sighed. "No commenting on any of the members of the family. Nor may you speak to them. They won't understand you."

The man shrugged. He was tall and broad shouldered.

Vater also ignored the man and led the way toward the field, followed by Sergeant Schwarz and the PWs.

Martha kept her thoughts to herself. It appeared this group of PWs would be trouble too. Trouble she'd have to figure out how to manage on her own.

7

When Vater, Zeke, and Martha entered the kitchen for their noon meal, Rosene stood at the kitchen window with an empty pitcher in her hands, staring at the PWs and the sergeant at the picnic table. Martha stepped beside her. There was no way to tell what they were saying, but the younger PWs laughed, and the sergeant smiled along with them. Then the older PW, who looked like an officer, frowned and said something. The others froze, even the sergeant.

"What's the guard's name?" Rosene asked.

"Sergeant Schwarz."

"Do you know anything about him?"

"No." Martha turned toward Zeke. "Did he tell you anything?"

Zeke rolled his eyes. "He couldn't stop talking." He dropped his voice. "His parents are from Germany and came here before the Great War. They only spoke German in the home. He graduated high school with honors and went to Yale on a scholarship, where he studied German. He graduated last year and was immediately drafted. He failed his physical and ended up as a guard in a PW camp."

Martha shook her head. "Figures." If she were

96

a man, she'd probably be a guard in a POW camp too. Unless she was a CO working with Jeremiah at Byberry.

That was nearly the story, minus Yale, of the guard who watched the PWs on the farm last fall. Martha stepped away from the sink. Rosene filled the pitcher and then poured the water in the glasses as everyone sat down at the table, except for Clare, who put the meatloaf, mashed potatoes, and gravy on the table.

Everyone dropped their heads as Vater prayed. Mutter slipped in the back door and to her place at the end of the table as he said, "Amen."

"Thank you, Clare," Mutter said as she dished up a slice of meatloaf. "It all looks and smells delicious, as always."

Clare was an incredible cook, making do with the ration cards and less meat during the war. It took a lot to keep everyone fed. She'd had a difficult pregnancy, then a newborn, and now a rambunctious toddler. On top of all that, now a second pregnancy.

When Arden threw his spoon on the floor, Rosene retrieved it and then fed him a bowl of mashed potatoes using hers.

"How did the PWs do this morning?" Clare asked.

"Good," Vater replied.

"Any problems?"

"No." Vater took a bite of meatloaf.

Martha leaned toward her father, around Zeke. "What about the officer?"

Vater played dumb. "Which one is the officer?"

Martha shook her head. "You know. The big one."

Zeke said, "Dirk. Dirk Neumann is his name."

Vater shrugged. "He was fine."

"Sergeant Schwarz doesn't seem fine," Martha said. "He seems like a pushover."

Rosene asked, "What does that mean?"

"Weak. An easy mark," Martha answered, still looking at Vater. "Dirk is going to be running the show in no time."

Vater sighed and said, "I don't think so."

The conversation shifted to Mutter's store, which had been extra busy that morning. When the meal was over, Vater stood. "I'm going to go rest. Zeke, you go ahead and take over the plowing."

Mutter stood. "Are you feeling all right, Ervin?"

"I'm fine," he answered. "Just tired." The doctor had diagnosed Vater with hypertension three months ago. He'd gone to the doctor because he was short of breath and tended to fall asleep every evening in his chair. Treatment included resting, avoiding stress, and taking a bromide. *"I don't have anything worse than our own president,"* Vater said after he was diagnosed. *"And look at what Mr. Roosevelt is getting done."*

Vater walked around the table and patted

Mutter on the shoulder. It was the most affection they showed in front of others.

Clare gave Arden a cracker and began stacking the plates. "Rosene," she said, "would you hang the diapers on the line before putting Arden down for his nap?"

"Sure." Rosene stood. "Then you should nap too." Clare was quite ill during her pregnancy with Arden, and they were all concerned about her now, but Rosene was especially concerned. "I'll do the dishes once Arden is down." She took off down the basement stairs.

Martha headed to the back porch. Zeke followed her down the outside stairs as Rosene started up the basement steps with the basket of wet laundry.

Zeke called out to the PWs, "Time to get to work!"

The guard translated what Zeke said into German. Martha guessed, if the PWs knew much about the Amish or the Mennonites, they might suspect Zeke spoke German, although perhaps not the dialect the PWs spoke.

As Rosene reached the clothesline, the PWs began standing. The sergeant gathered up their pails from the picnic table that had held their lunches. Dirk washed his hands in the bucket of water on the table. Another PW, one with dark hair, headed toward the outhouse.

The other PW with the dark hair yelled in German, "Pavlo, hold your nose!"

Pavlo turned toward him, his nose pinched with his right hand.

"Andreas," Dirk barked. "Clean up the table."

Now Martha knew the names of three of them—Dirk, Pavlo, and Andreas. Clearly Dirk was in charge. Pavlo and Andreas appeared to be twenty-two or so. The youngest, the light-haired blond boy, looked to be perhaps twenty.

He stood and said to Andreas, "I'll help you, Witer." That must have been his surname.

Zeke waited at the edge of the yard. Martha started toward the barn, but then stopped and turned, not wanting to leave Rosene unattended.

Rosene placed the basket on the ground, picked up a handful of diapers, and began pinning them to the line.

"There's a baby in the house." Martha couldn't see him, but Dirk was the one who spoke.

Rosene had her back to them and kept pinning.

"Maybe Martha has a baby," Dirk said. "Or maybe the little one hanging the diapers is the mother."

The youngest PW laughed nervously. Martha took a step toward the birch tree. The sun had come out, and the tree cast a bit of a shadow.

Dirk passed by and then stopped once he reached Zeke. Rosene continued pinning the diapers, one by one, and ignored the PWs.

Dirk asked Zeke in German, "Are you the boss now?"

Zeke stared at him blankly.

Dirk smirked. "I know you understand what I'm saying."

Zeke shrugged as he continued to stare at him.

Mutter came down the back steps and turned to the right, toward the store.

"I can't figure this family out," Dirk said as Andreas and Pavlo joined him. "Who's who? Are they Amish or Mennonite? Or German?"

He stared at Rosene as she pinned the last diaper, grabbed the basket, and headed back toward the basement.

Dirk asked Zeke, "How about the girl? Is she your wife?"

The other men laughed.

Zeke was younger than Rosene, but no one would have guessed she was nineteen. She was barely five feet tall and thin. Most guessed she was fifteen or so, while Zeke was over six feet and broad shouldered like Jeremiah. But he did have a baby face.

Vater said this group of PWs seemed fine, but Martha disagreed. Dirk was trouble. She was sure of it.

Martha was tending to a cow's hoof when Rosene hurried into the barn, out of breath.

Martha looked up in alarm as Rosene took a ragged breath and said, "Mutter came to the house—she had a message from the Zimmermans.

Their Mamm's cough is worse, and she needs to go to the doctor. Zeke needs to take her. I didn't want to go straight to the field to tell him and have Zeke leave the PWs there with nothing to do because no one was there to drive the tractor."

Martha let go of the cow's leg and said, "Come with me to the field." Elizabeth Zimmerman must not be doing well. She wouldn't agree to go to the doctor unless she was truly ill.

"I have a kitchen full of dirty dishes."

"They'll have to wait." Martha wiped her gloved hands on her overalls. "We'll have to do the plowing together. I'm not afraid of any physical harm from the PWs, but I think they'll be more likely to harass one of us than two of us together."

Martha thought of the verse Clare often quoted from Ecclesiastes. *Two are better than one; because they have a good reward for their labour.* They had to work together.

She finished up with the cow, and then they both headed toward the field. When they arrived, Zeke was at the far end, turning the corner on the tractor. The four PWs were spread out in the field behind the tractor, picking up rocks and putting them in burlap bags. Sergeant Schwarz plodded along behind the PWs, his rifle slung over his shoulder.

The youngest one tossed a dirt clod at Andreas, who turned quickly. Still, it hit him in the side of the head. He picked up something—a rock?—to retaliate. "Otis!" Andreas yelled.

Sergeant Schwarz yelled in German for the men to stop. Dirk crossed his arms as a smirk settled on his face.

Andreas tossed the rock into the air, caught it, and then wound up as if he were going to hurl it at Otis, who was only ten feet away from him. Martha shouted, "Knock it off!"

All the men turned toward her.

Zeke had the tractor turned around. He waved, and Martha motioned for him to stop. She marched toward him as she called out to Sergeant Schwarz, "Zeke is going to take a break. We'll be driving the tractor. Keep the men in line."

Zeke stopped the tractor and turned it off. Martha veered toward him, across the already-plowed rows. Rosene followed. When they reached him, Martha explained he was needed at home.

"Is it Mamm?"

"Her cough is worse," Rosene said. "She needs to go to the doctor."

Zeke jumped down. "I'll come back as soon as I can."

"We won't plan on seeing you this afternoon," Martha said. "If you can't work in the morning, let me know."

He nodded and gave Rosene a little wave. She gave him a sympathetic smile, which didn't go unnoticed by Martha.

The PWs had reached them, and Martha said quietly to Rosene, "Climb up on the other side."

She did, holding her skirt close as she landed next to the tractor seat.

Dirk stood back, but the younger PWs stepped closer to the front of the tractor. One of them—Pavlo—went around the side, then to the back, then ran up the wheel of the tire and slapped the exhaust pipe that stuck up along the side of the seat.

"Hey!" Martha barked. "What are you doing?"

He came around the other side and grinned, without saying anything. Dirk said, in English, to Martha, "You are much better to look at than Zeke, even in that ridiculous outfit." Then he repeated what he'd said in German.

They all laughed loudly. Except Dirk—he kept a straight face. Sergeant Schwarz smiled but stopped when Martha scowled at him.

"Get away and stay away from the tractor. All of you." She stepped toward Sergeant Schwarz and told him quietly to control the PWs. Rosene sat down on the tractor seat. When Martha started back to the tractor, Sergeant Schwarz ordered the PWs over to the row Zeke had just plowed.

Martha jumped up on the tractor, and Rosene moved off the seat to where she could hold the back of it and stand.

"Don't look at them." Martha gripped the steering wheel. "We have the rest of the afternoon to set the tone for the next eight months. We can't let them think we're okay with the way they're acting."

Thankfully, the tractor started on the first try as Martha pressed the foot button. She shifted it into gear without as much as a lurch and eased it forward. As they began rolling along, Martha let out an audible sigh of relief. They passed the PWs going the opposite direction, headed toward the far end of the field. Maybe this wouldn't be such an ordeal after all.

But then the tractor began to sputter. It rolled a few more feet before it stalled. And then stopped. Martha put it in neutral and set the brake. Then she jumped down and opened the hood. Rosene sat down in the seat.

When Jeremiah took over the farm, besides getting rid of the electricity, he'd also sell the tractor. The Amish didn't allow them in Lancaster County. Jeremiah said he wouldn't mind not having it. He'd never lost work time, at least not much, because a horse wasn't working right.

Martha slammed the hood shut.

Dirk had left the group picking up rocks and spoke in English. "I know engines. I can help."

"No." Martha's voice was low and firm. She marched around to the side of the tractor and climbed back up in the seat, but then she stood.

"What are you doing?" Rosene asked.

"Checking the exhaust pipe." She reached up

and felt the top of the pipe and then said, "Maybe you can get it. It's wedged in there pretty tight, and my hand is too big."

"What is it?"

"A potato."

"A potato?"

She nodded. "It's a prank. They clogged the exhaust pipe—that's why the engine stopped. You'll have to stand on the seat. I'll give you my gloves and knife—if you can pull the potato up a little and then stab it, maybe you can lift it out. Then slip it in your pocket. Don't react. I'll stand between you and the men." She turned and called out, "Back to work! All of you!"

They stood about twenty feet away, staring. Sergeant Schwarz translated what Martha had said.

Martha put one foot on the tire and another on the platform, blocking their view of the exhaust pipe. Then she took off her gloves and pulled her knife from her pocket, handing them both to Rosene.

Rosene put on the gloves and held the knife in her right hand as she climbed onto the seat. She stood on her tiptoes and reached into the pipe. "What if I knock it down into the engine?"

"It's too big." Martha spoke quietly as she stared at Rosene's hand. "But be careful."

She was able to get enough of a wiggle on it to move it upward, and she stabbed the potato and worked it in deeper as she held the potato with her other hand. Then she lifted it out and slipped it into her pocket.

"Thank you," Martha said. "Let's wait a few minutes and then I'll start the engine again. The main thing is to not react— and hope they haven't sabotaged anything else."

"How did Pavlo do that," Rosene asked, "when we were all here?"

"Maybe he did it earlier when Zeke stopped the tractor. Perhaps we didn't notice. Or maybe when he ran up on the tire."

After a couple of minutes, Martha pushed the start button with her foot again. It took several tries, but it finally started. The tractor lurched forward. "I hope Jeremiah has some ideas for me when he comes home tomorrow," Martha said. "I don't know how we're going to do this without him."

"I don't know either," Rosene said. "But if anyone can figure it out, it's you."

8

Brenna

"The milking crew will be in soon," Rosene said. "We need to stop the story."

I agreed, although I was fascinated by it. And not just hearing about the PWs and the farm in 1945, but also by the people. Dawdi Arden was a baby. Rosene was nineteen. It was a lifetime ago. Would I remember stories about my sisters and the farm in seventy years?

Rosene and I had worked as she told the story, and we had a large pan of lasagna baking for dinner and two smaller pans in the refrigerator for Rylan. I'd put them in his freezer for later.

Treva was the first one in from the milking, practically skipping into the house in her work dress, covered by a black apron. She wore a scarf on her head instead of a Kapp.

"Are you packed?" I asked.

"Of course not." She gave me a sassy smile.

I groaned.

"Go do it now," Rosene said. "And get it done. That way no one will be in a panic in the morning."

She meant me.

"What time do you have to be at the airport?" I asked Treva as we started up the back stairs.

"I'm not sure."

"Is your ticket on your phone?"

"Not yet," she answered as she reached the second floor and walked down the hall to the room we shared until I moved out with Ivy.

I stood in the doorway of the room as she flopped down on the bed—on top of a load of clean laundry. Treva was many things—kind, empathetic, generous—but she wasn't organized. It was her only fault, as far as Mammi was concerned.

"Eww," I said. "Get out of your choring dress before you get your clean clothes dirty." I stepped to the bureau and opened the bottom drawer, where I found a few pairs of jeans. "You'll need these," I said. "And sweatshirts." I opened the other bottom drawer and grabbed four sweatshirts. I wasn't sure why Rosene thought I could help Treva pack. I usually needed Ivy to help me.

But maybe that was the thing—it was easier to pack for someone else.

"How do you feel about going home?" I asked.

Treva unpinned her work dress and stepped out of it. "*Gut*." She had a habit of weaving Pennsylvania Dutch words in with English. "I'm looking forward to being with Gran and living at our place."

Our place. Both Ivy and Treva had gone home since we'd moved to Pennsylvania, but I had no desire to. Ivy said I was avoiding the situation. Rosene told me I'd go home when I was ready. I spoke with my therapist about it once, and she too thought I'd know when it was time to return. I hoped she was right, but I didn't believe I'd ever be ready. What would happen if I went at Christmas and I wasn't?

Treva pulled a clean dress from the pegs along the wall and stepped into it while I pushed the pile of clothes to the end of the bed and put the stack of jeans and sweatshirts on the edge. Then I started folding her clean clothes, which smelled like woodsmoke, fresh air, and earth—as line-dried clothes do.

As Treva pinned up her clean dress, she said, "Thank you for helping me." She turned toward me. "And thank you for taking me to the airport. I know it's not easy for you."

I gave her a smile as I kept folding and thought of nineteen-year-old Rosene. She'd essentially lost both of her parents too and, like me, had moved to Lancaster County. But she and Clare had fled Germany to save her life from the Nazis, while my life—once I survived the accident had never been in danger. I was two years older than Rosene at the time of her story, and yet everyone was still coddling me, afraid I might fall apart or have another panic attack or lose it altogether. On the other hand, Rosene had been working in my great-great-grandmother's store,

110

helping to run a household, taking care of Baby Arden, and helping to farm.

Maybe it was time, like Ivy said, for me to step up and stop thinking about myself all the time. I wanted to be a better person. I'd start by taking Treva to the airport tomorrow, without complaining. Then I'd go by the hospital on the way home and see how I could help Rylan. Then I'd look for ways to help Ivy. Grad school, as she'd told me more than once, was stressful.

Treva started digging in her top drawer. "I printed out my itinerary at the library. . . ." She pulled out a piece of paper. "Here it is. My flight leaves at ten."

"Which means we should be there by eight. Which means, with traffic, we should leave by six." Which meant I needed to leave my apartment at 5:30 to pick her up on time.

"You don't have to take me," Treva said. "I can ask Gabe."

"No." I matched a pair of her socks. "I want to."

The next morning, as I stumbled up the steps to the back porch of the farmhouse, Rosene swung the door open. "*Gute Maiye.*"

"Good morning," I muttered.

"How about some breakfast?" Rosene asked.

"I don't think we have time." I followed Rosene into the warm kitchen. "Is Treva ready?"

111

"She ran upstairs to grab something." Thankfully Treva's duffel bag was by the door.

Dawdi sat at the table, eating a bowl of oatmeal. I suddenly had an image of him as a toddler at the same table and quickly turned my head, afraid I might giggle.

"Brenna," he said, "how are you this morning?"

"Good."

"Have you had breakfast?"

I shook my head and pulled a protein bar from my pocket. "I'll eat in the car."

"That's not enough. . . ." It was a conversation Dawdi and I had over and over. I knew he said all the same stuff each time because he loved me. I wished he could just say it the way Dad used to.

I heard thumps coming down the stairs and then Treva appeared, followed by Mammi.

"Brenna," Mammi said. "You're here." She looked sad.

"Jah," I answered. "Is everything all right?"

"Of course."

Treva, who wore jeans and boots, had her coat and backpack on. I told her one time that she had fashion confusion, and she'd laughed. She was like a five-year-old, changing clothes all the time, going from Amish dresses to ratty jeans within a couple of days. I hoped she didn't feel as confused about her identity. "Ready?" she asked.

"Are you?"

"Yep."

"Did you tell everyone good-bye?" Our Amish grandparents weren't very affectionate, but she at least needed to give them a formal farewell.

She patted Dawdi on the shoulder. "See you later."

He reached up and grabbed her hand and squeezed it. "Call every once in a while. But not at milking time."

Englischers sometimes thought Amish people didn't keep in touch by talking on the phone. That wasn't true. They weren't opposed to talking on the phone—they just couldn't have a phone in the house where it would interrupt family life. Mammi chatted over the barn phone with Gran once a week. And Dawdi talked with friends and neighbors all the time. Both of my Amish grandparents felt far more comfortable talking on the phone than I did.

Treva laughed and said to Dawdi, "I know you're going to miss me."

He would. I didn't know how Dawdi was going to get his work done without Treva's help. She'd turned out to be quite the farmer. And teaser. Dawdi and Treva had a fun relationship. I tried not to be jealous.

Next, Treva told Mammi good-bye, and then Rosene.

I grabbed Treva's duffel bag and said, "I'll stop by soon."

"How about later today?" Rosene asked. "It's going to be awfully quiet around here." Mammi nodded in agreement.

"That'll probably work." I didn't remember either of them ever looking so needy.

Once we were in the car, I pulled up the directions to the airport on my phone.

"How are you feeling?" Treva asked.

"I'm doing great."

"Great? You've never been great before."

I sighed as I pulled out of the driveway onto the road. "I'm trying to do better. That's all."

"Oh. Is it because of Johann?"

"What do you mean?"

"Ivy thinks you have a crush on Johann."

"I don't have a crush on Johann."

"She said he calls a lot, that she can hear the two of you chatting."

When I didn't answer, Treva said, "Brenna?"

"I don't have a crush on Johann."

"Okay," Treva said. "If you did, it would make sense. He sounds like a great guy."

"He is," I said. "But he's not interested in me. I just want to be his friend."

"What if he was interested in you?"

"He's not." We drove in silence after that. Once we were on Highway 30, I took a drink from my water bottle but kept my eyes on the road.

I thought Treva had fallen asleep, which I preferred. I wish she hadn't told me Ivy could

114

hear my conversations with Johann. I found that creepy. And I didn't want to talk about him with Treva. Johann was the bright spot in my life. I didn't want to jeopardize that by having Ivy tell him I had a crush on him.

"You know—"

I jumped and gripped the steering wheel more tightly.

"What's wrong?" Treva asked.

"I thought you were asleep."

She groaned. A minute later, she said, "What was I saying?"

"You know . . ."

"That's right." Treva twisted toward me in the seat. "Ivy and Conrad are serious. She and Johann were never interested in each other, and they definitely aren't now. If you like him, you should go for it."

"Go for it?" Befuddled, I asked, "What does that even mean?"

"You know, let him know you're interested."

"He lives in Ukraine. I haven't seen him in three years. He's been a soldier, graduated from college, and now he has a successful career. He's just being nice to me, which I'll take. He definitely isn't interested in me."

"You're selling yourself short," Treva said.

I groaned. "I'm not selling myself. I'd rather have him as an online friend than risk not having him as a friend at all."

Treva went quiet. I stayed on Highway 30 instead of going north to the interstate.

Treva spoke again, but this time she didn't startle me. Her voice was low and gravelly. "Yesterday I said I was feeling good about going home, but I'm not. I'm worried."

I'd be worried too, but I didn't say that to her. When I thought of home, I recalled the dark forest, the emergency lights, and the worst night of my life.

"What worries you the most?" I asked.

"That all the pain will come back. That I'll miss Mom and Dad. And you and Ivy too."

I reached over and took her hand, while keeping my eyes on the road. "The pain probably will come back."

Treva pulled her hand away and then, with a hint of sarcasm, said, "I can always count on you to look on the bright side."

"I'm being honest. The pain isn't a bad thing. That's how it works with grief. It gets easier and then harder and then easier again," I said. "It's all part of the healing process."

"I hope that's true," she answered. I'd encouraged Treva to go to counseling, but she didn't want to.

"How about your friends back home? Do they know you're coming?"

"Most are away at college," she said. "At least the ones I've kept in touch with." She sighed.

"The truth is, I didn't do a very good job keeping in touch, and I think most of my friends don't have any idea what to say to me."

"I'm sorry," I said. Treva always seemed so gregarious, so blessed with friends, that I'd expected she'd kept hers. I'd only had two friends in high school, and I hadn't kept in touch with them either. It felt awkward, even more awkward than normal life, and a reminder of what my life used to be. Not that it had been all roses. I'd been depressed. But at least I had my parents.

Even amidst my thoughts of the past, as I drove through the countryside and the sun began to rise, I felt a sense of peace. But once we reached I-476, my anxiety increased as I merged onto the freeway. The morning traffic inched along.

"Thanks for bringing me," Treva said.

"You're welcome." I concentrated on keeping a good distance between the van and the semi ahead of us. "I hope you know—" my voice cracked—"how much I'll miss you and how much I love you."

Treva didn't answer, but when I glanced quickly at her, a tear was sliding down her cheek.

When we reached the airport, I jumped out of the van and gave her a big hug. "Text me when you get to Denver," I said. "And when you get to Portland. And when you get home."

"I will." She hugged me back.

"*Sei gut!*" Be good.

She laughed.

That was what Rosene would tell us when we left the farmhouse when we first came to Lancaster County, even if we were only going to do the milking.

As I drove away, following the directions on my GPS to get back to Lancaster County, a tear trickled down my cheek and then another. Driving Treva to the airport had been the easy part. Telling her good-bye was much harder than I thought it would be.

9

Two hours later, I was in Lancaster, back at the hospital, yawning. If I stopped by the farm on the way home, I wouldn't stay for long. Helping other people was tiring. And helping someone who talked about suing my family was intimidating. But I couldn't imagine Rylan was serious. He was the one who went up the staircase. I couldn't imagine he'd have a legitimate case.

When I reached his room, Rylan was in a wheelchair. He wore the shirt and coat he had on the day of the accident and the sports pants, which were cut at the knee on the right side, just above where the cast ended.

"What's going on?" I asked.

"I'm going home."

"Home?" I stammered.

He nodded. "You're taking me."

"I am?"

"Just kidding. I mean you could, but the nurse already arranged for transport."

"What about once you're home? Who's going to care for you then?"

Rylan shrugged. "You are."

"Right," I said. "I'll help with your classes, but who's going to help with other—" I paused— "stuff?"

He grinned. It seemed his pain meds must be doing the trick. "Like bathing and dressing?"

I nodded.

"Here's the thing," he said. "They wanted me to go to a care center for a couple of weeks, but they couldn't find one with an opening. They'll have home health come in to shower me a couple of times a week." He shrugged. "Hopefully my brothers will step up for the rest of it."

"Your brothers are coming?"

He frowned. "Not literal brothers. Viktor, Marko, Gabe."

"Got it." I took his key from my purse. "You'll need this."

"Hold on to it for now."

I put the key back in my purse. "Who is going to meet you at your apartment?"

"What do you mean?"

"Will Marko and Viktor be there?"

"I haven't texted them."

"How about if you text them so they can help get things set up in your apartment for you? I can go to the store. I put two lasagnas in your freezer last night. I can take one of those out to thaw. I dropped off a loaf of homemade bread too."

"Thanks," he said. "I'll text Viktor."

"I'll leave now instead of following the ambulance," I said. "I'll be at your apartment when you arrive."

When I reached the complex, I went up to our apartment first and found Ivy, Conrad, and Gabe all eating pizza at our little table.

Surprised not to have the apartment to myself, I asked, "Why are you home?"

Ivy answered, "My class got canceled."

I turned toward Conrad. "Why are you here?"

"Fall break."

"Oh, right." I turned to Gabe. "Why are you here? You're supposed to be working at the store."

"Priscilla closed it for the day."

"What?"

He nodded. "She said she needed the day off."

That was strange. I didn't remember Mammi closing the store on a regular day since we'd moved to Lancaster County.

Gabe stood. "Is Rylan here?"

"Not yet," I said. "But he will be any minute. Did he text you?"

"No," Gabe answered. "Marko did. He said someone needed to get Rylan situated."

I put my backpack down in the entryway. "Let's go down."

Ivy stood. "We'll come too."

Conrad gave her a questioning look.

Ivy said, "I'd like to meet Rylan. And maybe I can help."

I suppressed a groan. "Meet us down there." I

grabbed Gabe by the arm. "Come on. No doubt the ambulance driver drove faster than I did. They could be here any second."

As I dragged Gabe out the door, I asked, "Did you tell Conrad you joined up?"

He quickened his step, now dragging me along. "Shh."

"Guess that means no." I concentrated on going down the steps, feeling as if he might pull me down. "Don't you think it's going to come up?" I let go of Gabe's arm as we reached the first level.

I turned toward Rylan's apartment, and Gabe followed. "I didn't think Ivy would suggest that she and Conrad actually meet Rylan."

"So you think you can compartmentalize all of this? Job. Army. Family. Church."

"I'm not going to church anymore."

"I noticed. Why?"

He shrugged.

I wasn't going to press Gabe if he didn't want to talk about it, so I changed the topic. "What happened in Afghanistan to Rylan?"

"I don't know," he answered. "We have drill Saturday and Sunday. Maybe I can figure it out then."

Beyond us, in the parking lot, an ambulance turned in. "You meet Rylan," I said. "I'll go unlock his door."

Gabe followed my instructions.

I unlocked Rylan's door and stepped inside, noting the chill in the air. I turned up the heat and then opened the window covering over the sliding door to his patio. Then I stepped back out the front door.

Gabe came toward me from the parking lot. "Rylan needs his wheelchair. It's in his bedroom closet."

I headed back into the apartment and into the bedroom. He had a bed and a dresser. That was it.

I slid open the closet. Inside was a sleek wheelchair that was much lighter than I expected. I wheeled it through the bedroom door and out of the apartment.

Gabe still stood at the edge of the parking lot, so I wheeled it to him. Once the attendant had transferred Rylan into his chair, he grabbed a white pharmacy bag from the back of the van and handed it to Rylan.

"Thanks." Rylan fist-bumped the attendant.

Gabe undid the brakes, grabbed the back of the chair, and wheeled Rylan onto the sidewalk as Ivy and Conrad came down the stairs.

"Hey," Ivy said. I hadn't noticed what she was wearing before, but now I did, aware of what Rylan saw. She wore a jean skirt, a green blouse, and a black scarf on her head.

When Gabe didn't say anything, I called out, "Rylan, this is my sister Ivy. And Gabe's brother, Conrad."

"Say what?"

"My sister Ivy. She's my roommate. And Conrad is Gabe's brother."

"Seriously?" Rylan turned his head back toward Gabe. "You didn't tell me you have a brother."

Gabe's face reddened. "I have a brother. His name is Conrad." He ducked his head. "Now you know."

Conrad stepped forward with his hand extended. "Nice to meet you, Rylan."

Rylan shook his hand and smiled. "Same."

After we entered Rylan's apartment, Gabe pushed him to the recliner. I held my breath, sure Rylan would say something about knowing Gabe through his buddies who were in the Army Reserve and giving away Gabe's secret. But he didn't.

"I can't put weight on my leg, and I can't transfer without my prosthesis," Rylan said. "I don't have anything to pivot on. You two are going to have to make a chair for me."

"A chair?" I stammered.

"Like a sling." Rylan looked at Gabe. "Do you know what I mean?"

Gabe nodded and then grasped both of Conrad's wrists with his hands and said, "Grab my wrists." Then they stepped toward the wheelchair and Rylan scooted into the chair they'd made.

"We need to turn around," Gabe instructed.

They did and then took a step to the recliner,

lowering Rylan onto the seat. I felt relieved as Gabe and Conrad stepped away.

"Put my wheelchair back in my bedroom," Rylan said to Gabe. Then he looked at me. "It's time for my meds." Rylan still held the white bag on his lap. "Could you get me a glass of water?"

As I retreated to the kitchen, Gabe came out of the bedroom and inched toward the door.

"Don't you dare leave," I whispered as I walked by. He froze.

"What services do you have set up?" Ivy asked Rylan.

I rolled my eyes. She hadn't wasted any time getting into her social worker role. I filled a glass with water and returned to the living room.

"Make sure and contact your college counselor," Ivy said after he explained he'd have home health visits. "They can help make sure you get what you need there, including any mobility help."

"I've got Brenna for that." Rylan smiled wryly as I approached with his water and put it on the table beside his recliner. He took a bottle out of the bag. "Although I need to get my prosthesis evaluated before I can think about going back to school. Unless I use a medical transport."

"What do you need at the store?" I asked.

Instead of answering me, Rylan asked, "What's for lunch?"

"We have pizza at our place," Ivy said. "We'll bring it down."

"I'll go get it," Conrad said.

Gabe started to the door. "I'll go with you."

I strode after both of them. "Don't let him leave," I said to Conrad. "I can't stay with Rylan all afternoon. Gabe or one of the other guys needs to."

"I broke my leg, not my ears," Rylan said.

My face grew warm again. Instead of responding to what he said, I stepped to his refrigerator and opened it. There was a quart of milk, ketchup, mustard, and pickles. That was it. I hadn't looked in the fridge when I put the lasagnas in the freezer and the bread on the counter the evening before. "What do you eat?" I asked.

"Food."

"There's a service that can help with that." Ivy had her phone in her hand, Googling away. "Or we could start a meal train."

"Or I could go to the store." I needed to get out of Rylan's apartment. "What do you need?"

"Your grandmother's phone number. The one at the store."

"She doesn't have a phone at the store," I answered.

Ivy butted in. "I can give you the barn phone number."

I groaned. Ivy needed a lesson on boundaries. Sometimes in a new situation, she grew anxious and talked too much.

"Okay." Rylan took his phone from the pocket of his jacket.

Ivy rattled off the barn number, and Rylan added it to his phone. Then his phone beeped and he read what I assumed was a text.

I took out my phone. "Let's make a grocery list."

"Marko and Viktor are going to the store on the way here." Rylan glanced up from his phone. "They're going to make stuffed cabbage and dumplings for dinner tonight."

"Okay." He didn't need the lasagna after all, at least not tonight. "What about groceries for lunches and dinners?"

"I'm good," he said.

He wasn't good—he couldn't live off condiments. But I didn't say that. I turned toward the door, wanting to leave, as Conrad and Gabe came through it. Each carried a pizza box.

I had to get out of the apartment. Rylan's injury. Gabe's secret. Ivy in her take-charge mode. It was all too much. "Well," I said to Rylan, "if you don't need any groceries and the guys are all coming, I'm going to go ahead and get going."

Ivy crossed her arms. "Brenna, what's going on?"

"I told Rosene I'd stop by," I answered. "Rylan, if you need anything, call me." I took his key from my purse again. "You should take this."

"I'm not going anywhere," he smirked. "You

keep it. If I need help during the middle of the night, you'll have to let yourself in."

He must be teasing. Viktor and Marko lived in the complex. There was no reason for me to show up in the middle of the night. I didn't like his teasing—it made me uncomfortable.

"Bye." I headed for the door.

As I was backing out of my parking place, Gabe appeared at the passenger window.

I jumped as he slapped the window with his hand.

I rolled it down. "What do you want?"

"Where are you going?"

"To the farm."

"You can't leave."

"Why not?"

"You didn't want me to leave."

"Yeah, because you can help Rylan get to the bathroom. I can't."

"Ivy thinks you're mad at her."

"I'm not mad at Ivy." I sighed. "It sounds as if Rylan has everything covered for today. Marko and Viktor are doing dinner. I'm not needed. I want to go see Rosene."

He took a step backward.

I waved. He turned and marched back toward the apartment. I put a stick of gum in my mouth and continued backing out of the parking space.

I wasn't mad at Ivy, but she'd certainly inserted

herself into the situation. She was in charge now. I should have been relieved, but I felt replaced. Which was actually a new feeling for me.

I turned onto the highway, heading west. I'd made the trip to the farm so many times in the last month that I should have been able to drive it without a second thought. But I couldn't. My therapist told me I was hypervigilant, which I thought was a good quality when it came to driving. She said it took a toll on me. *"It's okay to relax,"* she said. *"To enjoy the scenery."*

My phone dinged. I glanced at it quickly. Treva. She'd made it to Denver.

She'd be in Oregon soon.

Everyone was surprised by how much I liked Lancaster County. I couldn't explain the comfort it brought me. It was open and organized. Beautiful yet predictable. Tidy and appealing. And aesthetically interesting. Every farm was well kept, yet each one was different in some way. Especially on laundry days.

The land was flat to gently undulating, and underneath was limestone and dolomite, creating some of the most fertile soils in the eastern United States, which the Zimmerman farm benefited from.

When I reached the farm, I parked by the shed. Dawdi stood next to the barn door, and as I walked toward the house, he called out, "Did you come to help me?"

"No," I called back. I knew I was supposed to

say something more, but I wasn't sure what that would be.

He laughed, waved, and stepped back into the barn.

When I reached the kitchen, no one was in it. My heart fell. I hoped Rosene wasn't resting. But then I chastised myself. If she needed to rest, she should be resting.

"Brenna? Is that you?"

Relieved, I said, "Jah."

Rosene appeared, one of her old scrapbooks in her hand.

"Is Mammi around?"

Rosene shook her head. "She closed the store for the day, but she's there doing inventory."

"Oh." I usually helped with inventory, but Mammi would have told me if she needed me.

"This is the scrapbook I kept from 1940 to the end of the war." Rosene held it up. "Let's sit at the table."

I eyed the coffeepot on the back of the stove. The early morning was catching up with me. I stepped to the stove and lifted it—it felt about half full. "Want some?" I asked Rosene.

"No, thank you," she said.

I poured myself a cup and then sat beside Rosene. She had the scrapbook open to the first page. There were pressed flowers between pieces of some sort of paper and then a newspaper article about Pearl Harbor being bombed.

"I don't know if I can explain this," Rosene said. "I was absolutely horrified by the attack on Pearl Harbor, and as someone who believes in nonresistance, I dreaded the US going to war. On the other hand, I was relieved that my adopted country was standing up to German fascism and Japanese imperialism at last. There were times in the late thirties and early forties when it seemed citizens in the US who embraced isolationism at home and authoritarianism abroad might sway the entire country. Even members of our own Congress invested in companies that profited from Nazi Germany. Prominent Americans like Charles Lindbergh, Henry Ford, and the Catholic priest Father Charles Coughlin, who had a radio program, were vocally anti-Semitic. Groups like America First, the German-American Bund, and the Christian Front embraced fascism." Rosene paused a moment. "Do you find these details boring?"

"No," I said sincerely.

She continued. "There were even elected federal officials who seemed willing to hand over our country for their own gain. I wasn't sure the US would stand up to fascism—until the day after the attack on Pearl Harbor, when FDR declared war on Japan. Three days later, Germany and Italy declared war on us."

Her explanation reminded me of Dad's spontaneous history lessons.

She continued, "So many people around the world had been swayed by Adolf Hitler. Christians in Germany and in other countries, including the US, identified with his Aryan supremacy and nationalism. I was relieved that the US, as a whole, chose not to."

"Me too."

"I hope history isn't repeating itself," she said.

I didn't follow current events much, but I had taken notice of the Unite the Right rally in Charlottesville, Virginia, in August where marchers chanted, "Jews will not replace us." Then a counterprotester was killed and many more were injured when a car driven by a neo-Nazi plowed into a crowd of people.

I'd also noted the immigration ban last January—how could I not? Ivy and Conrad had gone to the Philadelphia airport to protest. I'd heard on the radio that our new president's international policy was based on his America First doctrine. The fact that "America First" was chosen as a contemporary slogan certainly made a connection to the 1930s and '40s and those ideologies that had frightened Rosene at the time.

The young man who rear-ended Dad's car that I was driving the night of the accident also had neo-Nazi ideas. History did repeat itself, all too often. Or sometimes a dangerous ideology remained latent for periods of time, only to rear its ugly head again.

Rosene turned the page of the scrapbook. Next was Dawdi's birth announcement and Rosene's high school graduation announcement and a photo of her wearing a cape dress and Mennonite Kapp and holding a bouquet of flowers.

"That was taken at my graduation," Rosene said. "By an Englisch friend. It's the only photo I have from that period of my life."

Rosene flipped through the scrapbook. There was a photo of Martha in front of a sign for Franklin & Marshall College, wearing a Mennonite dress and her hair in a bun at the nape of her neck with a sheer cloth pinned to the crown of her head. "A friend of hers took the photo too," Rosene explained.

"I'm surprised your Mutter didn't have a camera."

"She either wasn't interested in photography or decided she'd made Vater compromise on enough things and didn't want to force another."

That made sense.

There was an article in the Lancaster newspaper about the Red Cross with a photo of a young woman. I leaned closer. "Is that Martha?"

"Jah," Rosene answered. "She was delivering a Christmas box to the family of a veteran who was in a POW camp in Germany."

Next was a sketch of a pond. Then recipes for Sauerbraten, Rouladen, Spätzle, apple strudel, and Black Forest cake. Then a bookmark, a handmade valentine from Martha, and a birthday card to Rosene from Clare and Jeremiah. The next page was an article from the *Philadelphia Inquirer* on Wednesday, August 15, 1945, with the headline "Peace."

"The war had finally ended." Rosene closed the book.

I asked, "What about the other pages?"

She grinned. "They'd give the story away."

I crossed my arms. "Didn't you already give the story away, with the article about the end of the war in the Pacific?"

"I'm pretty sure you already knew about that."

I rolled my eyes. "So what's on the rest of the pages?"

"An article or two, but mostly postcards."

"From where? And who?"

"You'll find out." She pushed the scrapbook toward the middle of the table. "Did you see Dawdi when you arrived?"

"Yes."

"Did he tell you Rylan left a message?"

"No."

Rosene stood and walked to the counter, where she kept a notebook. She took a slip of paper from it. "Arden hasn't told Priscilla yet." She held the piece of paper close enough so she could read it. "This is what he said: 'I wanted to let you know that I'm thinking about contacting a personal injury attorney about the accident. If you would

134

like to contact me, you can get my number from Brenna.' "

"Wow." I wasn't sure how to respond. Maybe he was serious about suing Mammi. "Does Dawdi want Rylan's number?"

"No," Rosene said.

"Why not?" I rubbed the scar on my forehead.

"He said what Rylan wants to do is up to him."

"I feel horrible."

Rosene smiled kindly. "It's not your fault."

"I'm the one who brought him on the property."

"You know," Rosene said, "most things in life aren't anyone's fault. They just happen."

"I should go back and talk with Rylan," I said.

"No." Rosene placed the piece of paper back on the notebook. "You should stay here and not get involved in this. It's not your responsibility."

But I felt it was my responsibility.

"How about a piece of apple strudel? And then more of the story?"

I couldn't pass up Rosene's apple strudel. Nor her story.

10

Martha

Zeke was on time for the milking the next morning and said the doctor had examined his Mamm and then given her a tuberculosis test. "She tested positive."

"Oh no." Martha's heart sank for all the Zimmermans.

"Jah," Zeke said. "But the doctor also said there's a new treatment he wants to try. He said to bring her back next week."

Martha hoped the treatment would work. Rosene came out to help a few minutes later, and the three worked without speaking much.

An hour and a half later, as she connected a pump to the last of the cows, Rosene said, "I'm going into the house to help Clare finish breakfast."

"Good," Martha said. "The PWs will be here soon."

A few minutes later, Zeke shouted, "Martha! We have a leak!"

She scooted back on the stool. From time to time the old aluminum milk cans, which were hard to replace since the war started, sprung leaks. Vater welded the holes shut, but he couldn't do that

136

when the can was full. "Pour the milk back into the holding vat," Martha called out as she ran toward the milk room.

"There are more leaks!"

She quickened her pace. The cans, with brass tags engraved with the name *Simons* on them, were lined up on a low shelf, ready for the driver to pick up. Milk covered the shelf and dripped down onto the concrete floor.

"These are leaking." Zeke pointed to the first one and then the second one. "And this one too." He moved to the third can and shifted it around, showing the leak. Martha looked closer. It was more than a leak. A hole had been punched in the bottom of the can with some sort of tool. And in the fifth can and the eighth one too. Half of the cans had holes punched in them and were leaking.

"Someone did this on purpose." Zeke took the lid off the first one and quickly dumped it into the vat.

Martha nodded. The PWs had left yesterday before they'd finished the milking. And they hadn't arrived yet. Or had they?

She heard voices outside. Was that German? "Are the PWs here already?" She grabbed the next can.

"Jah." Zeke stepped to the door. "They've been here for fifteen minutes or so. Your Dat is talking to them."

Martha groaned. They were an hour early. She grabbed two twenty-gallon cans that they used when she was a girl. "I'll sterilize these in the house. Hopefully Clare has water boiling. Pour all the milk into the vat for now. We can't take any chances. I'll send Rosene out to help."

She ran as fast as she could toward the house with the cans. Dirk stared at her while Otis grinned.

"Why are you here so early?" Martha yelled at Sergeant Schwarz.

"We were dropped off first," he responded. "Before the neighbors."

"Go to the field and continue picking up rocks." Martha gestured toward the shed with one of the cans. "The burlap bags are just inside the door."

"Yes, ma'am," he said.

When Martha reached the house, she barreled in without taking off her boots. "I need boiling water," she said. "Now."

Clare, with Arden on her hip, said, "The kettle is hot, and I have a pot nearly boiling." As Clare spoke, Rosene began scrubbing the sink.

When she finished, Martha told Rosene to go to the barn and help Zeke. "He's pouring all the milk back into the vat. We can't take any chances. Bring me another twenty-gallon can to sterilize."

Martha got to work, first testing the twenty-gallon cans to make sure they didn't have any leaks. They didn't. Then she scrubbed the cans

138

with soap and water and rinsed them with the boiling water from the kettle and then the pot on the back of the stove. After she dried them carefully, she started back out to the barn, meeting Rosene halfway, who was carrying another twenty-gallon can. "Three more of the cans have holes."

"Thank you," Martha said. "Are the PWs all out in the field?"

"All except Pavlo. I saw him behind the barn a few minutes ago."

Martha groaned. She needed to find him. The milk truck turned the corner of the lane and headed toward her. "I'll tell the driver we have one more can coming. Hurry."

Fifteen minutes later, when they had all the milk on the truck, Martha asked Zeke if he'd seen Vater.

"He followed the PWs to the field."

When Martha found Vater, he was breathing heavily. As she took his arm, she asked Sergeant Schwarz where Pavlo was.

"In the outhouse."

"Rosene saw him behind the barn."

Sergeant Schwarz shrugged. "Then why did you ask me?"

"Because you're responsible for him."

"I can't walk each of the men to the outhouse."

"Reprimand him when he comes back," she said. "Zeke will be out soon."

When she got Vater to the house, Mutter had already left for the store. Martha told Clare to make sure Vater ate and rested, and she told Zeke to go to the field and continue plowing. Then she gulped down a bowl of porridge and went back outside to look for Pavlo. She found him just then coming out of the outhouse.

"Stomach problems," he said in English as he took off jogging toward the field. Martha followed him at a swift march. When she reached the field, Pavlo was trudging across the plowed furrows toward the others.

Martha waved at Sergeant Schwarz and then beckoned him toward her where they could speak in private. It seemed to take him forever, but finally he reached her. She told him about the punctured milk cans.

"You think one of the PWs did it?" he asked.

"Yes."

"Do you have any evidence?"

"That's what I'm looking for," she responded. "You need to search them."

"If one of them did do it, they wouldn't keep the tool."

"You need to search them anyway."

He squinted toward the men. "What about the Amish boy you have working for you. Does he live close by?"

"What does that matter?"

"He could have snuck over and done it in the

140

middle of the night. Or while you were out of the milking room."

"Don't be ridiculous." Martha nodded toward the PWs. "Go search them."

"I'll search them during our lunch break."

"Search them now," Martha said.

He started toward the men, calling out in German, "We've had some mischief in the milk room. . . ." The men turned toward him, and he started back across the plowed part of the field.

Pavlo nudged Otis, who turned his back to Sergeant Schwarz—and Martha. Dirk took a step forward and called out in German, "What are you looking for?"

"Something sharp," Sergeant Schwarz replied in German.

Pavlo stepped in front of Otis. Otis's leg moved. And his foot. Was he stomping something into the soil?

Martha watched as Schwarz patted the men down and then lifted their pant legs and checked their socks. When he finished, he turned toward her and shrugged.

Not bothering to respond, she turned.

Zeke stood a few feet away. "What was that all about?"

"He was looking for something sharp that could have punctured the milk cans."

"But he didn't find anything?"

Martha nodded. "I was sure he wouldn't, but

141

I wanted the PWs to know we aren't going to pretend as if nothing happened. Not this time. They caused a lot of unnecessary work." She met Zeke's eyes. "Are you okay doing the plowing this morning? I don't want Vater to do it."

"I'll be fine," he said.

When they all gathered in the kitchen for their noon meal, after Vater prayed, Zeke told everyone about his Mamm's diagnosis and that the doctor hoped to try a new treatment.

"Streptomycin, most likely," Mutter said. "I read about it recently. They've just started using it with good results. She's fortunate."

Zeke nodded. "That's what the doctor said."

The rest of the day passed by without any further incidents. By three o'clock, Zeke had finished the plowing, and the PWs would finish picking up the rocks by four, when they were scheduled to leave. There were several large piles by the side of the field that would need to be moved.

Martha returned to the house, quickly washed, and changed into a dress. The day had grown surprisingly warm, and she didn't need a coat. As she came down the back stairs to the kitchen, she overhead Clare cooing to Arden, "Your *Dat* will be home soon."

Arden squealed in reply.

"Where's Rosene?" Martha asked as she stepped into the kitchen.

"Helping Mutter." Clare turned toward Martha. "Thank you for getting Jeremiah. Vater wanted to go back out and give Zeke a break, but I convinced him to rest again."

"That sounds like a good idea." Martha poured a glass of water from the pitcher by the sink, drank it, and then grabbed the keys to the Studebaker off the hook by the back door. "I imagine Jeremiah will want to see his Mamm too. Do you want to tell him about the doctor's visit?"

"Jah," Clare said. "We'll go over on Sunday after church to see her—at a distance."

"When will Jeremiah have to return?"

"Sunday evening."

"I'll give him a ride. You and Arden should come with us."

Clare smiled. "I'd like that."

Twenty minutes later, Martha approached the train station and found a place to park. She'd always admired the brick building with the columns in the front and remembered when it first opened when she was seven.

"Martha!" Jeremiah walked through the vast lobby, bathed in the late afternoon light streaming through the windows. He wore trousers, a handmade shirt, and a wool coat. He clutched the strap of the bag he carried in one hand and held a magazine in the other. His beard touched his chest, and his eyes twinkled.

Martha adored Jeremiah. He was the older brother she never had. "You're here already."

"The train was early."

"Ready to go home?"

"Jah." He sighed. "I just wish it was for longer."

"I can imagine," Martha said. Here she longed for some sort of life away from the farm when all Jeremiah wanted was to be with his little family.

Once they were in the car, Martha noticed he still held the magazine in his hand. On the front cover was an ice skater. "What do you have there?" she asked as they turned onto the highway.

"The March edition of *Life* magazine. I bought it at the Thirtieth Street Station." He opened it. "There's an article about the bombing of Cologne. Twenty thousand civilians were killed, and sixty percent of the city destroyed."

Martha glanced at the photo. It appeared to be miles and miles of rubble. They already knew thousands of people had been killed in Frankfurt in bombings over the last few years, and the city's central old city, which was close to *Onkel* Josef and *Kuisine* Lena's house, had been nearly destroyed.

"Every day I'm thankful Clare and Rosene came home when they did," Jeremiah said. "Whenever I question how God can use me where I am, I think of how He used Clare, and continues too. And Rosene too."

Martha agreed. It was a good reminder for her as

well. "How are things at the hospital?" she asked.

Jeremiah hesitated a moment and then said, "You don't want to know."

"No, I do," she replied. "Tell me."

"Horrible," he answered. "The patients are treated worse than animals. There's no dignity for them." He shuddered. "I'm not certain what to do, but I know I need to do something."

Martha wasn't sure how to respond.

Jeremiah asked, "How do I smell?"

She laughed. "What do you mean?"

"I can't seem to scrub away the smells of the hospital."

Martha smiled. "Surely it's not worse than the farm."

"It's a hundred times worse."

"What kind of smells?"

"You don't want to know."

"Jeremiah," she said. "Of course I want to. I don't think you can shock me."

He grimaced. "Urine, feces, vomit. Rotting flesh from bedsores."

She wrinkled her nose.

"The odors permeate the entire place."

"That does sound horrible."

"It's a hellhole," Jeremiah said. "And many of the regular attendants come to work drunk. I think it's to numb themselves, but then they beat the patients."

Martha winced.

Jeremiah said, "I don't mean to complain. I know others have it far worse than I do, including the patients. And people in war zones all around the world."

"What do you think can be done?"

He held up the magazine. "Some of us think *Life* needs to be told how horrible things are."

"You could send a letter," Martha said. "Or send one to the *Philadelphia Inquirer*."

"One of the Quaker men I work with grew up in Philadelphia and contacted a reporter from the *Inquirer*. The response was that there were far more important things to investigate than a mental hospital."

"I'm sorry," Martha said. "Maybe after the war . . ."

Jeremiah nodded. "But that won't help the ones who won't last until the war is over."

"It's that bad?"

"Jah. And worse."

After a moment of silence, Martha said, "We have PWs again."

Jeremiah's voice rose. "We do?"

"Yes. Vater requested them without telling me. It's complicated, but it does mean Rosene should have more time to help Clare."

Jeremiah crossed his arms. "Hopefully it won't be more complicated than it became last time."

Martha didn't have the heart to tell him that it already was.

When they reached the farmhouse, Clare handed Martha a folded piece of paper. "Your friend George left a message for you with Mutter. Rosene ran it over."

Martha unfolded it. *I need your help translating. I'll come by to pick you up at 5:30. I'll explain once we're on our way.*

It was 5:15. She ran upstairs to change into a skirt, blouse, and sweater. And her new hat.

11

Martha waited on the front porch for George, not wanting him to come to the door. Martha had told Clare she was leaving and to tell the others at dinner, because she didn't want to get in a discussion with either of her parents about her work with the Red Cross—or about George.

As a car, a black Ford, turned into the drive, Jeremiah came around the side of the porch. Martha started down the steps, squinting into the lowering sun.

"Where are you going?" Jeremiah asked.

"On a Red Cross assignment," Martha said. "I'm doing some translating. Are you done with the milking?"

"I wondered what you were doing," Jeremiah said, "when you didn't come out to the barn."

The car turned toward the house. George stopped the car and climbed out of the driver's seat. He wore a suit and hat, which he took off as he said, "Hello, Martha!"

She smiled and then nodded toward Jeremiah. "George, I'd like you to meet my brother-in-law, Jeremiah Zimmerman. Jeremiah, this is George Hall."

The two shook hands as they both said, "Nice to meet you." They were about the same height and locked eyes as they spoke.

"I appreciate Martha's help this evening," George said. "Something has come up at the POW camp north of here, and I need a translator. One I can depend on."

Martha's stomach fell. At a PW camp? Was it where their PWs lived? She'd ask George once they were in the car.

"It won't take long. We won't be late." George put his hat back on his head.

Jeremiah said, "Drive carefully."

Martha gave Jeremiah a strained smile. "Have a good evening with your family."

He smiled back, but genuinely. "Oh, I will. See you soon."

As George pulled the car back onto the road, he drove slowly along the fields. "Is all this land your family's?"

"Yes."

He pointed toward the store. "What's that?"

"A mercantile my family owns."

Mutter stood near the back of the store by the outside staircase, speaking with a man who wore a suit and hat. On the other side of them was a large car. "That's my mother," Martha said. "She must be talking with a salesman."

She also recognized Franz Richter, a German man who owned an acreage nearby, as he turned from the parking lot onto the highway in his roadster. He had moved to Lancaster County from New York after the war started. He was older, probably in his late sixties, and seemed fond of Mutter. She humored him.

As they passed the store, George said, "The Red Cross is taking applications for positions in Europe to settle refugees. I have an extra one— would you like it?"

Martha asked, "Did you send one in?"

"Yes."

She stayed silent a moment and then said, "I'll think about it." She turned toward him. "What's going on at the PW camp?"

"A couple of things," he said. "First, the camp does classes on Friday evenings. Usually, someone from the YMCA teaches a class on writing poetry. Someone from the college teaches a class on democracy. Often, someone from the community teaches a painting class. Nobody has a reason to be bored in the camp. POWs are provided with writing material, art supplies, woodworking tools, and musical instruments. They're allowed to correspond with their families in Germany, and they perform musical performances too. Oh, and they show at least one movie a week— sometimes more."

The PWs last fall hadn't mentioned any of that.

"I usually work as a Red Cross inspector, but tonight I'm going to teach first aid since the usual instructor couldn't make it. I need you to translate for me. And I also need to interview a POW who says he's been mistreated by a guard."

"There may be a problem." Martha told him about the PWs who were working on the farm. "Their camp is ten miles north. I'm guessing it's the same camp."

"Probably. It's a branch camp, so it's still fairly large. Chances are you won't see any of them. If you do, will they recognize you?"

"I'm not sure. . . ." On the farm, she wore overalls that were too big and a bulky coat. And a stocking hat over her pinned-up hair. "Maybe not. And there are only four of them." She explained that she didn't want any of them to know she spoke German.

"Why not?"

"Things got awkward last fall when the PWs figured out most of us on the farm spoke German. It got even worse when they figured out Mutter and Rosene, my little sister, are from Germany."

"Your little sister is from Germany?"

"Yes. My older sister went to Germany in 1937 and came back in 1939 with Rosene, our cousin. My parents adopted her."

"I see." George turned north.

"Anyway, the last group of PWs tried to get chummy once they realized we could understand German. They expected Mutter to listen to their problems. They expected me to give them more breaks. One tried to flirt with Rosene all the time. They often hid from the guard. I found one in the barn taking a nap."

George glanced toward her. "Are things going better with this new group since they don't know you speak German?"

Martha gave him a wry smile. "Not really. Yesterday one of them put a potato in the exhaust pipe of the tractor. This morning, someone punctured half of our milk cans, and we had to scramble to sterilize some old ones to get the milk to the truck on time."

"So, they're acting worse than the group before who did know you spoke German?"

"Perhaps." Martha tugged on her hat. "But I'd still rather have them think I can't understand them."

"Don't take anything they do personally," George said. "Think of it as part of a game. As POWs, they're expected to be disruptive. Some even feel a responsibility to escape."

"Really?"

He nodded. "They're encouraged to by the German government. In fact," he said, "it's not a crime for them to escape, although there are cases of POWs who are trying to escape being shot by guards."

Martha grimaced.

"However," George said, "it is a crime to help a POW escape. An American in Detroit helped a German POW who escaped a camp in Canada. He was arrested, tried, and sentenced to death by hanging."

Martha wrapped her arms around her middle.

George continued, "The good news is that not many POWs try to escape. Many are shocked by just how large the US is. Getting to Canada, our ally, isn't going to do them much good, and it's a long trip to Mexico. The POW helped in Detroit got as far as San Antonio before he was captured. Very few cross the Mexican border. The fear is that they'll connect with the German underground in the United States. Complicating our work further, there have been rumors of a German spy in the area. We need to be extra vigilant in dealing with the POWs and any suspicious behavior."

Martha didn't respond.

George looked at her. "What's really bothering you?"

"Honestly?"

He nodded.

"I worry that someone in my family could get too close to one of the PWs."

"Your little sister?"

"Perhaps," Martha said. She couldn't tell him she worried about her mother the most. Was she really speaking with a salesman when they drove by? Or someone else?

The military police at the gate checked George's identification and then allowed them to proceed. Watchtowers stood at the corners of the camp, and a high barbed-wire fence encircled the property. George parked in front of a large building where a few other cars were parked. "The first aid class will be held in the corner of the mess hall," George said, "and starts at 6:30."

A few PWs, still wearing their dark blue work uniforms, walked by. Then another who was wearing a faded German uniform.

"They're allowed to wear their uniforms here?" Martha reached for the door handle.

"Yes," George answered. He stepped out of the car, walked around the back, and opened Martha's door. She stepped out to a whistle from across the street and nearly laughed. None of the PWs who worked on the Simons farm would recognize her.

George smiled at her, and she met his gaze and smiled back but neither of them spoke. She didn't look across the street to see who had whistled. She guessed the PWs didn't see many women, at least not ones who weren't dressed in overalls and oversized coats. Or work dresses.

George grabbed a box from the trunk of his car. When they reached the mess hall, a few PWs were eating, but none were in the far corner where George set up for his class.

Soon, twelve students gathered. George started by saying that millions of accidents occur in the US each year—in homes, on farms, and on highways. "The more you know what to do if you or someone you know has an accident, or if you come upon one, the better your chances of saving someone's life—maybe even your own."

Martha translated. George showed how to check if someone had a pulse and if they were conscious. He explained when to move someone—if there was a fire or another threat—and explained when to immobilize someone who might have a head, neck, or back injury. He took out a hand towel and demonstrated how to stop bleeding, and then took out a handkerchief and a stick and showed how to make and apply a tourniquet.

As Martha translated, she was grateful for the German songs Mutter and Rosene had taught her about body parts.

"Don't forget our smallest friends," George said. "More children die in accidents than from anything else." Martha winced as she translated George's words. "Never leave a child unattended around water, and if a child disappears, immediately check any nearby ponds, creeks, and rivers."

As he wrapped up, he talked about preventing injuries, especially on worksites, saying, "If you see anything dangerous, point it out to your guard, supervisor, or the owner of the business."

They'd been fortunate on their farm, partly due to Vater's diligence in enforcing safety, but she'd certainly heard of horrific farm accidents. And she knew how easily they could happen. Zeke had nearly been trampled by two workhorses a few years ago. He'd rolled out of the way just in time.

George glanced at the clock at the end of the hall. "We have just a few more minutes. Any questions?"

"I have something to say," one of the PWs said in German. Martha translated.

"Go ahead," George said.

The man turned toward Martha. "Your accent is horrible. Where did you learn German?"

"Could you understand me?" Martha asked him. "Jah."

Martha shrugged. "Then I did my job."

Another PW added, "Your accent isn't that bad." He pointed to the man who'd criticized her. "He's always trying to kick up a row." Martha thought of the PWs on the farm.

George gave Martha a questioning look. She shrugged again and in German told the PWs, "The class is over. Thank you for attending."

The PWs began moving the tables to the sides of the mess hall and setting up the chairs in rows. George packed his supplies in his box and then said, "We'll go out the back door and up to the infirmary."

Dusk was falling as they walked along a trail up the hill through the trees. The evening had grown chilly, and she wished she had more than a sweater. When they reached the infirmary, which was a large cabin, George held the door open for

Martha and she entered first. A nurse wearing a white dress and a cap on her auburn hair sat at a desk. "Hello, George," she said as they walked in.

He said, "Hello, Nurse Olson," and then introduced Martha. "She's going to translate for me."

Nurse Olson said, "Lothar is waiting for you in the last room on the right."

Relief swept through Martha. She wouldn't see any of the PWs who worked on the farm tonight.

George led the way, and Martha followed. There were eight rooms in all. The doors to five of them were closed, and the ones with the doors open were empty. The last door on the right was also closed. George knocked on it.

"*Komm herein*," a deep voice said.

George opened the door and motioned for Martha to enter. There was a table in the room with several chairs around it. A man sat on the far side.

"Hello," George said.

"*Guten Abend*," the man said. "I am Lothar Huber."

George introduced Martha and then himself. He began to question Lothar, who at first answered in halting English but then switched to German.

Martha listened to his story and translated a few sentences at a time. George took notes.

"I've been beaten twice by the same guard," Martha translated. "I work in the kitchen and report at four in the morning. Three weeks ago,

I was walking in the dark when someone tackled me and then kicked me in the side repeatedly while I was on the ground. I didn't recognize the guard. I'd never seen him before. He called me names and then said it wasn't fair we had heated barracks while he was sleeping in a cold tent. It was dark so I couldn't see his face.

"But then Thursday morning, the same man attacked me again. Later, during breakfast, I saw him in the mess hall, speaking with another guard. I recognized his voice—and his height and body weight and mannerisms." The man paused and then said, "His name is Sergeant Schwarz."

Martha forced herself not to react to Lothar's words. She needed to remain completely disengaged. But she couldn't believe Sergeant Schwarz would beat anyone. He was so mild. Too mild.

George asked questions to verify the day and time of each attack and where he was struck. Lothar stood and lifted his shirt, showing bruises on his right side. He also pushed up his sleeve and showed a scrape on his left arm.

George wrote down the information and then asked, "Do you have any idea why Sergeant Schwarz would attack you?"

"No."

"Have any other POWs mentioned being attacked by Sergeant Schwarz?"

"No."

"Thank you," George said. "I'll submit your

158

complaint and my report to my supervisor by Monday."

Lothar said, "*Danke*." He stood as he looked at George. Then he turned toward Martha. "Thank you too."

"You're welcome." She'd found helping Lothar rewarding. Perhaps she could be of help to PWs.

After he left, George said, "I've done a few of these complaints, but they were about the food or lack of hot water. Or that they didn't have enough blankets. That sort of thing. This is the first I've done about a beating."

Martha frowned.

"What is it?" George asked.

"Unless there are two Sergeant Schwarzes here, the guard is the one assigned to our farm."

"Really? What is your impression of him?"

"He seems overly mild. And lenient with the PWs—too lenient."

"Perhaps he hides his frustration," George said. "Sometimes a person snaps."

"Maybe." She still couldn't see Sergeant Schwarz beating anyone. She had to force him to search the PWs.

A few minutes later, as they made their way back down the dark trail, a rustling in the forest stopped Martha. She peered into the trees. Two men stood, staring at her. One was Lothar. The other, she was sure, was Dirk. She ducked her head and kept on walking.

12

Brenna

I didn't go back to the apartment after Rosene stopped telling the story. Instead, I changed into a choring dress and then helped Dawdi with the milking—one of my least favorite things to do. I distracted myself by thinking about how the whole process had changed. The biggest difference was that the herd was now sixty cows instead of fifteen, which meant nearly five hundred gallons of milk a day, if all the cows were healthy. That was a crazy amount.

The paperwork for a dairy was intense. Dawdi kept all sorts of information on the cows—daily stuff like health and milk production. Lifelong stuff like age, number of calves, and infections. Each cow had her own stall with a little sign with her name and number on it—Dawdi named all of them. Cosmos. Violet. Geranium. Poppy. Daphne. The older generations of cows were named Bossy, Dottie, Nellie, and so on. I liked the more recent names better.

Each cow marched directly to her own stall. Dawdi fed them while I dipped each teat into a mixture of iodine and hydrogen peroxide to help prevent the spread of mastitis. I'd dip them again when the milking was done. Once Dawdi had fed them, he hooked up the milkers to the cows, and then I started scraping the manure through the grates behind each cows' back ends. Dawdi would spread the manure on the pastures and use it as fertilizer in the fields and gardens.

There was never a shortage.

The milk went straight into a can, which Dawdi poured into a holding tank. The tank had a tube connected to it that traveled to the milking room, where the milk flowed into the larger, one-thousand-gallon holding tank. From there, the milk went straight into the milk truck when it stopped by, usually every day.

Once the first of the cows were done, I put more food in the holding pen and then began moving them out of the barn. The entire milking process took an hour and a half. The one and only thing I liked about milking was getting to know the cows. Overall, they were pretty awkward too, although it didn't seem to bother them. They had some things down, like finding their stall two times a day. Other things didn't come as easily.

It wasn't that I thought they were dumb. They definitely had emotional intelligence. They made special friendships and protected the weaker ones. But other things, like loud noises or unfamiliar people, would set them off. One—Daphne—got her head stuck in a fence in the middle of the night and bawled so loud that Dawdi woke up.

When we were nearly done, Dawdi poured some milk onto a plate for the cats—the majority of which were gray—that had been milling around, waiting for it. They did a good job keeping the mouse population down and keeping us entertained.

When we finished, Dawdi said, "*Denki*. I appreciate the help."

"You're welcome."

"Can you help in the morning? Gabe asked for the weekend off."

"Sure."

I decided to spend the night. I'd left a toothbrush in the upstairs bathroom and could borrow some of Treva's extra clothes.

My phone dinged on the way back to the house. Treva.

In Portland. Gran is waiting for me at the curb.

Great. Give her a hug! Text me when you're home.

Then I texted Ivy to tell her I wouldn't be home.

She texted back.

What? I don't want to stay here by myself.

Then come stay at the farm.

I didn't hear back from her. Rosene had fixed taco soup and cornbread for supper, which was perfect for a quiet fall evening. Here, I didn't have to worry about Rylan. Or Gabe. Or anything. As I helped with the dishes, my phone dinged again. I took a peek. Treva and Gran were home. I sighed with relief.

I headed up to bed early, knowing I'd need to be out in the barn by five. When I reached the bedroom I'd shared with Treva, my phone dinged again, which surprised me. I didn't used to get service in the room. A new tower must have been put in nearby.

Ivy again.

You missed out. We all had dinner down at Rylan's. Gabe was there. We met Rylan's friends—I guess they are Gabe's too. How does he know all of them? Anyway, Marko and Viktor cooked Ukrainian food! You would have loved it. We missed you.

I wasn't sure what to text back. I was glad I missed out. JOMO. That was me. Finally, I replied.

I'm glad you all had a good time.

I didn't see how Gabe could keep his secret about joining the Army Reserve much longer. But who knew. Guys were weird that way. They

163

probably all successfully evaded Ivy's intrusive questions until she didn't notice she hadn't gotten a straight answer about their connection. And she'd never guess Gabe would have joined the Army Reserve. No one would.

I slept soundly, better than I had since we moved to the apartment. After Dawdi and I finished the milking the next morning, I took a quick shower and then ate dippy eggs, toast, and bacon, and then a cinnamon roll with Dawdi, Mammi, and Rosene. Over my second cup of coffee, I glanced from Rosene to Dawdi. This time I didn't think of them as nineteen years and eighteen months, sitting around the same table. Instead, I thought about how lucky I was to have them in my life. And Mammi too.

If Rylan was serious about suing, what would my grandparents do? What if they had to sell the store? Or even the entire property to settle the suit? What would my life be like without the store? It was my safety net. I had no plan other than to live nearby and run Amish Antiques.

A few minutes later, Mammi stood and said, "I'm going to the store."

I stood too and said, "I'll be there in a few minutes." I began clearing the dishes off the table.

"I'll do that," Rosene said.

"Let me help. I doubt there's a line waiting at the store." In the summer, sometimes there was but not in late October.

Once the table was cleared, I told Rosene good-bye. Business was slow all morning, so Mammi showed me her recordkeeping system for income taxes. She also showed me how she calculated withholdings from Gabe and me for our taxes, social security, and Medicare. I jotted down the information in my little business notebook, hoping I could remember all of the steps when needed. No doubt Mammi would be around and I could ask her for help, but she would expect me to know. Before we closed for the noon hour, Mammi said, "I want to tell you about one of these clocks. The one that's not for sale."

It was a mantel clock made out of dark wood, perhaps cherry, with a curved top, and it sat on the top shelf behind the counter. A little sign, made out of an index card folded in half, beside it read *Not for Sale*. We had to use a ladder to wind it every week.

"I want you to know where it came from." Mammi stared upward at it. "Rosene brought it back from Germany."

"In 1939?"

"No. In 1949."

"Oh," I replied. That meant Rosene wouldn't tell me anything more about the clock now. She'd claim that would be getting ahead of the story.

Mammi made a little murmuring sound. "I remember seeing it as a little girl, when I was six or so."

"What?"

"I grew up a mile from here. Coming to Monika Simons's store, and then Clare's store, was always a treat. Every once in a while, my father would buy a piece of stick candy for me—lemon was my favorite."

I struggled to process that bit of information. It was the first Mammi had mentioned her family.

"Anyway," Mammi said, "I want you to know how important this clock is. Don't ever sell it. Treasure it."

"I will." I hoped Rosene would tell me about the clock eventually.

Business sped up a little in the afternoon, but at four, Mammi said, "I'll finish up here. Would you go help Dawdi with the milking?"

"Sure." I headed to the house to change into a choring dress. Rosene wasn't in the kitchen. I guessed she was resting. Then I headed out to the barn. It was the most I'd helped with the milking in a row, ever. I wore an old coat over my choring dress. The temperature had dropped since the morning. I guessed it would freeze tonight.

As we finished up the milking and I led the last of the cows out to the holding pen, my phone dinged in my coat pocket. I pulled it out. Rylan.

I fell. I need you to help me get up.

I texted back.

> I'm at the farm. I'll text Ivy and see if
> she can.

I texted Ivy. She responded that she was at Conrad's.
I texted Rylan.

> I'll be right there.

I told Dawdi I needed to go.

"Denki for your help," he said. "Don't be a stranger."

"I won't." I ran to the house, kicked off my boots on the back porch, changed my dress, wadded up the choring dress to take to the apartment to wash, put on my shoes, and then darted out to the van without seeing Rosene again.

I left my choring dress in the van and headed straight to Rylan's. I knocked as I pulled out his key and let myself in, slipping out of my shoes. He sat on the floor with his back against the wall and his casted leg straight out.

"Hey," he said. "I scooted over here but couldn't manage to get myself up."

I pushed his wheelchair close, set the brake, and then squatted down.

"Eww," he said. "Were you shoveling manure?"

I glanced down at my coat. I didn't see any, but that didn't mean it wasn't there. "I'll take my coat off."

I wiggled out of it and put it on the tile by the front door, by my shoes. I returned to Rylan and crouched down to lift him up, thankful Ivy hadn't been home. I wasn't sure she had the height or strength. I wasn't sure I did.

"Place your arms around my chest and then clasp them behind my back."

I followed his instructions.

"Then lean back and shift your weight as you lift. I'll try to pivot on the foot of the cast. Then swing me around to the chair."

I followed his instructions. There was a moment when I thought we might both topple over, but then I lunged toward the chair and somehow he landed in it.

"Thanks," he said.

"You're welcome." I stood up straight and stepped backward.

He began wheeling toward the kitchen. "Marko took the lasagna you brought out of the freezer. I was going to cook it tonight. The guys are coming over."

"That's great." I followed him.

He asked, "Would you turn the oven on?"

I did as he requested.

He opened the fridge, which was now full. It

had milk and eggs. Hamburger. A deli container of mac and cheese. And fruits and vegetables in the drawers.

"There's bread too," he said. "But no salad." He looked up at me. "Want to stay for dinner?"

"Not really."

"Come on, Brenna." He pulled one of the pans of lasagna out and put it on his lap and then began rolling toward the oven. "You missed a fun time last night." He looked up at me with his big brown eyes. "Your sister—what's her name?"

"Ivy."

"Yeah. She was a lot of fun."

I rolled my eyes.

"She was. Her boyfriend—" He paused.

"Conrad."

"Right. Gabe's brother. Anyway, he was fun too."

I didn't really think of Ivy as fun, but it was probably her fear of missing out. It made her overly enthusiastic.

Rylan opened the oven door, even though it hadn't preheated yet, and then wheeled backward. He had to lean forward to get the lasagna on the shelf. Rylan wheeled back to the fridge and got the second pan of lasagna and repeated the process.

"I have salad," I said, surprising myself. "And dressing. I'll go get it."

"Great," he said. "There's ice cream for dessert."

Rosene's two lasagnas were enough for all of us. After we finished, Viktor and I cleaned up the kitchen, and then I claimed to be tired.

"Brenna was at the farm doing the milking," Rylan said.

"Really?" Viktor seemed surprised. "A dairy farm?"

"Yes," I answered. "Sixty cows."

Marko said, "That's a nice size herd."

I nodded, wondering if I was presenting my grandparents as wealthy to not only Rylan but to Marko and Viktor too.

"We had land back in Ukraine," Viktor said. "My grandparents raised wheat—they still do. They had a few cows but not a herd like that."

"My grandfather just has the dairy herd," I said. "He grows hay and feed for the cows, along with cultivating the pastures."

"Nice." Marko's smile held sadness in it.

I felt their losses. Land. Country. Grandparents. It had to be hard.

I went to church the next morning with Ivy, and then back to the apartment to rest.

At five, Ivy knocked on my door. "Ready?"

"For?"

"Sunday night fun."

I groaned. Conrad headed up a gathering of about fifty Mennonite youth—college-aged and a little older—every Sunday evening. When we first moved to Lancaster County, Ivy didn't like going, but now she loved it. She and Conrad were like the parents of the group. In good weather, they organized volleyball, softball, or soccer games. In bad weather, everyone gathered in a church hall for games or singing. Tonight, everyone was going to a corn maze at a Mennonite farm. There would be a pumpkin patch and a hayride, but no scary stuff.

"Come on," Ivy said. "Gabe is going to meet us."

I wondered if he would show up in his uniform. That I'd have to see. His secret would be out for sure. "All right." I made sure I didn't sound too enthusiastic about it.

I rode in the back seat of Ivy's Camry, holding the plate of pumpkin sugar cookies she made. I supposed, technically, I should have made something too.

The evening was clear and chilly but not cold. The perfect weather for an outing. The farmhouse had a covered area with an outside firepit and tables and chairs. The first group of people went on the hayride, and I grabbed some cookies and sat down at a table while Ivy and Conrad buzzed around and saw to everything.

A few minutes later, someone said, "Hello, Brenna."

I looked up. It was Marko, with Viktor and Gabe standing behind him. I'd expected Gabe but not the other two. All wore civilian clothes. "Hi," I said. "What are you all doing here?"

Marko jerked his head. "Gabe invited us."

"Nice," I said. "Grab some cookies and sit down."

On their way to the food table, Ivy saw them and gushed, "I'm so glad you two came with Gabe." It sounded as if she'd probably invited them, not Gabe. "The hayride wagon will be back in a few minutes. The corn maze is amazing." She hadn't actually seen the corn maze yet, or at least I didn't think she had.

The three guys returned with plates of cookies, apple and cheese slices, and popcorn balls and sat at the table with me. We didn't take the next wagon, but we did take the one after that. I sat between Gabe and Marko, while Viktor sat on the other side. At the last minute, Ivy and Conrad jumped up into the wagon.

"I feel bad that Rylan's not here," Viktor said. I did too, although it would be difficult for him to navigate the farm with his wheelchair.

"Brenna." Ivy leaned forward from where she sat on the other side of Viktor. "Wouldn't it be fun to have Johann meet Marko and Viktor?"

I smiled. She loved connecting people.

"Who's that?" Marko asked.

"Our friend from Ukraine," Ivy answered.

"Oh, that's right." Marko hit his forehead with the heel of his hand. "You met him when you traveled to Ukraine, right?"

"Yes," Ivy answered. "And then Brenna, Gabe, and Conrad met Johann a few years ago when we were all in Germany together."

"Is he coming to visit sometime?" Viktor asked. Ivy looked at me.

I shrugged. "Not that I know of."

Marko nudged me. "Oh, so he's your friend now?" My face grew warm.

"He's all of our friend." Conrad came to my rescue. "He's a good guy."

The wagon stopped, and we all clambered down into the maze. Gabe led the way at first, but we weren't making any progress. So I stepped forward, and after a few false starts, found the way through the maze. We ended up being the first group out.

"Wow," Marko said. "We could use you in our Army Reserve unit. You have a great sense of direction."

"She has a thing for geography," Ivy quipped.

"I guess so." Marko took out his phone. "How about a group selfie?"

We all posed, he shot the photo, and then he pointed across the field to where the vehicles were parked. "Let's get going," he said to Viktor. "I want to go check on Rylan."

They both said good-bye and waved and then started across the field.

Ivy waved back and said, "They're good guys."

I agreed silently.

The wagon pulled up, and we all climbed aboard. When we arrived back at the patio, only the parents were hanging around. Everyone else was in the maze.

"I have a paper due in the morning," Ivy said. "I should get going."

"Sounds good," Conrad said. "I still have lesson plans to do too."

"Let's go," Gabe said. "I'm hungry for more than cookies."

I needed to check with Rylan to see if he had any questions about the notes for last Thursday's class and if he planned to go to class the next day.

We piled into Ivy's car and headed back.

Gabe and I sat in the back, silently at first. But as Ivy started droning on about something to Conrad, Gabe leaned toward me and whispered, "I didn't get information out of anyone about what happened in Afghanistan. Sorry."

I wondered what all of them were hiding.

We dropped Gabe off, and then Conrad. When we reached the complex, I headed to Rylan's apartment as Ivy headed up the stairs to ours.

I knocked on the door and immediately Marko opened it. "Come on in," he said.

"Why no invite?" Rylan called out to me.

"What?"

"Viktor showed me the selfie at the corn maze."

"Oh, that," I said. "It was fun to have them join us."

Rylan exhaled. "But you didn't invite me."

I nudged Viktor. "I didn't invite them either."

"It was a last-minute thing," Marko said. "We were giving Gabe a ride."

"That figures that Gabe was behind all of it," Rylan said.

"Behind what?" I asked.

"Excluding me."

"We weren't excluding you," I said.

He crossed his arms. "You didn't invite me."

I rolled my eyes. "Stop. It just happened."

Rylan frowned. "Did you all have fun?"

"Yeah," I said. "I'll let you know when we have a similar outing. You can come with us."

Rylan wrinkled his nose.

"So," I said, "did you have any questions about my lecture notes?"

"No."

"Are you going to class tomorrow?"

He shook his head. "I need to get my prosthesis adjusted."

I hesitated, not sure what to say. Marko shrugged. I stepped away from Rylan.

"Okay," I said. "Let me know when you're ready to go back."

13

I took copious notes during classes on Monday and then stopped by Rylan's apartment again. I knocked and he called out, "Come in!"

I opened the door to the smell of something super savory.

Marko poked his head out of the kitchen. "Oh, hi, Brenna."

"Hello," I said. "What are you doing here?"

"Cooking mushroom soup." He nodded toward the counter. "And bread."

"Where did you learn to cook?"

He grinned. "My grandmother. Want to stay for dinner?"

"That's tempting," I said. "But I need to get home and study." I stepped toward Rylan, who was in his recliner with his prosthesis on.

"Is your prosthesis fixed?"

"Yep. Marko skipped class and drove me to the VA this morning. It needed to be adjusted but at least nothing broke."

"Nice," I said.

"While I was in the waiting room, one of the other patients warned me not to expect the VA to pay for my surgery. He said he fell on a friend's property and the VA wouldn't pay. They expected the home insurance of the friend to cover his

176

medical expenses." He looked pleased. "Most likely your grandmother's insurance will pay, right?"

I felt confused.

"I'll file a personal injury claim, and her insurance will dispute it. Then I'll sue your grandmother, and after a couple of years, the insurance company will settle—for less than I'm asking for, probably. But I'll still get a lot."

I stared blankly.

"She has business insurance, right?"

"I don't—I don't know," I stuttered. But I didn't think she did. The Amish had different ideas about insurance, or at least some of them did. In all of our "training," Mammi never mentioned insurance once. I hadn't seen any insurance bills. I knew Mom and Dad had insurance for our Christmas tree farm to cover workers and the public. But they were Mennonite.

"So you don't think she does?" Rylan's expression was serious. "I thought that might be a possibility. I feel sick about all of this—you're nice and have been good to me. But I can't pay my medical bills if the VA won't. So, I was thinking ahead today and had Marko drive by the law firm I used to work for."

My stomach dropped.

"He tricked me," Marko called out from the kitchen.

Rylan shrugged. "I'm just gathering information,

as of now. There's nothing to be alarmed about."

"Okay . . ." My voice trailed off.

"The attorney said if I do decide to sue, I have a good chance of winning."

I met Rylan's gaze and held it. Was he bluffing about the VA not paying?

"Why are you staring at me?" he asked.

"You went up the staircase. There was a rope blocking it off. And a sign to keep off."

He shook his head. "The rope was on the ground. And there was no sign."

"Did you notice the rope?" I asked.

"Sure. But I thought it being down meant it was okay for me to go up the staircase."

Had someone taken both down? Would any of us have noticed if they were no longer there? I crossed my arms. "What's the name of the law firm?"

"Oh, just one downtown." Rylan glanced toward the window. "How was class?"

"Fine," I answered, not trying to control the frustration in my voice. "I checked in with our instructor. He said he got your email. And I emailed you my notes. Do you want me to go over them?"

He shook his head. "Can you come over tomorrow afternoon after class? We could go over both sets of notes then." He sighed. "I'm tempted to drop out, but the attorney said I shouldn't yet, unless I want to go back to being a paralegal."

I froze, having no idea how to respond. Finally, I said, "I'll see you tomorrow."

As I headed past the kitchen, Marko followed me out the door and then pulled it shut behind him. "Collins and Collins." Then he quickly turned around and headed back inside.

When I reached our cold and dreary apartment, I second-guessed passing on Marko's soup and bread as I took a protein bar from the cupboard. It wasn't that I liked protein bars; it was that most of the time cooking seemed like an unsurmountable task to me. I headed to my bedroom, logged onto my computer, and sent Johann a message.

Want to chat?

My computer began to buzz. *Johann.* His face appeared a little distorted but then came into focus.

I clicked Video, and my face appeared in the upper corner.

"How are you doing?" I asked.

"Good. How about you?"

My phone began to buzz. It was Rylan. "Can you hold on a second? It's Rylan."

"Sure," Johann said.

"Hello, Rylan," I answered.

"Hey," he said. "I fell again, and Marko ran home for a spice or something. Do you mind helping me again?"

I was beginning to think that Rylan was coming

up with excuses for me to go to his apartment. Could he really not get himself back into his chair? Especially now that he had his prosthesis back on?

I didn't say any of that to Rylan, though. Instead I said, "I'll be right down." I hung up the phone and explained the situation to Johann.

"How is everything going with Rylan? Is he demanding too much of you?"

"No," I answered. "His friends are taking care of him. He fell is all."

Johann's expression turned even more caring. "Call me back when you're done."

"I will."

When I reached Rylan's, I tried the door. It was unlocked.

I stepped inside as I said, "It's me."

Rylan looked up from the recliner.

"I thought you fell."

"I did," he said. "I managed to pull myself up." He appeared unfazed, as if he hadn't just been straining to get back in the recliner.

"That's great. Do you need anything else?"

"How about a beer?"

"Are you taking any pain meds?"

He shook his head. "I haven't had any since last night."

I headed to the fridge. "When will Marko be back?"

"A half hour or so. You can stay, right? Just until he gets back."

I hesitated. I really wanted to talk with Johann, and it was getting late in Ukraine. On the other hand, I felt like I owed Rylan. "Sure," I said. "Just until Marko gets back. Then I need to go study."

I headed to the kitchen. The soup was on low and smelled even better than it had a few minutes ago. Two loaves of bread cooled on the counter.

I opened the fridge and grabbed Rylan a beer. I wasn't sure if I was supposed to put it in a glass or not but decided not to. I headed back to the living room.

"Thanks." He took the beer and opened it.

I stepped to the sliding door. The window covering was pulled back more than before. Dusk was falling, and it was hard to see. I flipped on the light. He had a patio but no furniture.

A gray cat jumped onto the patio and then rubbed against the sliding door.

"Is that your cat?" I asked.

"No," Rylan said. "She's a stray that hangs around."

"Do you let her in?"

"Sometimes," he answered.

"Do you want me to let her in now?"

He shook his head.

I turned off the light to the patio. And then I waited. After ten minutes, I sent Johann a message.

Hey, I'm not going to be able to get back on tonight. Can we chat tomorrow?

Everything okay?

Yes.

I didn't want to explain that I felt trapped, which I knew wasn't a good sign.

How about Wednesday?

Sounds good. Thank you.

Then I waited. And waited. Rylan nodded off. Marko didn't come back. Finally, the door opened, and Viktor walked in with a bag over his shoulder.

"Hello, Brenna. What are you doing here?"

"Waiting for Marko."

"He had to work." He lifted his bag. "I'm going to spend the night." He turned toward the kitchen. "Marko said he made soup. Have you had any?"

I shook my head.

"Stay and eat with us."

"Okay." I needed to study, but the protein bar hadn't lasted long.

Rylan stirred and then said, "Hey, Viktor. Where's Marko?"

"He had to go to work."

"I thought he was going to skip work."

"No. We have bills to pay," Viktor muttered. Then, in a cheery voice, he said, "Ready to eat?"

Rylan picked up his beer. "I'll just have this for now."

Viktor shook his head. "Suit yourself."

I stepped into the kitchen and took two bowls from the cupboard.

"He's either messing with you or me," Viktor said quietly. "He knew Marko had to go clean up a worksite and that I'd be here by seven."

I glanced at the clock on the stove. I'd waited an hour while Rylan slept. What was he up to?

Once I was back in my room, I Googled Collins & Collins. The opening paragraph on the website read,

When an Amish person is responsible for an injury, will the law assist the injured person? Yes. We can guide you through injury claims against the Amish.

Wow. We all wanted justice, but that sounded almost predatory. But perhaps I was biased. If Mammi was at fault, didn't Rylan deserve justice? But if he took the sign and rope down . . . what did justice look like then?

On Tuesday, I took notes in class, but when I stopped by Rylan's apartment, no one answered the door. I texted him. He returned the text.

I'm resting. I'll see you tomorrow.

Okay. I'll pick you up at 1.

On Wednesday, when I knocked on his door, Rylan called out, "Come in." I opened the door. He was in his wheelchair, heading toward the bedroom. "I'm almost ready. Hold on a second."

I waited and waited. Then I started doing the dishes in the sink. As I finished, Rylan came out of the bedroom in his wheelchair. His sports pants barely fit over his cast. "I need my backpack."

I grabbed it from the floor and handed it to him. He held it on his lap.

As Rylan wheeled himself outside, I slung my backpack over my shoulder and then locked the door.

Everything took longer than I expected. I had plenty of time when I left my apartment, but by the time we arrived on campus, we were already late for class. I parked as close as I could, yanked the wheelchair from the back of the van, and transferred Rylan. Then I put his backpack on his lap and mine on my back and began to push. When we reached the room, I struggled to keep the door open as I pushed Rylan through.

Once we were in, I paused a moment. All the seats in the back of the room and along the aisle were filled. The only open seat was at the front of the class. I began pushing as the instructor paused a moment, stared at us, and then started talking again. When we reached the front table, I positioned Rylan's wheelchair and then sat down in the chair beside him. I took out my laptop and began taking notes. A few minutes later, Rylan's head slumped, and he began snoring. Softly. But definitely snoring. I guessed he'd taken his pain meds.

He woke up when the teacher called for a ten-minute break. "Need anything?" I asked him.

"How about a cup of coffee?"

"I'll be right back." There was a line at the coffee kiosk. At the front were the two girls from the week before.

Once they had their coffee and started back, the shorter one stopped. "So what's up with Rylan?"

"He broke his leg," I answered.

"Why are you helping him?"

"He's my neighbor."

The short one gave me a puzzled look, as if she didn't believe me.

"What are your names?" If they were going to talk to me, I might as well know who they were.

"Ami," said the shorter one. She gestured toward her friend. "And this is Jessica."

"Nice to meet both of you." I smiled—or tried to. "I'm Brenna."

By the time I returned with the coffees, the professor was lecturing again. I took a tissue from my coat pocket, spit my gum into it, took a sip of coffee, and began taking notes again. Rylan held his coffee in both hands and took a drink every few minutes. When the instructor asked if we had any questions, Rylan asked if the midterm would include chapter twelve. It would. He had been listening.

When class ended, we waited until everyone else had left as I drained my coffee. Then Rylan held on to what was left of his while I pushed him out of the classroom. The two girls were waiting in the hall.

Ami said, "Hi, Rylan. Sorry about your leg."

"Thanks," he said.

She zipped her coat. "Don't you remember us?"

"No."

Ami's face grew serious. "My sister was a friend of Meg's. Jessica and I saw you a couple of times."

"Oh," he said.

"I'm really sorry about that too."

Rylan made a circular motion with his hand as if he wanted me to keep rolling him along. I started pushing his chair again.

Jessica shrugged as we passed by.

When we'd exited the building, I asked, "What was that all about?"

"I don't want to talk about it."

"Who's Meg?"

"I said, I don't want to talk about it."

I continued to the van, transferred Rylan, folded the wheelchair, and lifted it into the back. By the time I climbed up in the driver's seat, I was tired. I expected Rylan was too.

"I forgot to email you the notes," I said.

"Don't bother."

"Why not?"

"I should just drop out. . . ."

I wiped my sweaty palms on my coat and then started the van. Did that mean he'd decided to sue Mammi?

Saturday morning was one of those gorgeous early November days that seem like an extra gift before winter started. As Gabe and I sanded a table on the back porch of the store, I told him that Rylan had spoken with the attorney he used to work for about suing.

"Did you tell Priscilla?"

"No. I can't tell how serious Rylan is."

"It's odd," Gabe said. "People walk on eggshells around him. Viktor and Marko jump as soon as he texts or calls."

"Why do you think that is?"

"I think it has to do with what happened in Afghanistan. Their unit was under fire. I don't know what went down—"

I raised my eyebrows. *Went down?* I'd never heard Gabe use that expression before.

"—exactly, but Rylan lost his leg and a woman in the unit lost her life."

I winced. That sounded horrible.

"No one would tell me exactly what happened, though."

Mammi called me in to help a customer. I took off my gloves and put them in the work basin and then headed into the store. We stayed busy after that until it was time for Gabe to help Dawdi with the milking.

As Mammi and I left the shop, Gabe called out my name. I turned.

He ran toward me. "Can I get a ride?"

"Where to?" I asked.

"Rylan's. I'm staying over. Marko is working late."

"Sure," I said. "What about the home health nurse who is supposed to come in?"

"He canceled the visits."

That figured. "Does Rylan need you guys around all the time?"

"Marko says he doesn't like to be alone."

"And they're happy to accommodate him?"

"It seems so."

I wondered if it had to do with the secret Marko and Viktor were keeping. Or what happened in Afghanistan. Or both.

After I parked the van, I turned toward the stairway up to my apartment.

"Wait." Gabe grabbed my arm. "Can you come into Rylan's place with me?"

"No." I pulled my arm away from him.

"Brenna."

"I'm tired."

"So am I."

"I need to go—" I almost said *home,* but the apartment was far from that.

"Come on," Gabe begged. "I have no idea what to fix for dinner."

"I don't cook," I said.

"You do more than I do."

"No, I don't. I eat protein bars."

"But you're a Mennonite girl—"

"Woman."

"—young woman. You have to know how to cook."

"Order a pizza."

Gabe frowned but then said, "If I do, will you eat with us?"

I sighed. "I guess so."

A half hour later, Gabe and I sat on the floor in Rylan's living room, eating pizza.

"So . . ." Rylan looked down at Gabe from the recliner. "Did you tell Brenna about what happened to me in Afghanistan?"

"I don't know what happened," Gabe said.

"Marko said he told you."

Gabe shrugged. "Maybe generally. But he didn't give any details."

"So what happened in Afghanistan?" I asked Rylan.

His gaze drifted toward the sliding glass door. "I don't want to talk about it."

After a long pause, Rylan turned back toward me. "Do you guys have church tomorrow?"

I hesitated, waiting for Gabe to answer. When he didn't, I said, "Yes. It starts at eleven."

Rylan smirked. "I'll go if Gabe goes."

"I haven't gone for a while."

Rylan deepened his voice. "So?"

"Okay," Gabe said. "I'll go."

Now Rylan was looking at me. "Pick us up at 10:30. Gabe and I will be ready."

14

When I got back to my apartment, I sat at my computer, wishing Johann would come online. But he didn't. We hadn't been able to chat on Wednesday. He was on call at work and ended up having to resolve a server problem that had him working into the night. I hadn't heard from him since.

Ivy was out with Conrad. For once I wanted her opinion on why Rylan would want to go to church with us. I didn't trust him. It seemed he had some ulterior plan. Was he trying to sabotage the community around him? Marko and Viktor and Gabe. My family. I thought of Dirk in Rosene's story. It seemed he wanted to sow chaos on the Simons farm. Was that what Rylan wanted to do too? Maybe both were some sort of agents of chaos, an archetype Dad had told us about.

Both seemed to have a similar personality. Rylan had been traumatized by war. Had Dirk too? Or was chaos part of their personalities, regardless of their experiences?

The next morning, as I got ready for church, I had a call from the barn phone on the farm. I answered quickly, hoping everyone was all right. It was Rosene. "Want to come for Sunday dinner after church?" It was their district's off Sunday.

"I'm giving Gabe and Rylan a ride to church and home," I said.

"How nice," Rosene responded. "Bring them along."

"Are you sure?" I quickly explained about Rylan speaking to the attorney he used to work for about suing Mammi.

"Ach," Rosene said. "Well, regardless, bring him along if he wants to come. I'd like to meet him. Would you pass on the invitation to Ivy and Conrad too?"

"Yes," I answered. Ivy had already left, so after I told Rosene good-bye, I sent Ivy a quick text and then headed down to collect Rylan and Gabe. Surprisingly, they were both ready to go. Rylan was already in his wheelchair, waiting in the entryway.

"We all have a dinner invite from my grand-parents after church."

"Cool," Gabe said. "I hope Rosene is cooking."

"I'm sure she is," I said. "How does that sound to you, Rylan?"

He grinned mischievously. "Oh, I wouldn't pass that up for anything."

I wrinkled my nose. "What does that mean?"

He smirked. "What do you think it means?"

"You tell me."

"That I'm going to get a really good meal. Better than anything anyone makes around here."

192

I thought of Marko's mushroom soup. I hadn't had anything that delicious in a long time.

When we arrived at the church, Gabe transferred Rylan into his chair and wheeled him into the foyer. I led the way into the sanctuary, looking for a place in the back that would work with Rylan's chair, but he said, "Let's sit up front."

Gabe pushed Rylan ahead, and I followed. We ended up sitting in the front row—my least favorite place. Sharon, Gabe's mom, sat behind us. She was probably around fifty and had always been kind to me. I knew she adored Ivy, but it seemed she adored me too. Ivy and Conrad weren't sitting with her, which meant they were volunteering in the nursery or something. I couldn't keep track of all the church stuff Ivy was involved in and couldn't fathom how she pulled off graduate school and everything else she did.

The first song we sang was "All for Jesus! All for Jesus!" To my surprise, Rylan knew the words. " 'All my being's ransomed pow'rs; All my thoughts and words and doings, All my days and all my hours . . .' " He knew the words to "Gently Lord, O Gently Lead Us" and to "Depth of Mercy, Can there Be, Mercy Still Reserved for Me?" too.

They weren't popular songs like "Amazing Grace" and "How Great Thou Art," songs one might hear at funerals and that sort of thing. He'd either grown up attending church or had someone who sang the old hymns to him. I hadn't even thought to ask about his background when it came to faith.

The scripture for the day was 1 Peter 2. The pastor read, " 'Therefore, rid yourselves of all malice and all deceit, hypocrisy, envy, and slander of every kind. Like newborn babies, crave pure spiritual milk, so that by it you may grow up in your salvation, now that you have tasted that the Lord is good. . . .' "

Malice, deceit, hypocrisy, envy, and *slander.* All were used by agents of chaos. We were commanded to rid ourselves of all of them. Did Rylan have any idea what he was doing when it came to his relationships with Viktor, Marko, and Gabe? How his gossip and snarkiness affected the people who were trying to care for him?

I hoped he was listening to the sermon.

He wasn't. A few minutes in, his head tipped to the side and he began to snore softly.

When the service ended, Gabe wheeled Rylan around the pew and started for the exit. The congregation, just as they had the first time Ivy and I attended, greeted Rylan warmly. Thankfully Gabe interacted with them while I headed to the foyer in search of Ivy. I couldn't find her, so I headed down the hall to the nursery. There she was, handing an infant to a father. Behind her, Conrad held a screaming toddler.

After the father and baby walked away from the door, I asked Ivy if she'd received my text.

"Yes," she said. "I just didn't have a chance to answer. We'll be there."

"Rylan and Gabe are going too," I said.

"That's great."

A mother approached the door.

"See you soon," Ivy said to me.

By the time I reached the foyer again, Gabe had Rylan at the exit. "Let's go," I said, feeling apprehensive about having Rylan around Mammi. I hoped I wasn't catastrophizing what might happen—something my therapist pointed out that I did regularly. I wanted to be optimistic. Good could come from the Sunday dinner, right?

Once Rylan, Gabe, and I were in the van and I pulled away from the church, I asked Rylan if he grew up in a church.

"Why do you ask?"

"You knew the words to all of the hymns."

"Ahh," he said.

When he didn't say anything more, I asked, "So did you?"

"Some," he answered. "My grandmother used to take me. I always liked the singing."

Again, I waited for him to say more. When he didn't, I didn't ask a follow-up question. I wanted to respect his wishes if he didn't want to talk about it anymore.

As we entered the kitchen, we were met by

the savory smells of Rosene's chicken potpie. I introduced Rylan to Rosene. "She's my great-great-aunt," I added.

"Oh." He smiled at Rosene. "I didn't think you were Brenna's grandmother."

"No," Rosene answered. "That's Priscilla."

He nodded. "I'm sure I'll recognize her when I see her."

I didn't ask where Mammi was, but I wondered.

"Are Ivy and Conrad coming?" Rosene asked.

"Yes. They'll be here soon."

Rylan said he needed to use the restroom, so Gabe pushed him down the hallway.

"Did you tell Mammi about Rylan speaking with an attorney?" I whispered to Rosene.

She nodded.

Mammi came in from outside, followed by Dawdi. She gave me a terse greeting. "So, Rylan and Gabe decided not to come?"

I shook my head. "Rylan's using the bathroom. Gabe's down the hall with him."

She pursed her lips. "I see."

A couple of minutes later, Gabe pushed Rylan into the kitchen just as Ivy and Conrad arrived, and we all gathered around the table. Dawdi led us in a silent prayer and then, after he said "Amen," Rylan said, "That was weird."

"How so?" Dawdi asked.

"You didn't say anything."

"It was a silent prayer."

"Oh."

Rosene's chicken potpie, which was more like a really thick chicken noodle soup, was always delicious. She'd also made homemade biscuits, a green salad, and roasted acorn squash. It was the perfect autumn meal.

Dawdi took a half of squash and asked Ivy, "Have you bought tickets for you, Brenna, and Conrad for your Christmas trip?"

"Jah." She took a biscuit and passed the basket to Conrad. "Sharon said she'd give us a ride to the airport."

"It's going to be so quiet around here." Mammi sighed.

I imagined it would be.

She added, "It's already so quiet without Treva."

"Where are you going?" Rylan asked Ivy.

"Oregon," she replied. "Our other grandmother—Gran—lives in the cabin where we grew up. Our little sister Treva is already there, working on our Christmas tree farm."

"I think I remember her," he said. "From the day I fell. She was wearing an Amish dress." He looked at me. "Right?"

I nodded.

Conrad asked Rylan how he liked church.

"The singing was great," he said. "But I dozed a little during the sermon."

I didn't correct him that he'd dozed through the entire sermon.

The conversation turned to the farm and how Dawdi was managing without Treva. "Gabe helps with the milking in the morning and the afternoon," Dawdi said, "when he's not busy with other things. I appreciate Brenna's help when she has the time."

"I wish I could help," Rylan said. "My grandparents had a dairy when I was growing up. I really enjoyed the work."

"How old were you?" Ivy asked.

"From when I was little until I was thirteen. . . ." His voice trailed off. "When we moved."

"Where was the farm?" Dawdi asked.

"Ohio."

"Where in Ohio?" Dawdi asked.

"Out in the boonies. You wouldn't have heard of it."

I grimaced. Dawdi might have.

Ivy leaned closer to the table. "Do they still have the farm?"

He shook his head.

I hoped Ivy would stop asking questions, but she didn't.

"Are they still alive?"

He shook his head again.

Thankfully, Ivy finally read the room and kept quiet.

Rylan directed his attention toward Mammi. "Brenna wasn't sure whether you had business insurance or not."

Mammi wiped the corners of her mouth with her napkin and then said, "I do not."

"That's too bad." Then Rylan turned toward Dawdi. "I imagine this place must be worth quite a bit with the land, the dairy herd, and the store and everything."

No one spoke.

"How many acres is it?"

"Seventy," Dawdi answered.

Rylan whistled. "Land around here must be worth a fortune."

"Well," Dawdi said, "I know what I pay in property taxes, but we haven't had any reason to have the land appraised lately."

"I bet it's been paid off for quite a while."

Dawdi didn't answer.

Conrad said, "That's a little personal, don't you think?"

Rylan grinned.

"Lots of us Amish are land rich but . . ." Dawdi looked at Rosene. "How does the saying go?"

"Cash poor."

"That's right." Dawdi frowned a little.

Rylan shrugged and then turned toward Rosene. "My grandmother used to make chicken potpie like this. Yours is delicious. As good as hers, I think."

After we dropped Rylan back at his apartment, where Viktor met us, Gabe followed me.

"What are you doing?" I asked.

"I need to talk with you."

"What about?"

He nodded toward Rylan's apartment.

I exhaled. "I'm tired."

"I won't be very long. I have some new information."

When we reached the apartment, the door was unlocked, and I could hear voices inside. Ivy and Conrad. We must have been at Rylan's long enough for them to arrive and get up to the apartment, even though we'd left first.

I opened the door. They were in the kitchen, talking.

"Hi," Ivy said as we walked in. "What's up?"

I took off my coat. "Gabe wants to talk with me."

Ivy's eyes brightened. "What about?"

"Rylan." Gabe's voice was like a growl.

"Dinner was so awkward." Ivy crossed her arms. "What was with him today?"

"He's scheming." Gabe sat down at the table.

"What about?" Ivy asked.

"He's met with an attorney," I said. "One he used to work with who specializes"—I made air-quotation marks with my fingers— " 'in holding Amish people liable.' "

"Really?" Ivy asked.

"Yes." I sat down at the table. "I hoped he wasn't serious at first, but he seems to be."

"He shouldn't sue her," Ivy said. "It's not like he needs the money, right?"

"He doesn't think the VA will pay for his surgery."

Ivy's eyes widened. "That could be thousands of dollars." She uncrossed her arms and drummed her fingers along her jaw. "He should speak with his caseworker before he assumes they won't pay."

I had no idea how the VA worked. I glanced at Gabe. "Besides the medical costs, why does Rylan need the money?"

"Who doesn't need money?" Gabe shrugged. "Anyway, Marko stopped by after Rylan was asleep last night."

Ivy and Conrad both sat down at the table.

"Marko told me about what happened in Afghanistan." Gabe put his hands flat on the tabletop. "Rylan was in a relationship with a woman named Meg, but she died during an attack and that really messed him up."

I asked, "Was she from around here? There's a girl in one of my classes who said her older sister was a friend of Meg's."

"I'm not sure," Gabe said. "I'll ask Viktor." He took out his phone.

"What does this have to do with Rylan suing Mammi?" Ivy asked.

"Maybe nothing," Gabe said. "Or maybe it has something to do with his motivation. He doesn't have any family support. He lost someone he loved. . . ."

"Has Marko or Viktor said if Rylan was always the way he is now?" I asked Gabe.

"What do you mean?"

"Talking about people behind their backs. Snarky. Manipulative."

"I don't know." Gabe kept texting. "You put that well. I'll ask."

Ivy stood and said, "I'll make some coffee."

Conrad gave me a kind smile. "Sorry you have to deal with all of this."

"Thanks," I said. "It's just really hard to know what the right thing to do is."

He nodded. "Have you talked to"—I thought he was going to say God—"Johann about it?"

"A little," I said.

"What was his response?"

"He said not to get pulled into Rylan's drama." Well, he hadn't said that exactly, but that's what he meant.

"That's good advice," Conrad said.

I thought of Martha not reacting when the PWs put the potato in the exhaust pipe of the tractor but then making Sergeant Schwarz confront them when the milk cans had been punctured. It was hard to know when to ignore something and when to speak up about it. But Martha seemed to have a gift when it came to dealing with difficult people.

"It's hard for me to help Rylan and know what the best course of action is, and also not be affected by his behavior," I said. "For example, I'd prefer he didn't talk when I drive him to class, but I don't think I can enforce it."

Conrad laughed.

"I'm serious," I deadpanned. But it really had been a joke.

He stopped laughing and then smiled and then tried not to laugh. "I'm sorry," he said. "That just struck me as funny."

Gabe's phone dinged. He looked down and then said, "Meg was from Lancaster County."

"Interesting," Conrad said.

"And, yes, Marko said that Rylan was always kind of snarky and mean, but in a joking way." Gabe looked up. "He behaved better when Meg was around. Now he seems worse than ever."

"Maybe we should hire a lawyer," I said as Ivy returned to the table.

"I can't imagine it will come to that," she said. "I think finding out what the VA will pay for and having a heart-to-heart with Rylan is all that it will take. I'm happy to talk with him, but you know him better. He's more likely to listen to you."

"Oh no. I think he'd be more likely to listen to you."

"You should talk to him. You have more at stake. Well, I mean, we all do, but what if Mammi loses the store? What will you do for work?"

I'd been worrying about the same thing, but I didn't want to admit it.

"Talk to him on the way to class tomorrow. Send him a text to make sure he's going."

I sent him a text that I'd pick him up at nine a.m.

He texted right back. I read the text out loud. " 'See you then.' "

Ivy rubbed her hands together. "See? He just needs someone to be his friend," she said. "You'll be able to talk to him. Tell him to speak with his caseworker. Everything will work out."

15

After Gabe and Conrad left, I called the barn just before milking time, and Dawdi answered.

"So," I said, "what happens if an Amish business gets sued?"

He answered, "I don't know of an Amish business that's been sued."

"What about Amish people?"

"I've known one."

"What happened?"

"His horse bolted and caused a car accident on the highway," Dawdi explained. "They negotiated the amount down and the mutual aid fund helped pay for it."

"Would the mutual aid fund do the same for Mammi?"

He paused and then said, "Our fund is a little low at the moment. We have a couple of people going through cancer treatment. A baby who just had heart surgery. A family who was in a buggy accident." He paused and then said, "I'd better get to the milking. Gabe just arrived."

"One more thing," I said. "Did Mammi tell you Rylan has actually talked with an attorney who thinks he has a good case against the store?"

"Nee." He sounded down, especially for

Dawdi. "We'll have to see what happens. Talk to you later."

As I drove Rylan to class the next day, he said, "I had a great time at your grandparents' place yesterday. The house is beautiful. So is the land. You know, I'd only seen the store and the parking lot before today. . . ." He kept talking.

He exhausted me. He was unpredictable. I never knew what to expect. Would he be in a good mood? Or a bad one? Talkative or surly? Kind or mean?

It was one thing to be kind to him when I had nothing to lose, but what if I had the store to lose? Could I still be kind to him then? And how could I bring up the topic in a natural way? I said a silent prayer that God would show me what to do.

"I really enjoyed church too," Rylan said. "Thank you for including me."

"You're welcome."

Before I could come up with anything more to say, he said, "Hey, I know Gabe asked what I was like before I lost my leg."

I stared straight ahead. "Oh?"

"Marko texted Viktor about it. I saw the text when it popped up on his phone yesterday afternoon."

"So what were you like before you lost your leg?"

He pulled his beanie down on his head with

both hands. "The same way I am now. Charming as can be."

I groaned.

"You're not easily impressed, are you?" Rylan asked.

"Probably not," I answered.

There was a lull in the conversation.

"It's too bad your grandmother doesn't have business insurance." He fidgeted with his beanie again. "Maybe you and your sisters can help her out."

"What do you mean?"

"It sounds as if the three of you are always flying here and there. You and Ivy each have a car. It seems as if you have plenty of money. Some sort of inheritance from your parents or something?"

"It's not an inheritance." I gritted my teeth. "It's life insurance money."

"So your parents believed in insurance, but your grandparents don't?"

"My parents were Mennonite. My grandparents are Amish."

There was another long period of silence. Finally, as I pulled onto the college campus, Rylan said, "You have a lot. More than you realize." He exhaled again. "I have nothing."

I finally connected with Johann that evening. I intentionally asked how he was doing—how his job was, how his mother was doing, how his army buddies were. I didn't want the focus to always be on me.

"How are you?" he asked when there was a lull in the conversation.

I made a face. "Do you really want to know?"

He nodded.

I told him everything that had happened lately. "He said he has nothing," I concluded, "while my family has so much."

"Doesn't he have disability from the government?"

"He must," I said. "And he has the GI Bill for school. It pays for tuition and helps with living expenses."

"That's not a lot," Johann said, "but it's not as if he has nothing. Unless he's talking about not having a family."

I explained what I knew about Meg.

Johann grimaced. "That certainly makes his losses more complicated."

"True." I went on to explain that it felt as if he were manipulating his friend group. "He bad-mouths everyone behind their backs. Then they tell each other, and everyone feels bad."

"It sounds as if Rylan has several problems."

"It seems so," I said. "And my family is going to have problems too if he sues. And so will I. Mammi wants me to take over the store in a couple of years."

"Really?"

I hadn't told Johann that before. I was afraid it made me sound like a loser. Here I was studying internet security, but all I planned to do was manage my grandmother's antique store. That's why I'd added the business classes.

I nodded. "Yes. That's the plan."

"Do you want to take over the store?"

I shrugged. "I don't have any other ideas."

"But does that mean you want to?"

I pursed my lips together. What other choice did I have? "Yes," I answered. "I want to." But I had a sinking feeling in my stomach as I said it.

Johann smiled, his eyes full of compassion. After a moment of silence, he said, "Don't expect the worst when it comes to Rylan. The attorney he met with might decide the case isn't worth it."

"That's true." I forced myself to smile.

"Change of subject," he said.

I smiled genuinely in relief.

"I hesitate to ask this, but I am going to force myself to."

I braced myself. Did he not want to spend time with me online anymore? Was I too depressing to be friends with?

"I have time off at Christmas, but Mama has to work. She wants me to go on vacation and have fun. I don't want to invite myself . . ."

What was he saying?

"But what do you think?"

"I'll be in Oregon," I said.

"Oh."

"But you could meet us there," I added quickly, noticing how defeated he looked. "Conrad is coming too. We can go up to Mount Hood. Maybe spend a day in Portland. What do you think?"

"I think I'd love that," he said. "If you're sure."

"Positive." While I seldom felt positive about anything, I actually did feel positive about Johann spending Christmas with us. Maybe not one hundred percent. But at least ninety-five percent. That felt like a miracle for me.

Johann made me feel safe. Not quite comfortable, but less awkward. Just the thought of him with me in Oregon brought a sense of peace.

But as soon as we ended the call, I began to second-guess my enthusiasm. Would Gran be all right with Johann coming? What if sparks flew between him and Ivy? I'd be hurting Conrad.

"Not your fault." The three words were in my therapist's voice. It wouldn't be my fault. I didn't have nearly as much power as I gave myself credit for. On the other hand, I did have power over myself. I could decide what was best for me.

I decided to call Gran. It was only three p.m. in Oregon. She finally had a cell phone and answered on the second ring. I got right to the point. "Would you mind if Johann came for Christmas?"

"Well, that's an idea," Gran said. "Let me think.

You girls can share your room. Brooke and Daniel are staying in Ivy's, as you know. Their kids are staying in Treva's. Conrad and Johann can have the basement room. How does that sound?"

It sounded crowded. "Will Brooke and her family be at our house for Christmas?"

"No, they'll go down to Eugene to her parents."

"Right," I said. "I think it will be fun to have Johann meet you and see Oregon."

"Is there anything I need to know?" Gran asked gently.

"About?"

"Johann."

"What do you mean?"

She sighed. "Are you interested in him? Is he interested in you?"

"No," I said. "He just wants to visit is all."

"Okay," Gran said. "How are you feeling about coming home?"

The thought of Johann meeting us in Oregon had distracted me momentarily from thinking about what it would be like to be back home.

"Have you talked with your therapist about it?" Gran asked when I didn't answer.

"I'm not seeing my therapist anymore."

"Do you want to schedule an appointment to talk things through?"

"No."

Gran sighed. "I respect your decision, but remember that it's an option to speak with your therapist if the thought of coming home starts to feel overwhelming."

"I'll keep that in mind," I answered.

"Let Johann know your flight schedule in case he can coordinate his arrival close to yours," Gran said. "Last I checked with Ivy, she hadn't rented a vehicle. Make sure she does that soon and gets one large enough for all of you and your luggage. Tell her to get an SUV in case you want to go up on the mountain while you're here."

"Jah," I said. "We do."

On Tuesday morning, Rylan needed a ride to the VA hospital in Philadelphia. Marko and Viktor had class. If Gabe took off work to take him, then I'd need to work in the store. I decided to be brave and drive him, even though it meant going all the way into the city.

Once we were on the highway, he asked, "Any more thoughts on me suing your grandmother?"

"No," I answered.

"You shouldn't worry about it. It's a slow process. Don't even think about it."

"We're not dwelling on it," I said, even though I was.

"Your grandmother should hire counsel." He sounded like he knew what he was talking about. "I don't want her to be at a disadvantage."

I doubted Mammi would hire a lawyer, but I didn't say so. He would likely know that, anyway, given his work as a paralegal in a law firm that targeted the Amish.

"Gabe is the one who told me about the money you and your sisters have."

"What does Gabe know about it?" Had Ivy told Conrad about our insurance money? Did Conrad then tell Gabe? That made me uncomfortable.

I didn't even know what we had. Gran said we had "enough" to cover our education and living expenses. When we were twenty-five, we'd be given a lump sum to help us get established as adults.

"Look," I said. "This isn't any of Gabe's business. Nor is it yours."

Rylan crossed his arms. "Don't worry, I won't go after it."

I exhaled loudly. "Why would you? What does our money have to do with you going up an obviously rickety staircase that was roped off— or at the very least had a rope on the ground in front of it?"

He didn't respond.

I kept vacillating between blaming Rylan for his fall and blaming Mammi and Dawdi for not repairing the railing.

Trying to change the subject, I asked, "Would you tell me more about Meg?"

"No." He looked out the passenger window.

I didn't mean to hit a nerve. Or had I? "I'm sorry," I said.

Neither of us talked for the next thirty minutes. The only sound in the car was my GPS telling me to turn east onto 202. When I turned south onto I-76, which I'd stay on until I was a few blocks from the VA Medical Center, he said, "You bringing up Meg isn't the same as me bringing up your money."

"Actually, it is," I said. "We wouldn't have the money if it wasn't for our parents dying."

"But they were your parents—not the person you hoped to spend the rest of your life with."

"Look," I said. "I'm really sorry about Meg. Truly. But I don't think it serves a purpose to compare our losses. It's not a competition. Both are huge losses. And obviously it's hard on both of us."

"Fair enough," he answered.

The next time he talked was when I turned off the freeway. "Go straight," he said. "I'll show you where to turn for the handicap parking."

He didn't want me to go into his appointment with him, which was fine with me. I'd brought my network securities textbook and planned to get caught up on reading. On the way home, I intended to go over the material with Rylan once we were out of the city and I wasn't as anxious. But the traffic was slow, and he soon fell asleep. He didn't wake up until we were near the apartment.

"Would you drop me off?" he asked. "I'm too tired to go to class." He took out his phone and texted someone. By the time I had pulled up to the complex and gotten the wheelchair out of the back of the van, Marko appeared, ready to transfer Rylan.

"How did it go?" he asked Rylan.

"Fine. I'm just really tired."

I wanted to skip class too, but I didn't. The sight of Rylan exhausted and dependent on Marko stayed with me. Rylan annoyed me, but I couldn't help but feel concerned for him. Maybe his behavior came from a mixture of anger and anxiety. I knew what it was like to be anxious. I couldn't imagine adding anger to the mix. I felt sorry for him. I'd never had anyone tug on the full spectrum of my emotions the way he did.

The next day, when I arrived at Rylan's apartment to take him to class, no one answered the door. Finally, I called his phone, not wanting to barge in with my key.

He answered with a groggy "Hello?"

"I'm here to pick you up."

"I'm not going today," he said.

"Do you need anything?"

"No. I'm just going to sleep."

I didn't hear from Rylan the rest of the day, so I assumed everything was fine.

I'd gotten our itinerary for Oregon from Ivy and emailed it to Johann, but I hadn't spoken with him. As I was cleaning up my notes for Rylan at my desktop in my room, a video call rang from Johann.

I accepted it, and his face slowly materialized. It wasn't a great connection. At last, I could hear him say, "I got your email. I just wanted to double-check that it's all right with your grandmother from Oregon."

"Yes," I said. "She's fine with it. You and Conrad will share the basement area. There's a family room down there with couches and stuff. And a bathroom. The two of you will have that entire space."

"Nice," he said. "There's a flight that arrives in Portland two hours after yours. Is that too long for you to wait?"

"No. That will give us time to get the rental." I paused a minute and then said, "Did Ivy tell you she and Conrad are dating?"

He grinned. "Yes. A long time ago. That's really old news."

My face grew warm. "I just wanted to make sure. I know you and Ivy are close."

"Yes," he said, "as friends." Was his face growing red, or was it the bad connection? "I'm not coming to see Ivy. I'm coming to see you."

I froze. It made me happy to hear that—but sad too. Once he spent time around me, I doubted we'd ever be more than friends. He'd know the true me. Neurotic. Awkward. Weird. Everything he wasn't.

"We can talk more in Oregon," he said.

"Okay," I croaked.

Thankfully, he changed the topic and asked me about my classes. Then he asked how Rylan was doing.

"I'm not sure," I said. "He didn't go to class yesterday or today, and I haven't heard from him since this morning." I didn't tell Johann about Rylan's reaction to me bringing up Meg.

"Is he treating you right?" he asked.

"Mostly . . ."

"What does that mean?"

"He doesn't treat anyone great. But I think he's in a lot of pain, physically and emotionally. And I think he's angry and anxious. And depressed too."

"I'm sympathetic toward him, but losing a limb—even losing someone you love in battle—isn't an excuse to treat others badly. Don't let him get away with it."

I was too embarrassed to ask Johann how *not* to let Rylan "get away with it." I felt as if I should know. I didn't want Johann to know how helpless I was at this sort of thing—or how helpless Rylan made me feel. Should I refuse to help him? That was the only thing I had any control over.

We ended the call, and I went to bed early. The next morning, I went to Mammi's shop to work for the day because Thursday's class was canceled. Gabe was working with Dawdi, and the shop was slow and pretty boring. Mammi spent the morning showing me her inventory system. I'd helped her take inventory several times, but I hadn't seen the ledgers where she kept the final details.

"When do you plan to retire?" I asked.

"Why? Are you ready to take over?"

"Not yet. I just wondered if you have any immediate plans."

"No," Mammi said. "I'll wait until you're ready and it seems like it's time for me."

"Are you thinking within the next year? Or five? Or ten?"

"Certainly not ten," she answered.

"So, five?"

"Perhaps less."

In five years, I'd be twenty-six. I'd started out taking business classes in college, thinking that would help me the most with the store. But an instructor in my marketing class suggested taking computer classes too, including website development and internet security classes. I had an idea of putting Mammi's store online someday—after she was out of the business, of course. That interested me more than the day-to-day operation of the store.

Around one, after we'd returned from lunch, Mammi asked how Rylan was doing.

"I don't know," I said. "I haven't heard from him in a while."

"Should you check in with him?"

"I don't think that's necessary."

"Why don't you call him on the way to the house?"

"The way to the house?"

"Jah," she answered. "Go back to the house and help Rosene with the rest of the housework and getting supper ready. She's been tired lately."

I called Rylan as I walked. It rang and rang. Finally, he answered. "Brenna," he said. "I was just thinking about you."

"How are you doing?"

"Better. I just got off the phone with my attorney. He needs information from you."

"What do you mean?"

"He's going to depose you about my accident. Under oath."

I felt ill.

"All you have to do is tell the truth."

I stumbled as I reached the yard. "Well, I guess I'll talk to you later."

"Don't take it personally," he said. "It's just business."

"Bye." I ended the call. Even though it was cold and spitting snow, I was sweating. Even my hands.

I decided not to tell Rosene about the phone call. Instead, after I'd hung up my coat and slipped out of my boots, I stepped into the kitchen with a forced smile on my face.

Rosene sat at the table, peeling potatoes. "What's wrong?" she asked.

I reached for my forehead, touching my scar. "What do you mean?"

"You usually only smile if something's wrong."

I hadn't realized that, but I believed her. "Mammi sent me to help you."

Rosene cocked her head. Maybe she expected me to say more. After a long pause, she said, "How nice. We can peel potatoes together. Would you like me to tell you more of the story?"

"Yes, please." Anything to take my mind off Rylan and his plan to ruin my future.

16

Martha

The next day, after the morning milking, Jeremiah plowed the garden and Martha and Rosene raked it, tossing rocks out of the soil. Then they began lining the rows. As they worked, Martha asked, "Who was Mutter talking to outside of the store late yesterday?"

"She said he was a businessman looking for directions." Rosene maneuvered a large rock out of the soil. "How was your time with George?"

"Good. We went to a PW camp, where I did some translating. I didn't see any of the PWs who've been working on our farm." She didn't mention she thought she might have seen Dirk.

"Be careful," Rosene said.

"I will. I doubt I'll do more translating, though. George understands the risks."

Three hours later, as they finished lunch and Rosene started to clean up the table, Mutter said to her, "I need your help in the store to stock the shelves. We were busy this morning."

Rosene turned toward Clare, who was yawning. Her face was pale and drawn. "I'll hurry with the dishes," she said to Mutter. And then to Clare she said, "You should put Arden down for his nap and then rest."

Martha headed out to the garden to finish the rows. She and Clare were very different people and always had been. Clare had always enjoyed keeping house and cooking, while Martha had always preferred working on the farm and in the store. They hadn't been particularly close before Clare left for Germany.

When Clare returned with Rosene, Martha was overwhelmed with relief that Clare was safe. It took a while for Rosene to trust Martha, but slowly they developed a relationship. Rosene would never be as close to Martha as she was to Clare, but Rosene's arrival had drawn Martha and Clare closer together. Martha and Clare couldn't help but be thankful for each other. Rosene had lost her mother and twin sister, Dorina, to death and then her father and oldest sister to working with the Nazis.

A car door slammed, and Martha turned toward the driveway. She couldn't see a car, but Mutter came toward the back porch from the direction of the store. She didn't look Martha's way and walked up the steps. A minute later, Mutter headed back toward the driveway.

Martha stepped away from the garden and toward the side of the house. In the driveway, the man from the day before stood beside his black car.

Martha slipped back to the garden. Who was the man? Surely not a businessman looking for directions.

What if the man had something to do with the German underground in the United States? Prior to the US entering the war, the America First movement collaborated with the German government to promote Nazi propaganda in the United States. In 1940, the Christian Front organization conspired to overthrow the US government and had plans to steal weapons and ammunition.

In December of 1941, Martha hoped that Japan attacking the US and Germany declaring war on the US would put an end to the fascist groups in America, but since then she'd read about spies who were American but working for the Nazis. And German spies too. In the summer of 1942, eight Nazi agents had been arrested on US soil with explosives to blow up railway bridges and New York's water supply, among other things. They'd been ferried by U-boats to beaches on Long Island and Florida by the Germans. Had more arrived? Or were Nazi sympathizers in the US continuing to plan havoc?

But why would they contact a middle-aged Mennonite woman in rural Lancaster County? It didn't make sense. Unless it had something to do with Mutter being German and her relatives back in Frankfurt. Both Uncle Josef and Cousin

Lena worked for the Nazis. Were they trying to contact Mutter for some reason with information they couldn't write in a letter—one that might or might not get across the Atlantic intact?

On Sunday, Jeremiah, Clare, and Arden rode in their buggy to church in their district, while Mutter, Vater, Rosene, and Martha piled into the Studebaker to go to church at the Mennonite meeting hall five miles from the farm.

Martha, with her eyes on the store as they drove past, said, "I see the businessman who asked for directions stopped by again yesterday."

Mutter didn't respond.

Martha continued, "I saw him in the driveway. Mutter, you were talking with him."

Mutter answered immediately. "He seems to be bad with directions. He'd asked for directions to the mercantile in Paradise but somehow he missed it. So he stopped and asked for directions again."

"You were deep in conversation," Martha said. "Although he seemed to be doing most of the talking."

"Jah, he's a talker," Mutter said. She seemed a little flustered. She was usually better at—lying? Not revealing information? Keeping secrets?

When they reached the church, Rosene sat in the middle between Mutter and Martha on the women's side, while Vater sat with a couple of men who were near his age on the men's side.

Mutter and Martha both wore their hair in buns at the napes of their necks with sheer cloths pinned to the crown of their heads. Rosene, like most of the other women in the congregation, wore a traditional American Mennonite Kapp.

Martha appreciated her community. She'd been loved and supported, even though her family—with her immigrant German mother and adopted German sister—was different. But she couldn't help but long to see and experience more of the world. Especially now when more people than ever around the world were displaced and struggling to find any community at all.

After the service, the congregants gathered under the oak tree in the churchyard. She overheard Elmer Yoder, who was speaking with Vater, say, "I've heard rumors of a German spy in the area. I'm afraid Englischers will grow even more suspicious of us Mennonites."

Martha shifted a little so she could hear better.

"I haven't heard any rumors," Vater responded.

Martha, feeling badly she was suspicious of her own mother, stole a glance at Mutter. She and Rosene were talking with Tabitha Yoder, who was hard of hearing and speaking loudly. Mutter had defended Hitler and the Nazis when they first came to power. She claimed Clare was safe in Germany long after Vater wanted her to return home. After Dorina's death and when Germany declared war on the US, Mutter ultimately gave up hope that good would come from the Nazis—at least that was what she'd indicated.

Mutter had always missed Germany, always been proud of her German heritage, always believed German music, literature, and schooling were superior. It had seemed, quite a few times, that Mutter regretted marrying Vater and raising her family in the US. It wasn't until she opened the store that she seemed to have gained any sort of contentment living in Lancaster County.

Elmer said, "Well, keep your eyes open. With all these PWs around, there's bound to be trouble. If a spy coordinates with one of those Nazi officers, who knows what might happen."

Vater said, "I'll keep my eyes—and ears—open, Elmer."

Elmer tugged on his beard. "It's hard to know who to trust these days."

"The Lord," Vater answered. "He's the only One we can trust. Hopefully the war will soon be over."

That afternoon, after Jeremiah, Clare, and Arden had returned from church and visiting Jeremiah's family, they all piled into the Studebaker to take Jeremiah back to the train station. As Martha turned down the driveway, Rosene and Zeke came running from the barn and asked if they could ride along too.

"Did you finish the milking?" Martha asked.

"Jah," Rosene said. She smiled. "Hopefully we don't stink."

Jeremiah sat in the back with Clare and Arden. Zeke climbed in the back with them, and Rosene climbed in the front.

Arden laughed. In the rearview mirror, Martha watched him crawl out of Jeremiah's arms, across Clare, and onto Zeke's lap. As Martha directed her attention forward, Rosene turned her head and watched the antics in the back seat. She was crazy about Arden—it was obvious she wanted to be a wife and mother someday. She enjoyed keeping house and cooking, just like Clare.

When they reached the train station, Martha parked on the street, and they all climbed out of the car. Jeremiah hoisted Arden onto his shoulders. Clare walked beside them, slowly. Jeremiah met her pace, so Martha led the way to the station, with Zeke and Rosene walking behind her.

As they neared the station, Martha glanced down the side street. There was George. She started to wave, but then she noticed the woman beside him. She wore a mint green hat over her auburn hair. Was it Nurse Olson from the camp?

Martha realized that she had stopped, and the others had too. She started walking again. Jeremiah gave her a sympathetic smile. Had he seen George too?

When they reached the station, Jeremiah bought his ticket with Arden still in his arms, and then told everyone good-bye. He and Clare didn't show much affection to each other, but he kissed her on the forehead and then kissed the top of Arden's head. Then he slipped him into Clare's arms.

"Dada!" Arden called out.

Clare bounced him on her hip. Jeremiah turned and waved and then continued to the platform.

Arden began to fuss, and Zeke whooshed him away from Clare and lifted him to his shoulders. Arden began to laugh, and Rosene reached up and steadied him. Martha put an arm around Clare and walked with her out of the station and toward the car.

Zeke and Arden led the way, bouncing along the sidewalk, with Rosene running alongside.

When they reached the car, Rosene climbed in the back seat with Zeke and Arden, and Clare rode up front. Martha started the car and eased away from the curb as she said to Clare, "Are you all right?"

"I will be," she answered.

When Arden began to fuss, Zeke passed him up front to Clare, who settled the boy atop her belly.

In the back seat, Zeke asked Rosene, "Do you think about your life in Germany much?"

"No," she replied. "Not really. Except to thank the Lord for bringing me here." There was a pause and then Rosene said, "I'll always be indebted to Clare for saving my life."

Martha glanced toward Clare. Her head was tilted back against the seat, and her eyes were closed. Arden slept soundly in her arms.

On Monday, as Martha finished the last of the egg noodles on her plate, Clare said she'd do the dishes after she put Arden down for a nap. "I'm feeling better," she said to Rosene. "You go work in the garden. It looks as if we'll get rain by this evening."

After Martha cleared her plate from the table, she followed Mutter down the back steps. As Mutter turned toward the store, she stopped and spoke with Dirk. Martha couldn't tell if they were speaking in German or English.

After a few minutes, Mutter continued on, and Martha ran after her. When she caught up with her, Martha asked if she was speaking German with Dirk.

"Of course not. We were speaking English. These boys are disturbed," she said. "Dirk was saying that his father is a high-ranking Nazi officer—a general, I think—who is ashamed of him for being captured. No wonder he's so unsettled. He said if Germany loses, his father will most likely disown him."

"Why?" Martha asked. "Won't his father, as a high-ranking officer, be even more responsible?"

"You would think," Mutter said. "But the father sounds like a horrible bully."

"So the apple didn't fall far from the tree," Martha said.

Mutter took out a pin from her hair and then repositioned it. "Dirk isn't that bad. I hope mothers in Germany are being kind to our boys who are POWs too."

Martha doubted any mothers in Germany had contact with American POWs, unless the mothers worked in POW camps.

She headed back to the milk room and examined the patched cans. Martha guessed Rosene had reached the garden because she heard Dirk say in German, "Ah, look. They let the little girl out of the house today."

Someone laughed. Was it Sergeant Schwarz?

"She's German," Dirk said.

"Well," Sergeant Schwarz said, "everyone on this farm is Mennonite or Amish. Most of their people came from Germany, as did most of the people in Pennsylvania."

"Jah, I realize that," Dirk said. "But the older woman *is* German and so is the little one."

"Why do you say that?" Sergeant Schwarz asked.

"They both have slight accents. Both carry themselves like German women—with confidence." Martha stood up straight, as her mother was always telling her to do, as she listened. "It's obvious the younger one understands us when we

230

speak German. So does the older one. Actually, they all do."

"I don't think they do," Sergeant Schwarz said.

Dirk laughed. "Believe what you want."

Sergeant Schwarz didn't respond, at least not verbally. "I'm going to go use the outhouse," he said. "Be ready to go to the field in five minutes."

Martha continued examining the cans. The first one had held. The second one hadn't. Neither had the third. Perhaps Vater would feel up to repairing them again.

Dirk spoke again. *"Guten Tag."*

"Hello." It was Rosene.

"Sprichst du Deutsch?"

"I don't understand German," Rosene answered.

There was a pause and then Dirk laughed and asked in English, "Could you teach me to speak—American?"

"American?" Rosene paused. "English."

Dirk laughed again. "Jah, English."

"Absolutely not."

Martha's face grew warm. She marched out of the milk room and turned toward the garden. But as she did, she heard Clare yell, "Arden!"

17

"He's not in the house," Clare yelled. "I can't find him anywhere."

Dirk stood by the garden, smoking a cigarette.

"Have you seen the baby?" Clare asked in English.

Dirk gave Martha a questioning look.

Martha shouted, *"Hast du das Baby gesehen?!"*

"Aha." He grinned and answered in English. "No, I haven't seen the baby."

Martha started running. Arden was fascinated by the pond, and it posed the most danger. How long had he been gone from the house?

There was a commotion in the horse barn, which was another of Arden's fascinations. He called the horses "neigh neighs."

She turned around and yelled at Dirk, "Go check the pond!"

He dropped his cigarette and ground it into the soil. Rosene ran past him.

Martha took off for the barn. The last stall was open, and the yearling bellowed. She heard hooves against the wooden wall, and then the yearling came tearing out of the stall toward Martha. She jumped onto the railing of another stall as the horse tore by. As it bolted out the door, she ran to the last stall.

Arden lay crumpled in the corner. She rushed to his side. His eyes fluttered and then opened. Martha ran her hands over his head. He began to whimper.

"Martha!" Clare yelled.

"He's in here." Martha ran her hands over his body. Arden whimpered louder. She pulled up his shirt. There was a red mark on his chest.

She scooped him up and stepped out of the stall as Clare and Vater rushed in. Clare began to sob and ran toward them.

"The horse kicked him in the chest, but I think he's okay."

Arden fell into Clare's arms. Vater staggered. Martha caught him and directed him to a hay bale. Clare slumped beside him, clutching Arden. He began to cry.

Martha stepped out of the barn to find Rosene and Dirk to tell them the baby had been found. Just beyond the picnic table Dirk stood, talking with Otis. She couldn't tell what he said, but he was calm and collected, as if he didn't have a worry in the world.

Either he didn't care Arden might be drowning in the pond or he'd known all along the baby was in the horse barn.

Zeke managed to catch the yearling and coax him back. At lunch, he said, "I asked Dirk to put the yearling in the pasture this morning. When

I confronted him about it a few minutes ago, he said he forgot." Zeke glanced at Clare, who sat in her chair, still holding Arden. "I'm really sorry."

"It's not your fault."

"We need to watch Arden," Martha said, "and make sure he doesn't have any internal injuries." She looked at Mutter at the end of the table. "Would you call the doctor? Ask if we should bring Arden in to be examined?"

"I'll do that," Mutter said.

Rosene reached for Arden and said to Clare, "You need to eat."

"I'm going to work with Dirk this afternoon," Martha said. "Mucking out the dairy barn."

"Are you sure?" Vater asked.

"Yes." She needed to see what he would say about her speaking German. And try to figure out if he'd left the horse barn door and stall door open on purpose. Perhaps he thought the yearling would have escaped hours earlier. But what she really wanted to know was if he'd watched the baby go into the horse barn and hadn't done anything to stop him. Was the man without a heart? Or just a cold-blooded enemy? Was he so full of anger that he'd sacrifice a child to reach his goal of disrupting an American farm?

A half hour later, as they shoveled manure into separate wheelbarrows, Dirk said in German, "I'm thankful the baby was not harmed."

"Jah," Martha said in English. "Did you leave the barn door and stall door open?"

"*Ich spreche kein Englisch,*" he responded.

"And I don't speak German." Martha held his gaze as she spoke.

He thrust the shovel forward, scraping it on the cement as he filled it with manure.

"Let's get past this—" Martha hesitated— "pretense." Then she repeated what she'd said in German. She continued speaking in German, "We've both been trying to fool the other. It hasn't worked."

Dirk stood up straight, pursing his lips. "All right," he said in English.

She leaned against her shovel. "What are you up to?"

"Up to?"

"What are your intentions while you're on our farm?"

"To do my duty," he said. "And work with our"—his lip curled in distaste—"small group."

Martha paused. Did he resent being assigned to a small farm with only three other PWs? That would certainly limit his influence.

"Have you been put in charge of them, as an officer?" Martha asked.

"I'm not an officer."

"I don't believe that."

He shrugged. "I'm only twenty-one."

"I don't believe that either."

"It doesn't matter whether you believe it or not," he said. "It's true. My duty is to work with my countrymen—even Andreas and Pavlo."

"What do you mean?"

"They're Russian peasants. They headed west to fight for the Reich after we invaded Russia. We'd rather have them fighting for Germany than Russia, but I'm not sure I trust them. Not entirely."

"Oh." Martha hadn't realized Andreas and Pavlo weren't German. "Well," she continued, "you must not leave barn doors or stall doors open while you're working on our farm."

"That's offensive," he said. "Clearly someone wasn't attending the baby as they should have been. And now you blame me."

Martha pursed her lips together. "And stay away from my little sister."

"From Rosene? She's such a lovely German girl."

"Leave her alone," Martha hissed.

Dirk smirked. "Or what?"

"I'll report you," she said. "You'll be punished at the camp."

"Unlikely."

They continued shoveling. Martha poured her angst into the movement of the shovel. Down. Scrape. Lift. Dump.

After a few minutes, Dirk stopped and said, "My other goal is to await the Reich."

"What?"

236

"Watch the skies," he said in English. "There will soon be an invasion."

Martha stifled a laugh. "Germany will invade the United States?"

He nodded. "By air and sea."

"But the war has turned. It will soon be over."

"That's propaganda," Dirk said. "Created by your government. Our Führer will not be deterred. Our Thousand-Year Reich will happen as planned, thanks to the resources of your nation."

The next day, the temperature reached seventy. Martha wore overalls and a work shirt as she walked toward the barn for the afternoon milking. She was interrupted by the truck arriving early for the PWs. She waved at the driver and then started toward the field instead of the barn. Zeke would have to help with the milking and finish the field dragging the next day.

Once she notified Dirk and Otis, she headed to the milking room, where Andreas and Pavlo were sterilizing the milking cans. "The truck is here," she said.

Pavlo asked in English, "So soon?"

She nodded. "You'll have time to enjoy the sunshine at the camp."

"I would rather stay here," he answered.

There was a commotion outside as someone—was it Mutter?—called out, "The president has died!"

Shocked, Martha stepped out of the milking room. Mutter was standing at the back porch. She turned around as Clare and Rosene came out the back door, then called out so Martha could hear. "President Roosevelt has passed away, down in Georgia. Of a stroke. It was on the radio."

Martha wrapped her arms around herself. The air had turned cold. President Roosevelt had high blood pressure, like Vater. He had the best medical care in the world, and it still couldn't stop a stroke. What would happen with the war? And the country?

Someone behind her began to clap. She turned. Dirk had a smile on his face and was clapping slowly and rhythmically. Otis made eye contact with Martha and began clapping too. *"Don't take anything they do personally,"* George had said. *"Think of it as part of a game."*

Andreas and Pavlo reached the truck. Dirk nudged Andreas, but he stepped away without responding and climbed into the back of the truck first. Clearly he was ignoring Dirk and Otis.

Martha started toward the house, toward her family. It seemed wise to spend a few minutes with them in prayer for their country before starting the milking.

18

The next evening, Martha left after supper for town to go to the Red Cross meeting to assemble packages for American POWs in Germany. She'd been tempted not to go. It had been a hard day of work, besides the worry of the president dying. Andreas didn't come with the rest of the PWs that morning, which meant the rest of them had to work harder to get everything done.

By the end of the day, she decided to go to the meeting even though she was exhausted. When she arrived, George asked if she could accompany him back to the PW camp instead of helping with the packages. "We've had another complaint." George dropped his voice. "Another beating by a guard."

Martha took a step backward. "What came of the last complaint?"

"Nothing. Sergeant Schwarz claims it was a fabricated charge. Since there were no witnesses, the POW's account couldn't be verified," he said. "Hopefully this latest charge will clarify what's going on. Can you go with me?"

"Yes," she said. "I can."

When they reached the camp, they walked up to the infirmary again and were greeted by Nurse Olson. She seemed warm to George but not overly so. In fact, she seemed upset. "The POW is in the back room," she said. "Andreas is the one I told you about."

Martha wondered what Nurse Olson would have told George about a PW. And then she realized the nurse said *Andreas*. Surely there were several PWs by the first name of Andreas in the camp.

Martha led the way and opened the door first. The light was dim. She squinted. "Andreas?"

He nodded.

She stepped closer. It *was* Andreas. There was a lamp on the table. She tilted it toward him. He had a black eye, and his arm was in a sling.

George stepped into the room.

"Andreas is one of the PWs at our farm," Martha said to George.

"Will you translate for him?"

"Yes," Martha said. In German, she asked Andreas if he approved of her doing the translating.

"Jah," he answered, after he recovered from his surprise that Martha was in front of him.

Martha sat in the chair by the window and then George sat beside her.

"Tell me what happened," George said.

In German, Andreas said he was walking down to the mess hall that morning when someone rushed him, flung him to the ground, and then beat him, hitting him in the face and eye and then kicking him in the side, which bruised his arm badly enough for the need to wear the sling.

"Can he identify the attacker?" George asked.

"Jah," Andreas answered. "It was Sergeant Schwarz."

George jotted down notes as he spoke. "Did the sergeant say anything?"

"*Nein.*"

"Did you fight back?"

"I tried," Andreas said. "But I was on the ground and at a disadvantage. He's stronger than he looks."

"How did you get him to stop?"

"Someone coming along the trail yelled, and he stopped kicking me and then disappeared into the trees."

"Who yelled?"

"I don't know." Andreas leaned backward. "They kept going."

"How sure are you that it was Sergeant Schwarz?"

Andreas gestured at Martha with his good hand and then said, "*Fraulein* Simons knows how well I know Sergeant Schwarz. It was him."

"Any idea why he would attack you?"

"Nein," Andreas answered. "He caught me by surprise."

"What did you do after the attack?"

"I came here."

"Who cared for you?"

"The nurse on duty."

"Not Nurse Olson?"

"Nein. Another nurse was working, the night shift."

George made a note and then said, "I have just a few more questions. Do you see Sergeant Schwarz outside of your work situation? Do you see him much here at the camp?"

"Occasionally," Andreas answered. "At the mess hall. He watches us play *Fußall* on Sunday afternoons. He also attends concerts other POWs put on, ones that I attend."

"How does he treat you when you're working on the Zimmerman farm?"

"Decently."

Martha thought of Dirk saying he didn't trust Andreas and Pavlo because they weren't German. Did Sergeant Schwarz feel the same way?

George asked, "Is there anything else I should know?"

Andreas shook his head. "Just that I'm in a lot of pain. If you're done, could I get my medication from Betsy—I mean, Nurse Olson?"

Martha translated the request, and George said, "Yes. Go ahead. I'll finish up my notes."

Andreas excused himself and George took a minute to write a few more things down. When he pushed back his chair, Martha said, "An interesting thing happened on the farm yesterday." She told him about Dirk saying that

242

Andreas and Pavlo were Russian and nudging Andreas, trying to get him to clap at the news President Roosevelt had died.

"Where was Sergeant Schwarz when that happened?"

"He wasn't there," Martha said. "He must have been coming back from the pasture."

"When all the PWs were already at the truck?"

Martha shrugged. "Yes."

George made note of that, collected his things, stood, and then held the door for her. She walked into the hall.

When they reached the lobby, Andreas was tipping a paper pill cup into his mouth while Nurse Olson sat back down at her desk.

"Thank you for the use of the room," George said as he opened the door for Martha. She stepped out onto the porch and then down the steps. Andreas followed but kept a distance between them.

"Why did Nurse Olson speak to you about Andreas?" Martha asked once they were in the car. George pulled out and headed toward the highway. Finally, he said, "Did she mention that?"

"Yes. And I saw you with Nurse Olson in Lancaster two weeks ago on Sunday."

"She goes to my church when she's in town."

Martha folded her hands in her lap. "What's going on?"

He gave her a quick glance, followed by a

smile. Then he returned his attention to the road. "I'm not at liberty to say."

On Monday, Andreas arrived with the others, including Sergeant Schwarz. Martha searched the two for any signs of animosity. They didn't interact, so she couldn't tell. Andreas no longer wore the sling, but his movements seemed stiff.

Martha sent Zeke, Dirk, and Otis, along with Sergeant Schwarz, to seed the field while she took Andreas and Pavlo to mend the pasture fence with her. On the way, she asked Andreas how he was feeling.

"Okay," he answered in English.

"Are you comfortable being here with Sergeant Schwarz?"

"Jah." He dropped his voice and spoke in German. "He denies it was him."

The morning proceeded without incident. Martha enjoyed working with Andreas and Pavlo. She relaxed a little and asked the two if they knew each other before they arrived in Pennsylvania. Pavlo gave Andreas a furtive glance.

"No," Andreas answered in English. "But we came from the same area back home."

"Where is that?"

"Near Medyka."

"Where is Medyka?" Martha asked.

"In Poland."

"Oh." Why did Dirk say they were Russian?

"Both of our families farmed." Andreas paused a moment and swiped his hand across his forehead. "We were invaded by the Germans and Soviets in 1939, then occupied by the Russians, and then invaded by the Germans again in 1941."

Martha's stomach lurched. Dirk must have deemed them Russians because Poland had been occupied by Russia. And because if he thought of them as Russian, he could look down on them even more than he already did due to them not being German.

Andreas continued, "We met after we were both forced into the German army in 1941. We were sent west to fight. We were captured by the Americans last summer in France, shipped to England, and then here. We arrived in January."

"Are you anxious to return home after the war ends?"

Again, Andreas glanced at Pavlo and said something in their dialect. Pavlo's face grew serious, and he shrugged.

"There's nothing to return to. Our farms were destroyed by the Russians. The buildings and crops were burned." Andreas pursed his lips together. "My parents were killed; Pavlo's died a few years before. Now Poland is again under Russian occupation." Andreas shrugged. "We like America. We wish we could stay. We have nothing to go back to Poland for."

Martha said, "I'm sorry."

Andreas held a fence post with his good hand as Pavlo drove it into the ground.

"At best," Andreas said, "we'll be sent to Germany, where we won't belong. At worst, we'll be sent to Poland, where the Russians will treat us badly. They'll know we fought for the Germans."

That evening, Martha went back outside to check on a cow that was due to calve. As she started back to the house, a car drove down the driveway. *George.* What was he doing at the farm?

She glanced at her blue shirt, with the sleeves rolled and pushed up over her elbows, and overalls that were covered with mud and manure. She didn't have time to change. Her hair was in a bun at the nape of her neck, but strands had come undone.

He climbed out and started toward the porch, but Martha waved and called out, "George!"

He turned toward her. "Martha?"

She laughed. "Yes, it's me."

He smiled. "I have some questions for you." That sounded serious. He spoke quietly. "A German-American was arrested for spying a couple of days ago in Washington, DC. A person came forward and said he'd been seen here in Lancaster County a few times. Perhaps visiting someone who lives near here."

"Goodness," Martha said.

"He also had contact with a guard at the camp."

"Sergeant Schwarz?"

George shook his head. "I clarified it wasn't Schwarz."

Martha wasn't sure what the case had to do with her. She must have had a puzzled expression on her face because George said, "A volunteer told me he saw someone who looked like the alleged spy at your mother's store recently."

"How could this person identify the alleged spy?"

George folded his hands. "He recognized him from a photo in the *New York Times*. The spy was with someone who lives around here—a German man."

Martha felt ill as she immediately thought about Franz Richter stopping at her Mutter's store.

"I'm just wondering if you've seen anything suspicious. And I wanted to warn you that someone—probably with the FBI—may be coming around to ask questions. The volunteer who believes he saw the spy at the store reported it."

Martha couldn't bring the issue up with Vater— it would be too stressful for him. She wished for the hundredth time that Jeremiah was home.

George gave her a sympathetic smile. "Call me if I can help in any way."

"Thank you." Martha closed her eyes a moment

and upon opening them asked, "Have you heard any more about going to Europe?"

"My application has been accepted, but I don't have a position yet. Will you apply? I still have the extra application."

Tears threatened, and she blinked quickly. "I'll think about it more. . . ."

He leaned toward her. "Your family is fortunate to have you."

"Thank you," she said. "I'm fortunate to have them." And she was. Yet she longed for more.

The next morning, Rosene returned to planting the garden now that the chance of frost was gone. At lunchtime, as Martha headed to the house, she spotted a piece of paper on the other side of the walkway. As she bent to pick it up, Dirk—who sat at the picnic table—smirked. At least it seemed he had. Or had she imagined it?

She stood and slipped the paper in her pocket. When she reached the house, she read it. *Women's clothes. Shoes. Hats.* She didn't recognize the handwriting, nor did she say anything about it.

After lunch, Mutter left the house first. When Martha came down the steps, Mutter seemed to be searching for something by the driveway

"What are you looking for?" Martha asked.

"A list for the store," Mutter answered.

Puzzled, Martha walked toward her and asked, "Are you thinking about carrying women's clothes?"

"Jah," she answered. "Why do you ask?"

She showed Mutter the list. "Whose handwriting is this?"

"Mine," Mutter said. "Rosene and I were brainstorming ways to expand. I put the piece of paper in my pocket. It must have fallen out."

"It doesn't look like your handwriting. Yours is usually not as neat."

Mutter smiled. "I've been trying to improve." She took the list. "Thank you."

Martha headed toward the field, passing through the barnyard. Sergeant Schwarz and Dirk were speaking German but softly enough that she couldn't hear what they were saying. Sergeant Schwarz held his head high and his shoulders squared. Martha stepped under the eaves of the milk room to watch the men.

Pavlo and then Andreas, who held a shovel in his good hand, approached Dirk and Sergeant Schwarz.

Dirk hissed something. She made out, in German, ". . . you must do what I tell you to."

19

Brenna

Rylan went to our classes the next week. We didn't talk any more about his attorney or his plan to sue Mammi. Or me being deposed. He seemed to be doing better. He was able to transfer himself from his wheelchair into my van. Around the apartment, he could now use a crutch to get around when he had his prosthesis on, but it was too difficult to go a long ways with that method.

It was only a couple of more weeks until his cast came off. I knew he looked forward to it, and so did I. By winter term, he'd be driving himself to classes. If he didn't drop out.

The following Monday, the third week of November, as I drove us back to the apartment complex from class, I asked, "What are you doing for Thanksgiving?"

He shrugged. "Maybe Viktor and Marko will invite me to their family dinner."

"What about your family?" I asked.

"Would you stop asking about them?"

It wasn't as if I asked about them much—just a time or two.

Impulsively, I blurted out, "You can come to Mammi and Dawdi's if you want."

"Why would you ask me to come to your family's Thanksgiving? Are you as naïve as you seem, or do you have something up your sleeve?"

"What do you mean?"

He shook his head. "You're either a really good actor—or really stupid."

"Thanks," I said. "Everyone knows I'm no actor."

He smirked. "That's an understatement."

I wasn't exactly sure why I asked him. Yes, I felt sorry for him. But I also knew what it was like to be floundering. No matter how off-putting Rylan was, he still needed connections with others.

That Saturday, Gabe had drill again. I spent Friday at the farm and helped with the milking in the morning. It snowed a couple of inches during the night. The cows were waiting when we went out at five and were extra anxious for their feed. My hands were cold and stiff as I fed the first group and dipped their teats and then helped Dawdi get them hooked up to the milkers.

By the time we finished, the temperature had dropped more, and I was chilled by the time I got back into the house. Rosene poured a cup of coffee, handed it to me, and said, "Go get a shower. I'll have hotcakes and sausage ready by the time you're done. And then I want to talk about Thanksgiving with you."

I took the coffee. "I asked Rylan to join us. Is that okay? He probably won't come. He'll probably go with Viktor and Marko instead."

251

"It's fine if he joins us. Invite Viktor and Marko too. Gabe and Conrad are coming, along with their mother." Rosene glanced toward the hallway. Dawdi hadn't come in from the barn yet, and Mammi must have still been in their room. She lowered her voice. "Priscilla and Arden are going to go spend a few days with Janice and Roy up in the Big Valley over Thanksgiving."

"Janice and Roy? Who are they?"

"Arden's sister and brother-in-law. Janice is the oldest girl in the family."

"Why haven't I heard of her?"

"We've talked about her when you've been around."

"Was Janice the baby Clare was pregnant with in the story?"

Rosene smiled. "I can't answer that."

I rolled my eyes. "I forgot."

A door opened down the hall.

"Go get your shower," Rosene said. "I'll have breakfast ready by the time you're done."

A half hour later, as we all sat around the table, I asked Mammi and Dawdi what made them decide to go up to Janice and Roy's for Thanksgiving.

Mammi turned toward Dawdi, deferring to him.

He gave her a pointed look and didn't say anything.

Mammi cleared her throat and then said, "We haven't seen them for a few years."

I asked Rosene, "How come you're not going too?"

"It's a long drive."

I didn't believe that was her reason.

"Who's going to do the milking?"

"Gabe," Dawdi answered. "With Conrad's help."

"And I'll need you and Gabe to operate the store the day after Thanksgiving and that Saturday too," Mammi said. "We won't come back until Saturday evening."

After breakfast, I spent the rest of the day dusting every single object in the shop. It was definitely the slow season. Everyone seemed to be getting ready for Thanksgiving—and were shopping for groceries, not antiques. Business would pick back up after Thanksgiving, at least that's what happened in the past.

As I dusted, I thought about the upcoming trip back to Oregon. I had no desire to return at all, even though it had been over three years. Now I was going back to a crowded house, including Johann. What if I had a panic attack?

Three years ago, I never would have expected to make the progress I had. But counseling, medication, and baby steps set me on a functioning path, along with the love of my sisters, grandparents, and Rosene. I just hoped it was a path I could continue to walk.

At three, Mammi said, "Go back to the house.

Maybe Arden will want to start the milking early."

"Denki." If he didn't, I could get a cup of coffee and a snack before we started. Dark clouds hung in the sky, threatening more snow as I reached the house, but all was quiet. I guessed Rosene was resting. I changed into my chore dress, grabbed a warm work coat off the back porch, put on rubber boots, and headed out to the barn.

Dawdi was cleaning the milk room. "You're early," he said.

"The store is really slow."

"I can imagine," he said. "I'll be done in a minute. You can get started."

We didn't talk much as we worked. The snow started again, and the cows who waited in the yard started to bawl. When we finished, I blew on my hands to try to warm them and then told Dawdi I was going to head to my apartment. "I need to get clothes for church tomorrow. I'll be back tonight," I said. "I'll go change and tell Rosene."

She had a pot of barley soup on the stove that smelled delicious, but I said I'd get something to eat at the apartment. Which meant a protein bar.

When I reached the stairs to our apartment, I heard voices and turned. Rylan's door was open, and Viktor stood outside of it, smoking. "Brenna!" he called out. "We just arrived. Marko is preparing chicken Kiev for dinner. There will be plenty."

"Thanks," I said. "I'm only here for a few minutes. I'm going back to my grandparents."

"Aww." He dropped his cigarette and ground it into the cement. "At least come in and say hello."

I considered declining but remembered I was still trying to be kind. I followed Viktor inside. There was a card table and four folding chairs in the space for a dining table. I guessed Marko had brought them.

Rylan was in his recliner with a beer in his hands, Gabe was loading the dishwasher, and Marko was chopping garlic. He saw me first and belted out a hearty "Hello, Brenna. How are you?"

"Good."

Gabe turned and smiled. "How was milking?"

"Cold," I answered. "How was drill?"

He grinned. "We were inside."

Technically I was too—although the barn was pretty drafty.

"Get Brenna a beer," Rylan called out.

"I don't drink," I answered.

"Well," Rylan said, "it's about time you start."

I turned toward him. "Um, no. I don't want to drink. I can't because of my medication. And I don't want to anyway." I shrugged. "It doesn't bother me if you drink. Please don't be bothered if I don't."

Rylan groaned. "You're such a killjoy."

I grinned. "I know." My JOMO loved being a

killjoy. I pointed toward the door. "I'm headed back to my grandparents. I just need to grab some things from the apartment."

"Are you going to give me a ride to church tomorrow?" Rylan asked.

"Do you want to go?"

He thought a moment and then said, "Nah." Then he laughed.

"Cool," I said. "I'll see you Monday." I turned back to the kitchen but then remembered Thanksgiving.

"Everyone here is invited to Thanksgiving at my grandparents. They won't be there, but my *Aenti* Rosene will be cooking. Ivy and I will be helping." I gave Gabe a nod. "Gabe and Conrad and their mom will be there." I turned toward Rylan. "Have you decided?"

He shrugged.

"Well," I said, "Rosene would love to have everyone."

"Wait, she invited us too?" Marko asked.

"Yes," I answered. "I told her you'd probably be with your families, but she said to ask you anyway."

Marko looked at Viktor and then back at me. "We don't really celebrate Thanksgiving."

"Then come to the farm." I waved as I headed out the door.

Just as I reached it, Gabe started after me. "I have a question for you."

I turned toward him. He motioned for me to keep going, and once we were both through the door, he pulled it closed behind us.

"How do you do it?" Gabe asked.

"Do what?"

"Not care about what they think of you."

I tilted my head. "I *don't* care. There's nothing to it." I kept walking, heading for the stairs as Gabe turned around and returned to Rylan's apartment.

Why did Gabe care what they thought of him? And why did he keep hanging around Rylan when it only made him feel bad? Why had he joined the Army Reserve when he couldn't talk with his mother about his decision? Didn't he realize what a red flag that was?

A half hour later, I was back at the farm with my church clothes. When I stepped into the kitchen, Rosene stood at the kitchen sink, doing the dishes.

"I'll help." I placed my bag by the back door.

"No," she replied. "Eat the soup I saved for you. There's bread too." She gestured toward the stove.

"Thank you." I'd forgotten to eat a protein bar.

"There are snickerdoodles for dessert."

"Yum," I said. "When did you make those?"

"Yesterday morning," she answered.

The house seemed unusually quiet. "Where are Mammi and Dawdi?"

"They went to a neighbor's for dessert."

I blinked. The entire time we lived with them, they'd never gone to a neighbor's house. "Which neighbors?"

"The Smiths."

I couldn't believe it. "The *Englisch* neighbors?"

"Jah," Rosene said. "They've been our neighbors for forty years. They invite us over from time to time."

It was hard for me to imagine Mammi and Dawdi having a social life. "Why didn't you go?"

"I wanted to be here when you got home."

"You didn't need to do that."

"I know." She looked over her shoulder and smiled. "I wanted to."

I concentrated on eating, and a few minutes later, Rosene drained the dishwater and then the rinse water. Once she dried her hands, she picked up a plate of cookies from the counter and sat down at the table.

"I asked Rylan, Viktor, and Marko to come for Thanksgiving. They'll let me know, but are you sure that won't be too much work for you?"

She shook her head. "Sharon will contribute to the meal. And you and Ivy will help."

I already knew I wouldn't be much help since I didn't cook. I changed the subject. "Were Dawdi and Mammi more social before we came to live here?"

"What do you mean?"

258

"Did they see Dawdi's sister more? Visit the neighbors? That sort of thing?"

"Well, yes," Rosene said. "They had more time."

"Do you think they're going to be more social again with all of us girls gone?"

"Most likely," Rosene said.

"So we were holding them back?"

"No," Rosene answered. "Their priorities shifted with the three of you here."

"Interesting." Not once had I thought about the sacrifices they made to care for us. Rosene too.

She smiled at me and pushed the plate of cookies closer. I took one.

"Want to hear more of the story?"

"Absolutely," I answered. "I've been wondering what that list of women's clothing was all about."

20

Martha

Nothing more came of George's warning about the arrested spy and the German man who the neighbor saw at Mutter's store. Mutter did look into adding women's clothes to the store but then decided to wait until after the war, saying she hoped rationing would end soon.

On the last Friday of April, Martha drove into Lancaster to collect Jeremiah from the train station. Once again, he held a magazine in one hand and his bag in the other.

When they reached the car, Martha asked, "Is there something special in the magazine?"

"Not special. Disturbing." He put the magazine on his lap. *Life* had a photo of General Eisenhower on the cover, dated April 16, 1945. "There's an article about concentration camps in Germany. The US soldiers found a pile of ashes and bones at one called Buchenwald. General Eisenhower and General Patton toured another concentration camp, Ohrdruf, and saw a burial pit."

Martha shuddered.

Jeremiah opened the magazine. "There are photographs of that, and of the Bergen-Belsen concentration camp too. It seems millions were killed. Talk about a hellhole. And more starved and died from disease," Jeremiah said. "Those who survived appear to be skeletons, barely clothed and wearing rags, with no shoes."

He flipped to another article, with the date of April 20, 1945. "Four photographers from *Life* accompanied the soldiers who liberated the camps." He read from the text. "The writer of this article calls it a 'barbarism that reaches the low point of human degradation.'" He looked up at Martha. "Remember the rumors about what the Germans were doing? Some said it was all American propaganda. But it turned out to be so much more brutal than anyone even guessed. Do you want to see the photos?"

She swiped her hand over her forehead. "Yes. Let's look at them now before we get home." Martha kept her eyes on the magazine as Jeremiah turned the page. A little boy walked down a road adjacent to a ditch lined with hundreds of bodies. There was a photo of open railway cars with half-dressed corpses stacked like firewood.

Martha wanted to look away—but couldn't.

Jeremiah turned the page again. Emaciated prisoners in striped pajamas hugged their liberators. He kept turning the pages, and as he reached the end of the article, he asked, "Do you think you can get me a camera?"

Feeling ill, Martha pulled away from the curb. "What for?"

"To take photos inside the hospital." He held up the magazine. "I'd heard some about what the Nazis were doing, but it wasn't until I saw the photos that I realized the depravity of what was happening. Some of our patients are as emaciated as the concentration camp survivors. Some are half-clothed and lying in filth. Some have died from violence. Others aren't getting the nutrition they need. No, it's not as bad as the concentration camps. But it's worse than words can describe, and so much worse than anyone who hasn't seen it could imagine."

"Would your bishop allow you to use a camera?"

Jeremiah shrugged. "I won't be taking photos of Clare or Arden. I won't be using it to make any graven images. It would simply be to provide evidence of a situation that must be remedied."

"I'll see what I can do." Martha admired Jeremiah for his empathetic heart and that he wanted to see the hospital change, even though he wouldn't be working there much longer. God willing.

Back at the farm, as Martha climbed out of the Studebaker, George drove up the driveway.

Jeremiah gestured toward the house. "I'll go tell Clare hello and then help Zeke with the milking. If George needs you to translate, we'll be fine."

"Thank you." She started toward George's car. As he climbed out of it, he asked, "Did you get my message?"

"No. I just got back from the train station with Jeremiah."

"I need a translator. I'm teaching the first aid class again—a last-minute request."

"I'll go tell Clare," Martha said. "And be right back."

She walked up the steps to the front porch and then through the door into the living room. Vater sat in his chair, his head resting against the back, his eyes closed. Hopefully he was asleep.

Voices came from the kitchen. "Are you getting enough rest?" Jeremiah was asking Clare.

"I'm trying," she replied.

Martha cleared her throat as she stepped into the kitchen. "I'm going with George to do some translating at the camp."

"Vater won't be happy," Clare said. "He's worried you spend too much time with George."

"He has nothing to worry about. George will be going to Europe to help with the refugees soon."

"Ach," Jeremiah said. "That's important work."

Martha agreed.

As she returned through the living room, she tiptoed, not wanting to wake Vater. He stirred but didn't open his eyes.

On the way to the camp, Martha told George about Jeremiah's need for a camera.

"I have one in my trunk he can use," George said. "And a roll of film."

The first aid class was the same as before, which made the translating easier. None of the PWs who worked on the farm were there. After the class, George said he needed to go up to the infirmary because he had a question for Nurse Olson. "Stay here," he said to Martha.

Clearly he didn't want her overhearing his conversation.

As she waited, two guards came into the mess hall.

"Martha?"

She stood. "Hello, Sergeant Schwarz."

"What are you doing here?"

"Working as a translator. I'm waiting for George Hall, the director of the Lancaster chapter of the American Red Cross."

"I see." He nodded toward the other guard, who gave him a wave and continued through the mess hall and out the back door. "Mind if I sit down?"

"Of course not," she said.

"I'm teaching a US history class in a half hour." He looked toward the far corner, where an English class was being taught.

"History? Did you study it in college?" Martha asked.

"Yes. However, my degree is in political science with a minor in German, from Yale."

Martha remembered that Zeke had told her

Sergeant Schwarz had graduated from Yale. They talked for a few more minutes, until George returned. After they exchanged greetings, George said, "We should get going."

Martha told Sergeant Schwarz good-bye. "See you on Monday."

"See you then."

She watched as he walked across the mess hall. He held himself higher and with more confidence than he did on the farm.

Once they were in the car, Martha asked George if everything was okay with Nurse Olson.

"Yes," he said. "She's fine. She's been documenting some concerns about what's going on here at the camp is all."

The following Wednesday, the PWs seemed restless. Had they been hearing the news that the Allies were making great progress? Martha doubted Dirk would believe it. Martha, Zeke, and all four of the PWs worked in the pasture, replacing a section of fence. The weather had turned chilly and had been near freezing that morning. But now it was warm enough for Martha to shed her jacket.

As she hung it on a fence post, Zeke showed Otis how to use the posthole digger. A half hour later, they had the fence closed and started back to the house for the noon meal.

As they neared the yard, the PWs split off

toward the picnic table and the bucket to wash their hands while Martha and Zeke continued toward the house. Rosene raced out of the back door, followed by Mutter.

Martha's heart began to beat faster. "Is Vater well?"

"Yes." Mutter turned toward Rosene.

Rosene folded her hands together as if in prayer. "Hitler is dead. Someone from the BBC heard it on the German airways. They reported he died in combat against the Bolsheviks—it was on the radio this morning."

"In combat?" Martha scoffed. "That seems highly unlikely. Are you sure he's dead?"

Rosene nodded, and her eyes sparkled with tears. "The war will soon be over, won't it?"

"I hope so. I'd better tell Sergeant Schwarz. He can tell the PWs." Martha turned toward the yard. As she neared the group, she motioned to Sergeant Schwarz to meet her by the garden. When he reached her, she told him what Rosene and Mutter had heard on the radio.

"Are you sure?" He seemed surprised.

"Mutter and Rosene said it was on the radio. The BBC, after monitoring the German news, reported it. They said he died in combat." She motioned toward the PWs. "You should tell them."

He hesitated. "They won't believe it."

"Dirk won't believe you," Martha said. "The others might."

"I'm going to wait. They'll get the news once they're back at the camp."

"Suit yourself." Martha turned back toward the house, but as she reached the back steps she glanced over her shoulder. Dirk had joined Sergeant Schwarz by the garden. The two were talking. Dirk laughed and pointed to Martha. Then he laughed again and shook his head.

"*Lächerlich*," he said, loudly enough for Martha to hear him. *Ridiculous*.

21

Brenna

"I thought Hitler committed suicide," I said to Rosene when she stopped the story.

"He did," Rosene answered. "The Germans falsely reported he died in combat. He shot himself in the temple and may have taken a cyanide capsule too. His wife of one day, who'd been his mistress for years, died from cyanide poisoning."

"Eva Braun, right?"

"Correct," Rosene replied. "The German public knew little of their relationship. That and their suicide came out later through testimony of those who were with him at his command bunker in Berlin. There were rumors that he'd escaped instead and there were many 'sightings' "—she made air quotes with her fingers—"over the years, some in Europe and some as far away as Argentina."

I had lots of other questions about Martha and the POWs but knew Rosene wouldn't answer them.

Rylan texted me the next day that he, Viktor, and Marko all wanted to come to our Thanksgiving.

It's nice of you to invite us. We're looking forward to it.

He was currently polite Dr. Jekyll instead of mean Mr. Hyde.

After class on Wednesday, I dropped Rylan off at his apartment. The snow from the week before hadn't lasted long, and now the weather had turned warmer. It was fifty degrees but overcast. Not cold—but not sunny either.

As Rylan rolled his chair toward his apartment, I walked alongside him. "I'll pick you up at noon tomorrow."

"No need," he said. "Marko and Viktor will give me a ride."

"Great. We'll plan to eat around one, but come before that. Twelve thirty or so."

"Are you going to the farm now?" Rylan asked.

"Yes." Mammi had closed the shop for the day. "I'll help Gabe with the milking, and then Ivy and I are going to make pies this evening with Rosene."

He unlocked his door, and I held it open while he wheeled inside. "Can you stay for a little while?" he asked.

I hesitated. Why was it so hard for me to tell Rylan no? Well, I knew if he asked me to do anything against my morals or values, I'd tell him no. But I couldn't seem to tell him no about the little things. And maybe being nice to him wouldn't make any difference in the long run. If he wanted to, he'd sue Mammi regardless of what I did.

Maybe I needed a pep talk from Johann on boundaries. He'd been the one most concerned about my relationship with Rylan. Or maybe I just needed a pep talk from myself. "I can't stay," I said. "Gabe's expecting me to help with the milking."

"Make him do it by himself."

I shook my head. "No. I told him I'd help. I need to go."

He turned his mouth down in a pout.

"Bye." I stepped out the door. "See you tomorrow." I closed his door and ran up to my apartment to pack. I'd be helping with milking through Saturday, in addition to working in the store, and planned to stay the entire weekend.

When I arrived at the farmhouse, Ivy and Rosene were in the kitchen, peeling apples.

Ivy picked up an extra knife on the table and extended it to me. "Want to help?"

"I'm going to help Gabe with the milking."

"Conrad's out there."

"He's done with school already?"

"Yep."

"So I really don't have to help?"

"Nope."

"Excellent." I grinned.

We had tomato soup and grilled cheese sandwiches for supper once Conrad and Gabe came in from the barn. After Rosene led us in prayer, Ivy asked, "Do we have a plan for dealing with Rylan tomorrow?"

I nearly choked on a bite of my grilled cheese sandwich. "What do you mean?"

"Should we smother him with kindness? Or confront him?"

"What happened to acting normal, like you're always telling me to do?"

"Well, sure. We'll act normal. We'll be authentic. But if he's coming to Thanksgiving dinner, shouldn't we try to make some progress on dealing with him?"

I thought of how lonely Rylan appeared when I left him at his apartment. "I think we should be welcoming. I don't think Thanksgiving is a good time to try to manipulate someone."

"We wouldn't be manipulating him," Ivy said. "We'd be trying to figure out what his plans are."

"Then just ask him," I said. "But not tomorrow."

"I agree," Rosene said.

I felt my anxiety rise with Ivy's questions. If Mammi lost the store, I'd have to get a different job. Work for someone else. I'd have to deal with other people, besides customers. Maybe I'd have to move away from Lancaster County and my family. The back of my throat grew thick. I took a sip of water and then another.

"Let's talk about our schedule in the morning," Rosene said, likely noticing my discomfort. "I'll mix up the breakfast casserole tonight. . . ." I silently blessed her for changing the subject.

Rylan was the biggest source of stress in my life right now. Where was the balance in that? My therapist had encouraged me to practice staying in the present. I took a deep breath. That would be my goal for the evening. And for tomorrow too.

After we finished eating, Gabe and Conrad stuck around, saying they wanted to help make the pies. While I did the dishes, Rosene began rolling out the dough for the crusts, and Ivy set Conrad and Gabe up with the recipe and ingredients for apple pie filling. We'd also make shoofly pie and pumpkin pie. I longed to hear more of Martha's story, but there was too much going on. I knew Conrad would enjoy the story, but I couldn't imagine that Gabe would.

On Thanksgiving morning, Gabe and Conrad did the milking again and then came in for a breakfast of cheesy casserole, sticky buns, and orange slices.

After Rosene led us in a silent prayer, she said, "We only had oranges on Christmas morning when I was a girl. We each were given one— Mutter brought them from the store. She'd get a box each December, and they'd sell out right away." She looked directly at me. "Isn't it odd how things change in a lifetime? Now we can buy oranges any day of the year."

I thought of her as a thirteen-year-old when she first arrived in Lancaster County, but I didn't know much about her then. As a nineteen-year-old, she seemed spunky.

"What do you remember about your first Thanksgiving?" I asked.

"By November, I'd been here eight months. Soon after I first arrived, I had a seizure. A month after that, Clare took me to a doctor in Philadelphia. He prescribed a medication that kept me from having any more."

"The medicine cured you?"

"I don't know. It could have been that I would have grown out of the seizures anyway. In September, I started school at the nearby one-room school for my eighth grade. The next year I went on to high school."

"How was that?"

"Good. But during my sophomore year, after the US entered the war in December, I feared my classmates would turn against me for being German," she said. "But by then everyone thought of me as the littlest Simons girl, as Clare and Martha's little sister. Because I'd started studying English when I was young, my accent was barely noticeable. No one associated me with Germany at all." She smiled a little. "It doesn't seem that long ago." She grinned. "Which I know none of you believe."

I smiled kindly. I couldn't imagine how it couldn't seem like a long time. It was. Nearly eighty years ago.

After breakfast, I cleaned up while Ivy started peeling potatoes. Rosene pulled three chickens out of the fridge. On our first Thanksgiving in Lancaster County, I was surprised to find out that Mammi and Rosene didn't cook a turkey. *"Too dry,"* Rosene had said. *"We always roast chickens instead."*

Conrad and Gabe added three more chairs to the table, leaving a place for Rylan's wheelchair, and then hung around for a while. It dawned on me how much Conrad and Gabe added to the farm, and to Rosene, Mammi, and Dawdi's lives. They'd been working for them, doing one thing or another, for years. Even though Gabe could be a little flaky, he was still a good employee.

After a while, Gabe went home to get their mother.

"You should sit down," I said to Rosene. "How about another cup of coffee?"

"Denki," she said. "I am a little tired."

By the time Gabe returned with Sharon, we had the table set and the broccoli salad made. The squash and the chicken were roasting in the oven. Sharon wore a clip in her short brown hair, which was streaked with gray. She brought cranberry

274

sauce, homemade pickles, and a large basket of yeast rolls.

It was twelve thirty. Rylan, Viktor, and Marko would probably show up any minute.

Sharon helped Ivy mash the potatoes, and Rosene made the gravy. I poured water into all the glasses. At one o'clock, they still hadn't arrived.

"Gabe," I said, "have you heard from Rylan? Or Marko or Viktor?"

"I'll text Viktor." Gabe stepped out onto the back porch. He came back in a minute later. "He said Rylan was out of sorts with Marko, but they're on their way now."

When they arrived, Gabe and Conrad went out to help carry Rylan and his chair inside. When they all entered, I introduced Rosene to Marko and Viktor, and Conrad introduced his mother.

"So you're the woman responsible for these two," Rylan said. "I mean, Conrad's cool." He shook his head. "But Gabe? Well, I'm not so sure yet." He grinned at Gabe, whose face reddened. "Just kidding."

I winced. Rylan was a perfect example of how *not* to joke.

Marko held a bowl in his hands. He held it up and addressed Rosene. "I hope you don't mind that I brought a Ukrainian harvest salad."

"I'm glad you did," she said. "Tell us about it."

"It's called a *vinegret*. It has beets, potatoes,

carrots, peas, and pickles, with a sunflower oil dressing." He put the bowl on the table and took the plastic lid off. Inside was a beautiful, fuchsia-colored salad. "Our grandmother used to make this for special dinners."

"*Wunderbar*." Rosene beamed.

A grin spread across Marko's face. "You remind me of her." He nudged Viktor. "Don't you think so?"

Viktor smiled. "Jah, although Rosene is a third the size of our grandmother."

Marko laughed. "That's true."

"And she's not as sad."

Marko's eyes grew serious. "That's true too."

Rosene's story certainly was sad, but she wasn't a sad person. She rarely referenced her story to those she didn't know, so Marko and Viktor would never know what her childhood in Germany had been like. But I liked to think that they, as people who had also left their homeland, would be sympathetic.

We placed all the food on the table, and then Rylan wheeled to his place and we all sat down. Rosene led us in prayer, and then we began filling our plates and passing the food around. The conversation stayed light while we ate. Sharon asked Viktor and Marko about their life in Ukraine. Marko did most of the talking, describing their grandparents' farm and their village. "Our fathers had a construction company," he said. "Our uncle now has the farm."

After the dinner dishes were cleared away and everyone dug in to the pie, Rylan said, "Marko and Viktor, you should share your news with the group."

"What news?" Gabe asked.

Marko leaned back in his chair and stared at Rylan.

Viktor shook his head.

"What's up, guys?" Gabe asked.

Marko sighed. "One of the captains in our unit texted me last night. There's talk of us being deployed next year."

Gabe's face turned white. I guessed he hadn't told Conrad or Sharon about joining the Army Reserve.

"I'm guessing Gabe really wants someone to change the subject," Rylan said. "I know I would."

I glanced from Conrad to Sharon. They didn't seem to be catching on to Rylan's subtext.

Rylan added, "Because Gabe will most likely be going too."

Conrad caught on first. "What are you talking about?"

By the expression on Rosene's face, she'd caught on to what Rylan was saying. Gabe's missed Saturdays at the store probably made sense to her now.

Gabe subtly made a motion of slashing across his neck, signaling Rylan to stop talking.

Rylan grinned. "Do you want me to tell them, or do you?"

Gabe muttered, "Mom, Conrad, I'll explain later."

Both Sharon and Conrad had concerned expressions on their faces, but they didn't press Gabe.

"I get it that no one wants to address the Army Reserve, the elephant in the room," Rylan said.

Sharon exhaled, as if she'd been kicked in the stomach.

Marko growled, "Knock it off, Rylan."

Gabe's face turned from white to red.

Rylan glanced from Ivy to Rosene. "Thank you for dinner. Of course, my gratitude doesn't mean that Brenna won't still have to testify against Priscilla."

Rylan was on a roll, causing chaos at every turn.

"What do you mean?" Ivy asked.

"Brenna was an eyewitness."

Ivy shot back, "So was Gabe."

Rylan said, "His testimony won't mean as much."

Marko stabbed a bite of pie so hard the fork screeched against the plate and then said, "This family has been nothing but kind to you and you plan to sue them, even though the VA will pay for all of your medical costs."

"Is that true?" I asked Rylan.

"No. I mean, I don't know," he said.

"They will," Marko said. "It might take a year, but they'll come through. Besides, you're the one who climbed those stairs."

"The rail broke," Rylan said. "Someone else could have been hurt—could still be hurt." He glared at Marko. "It's my duty to make sure that doesn't happen."

"Arden is making the repairs next week. The materials finally arrived," Rosene said. "The rope and the *Private! Do Not Enter* sign were in place that morning when I took my walk. The stairway wasn't open to the public."

Marko said, "Even if there hadn't been a sign—"

Rylan blurted out, "There wasn't."

"Well, you still shouldn't have gone up it."

Rylan glared at Marko again. "How did I know it didn't lead to another part of the store?"

Marko pushed his chair back. "How do we know you didn't take the sign off and undo the rope?"

Rylan's voice went low. "I can't believe you said that."

Marko met Rylan's gaze.

"Do you think I fell on purpose too? Broke my good leg for the fun of it?"

"I didn't say that."

Rylan wheeled his chair backward, away from

the table. "You didn't have to. It's obvious what you think." He looked around the table. "Is that what everyone else thinks too?"

"No," I said.

Ivy echoed my no, but more empathetically.

"I don't think you fell on purpose either." Marko sighed. "I just don't understand why you went up there. Why did you?"

Rylan didn't answer. Instead he wheeled backward farther, turning his head toward Rosene as he did. "Thank you for your hospitality. Make sure and tell Priscilla's attorney that you saw the sign that morning. Someone must have taken it after that."

Then he looked past Marko, as if he wasn't even there, to Viktor and said, "I'm ready to go."

On Friday, the store wasn't as busy as I'd anticipated, and Gabe and I had time to talk—or I had time to ask questions, starting with, "Did you explain everything to your mom and Conrad?"

He nodded.

I stood behind the counter, winding the clock Rosene brought from Germany. "How did it go?"

"Miserably." Gabe leaned against the counter from the other side. "Mom was hurt that I hadn't told her before, that I didn't trust her enough to say anything. But it didn't have anything to do with trust. I was too embarrassed to say anything."

I came down the ladder and stepped to the wall beyond the shelf that was lined with mechanical clocks. I started winding the first one. "What did Conrad say?"

"Not much. But he thinks I'm a fool. He didn't say that exactly, but I could tell."

I stepped to the next clock. "Why were you embarrassed to tell your mom?"

"Because it was an impulsive thing to do, and she'd warned me about not being impulsive—for as long as I can remember."

"Then why did you join?"

"Because my dad's dad had been in the army and served in Korea, and he talked about it the few times I saw him when I was little. It's not like it sounded like fun—but it sounded like *something*. Like adventure and discipline. Like comradery."

I wondered if Gabe felt he had been missing all of those things in his life. "Where is the unit being deployed to?"

He scooted down to the end of the counter, closer to me. "That's the thing, we don't know. We're just on some list."

I moved to the next clock. "What are the possibilities?"

"Syria. A few different places in Africa. Afghanistan. But maybe it won't happen at all, and especially not to Afghanistan. The army's been pulling troops out, not sending them."

"I don't think you can make assumptions about the military."

He grimaced. "I know that now."

I'd never seen Gabe so unsettled. "You'll figure it out," I said. "But don't count on it *not* happening." I moved on to the cuckoo clocks on the far wall.

A customer came into the shop and then another. Gabe waited on them as I kept winding the clocks. I loved the sound of them ticking, although I was ambivalent about the chiming. Some days it really got on my nerves, but nonetheless I appreciated the clocks. As long as they were wound, they were predictable. Trustworthy. I valued their constant presence, their witness to how quickly life passed by—and how quickly it could change.

Gabe and I took turns taking lunch breaks so we didn't have to close the shop. He left to do the milking at four, and I closed the shop at five. After he and Conrad finished the milking, Gabe went straight home. Saturday was a repeat of Friday, except we were swamped all day at the store. I was exhausted by the time the day was over and never so happy to see Mammi, who came straight to the store to help close as soon as they arrived home.

I headed straight for the apartment and felt so exhausted I didn't go to church the next day. The next afternoon, Dawdi made the repairs to the staircase and replaced the railing, working through the cold and snow. But it was done. It felt like a big step.

For the next two weeks I gave Rylan rides, doing my best not to speak with him about anything important. I saw Viktor at Rylan's apartment a few times but not Marko.

Two weeks later, on the Sunday evening before our finals, Rylan called and asked if I could help him review. I'd stayed home from the Sunday evening youth gathering to study, and the last thing I wanted to do was spend the time with Rylan.

But I had said I'd help him. I gathered up my laptop, books, and notebook and headed down to his apartment.

Viktor was there, cleaning up the kitchen. When I asked how he was doing, he grunted, "Fine."

"How's Marko?"

He grunted again, but I couldn't tell what he'd said.

I told Rylan hello and then said, "We should sit at the table."

He lowered the recliner, grabbed his crutch, and then shuffled to the table.

In the middle was a stack of documents. I concentrated on opening my laptop as Rylan pointed to the papers. "Bills," he said. "From the hospital. Over thirty thousand so far."

All I could do was mutter, "Wow."

I'd made a list of what to study for—account

takeover, authenticator, brute force attack, credential stuffing, DNS spoofing—so I concentrated on that, trying to not think about how much his surgery and hospital stay had cost so far. As I started quizzing him from the study notes on my laptop, a video call came through from Johann.

"You can answer it," Rylan said. "I need a break."

I answered the call. When Johann's face materialized, I said, "Dobryden. I'm at Rylan's—we're studying."

"Hello," Rylan called out. "I've heard more about you from Ivy than Brenna, just so you know."

I suddenly wished I hadn't accepted the call.

"Hi." Johann politely said, "I'm glad to finally meet you."

Viktor came out of the kitchen. "Dobryden!"

"This is Viktor," I said to Johann.

Viktor stepped forward and rattled something off in Ukrainian that I couldn't understand. Johann laughed and then answered in Ukrainian. They talked for a couple of minutes, and then Viktor said in English, "I'll let you talk to Brenna."

"Nice to meet you," Johann said.

I wasn't sure what we'd talk about in front of Rylan and Viktor, but Johann did his best to include Rylan in the conversation. "What's going to be on your test?"

When Rylan didn't respond, I rattled off what we were studying.

"What do you want to do after you graduate, Rylan?" Johann asked.

Rylan shrugged. "I may not need to graduate."

"What do you mean?" Johann asked.

I groaned. Not this again.

"We'll see how much money I get out of Brenna's fam—"

"Knock it off, Rylan." Viktor scowled.

Rylan smirked.

"Well." Johann frowned. It seemed interacting with Rylan had only confirmed Johann's concerns. He turned his attention to me. "I'll call back tomorrow."

As we ended the call, Rylan smirked again. "Your boyfriend seems nice."

"He's not my boyfriend."

"He's a gentleman," Viktor said. "Unlike you."

"I've never aspired to be a gentleman."

"And it shows." Viktor stepped into the entryway. "I'd leave, but I don't want Brenna to be alone with you."

Rylan yawned. "Brenna can leave. So can you."

I gathered up my things, hoping Rylan would pass the class whether he wanted to or not. I said, "Good-bye," and then Viktor followed me out the door.

Once we were on the walkway, Viktor said, "I can't blame Marko for being fed up with

Rylan. It seems he just grows more difficult."

I zipped my coat against the cold. "It seems as if he's worse with Marko than anyone."

Viktor shrugged. "Rylan has a lot of anger bottled up inside of him."

"What can be done?" I stood up straight and met Viktor's gaze.

"I have no idea. I thought kindness could heal him—letting him know he wasn't alone, that we cared, that we're his brothers. But it hasn't helped." He shrugged. "Do you have any ideas?"

"No. I also thought being kind, even if he planned to sue, might get through to him."

"He shouldn't sue," Viktor said.

"But the railing wasn't safe."

"At the least, Rylan took the rope down. Maybe even the sign too. He's never played by the rules."

"But we can't prove it."

"Maybe not." He shrugged.

"Do you have any photos of Meg?" I asked.

"I don't," Viktor said. "Rylan had some posted on social media, but he deleted all his accounts."

"Was Meg on social media?"

"If she was, I didn't follow her." Viktor paused a minute. "I'm guessing if she was, her parents probably deleted the accounts. Don't you think they would?"

I shrugged. I had no idea about that kind of thing. I wasn't on social media. Ivy used to be obsessed with it—part of her FOMO. My JOMO kept me totally disinterested.

Viktor shoved his hands into his pockets. "Why do you ask?"

"I was just wondering what she looked like. Is that creepy?"

"No." He leaned forward a little. "She looked like you. Tall. Thin. Light brown hair."

That caught me off guard. Without responding, I gave him a wave and started toward the staircase.

There was no need for me to worry about Rylan passing our final exam. He did—with a B, which meant if he'd actually studied, he would have had an A+. I had an A, but I'd studied. A lot.

A week later, I took Rylan to the doctor to have his cast removed. When he checked in, the receptionist asked if the injury was due to an accident.

"Yes," he answered. "It's been documented thoroughly."

"I'm verifying the information is all," she said.

He asked, "Does that mean the VA won't pay for it?"

"I don't have that information," she said. "You should speak with your caseworker."

"I left a message with her but haven't been contacted," he said.

"I'll make a note of that in your chart." Then

she looked past Rylan to the man behind him and said, "Next."

Without his cast on, Rylan could drive himself places. And with classes done, he wouldn't need my help anymore.

My time assisting Rylan was over. I'd successfully helped someone else for the first time in my life. Which was ironic, since he would soon be trying to take away my future livelihood. My thoughts now turned toward going home to Oregon, which made my heart race.

I concentrated on seeing Johann. That was something I could actually look forward to.

22

As the airplane neared Portland, I lifted the window shade and wished I could see Mount Hood, but it was dark. Instead, I saw the lights of the city and the blackness of the Columbia River. A few minutes later, the lights lining the runway came into view as we descended. Ivy, who sat between Conrad and me, touched my arm and whispered, "Are you doing okay?"

I nodded even though I wasn't. And it made me anxious to have her ask. An hour later, we had our luggage and our rental vehicle. An hour after that, we'd eaten at a franchise diner not too far from the airport, and then, as we headed back, Johann texted that his plane had just landed. We circled around to the arrivals, and there he was, carrying an olive-green pack on his shoulder and wearing a down jacket. I guessed the pack was army issued. His hair was short and looked as if it was army issued too.

"Get out and greet him," Ivy said from the driver's seat.

"Huh?"

"It's polite," she whispered.

I did as she said. Johann grinned and stepped forward, giving me a hug. As he stepped back, his blue eyes sparkled. He seemed genuinely happy to see me.

The hatch to the SUV slowly raised, and Johann stowed his backpack. As we climbed into the back seat, both Ivy and Conrad turned and said, "Hello, Johann!" in unison. Then they laughed.

As Ivy pulled away from the curb, she asked, "Are you hungry?"

"Starving. All they had on the plane was a cheese plate." He'd transferred in New York.

"We'll go through a drive-thru," Ivy said.

"A what?"

"A fast-food restaurant."

"Ah," he said. "McDonald's."

Ivy laughed.

By the time we turned off I-205, it was eleven, which meant two in the morning back in Pennsylvania and nine in the morning in Ukraine. Johann rested his head against the back of the seat and closed his eyes. I was wide awake. Ivy turned onto the highway and headed east toward our tree farm. It was cold out, thirty-three degrees, but there was no snow on the ground. Hopefully there would be soon. We climbed in elevation as we left Oregon City.

As Ivy slowed to drive through the town of Eagle Creek, Johann opened his eyes and lifted his head. Ten minutes later, Ivy turned onto Trillium Lane. As we passed the site of the accident, she glanced in the rearview mirror. I met her eyes and smiled sadly. Johann reached over and put his hand on my forearm. I realized I'd clenched my fist and opened it. No one said anything.

When Ivy turned into our driveway, I expected to feel panicky, but instead I felt relief. The back door to our cabin opened. How I wished Mom and Dad would walk out to greet us. But Gran stepped out and then Treva. I exhaled. The next best thing.

Ivy parked, and we all tumbled out of the car. And then Pierre, who lived in Haiti and was at the Global Gathering with all of us in Germany three years ago, came out of the back door too. We all hugged. It felt like a mini reunion. I wished Rosene had come with us, but then Christmas would have really seemed bleak for Mammi and Dawdi.

"What are you doing here?" I asked Pierre after I hugged him.

"Brooke and Daniel invited me," he said. "I arrived yesterday." He grinned. "We decided to surprise all of you."

Ivy stepped closer. "How long can you stay?"

"I have a tourist visa, so I could stay three months. But I'm only staying for a month. I need to get back home to help my parents."

Ivy had met Pierre and his sister, Adrienne, when she went to Haiti on a service trip. We'd met

291

Adrienne in Germany too. "Couldn't Adrienne come?" I asked.

"No. She's working as a nanny and couldn't get the time off." I thought it odd he came at Christmas but didn't say so.

Brooke and Daniel and their two little boys, who weren't so little anymore, came out and greeted us. Then we all went in the house for hot chocolate and cinnamon rolls and then shuffled off to bed.

I fell asleep in my old bed with Treva and Ivy on either side of me. In the middle of the night, I awoke to someone's hand on my arm.

"Brenna." It was Ivy. "Are you okay?"

"I'm asleep," I answered.

"No, you screamed, and you were thrashing around."

"Sorry," I muttered.

"Did you have a bad dream?"

"I can't remember." I rolled over toward Treva, who'd stayed asleep.

Ivy began to rub my back. I pretended she was Mom.

Gran fixed blueberry pancakes and bacon for breakfast. After we all ate, we went out to the Christmas trees and showed Johann around the property. Daniel, Treva, and Pierre were already helping a few U-cutters.

I breathed in the scent of the fir trees and then asked Johann if he wanted to walk up to the knoll where we might have a view of Mount Hood.

"Sure," he said.

I asked Pierre if he wanted to go with us.

"Let's all go," Ivy said, leading the way.

As we followed, Johann asked Pierre how things were back home.

"Bad," he answered. "The gangs are gaining more and more power. They control the roads, which interrupts transportation and the shipment of food."

"That's horrible," Johann said.

"Yes," Pierre answered. "I'm worried about my family."

"What about Adrienne?" I asked.

"The family she works for has security. At the moment she's safe, but in some ways she's also more of a target. Sometimes the wealthy are kidnapped in hopes of a ransom."

I couldn't fathom how it would be to live under that sort of a threat.

When we reached the knoll, both the peak and the middle section of the mountain showed, with a strip of clouds in between. It was completely covered with snow, which always gave me hope. No matter how much melted in the summer, revealing gray slabs of basalt and forests of emerald trees, the snow returned each winter.

For a moment, standing with my sisters—along

with Conrad, Pierre, and Johann—I felt hope for myself. For all of us. Maybe coming home hadn't been a bad idea after all.

A storm was predicted to come during the night, so right after lunch we went through our collection of snow parkas, pants, gloves, hats, and boots, and then through the cross-country skis in the shed, and came up with enough for the six us. As Ivy drove east over a back road that came out on Highway 26, snow started to fall.

"It's beautiful," Pierre said from the back seat. "But it looks cold."

"It's not bad." Ivy grinned. "Just a little below freezing."

By the time we reached Government Camp, which already had a couple of feet on the ground, it began to come down in buckets. We stopped at Trillium Lake, but the parking lot was full, so we continued to Frog Lake, the last place we'd gone on a hike with our parents. Dad had taken a selfie of all of us that day on his flip phone. It was the last photo we had of our family.

I tried not to think of it now. We parked in the lot off Highway 26, and we all put on our gear. Pierre turned his face up to the falling snow and laughed. And then shivered.

Johann had cross-country skied before, but Conrad hadn't and neither had Pierre, of course.

Frog Lake was a good place for them to learn. It was mostly flat, unlike the trail down to Trillium Lake.

When we reached the trailhead, which was really the gravel road that led down to the lake, Johann and I skied out ahead of the rest and broke two trails. Out of the three of us girls, I was the stronger skier—being taller probably helped. Ivy and Conrad followed, skiing side by side. And then Treva and Pierre. The snow began coming down even harder. It took me a few minutes to smooth out my stride, but soon I was moving back and forth as if I'd been skiing last week instead of four years ago. By the time we reached the south side of the lake, Ivy called out, "We should take a break."

I glanced over my shoulder. Through the falling snow, I could see that Conrad was a ways behind Ivy, and Pierre and Treva were quite a bit farther behind him.

"Johann," I called out, "we need to wait."

When Pierre finally reached us, he joked, "Is this really what you do for fun?"

"This and hiking," Treva said. "Our two big outings."

"It builds character," Ivy added. "At least that's what Dad always told us."

He was right. Plus, it built family memories and an appreciation of geography, or at least it did for me. I didn't realize it at the time, of course. After

Pierre caught his breath, we kept going. When we reached the lake, a beam of sunshine broke through the clouds and snow. Johann stopped, and then the rest of us did too.

"What a beautiful landscape," Johann said.

"Yes. I believe I understand the reason for this now." Pierre took off his gloves and took his phone from his jacket. He snapped a photo of the lake and then one of the rest of us.

"I'll take a selfie," Johann said, taking his phone from his pocket. "Everyone gather round."

I'd never told him about the selfie Dad had taken a month before the accident. Ivy, Treva, and I all exchanged glances, but then we scooted close to Johann, as did Pierre and Conrad.

"Say *fromage*," Johann said.

We all laughed and said, "Fromage," as Pierre said, "Cheese."

By the time we got back to the SUV, we were wet and cold. The sun was low in the sky, and the snow had started to fall again, even harder than before. We strapped the skis to the racks on the top of the vehicle, peeled off our parkas and snow pants, and changed out of our ski boots into regular boots. We pulled out the snacks we'd packed—crackers and cheese and grapes—and then Ivy pulled the SUV onto the highway. Quite a bit of snow had accumulated on Highway 26, and it was slow going. By the time we reached

Government Camp, it was dark, and the snow was coming down hard, like little white missiles aimed at the windshield.

Ivy pulled into the rest area. "I need to pee," she said. "Plus I can't see very well."

"Do you want me to drive?" Johann asked.

"You don't know the road," Ivy answered.

"I watched closely coming up," he said. "I have an idea."

"Maybe . . ." Ivy said.

We all piled out of the car and used the restroom. When we returned, Ivy climbed back into the driver's seat. The snow started coming down even harder.

After several miles, Ivy slowed. Then she said, "Brenna, do you know where the turn is?"

"It's about ten more miles."

"Are you sure?"

"It might be nine."

"Okay."

Five minutes later, Ivy pulled over and put on the hazard lights. "Johann, do you want to give it a try? Or anyone else?"

"I vote for Johann," Conrad said.

"So do I," Pierre said. "You definitely don't want me to drive."

"I don't want to either," Treva said. She didn't have a lot of experience driving in the snow. I had some, but I didn't want to drive either. But I didn't bother to say so.

"You sit up front," Conrad said to me. "You can help find the turn."

Once we were back on the road, Johann drove slowly but steadily. No one spoke. I took out my phone to make sure I knew where the turn was, but I didn't have service. The way the snow was coming down, in that mesmerizing way that threatened to lull the driver into believing it was harmless, I wondered if we should stay on Highway 26 instead of taking the cutoff.

I said so to Johann.

"The plow hasn't come through here yet."

"It won't have gone over the cutoff either."

"So it's not apt to be any deeper than here, right?"

"That's true. But there's less traffic on the cutoff. If we get stuck, there might not be anyone coming by for a long time."

"All right," Johann said. "I'll follow your directions."

We rode along in silence. I glanced behind me, and it appeared the others had fallen asleep. When I turned forward again, the car ahead of us was braking. Johann braked too, pumping the brakes slowly. There were more taillights ahead. The traffic was crawling along.

"There must be a wreck," I said. "If it was a weekend, it might just be ski traffic, but since it's Thursday, I don't think it is."

"This isn't good," Johann said. "A snowplow isn't going to be able to get through."

"The cutoff is a mile from here." I chomped down on my gum.

"I think we should take it," he said.

I agreed.

As we turned off, the SUV fishtailed a little, but Johann quickly recovered.

"Is there a lot of snow in Ukraine?" I asked.

"It depends on the area," Johann answered. "There was over fifty centimeters—a foot and a half, I think—in Kyiv a couple of years ago, but that was a lot. When I was in the Donbas, I drove a supply truck at first, during the winter. We had a few bad storms, so it was good practice for me."

I knew he did his basic training in the fall of 2014, after I met him in Germany, and then reported immediately to the front. I also knew that US military personnel helped train him, which surprised me at the time. I didn't talk with him much during his eighteen months of service, through April of 2016. We emailed back and forth some, and then after he was discharged was when we started video chats. There was a lot I didn't know about his wartime experience.

"Do you talk much about what it was like to fight?" I asked.

"Some," he answered.

"I'd like to listen," I said. "If you want to talk about it. Now or later. Anytime, really."

He smiled a little. "Thanks. I don't want to burden you, though."

"What do you mean?"

"Well, you're Mennonite. And nonresistant."

"You're Mennonite too."

"I was."

"You don't consider yourself Mennonite anymore?"

"I'm not nonresistant. I've served as a soldier. I don't know that I killed anyone, but I would have if I needed to."

"I think you can still be Mennonite. . . ." My voice trailed off.

"I still aim to follow Christ's teachings," he said. "I'll never stop. But I'm a little confused about the rest."

"I have no idea what it would be like to have my country attacked," I said. "To be part of a resistance. I know Jesus said, 'Blessed be the peacemakers.' I think that's what you were trying to do. Make peace."

"It wasn't as if I was trying to negotiate peace. I mean, our government was, through the Minsk II treaty. Once that was settled, the fighting died down some. But it didn't solve anything. Over ten thousand Ukrainian soldiers have died in the last three-and-a-half years."

That was far more than the number of American soldiers who had died in Afghanistan. Gabe had mentioned once while we were working, when

Mammi wasn't around, that 2,400 US soldiers had died in Afghanistan since the war started in 2001.

"Thank you for being willing to listen," Johann said. "I'll tell you more, I'm sure."

It seemed like the snow was letting up a little.

"Do you think it's snowing at your tree farm?" Johann asked.

"I hope so," I said. "I'd love for all of us to have a white Christmas."

Johann smiled broadly. "So would I."

By the time we neared our place, the snow had stopped, but it had already covered the ground with a couple of inches. "The turn to our farm is two miles from here," I said.

Johann let out a sigh of relief. "We made it."

"Thanks to you."

"No," he replied. "Thanks to us. We make a good team."

I nodded. We did.

My phone dinged. I expected it to be a worried text from Gran. It wasn't. It was Rylan.

Hey, I'm not doing so hot.

What's wrong?

Is life really worth it?

I hesitated, then I texted back.

301

Yes. Are you alone?

Yes.

Where are you?

At my apartment.

"Who are you texting?" Ivy asked in a groggy voice.

"Rylan. He's not doing well." I turned my head. "Conrad, would you text Gabe and ask him if he can get over to Rylan's? Or better yet, ask Viktor to."

"Sure."

I turned toward Ivy and read her the texts. Then I asked, "What should I text him?"

"Ask him who he'd like to be with him."

I texted the question to him.

He texted back.

You.

"What was Rylan's response?" Ivy asked.

"Turn here," I said to Johann, pointing to our driveway. The lights were on in the cabin. It looked so cheery. I didn't want to read what Rylan had texted out loud. I handed my phone to Ivy. I had no idea how to help Rylan. I was afraid I'd only make it worse.

"Brenna," Ivy said. "What's going on with you and Rylan?"

"Nothing," I said. "I promise."

Johann stopped the SUV next to Gran's Prius and gave me a questioning look.

I shrugged and turned to Ivy. "Pretend you're me and text him back. I have no idea what to do. He's creeping me out."

23

Gran opened the back door of the cabin as I climbed out of the SUV. "I was getting worried," she said.

"The storm blew in sooner than predicted." I gave her a hug. "Thankfully, Johann was able to get us home."

Ivy hopped out of the back of the SUV and thrust my phone toward me. "You should call him."

Conrad held up his phone. "Gabe texted that he and Viktor are on their way to Rylan's."

"Call him until Gabe and Viktor arrive," Ivy said. "Can you?"

"No," Ivy said. "He trusts you."

"Well, I don't trust him."

"You don't need to." Ivy opened the back of the SUV. "Just let him know he's not alone."

I gave Johann a questioning look.

He nodded and then said, "I'll stay beside you while you talk with him."

I held my phone as if it were a hot potato.

"You could put him on speakerphone," Johann offered. "I could talk with him too—unless you think it might make things worse."

I had no idea what might make things worse for Rylan.

Ivy had her phone out. "I'm texting you a

number to give him. It's for the suicide preven-
tion line."

"Thank you," I said.

Gran, who'd overheard the conversation, gave
me a sympathetic smile as we traipsed into the
house. "Go into the office," she said. "You two
can place the call there."

"Good idea." I led the way through the kitchen,
into the dining room, through the entryway, and
down the hall to what was Mom and Dad's office.
I collapsed in Mom's rocking chair, leaving the
office chair for Johann.

Then I placed the call, put it on speakerphone,
and put it on the coffee table in front of me.
Rylan didn't answer. After it rang ten times, I
hung up and then placed the call again. This time
he answered after the seventh ring.

"Why are you calling me?" he asked.

"Because I want you to know you're not alone."
I was grateful for Ivy's words. Wasn't that what
we all needed to know? That we weren't alone.

Johann said, "Rylan, it's Johann. I'm here too. I
want to help if I can. If this is about your service
to your country, I want you to know I can relate
to that."

Rylan didn't answer.

"Is this about Afghanistan?" I asked.

"Maybe," he answered. "But I don't want to
talk about it."

"I have a number for a professional you can

call," I said. "I'm texting it to you." I quickly forwarded the number Ivy had sent to me.

"I'd rather talk to you."

"How about if I tell you about our day?"

"Whatever," he responded.

I started by telling him about scrounging for coats and snow pants and skis and then heading up to the mountain. I told him about Pierre seeing snow for the first time, and then skiing around the lake. Next I told him about the snowstorm on the way home. As I got to the part about the wreck ahead, he said, "There's someone at my door. Did you send anyone?"

"Conrad texted Gabe to tell him you were having a hard time."

"I would have texted Gabe if I wanted him to come by."

"Well, you texted me, and I can't be there," I answered. "So we sent reinforcements."

There was rustling in the background. "Did you give him your key?"

"Yes," I said. "I did."

"Rylan. Hey, man, what's going on?" It was Viktor's voice.

I heard what sounded like a sob and then Rylan's muffled voice saying, "I gotta go. Viktor's here too." He ended the call before I could say good-bye.

I exhaled, trying to overcome the numbness that I felt.

Johann patted my shoulder. "You did a good job distracting him until Gabe and Viktor arrived."

"I hope so," I said. "I have such conflicting feelings toward him."

Johann's eyebrows shot up.

I quickly explained, "On the one hand, I feel sympathy for him. Losing his leg, losing the woman he loved, breaking his other leg. On the other hand, he's annoying. The way he pits people against one another, his toying with me and my family over suing Mammi, the way he manipulates his friends."

"He sounds broken. Like he's been through a lot."

"Yes. But he pushes people away, like his buddies who'd do anything for him." I stood, feeling as if we should join the others.

"Wait," Johann said. "I need to tell you something."

I sat back down, perplexed. He sounded so serious.

"First, I may be getting a new job in January. I can't tell you any more than that right now, and I won't be able to say more about it online—not until we see each other in person. But if I can't chat as much in the coming months, that could be why."

"Okay . . ." Was that an excuse to not spend as much time with me online?

He leaned forward. His voice wavered a little

as he said, "I can't tell you how much your friendship has meant to me." He took my hand. "Our chats have helped keep me sane over the last year. Your steady faith has kept me looking to the Lord."

"Really?" I hadn't once thought I was helping Johann. "You've done all of that for me, but I don't see how I've been a help to you."

"That's because you're an encouragement without trying. It's never pretentious. You're authentic. You're transparent. And honest."

I swallowed. Was I honest about how I felt about him? How did I feel? I hadn't *allowed* myself to feel anything for him.

He squeezed my hand. Was all of this platonic? Or something more? My heart raced faster.

The blue of Johann's eyes deepened. "I know we live across the world from each other, but I hope we can keep getting to know each other more and more, and visit again soon. Mama and I would love if you could come this summer."

I opened my mouth to speak, but no sound came out.

"You can think about it."

I nodded.

He leaned a little closer. Was he going to kiss me? There was a noise out in the hall and then Treva yelled, "I'll be right there."

Johann let go of my hand and said, "We should join the others."

I nodded again, both relieved and disappointed he didn't kiss me. But, surprisingly, more disappointed than relieved.

Johann stood. "Someone should text Gabe and see how Rylan's doing." For a blissful minute, I'd forgotten all about Rylan.

I stood too and led the way out of the office.

When we reached the kitchen, Conrad was texting someone. He glanced up at me. "Viktor called an ambulance for Rylan. It seems he took something—maybe pain meds—right before they arrived."

It wasn't until the next morning that I finally heard from Gabe. He said that the ER doctor had pumped Rylan's stomach and then sent him to the VA in Philadelphia. Marko and Viktor were going to see him that afternoon. I wasn't surprised that Marko would put aside his frustration with Rylan and go see him.

The next three days were filled with fun and worry. After a day of hanging out at our place, helping with the last of the U-cutters, Treva and Pierre stayed to help Daniel with the tree farm while Ivy, Conrad, Johann, and I went into Portland. It was sunny and clear and in the mid-fifties, quite the contrast to our day on the mountain. Johann bought a tile trivet with an image of Mount Hood on it for his mother. I bought Gran a handmade pine-scented candle.

And Conrad bought a pair of sterling silver earrings for Ivy, who had gotten her ears pierced a few months ago.

Afterward, we bought elephant ears and walked along the Willamette River. As we reached the Hawthorne Bridge, my phone dinged. It was a text from Marko.

Wanted to let you know that the VA doc finally convinced Rylan to go on an antidepressant. Would you pray that it will help? And pray for patience for Viktor and me? We're out of ideas to help him.

I texted back.

Thank you for the update. I'm praying for all of you.

Ivy asked, "News about Rylan?"

I nodded and relayed the information without saying who the text was from.

"That's good to hear he's getting the help he needs," Ivy said. Then she and Conrad increased their pace and moved ahead of us.

"Was the text from Gabe?" Johann asked.

"No," I answered. "It's from Marko."

"Wait, who's Marko?"

"Viktor's cousin."

"Oh." He smiled. "Got it."

I returned his smile. "You'll have to come to Pennsylvania to meet all of them in person."

His eyebrows lifted. "I'd like that. When? Before summer?"

"How about for my graduation in May?"

"And then you'll come to Ukraine in July or August?"

I wanted to, but I'd never traveled by myself. Softly, I said, "I hope so."

Ahead of us, Conrad reached for Ivy's hand. She turned her head toward him and gave him a sweet smile.

My heart lurched. Johann leaned toward me, and for a moment I thought he might take my hand again. I wanted him too. But he didn't. Instead, he said, "I like Portland. It's a beautiful city."

"It is," I answered as we passed an older man on a bench. He wore a tattered Vietnam Veteran hat and appeared to be homeless.

I dug a ten-dollar bill from my pocket and offered it to him.

He had a surprised expression on his face as he whispered, "Thank you." I hurt for the old man in front of me. And for Rylan. And for Johann too. I thought of Rosene's story and about Dirk, Andreas, and Pavlo. And of my great-grandfather Jeremiah too. He didn't serve in the war, but the hospital where he worked was its own kind of war zone.

I wanted to serve, but I didn't see how anything I did could compare to what those around me had done. And what Ivy would do. What kind of person did I want to be? I knew if I took over Mammi's store, God would use me. But was there something more He might have for me, regardless of my mental health issues and quirky personality? I knew God could do all things—but I still needed to be realistic.

What God might have for me was one thing, but I sensed perhaps there might be more I wanted for me too.

Brooke, Daniel, and their boys left Christmas Eve morning for Eugene. Pierre opted to stay with us, which seemed to make Treva happy. I helped Gran as much as I could and insisted she rest. Ivy, Treva, and I found Mom's fondue pots in the pantry. We grated cheese and cut apples, pears, broccoli, cauliflower, and bread. We also dug chocolate out of the baking drawer and made chocolate fondue too.

After we ate, we gathered in the living room around the fireplace, and Conrad read the Christmas story from the Gospel of Luke and then we exchanged small gifts. Johann brought carved and painted Ukrainian Easter eggs for all of us. Pierre gave us all French chocolates that I was pretty sure Brooke had donated to the cause. Conrad handed out packets of Amish peanut brittle. Ivy gave us personalized collages. Treva made a plate of her famous chocolate chip cookies for each of us. And I gave everyone a bookmark made from a map of an area unique to them. Ivy's was Portland. Treva's was Lancaster County. Conrad's was Goshen, Indiana, where he'd gone to college. Pierre's was Frankfurt, Germany, where we'd all met. Johann's was Berdyansk, Ukraine, where he'd grown up.

"Do you have the leftovers from the maps with you?" Ivy asked.

I nodded.

"I have the supplies to make collages," Ivy said. "Maybe we could do that tomorrow."

I doubted the guys would want to, but Johann said, "That sounds like fun."

The three of us girls fixed Christmas dinner, insisting Gran rest. We were all afraid of overtiring her. We decided to follow Rosene's menu for holiday meals and roast two chickens. I'd gotten the recipe for Marko's vinegret salad and also for Rosene's broccoli salad. Ivy made Haitian patties—pastry dough stuffed with sauteed ground beef, garlic, onions, and peppers.

As we sat around our family table, Gran said a beautiful prayer, thanking the Lord Jesus for His coming to earth to teach us how to live, thanking Him for each of us around the table, and then thanking Him for Mom and Dad and the legacy they left behind. After she said, "Amen," she lifted her head and said, "Conrad, Johann, and Pierre, I wish you could have known Isaac and Malinda."

Johann cleared his throat and said, "I think I speak for the three of us when I say that through their daughters, we have a glimpse of them. Because these three young women are good and kind and serve others. Your daughter and son-in-law raised them well."

"Amen," Conrad said.

Pierre added, "I'm in complete agreement."

I blinked back tears.

After we cleaned up from Christmas dinner and Ivy began pulling out her collage supplies, I stepped into the office and called Rylan.

When he answered, I said, "Merry Christmas."

He grunted.

"How are you?" I asked.

"Miserable."

"I'm sorry." Perhaps I shouldn't have called.

"I'm better than I was, though," he said. "Although I don't think the medicine is working yet. Viktor and Marko brought me Christmas dinner. Some weird Ukrainian food, but it was good."

"They celebrate this Christmas?'"

"What do you mean?"

"I thought they'd celebrate the Russian Orthodox Christmas."

"I don't think so. . . ."

That was interesting.

We talked for a little while longer and then he said, "I need to rest. I'll text you tomorrow."

I headed upstairs and grabbed a folder from my room and then returned to the dining room. Johann was cutting out pictures of snow scenes from an old skiing magazine of Dad's, and I sat down beside him.

"How's Rylan doing?" he asked.

"Better."

I hadn't made a collage with Ivy before, but I'd been watching her make them for years. She documented her own history that way, with collages about her childhood and our parents. She'd also made one for the history of our great-grandmother Clare after she heard her story. I'd been printing out photos, collecting maps, and saving verses and poems for a few years, thinking I'd like to try collaging. I'd put the maps in the same file.

I opened it and pulled out photos from Germany and a screenshot of video chatting with Johann. Then I took out the verses—*A friend loves at all times, and a brother is born for a time of adversity.* And *Greater love has no one than this: to lay down one's life for one's friends.* My favorite quote was *A map says to you, "Read me carefully, follow me closely, doubt me not. . . . I am the earth in the palm of your hand."* It was from Beryl Markham, adventurer and author.

I cut different shades of green paper and glued

those down first. Then I layered the maps, photos, verses, and saying.

"You came prepared," Johann said.

I nodded as I pulled out two final pieces from my folder. One was a saying by Lois Lowry from her book *The Giver*. "What do you think? Should I use this one?" I read, " 'The worst part of holding the memories is not the pain. It's the loneliness of it. Memories need to be shared.' " I flipped to the second piece of paper. "Or this one. 'Nothing is ever really lost to us as long as we remember it.' " It was from *The Story Girl* by L. M. Montgomery. Mom had read both books to us.

"Do you have room to use both?"

I examined my board. "You don't think it will be too crowded?"

"No," he said. "Both are important." He held up his finished board. It was all snow, trees, frozen lakes, and sections of Ukrainian maps with the saying, *Kindness is like snow. It beautifies everything it covers.*

"The quote is by Kahlil Gibran. I need to add that," he said.

"The board is lovely," I said.

He smiled. "Ukraine is lovely too."

"I hope I can visit. . . ." I wanted to meet his mother in person. I wanted to see what a country at war was like, even though I wouldn't be anywhere close to the war zone.

Johann put his hand on top of mine. I flipped mine over and grasped his. I didn't know if I'd go to Ukraine or not, but Johann was like a familiar landscape to me.

But landscapes could change in a minute— earthquakes, tornadoes, hurricanes. And lives could too.

If only I was normal. If only a visit could just be a visit. I let go of his hand and put the remnants of my maps back into my file.

24

Three days later, after we packed the SUV for the ride to the Portland airport, Gran called the three of us girls into Mom and Dad's office, leaving the three guys to chop firewood.

"I want to pray for the three of you before you go back to Pennsylvania."

Gran sat down in Mom's rocking chair, I sat down in the office chair and scooted toward Gran, and Ivy and Treva sat on the floor. Gran prayed for our studies, for our relationships with Mammi and Dawdi and Rosene, and for our other relationships too. After she said, "Amen," Gran said, "I've enjoyed having all of us together, and with Conrad, Johann, and Pierre too. It gives me a glimpse of the future."

Baffled, I left the room first. What was Gran talking about? Sure, Ivy and Conrad might end up getting married. But I hardly knew Johann. And Treva and Pierre had just met.

A few minutes later, though, as Treva hugged Pierre good-bye, I realized I was as dense as I'd always suspected. Clearly they had feelings for each other.

"Tell Brooke, Daniel, and the boys good-bye for us," Ivy said to Gran after she hugged her.

"They'll be here soon," Gran said.

Pierre grinned. "I'll watch over your grand-mother until they arrive."

I wished he could stay in Oregon instead of going home, but he'd be returning to Haiti in a couple of weeks.

Because our luggage filled up the back of the SUV, I sat in the middle of the back seat, and Treva and Johann sat on either side of me. Ivy slowed as we passed the accident scene, which was covered with snow. Tears stung my eyes, but I swallowed hard and managed not to cry. I felt the urge to rub my scar, but Johann reached for my hand before I raised it. Then we were on our way, leaving Gran and our forest home behind.

I didn't know what my future held, but I knew one thing. I'd make an appointment with my therapist when I returned to Lancaster County. I needed to figure out a few things—what to do about Rylan, how I felt about Johann, and what *I* wanted for my future.

Rylan texted the day after we arrived home that he needed a ride home from the hospital.

I texted back.

Can Marko or Viktor or Gabe give you a ride?

They're all working.

Obviously, I knew Gabe was. If he wasn't, I would be. And I should have known Viktor and Marko were.

I'll be there in two hours.

Hurry.

It was 10 a.m. I called my therapist's office and left a message to make an appointment, quickly showered, dressed, and then padded out to the kitchen to pour myself a cup of coffee for the road.

Ivy was making a second pot. "Good morning."

"Morning."

"Where are you going?"

"To pick up Rylan."

"At the VA in Philly?"

I nodded.

"Are you okay doing that?"

"I think so," I said. "I've been there before."

"It snowed during the night."

"Oh." I stepped to the window. The parking lot was covered. I checked my weather app. The temperature was twenty eight, and it wasn't going to get any warmer until afternoon.

I checked my traffic app. It didn't seem any worse than usual, but I texted Rylan and told him it might be twelve thirty before I arrived.

"Do you want me to go with you?" Ivy asked.

"Don't you have something going on today?"

She nodded. "I'm going to go observe a social worker at an elder care center for my thesis."

"I'll be fine." I didn't want her to cancel. Honestly, with so many elderly relatives and no one in our parents' generation around to help, I was relieved Ivy was focusing on helping the elderly. She would know what to do when we needed to care for Rosene, Gran, Mammi, and Dawdi.

The van slid going out of the parking lot, but I managed to make it out to the street. Once I reached the highway, I was fine. The traffic had melted the snow.

As I drove, I braced myself for seeing Rylan. He'd been through more trauma since I'd seen him last. A suicide attempt, Christmas in the hospital . . . I could listen and respond—not reacting was one thing I'd learned through counseling. I could say things like, *That must be hard* and *I'm sorry that happened.*

I didn't need to—I couldn't—try to fix Rylan.

I reached the hospital at twelve fifteen. I pulled into a parking space on the street and texted Rylan.

Come up to my room. The nurse wants to speak with you.

He texted his room number, and I parked in the garage. When I reached his room, he was sitting on the edge of the bed with his cane propped beside him.

"Look at you," I said. "Back to using your cane."

He simply nodded. His eyes appeared flat and his body tense. "The nurse will be right back."

"What's up?" I asked.

"He wants to go over my instructions with you. In case I forget."

I sat down in the chair by the window, which overlooked a snow-covered brick courtyard.

"How was Oregon?" Rylan asked.

"Good."

"How's Johann doing?"

"Good," I repeated.

"When is he coming to Pennsylvania?"

"Maybe for graduation, but I'm not sure."

"Oh, he will," Rylan said slyly, which gave me a creepy feeling. My friendship with Johann wasn't his business, and I didn't want him to make it his business.

The nurse, a middle-aged man, came in and introduced himself.

I stood. "I'm Brenna Zimmerman—a neighbor and friend of Rylan's."

He shook my hand and then held up a packet of papers. "I wanted to go over Rylan's medication with you in case he has any questions once he gets home. He's on an antidepressant and anti-anxiety medications." He told me the names, explained the dosages, and then flipped the page. "He has an appointment with a therapist in Lancaster next Thursday. If at any time Rylan begins to feel suicidal, he should call this number. If he's unable to, you or someone else should call this number for him." The number was circled in red. "But call 9-1-1 if he's having suicidal ideations."

I glanced at Rylan as the nurse left. "How are you feeling?"

"Will you give me a ride to the therapist?"

"Sure," I said. Yes, he could drive himself, but going to a therapist was a big step for him. If it made it easier to have someone else drive, I could do that. I thought of all the help I had when I needed it—I don't know how I would have survived without it. "Are you good to be at home? Will the guys take turns staying at your place again?"

He made a sour face. "They're all mad at me."

I stifled a groan. What had he done now?

After I helped Rylan into his apartment, I texted Gabe and asked him to call me when he had a chance. Just after four, my phone rang. I guessed he was on his way to the barn to help Dawdi with the milking.

"What's up with Rylan?" I asked. "He said you and Viktor are mad at him now too."

"When we visited him in the hospital, he told Viktor he was a horrible friend for not inviting him to Christmas. Then he said he never wanted to see us again."

"Ouch."

"The thing was, Viktor was going to invite him—even though Marko didn't want him to—but then Rylan ended up in the hospital and Viktor didn't see what the point was," Gabe said. "He wouldn't be released by Christmas anyway."

"So Viktor is done helping Rylan?"

There was a pause and then Gabe said, "Well, if Rylan doesn't ever want to see him again, what's the point?"

"The point—probably—is that Rylan said it impulsively and didn't really mean it."

Gabe's voice grew louder. "Then he should apologize."

"Yes, he should," I answered. "But chances are he won't."

"I think he's pushed everyone to the limit," Gabe said.

"Yes. It sounds like it." I paused a moment and then said, "I'll let you know if I have any more questions. Bye." I hung up.

What was our responsibility to Rylan? What was my responsibility to him?

I wished I could talk to Dad about all of this. He would know what I should do. One of his many favorite verses was from Proverbs. *Whoever oppresses the poor shows contempt for their Maker, but whoever is kind to the needy honors*

God. Rylan wasn't poor in the financial sense, but he was definitely needy. One of the neediest people I knew.

I decided to call the barn phone and hope Dawdi would answer. Finally, after the tenth ring, he did. "Arden Zimmerman here," he said. "How may I help you?"

"Hi, Dawdi," I said. "I need advice."

"Brenna." His voice was warm and loving. "From me?"

"Jah." I explained my dilemma. "How long do I keep trying to help Rylan?"

"I have a verse for you," he said. "Luke 6:31. 'And as ye would that men should do to you, do ye also to them likewise.'" He paused a moment and then said, "Our family went through a lot of trauma three years ago. I know that the threat of being sued is difficult—and that the reality of it would be even harder—but we lost our son." It was a complicated grief for Dawdi and Mammi because they hadn't seen Dad for years. "You and Ivy and Treva lost your parents. The threat of being sued or actually being sued doesn't compare to that. If God asks us to forgive seventy times seven, don't you think He would ask us to help seventy times seven too?"

"I hadn't thought of that."

"I'd like all of us to do what we can," Dawdi said. "But you're in a better place to help Rylan. He trusts you. Just be kind. God will show you what to do. Or else He'll bring someone else into Rylan's life. Maybe you're the bridge to something better for him."

God wanted me to be kind to Rylan. That honored Him.

I'd check in with Rylan. Listen when he needed to talk. Walk away if he was snarky. Being kind also meant setting boundaries and not letting him get away with being mean.

I thanked Dawdi for his help.

"I love you, kid."

Tears sprang into my eyes. It was the first time either of my Pennsylvania grandparents had said anything like that. "I love you too," I responded. "Thank you. I'll see you soon."

After I hung up, I texted the guys and asked them to come over for pizza at eight because I wanted us to chat about Rylan. They all texted back and said they'd be there. When Ivy arrived, I told her what was going on with Rylan. "He's pushed everyone away," I said. "And now he feels isolated. I invited the guys to come over tonight, but I'm not sure what to even say to them."

"Rylan is like a toddler pitching a fit because his parents have put him in his room for a timeout—for pitching a fit," Ivy said sensibly. "Everyone's most basic need is to belong, like I said before—from a tantrum-throwing toddler to a veteran with PTSD. I think the key is to let Rylan know he belongs without condoning his behavior."

That was pretty much what I was already thinking. But there was one more issue. "Do I accept him even if he goes through with the lawsuit against Mammi?"

"Maybe separate the two things as best you can," Ivy said. "If he has a valid suit, then we need to let it progress through the justice system. But no one should tolerate him being manipulative." Ivy wrinkled her nose. "The key to belonging is to find the right group to belong to. Maybe Rylan hasn't found the right one. Maybe hanging with his Army Reserve buddies isn't the healthiest place for him."

I couldn't imagine anyone being more tolerant of Rylan than Marko, Viktor, and Gabe had been. Viktor and Marko's commitment to him when I first met them was unbelievable. And that Gabe would adopt that same commitment was a surprise too. Rylan was a fool to alienate them.

But on the other hand, I hadn't kept in touch with the few friends I had in Oregon after Mom and Dad died. It was too painful. Maybe Ivy was right.

Marko, Viktor, and Gabe arrived together. I hoped Rylan hadn't seen them come up the steps to my apartment. He'd be paranoid and surly if he had. The pizza had already arrived, so I invited everyone to sit at the table and eat.

They each scarfed down a piece in record time, followed by another. While they chewed, I said,

"Rylan said all of you are mad at him now, but Gabe explained Rylan said he doesn't want to see any of you 'ever again.' " I made air quotes around the last two words.

Marko nodded. After he swallowed, he said, "I don't mind so much if Rylan misconstrues the truth concerning us, but I can't stand what he's trying to do to your family."

I sighed. "Our family has been through a lot in the last three years. Things have become less black and white. We value one another more, and I think that's made us want to value Rylan too, even though he can be a pain. If nothing else, the Lord wants us to be kind to him."

Marko helped himself to a third piece of pizza. "What if he goes through with the lawsuit?"

I turned my plate, with its half-eaten piece on it, clockwise. "We need to let the lawsuit work its way through the system. If my grandmother was negligent, then the suit will show that. If they took reasonable steps to keep the public off the staircase, hopefully that will be revealed too. I need to separate the possibility of the suit from Rylan being needy."

"So basically turn the other cheek," Gabe said.

I took a bite of pizza and then said, "There's a pattern here. Forgive. Do unto others. Be kind to the needy."

"We grew up with those teachings too," Marko said. "But you can't encourage Rylan with your kindness. He doesn't operate the way most people do. For example, he lied about his grandparents having a farm."

I nearly choked. "What?"

Marko nodded. "He started telling that story after he found out our grandparents had a farm. It's as if he wished he had grandparents who had a farm so he made up the story."

"That's weird. Why would he do that?"

"Because his family sucks," Gabe said.

I turned my attention back to Marko. "What is the story with his family?"

"Who knows. I can never get a straight answer from him, except I think his mother lives in Maine. That's all he's said that actually sounds believable."

I put my pizza back on my plate. "I know we can't fix him, but being on medication and seeing a therapist is a positive step for Rylan taking care of himself."

Viktor gave Marko a questioning look. Marko leaned back in his chair.

"I'm trying to set boundaries with him," I said. "I'm going to get back into counseling myself to try to figure this out." My therapist had called back, and I had an appointment for the next Wednesday. "But there's a lot I can't do."

Viktor glanced at Marko again, who exhaled loudly. "If we continue to put up with his abuse, we're just going to postpone the inevitable."

Viktor asked, "Which is?"

"That Rylan has to hit bottom and take responsibility for his own life. I'm sorry for all his losses, but he needs to man up. The sooner, the better. And I don't care if he finds out the truth. Maybe it's time."

When no one reacted, I asked, "What exactly do you mean by that?"

Marko shook his head. "Nothing." Then he stood and said, "I need to leave." He grabbed his coat and headed for the door.

Viktor sighed as he stood and cleared the table. When he returned, he said, "I need to get going too."

After he left, Gabe asked, "Any other questions?"

"No." My voice revealed my defeat.

"I need to get the van back to Mom."

"Bye."

I sat at the table a long time after they all left. So much for me trying to bring everyone together. I didn't know what to do. *God,* I prayed, *regardless of what the guys decide to do, if you want me to be Rylan's friend, show me how.* It was as simple as that. I had no idea what the right thing to do was

Five days later, I was back at Edenville, relaying the conversation with Marko, Viktor, and Gabe to my therapist. I finished by saying, "What do you think is going on with all of them?"

She gave me a sympathetic smile. "What do you think is going on?"

"I think it has to do with what happened in Afghanistan. With Meg, Rylan's deceased girlfriend. Rylan blames someone besides himself for her death—but Marko and Viktor are keeping a secret from him."

"If you knew what happened, would it change how you feel about Rylan?" my therapist asked.

"I don't think so."

"What is your main objective?"

"To figure out how to help Rylan without being manipulated by him."

"Let's work on that." She gave me a few ideas on how to end conversations with him and direct the attention away from him suing Mammi and onto what his needs were. "But keep in mind you're not responsible for him," she said.

"I don't want to be. I want him to be responsible for himself."

I only had ten minutes left in the session, so I changed the subject to Johann. "I've liked him for a while, but I never thought he might like me. I'm sure once he gets to know me, he won't. Which makes me not want to go to Ukraine. Nor have him come here, even though I invited him."

"Because?"

"I don't want to give him the chance to get to know the real me."

"Do you think he might already know the

real you? You met three years ago. You've been messaging and chatting. You spent a week together." She smiled. "You're transparent, Brenna. And honest."

"That's what he said."

"Do you feel as if you know him?"

I nodded. "Definitely."

"Going to Ukraine for a visit isn't any sort of a commitment. Getting to know someone better, even if you feel as if you know them, is a good thing. But it doesn't mean anything more than that. If you're interested in him romantically, then getting to know each other simply gives you a chance to find out if you're compatible."

She was right. I sighed. "I wish I could talk to my parents about all of this. I've really been missing them."

"That's understandable," she said. "You're a young adult, and you should have the advice of your parents as you transition into adulthood and navigate relationships."

My eyes filled with tears.

"Not only does all of this activate your grief, but it leaves a dearth of resources for you, ones that you'll have to fill through other ways." She leaned forward a little. "Besides therapy, you need to find trusted adults to help you navigate this time in your life."

A tear spilled over and fell down my cheek.

"Does anyone come to mind?"

"My sister."

"Treva?"

"No. Ivy."

It seemed my therapist was trying to hide her surprise. The first year of our sessions was mostly me ranting about Ivy—probably as a deterrent to grieving the loss of Mom and Dad.

"She's given me some good advice a couple of times lately. I think she knows more than I thought."

"Good," she said. "Who else?"

"Rosene."

My therapist nodded.

I was impressed with how she remembered everyone in my life. "She's ninety-one, but she seems to understand me better than anyone. She's been telling me a story about her sister. Even though everything happened seventy-five years ago, the story is helping me try to do the right thing."

"Good."

I glanced at the clock. Our time was up. I made another appointment for two weeks from now, and then trudged out to the van. I didn't want to go back to the apartment. I decided to go to the farm. Hopefully Rosene could tell me more of Martha's story.

25

Martha

After the news of Hitler's death, Mutter brought an extra radio from the store to the house. Moscow reported that Berlin had fallen, and then more reports came in about units of the *Wehrmacht*—the regular German army—surrendering. There was speculation about when the war would end. Vater thought it would be soon. Clare said the family should brace themselves for it taking longer than expected.

Martha couldn't imagine the war in Europe would last longer than a few more days. Maybe a week. She wished she could ask George his opinion, but she'd been too busy to attend the last Red Cross meeting.

Dirk didn't believe Hitler was dead and told Martha, again, to expect an invasion. "Don't turn your back to the east," he said. "Any day now, a sky full of *Messerschmitts* will arrive, leading the attack on the US. The war will end with a victory for the Third Reich."

Martha simply smiled and told him to start mucking out the stalls in the dairy barn with Zeke. She couldn't leave Dirk alone anywhere on the farm.

On Monday morning, after they'd eaten break-fast and Vater had led them in devotions, Martha started out to the milking room to finish cleaning as the truck arrived with the PWs. It was late.

She stopped and waited by the garden. One by one, as they climbed down from the back of the truck, they joined her. First Andreas and then Pavlo. Then Otis. And finally Dirk, with Sergeant Schwarz following him.

Martha started to give them their assignments for the morning when Clare yelled, "Martha!" Again, Martha thought something had happened to Vater. But Clare said, "There's an announce-ment on the radio."

She started toward the house with the PWs and Sergeant Schwarz trailing along behind her. Clare had left the door open, and the radio was blaring. "The unconditional surrender of the German Third Reich was signed in the early morning hours at Supreme Headquarters, Allied Expeditionary Force at Reims in northeastern France."

Rosene let out an uncharacteristic whoop, Martha stepped into the kitchen, and the PWs and Sergeant Schwarz crowded onto the back porch.

The report on the radio continued. "Represen-tatives of the four Allied Powers—France, Great Britain, the Soviet Union, and the United States—and the three German officers delegated by German President Karl Doenitz . . ." Names of other officials involved in the negotiations were read. The broadcaster concluded by saying, "President Truman will address the nation tomorrow morning with additional information."

"It's over," Vater said.

"No!" Dirk spoke in English. "It's American propaganda. Germany would never surrender."

Martha turned toward Dirk. He'd been completely brainwashed. She glanced from him to Sergeant Schwarz. He had a frown on his face, perhaps at Dirk's response.

The next morning, before President Truman addressed the nation just after 8:30, they all gathered around the radio again. This time, Sergeant Schwarz stepped into the kitchen, followed by the PWs. Vater motioned toward the table and the empty chairs and said, "Sit down. Clare, pour everyone a cup of coffee."

The speech began with, "This is a solemn but glorious hour. I only wish that Franklin D. Roosevelt had lived to witness this day. General Eisenhower informs me that the forces of Germany have surrendered to the United Nations. The flags of freedom fly over all Europe." He mentioned the terrible price the country had paid to rid the world of Hitler and his evil band and went on to talk about the Japanese leaders not surrendering and that the war in the Pacific would steadily increase.

Dirk seemed to be comprehending President

Truman's words, and so did Andreas. Their English had improved significantly. Pavlo and Otis were more interested in their coffee than the speech.

Dirk crossed his arms and leaned back in his chair as President Truman said, "The Allied armies, through sacrifice and devotion and with God's help, have wrung from Germany a final and unconditional surrender. . . ."

Dirk jumped up and marched to the porch. Sergeant Schwarz leaped to his feet, knocking his chair over as he rushed after Dirk, who was pounding down the steps.

Martha stepped to the open door and watched Dirk stop at the picnic table and then pound his fist on the wood until Sergeant Schwarz joined him and blocked her view.

She kept her eye on them as she continued to listen to the speech. "The whole world must be cleansed of the evil from which half the world has been freed." President Truman went on to declare Sunday, May 13, a day of prayer.

As the president finished the speech, Vater turned off the radio. He said to Mutter, "Take it back to the store."

Andreas stood and said slowly, "Thank you for the coffee and for sharing your home."

"You're welcome," Vater said. "I hope your homeland will soon recover from all of this."

Andreas gestured toward Pavlo. "Our home is

Poland. There's nothing for us to return to."

"We need to get back to work." Martha motioned toward the PWs and stepped onto the back porch. The last thing she wanted was for Andreas to ask Vater to help them stay.

In the late afternoon, after the milking was finished and the PWs left, Clare asked Martha to walk with her to the store to see if she could place a call to Jeremiah. Martha took Arden and lifted him to her shoulders.

She asked Clare how she was feeling.

"Better," she answered. "I just hope Jeremiah is home by the time the baby is born."

"So do I," Martha said.

"When he comes home, what do you plan to do?" Clare asked.

"If I could do anything?"

"Jah," Clare answered. "Anything."

"I'd like to work for the Red Cross in Europe. I'd like to help resettle refugees."

"Ach," Clare said. "You would be good at that."

"But it's not possible."

"Perhaps it will be."

Martha didn't respond. Even with Jeremiah home, Vater would still be ill. And Clare would be busier than ever with another baby. Rosene would need to do more of the housework, and Mutter would need Martha's help again.

When they reached the store, the big radio

was on, and several people had gathered around it at the back of the store. It was turned up loud enough to hear, "The celebration continues around the world, including in New York City where the streets are filled with people. . . ."

The excitement in the newscaster's voice matched the excitement in Martha's heart. Yes, she wouldn't be able to leave the farm, but the horrors of the war in Europe would stop. Now, as President Truman said, was a time to pray for the war to end in the Pacific, to mourn all who died, and to begin to rebuild. Even if she wouldn't have a role in doing that in Europe, God would use her to help her family move forward.

Rosene waited on a customer, and Mutter stood in the back, listening to the radio. Clare stopped at the far end of the counter, where the phone was, while Martha continued toward Mutter.

The bell on the door jingled, and a man stepped inside. It was the businessman who had spoken with Mutter before. Mutter turned toward the door and then said to Rosene, "I'll be back in a minute."

Mutter approached the man. He said something Martha couldn't hear, and Mutter said, "I'll show you." She led the way, and he followed.

Distantly, Martha heard Clare say, "Hello, Jeremiah. How are you?" After a pause, she said, "We're all so relieved. And praying . . ."

Mutter and the man spoke in the front corner of

the store, and then the man left without buying anything.

Clare continued speaking to Jeremiah.

And then Mutter left the store too.

Clare hung up the phone and said, "Jeremiah will be able to come home Friday again, but earlier in the day. He'll be on the noon train."

Martha said, "I'll pick him up."

Clare waved at Rosene. "We'll see you soon."

"Yes," Rosene said. "We'll close up in a few minutes."

As they left the store, Martha looked to the right. Mutter sat in the car with the businessman, deep in conversation. If she was working with a spy, she wasn't being very discreet.

Martha went back into the store, leaving Clare on the porch, and when Rosene had finished waiting on the customer, Martha approached her. "Does the man Mutter's speaking with stop by often?"

Rosene looked toward the door. "She's still speaking with him?"

Martha nodded. "She's sitting in his car."

"He's stopped by a few times."

"Mutter told me he's a traveling salesman. Is that true?"

Rosene's face reddened. "As far as I know."

Martha stepped closer to her sister. "Are you upset?"

Rosene shook her head. "I don't know what's

340

going on, is all. And I haven't known whether to say anything or not."

Martha said, "Please tell me if you have any concerns or see anything suspicious."

"I don't want to be disloyal to Mutter."

"I know." Martha put her arm around Rosene. "You won't be."

Then she joined Clare on the porch.

"Who's Mutter talking to?" Clare asked.

"A traveling salesman," Martha answered. The last person she wanted to worry was Clare.

On Friday, when Martha met Jeremiah in the train station, he held a roll of film in his hand. "Could we drop this off to be developed?" he asked before even saying hello.

She drove to the stationery store in Lancaster and took the film inside while Jeremiah waited outside. The clerk said the prints would be ready in a week.

On the way to the farm, they talked about the war ending and President Truman's speech. Martha told him that Mutter had brought a radio to the house for news of the end of the war. "But she's taken it back to the store now."

"*Gut*," Jeremiah said. "I don't want Arden to get used to having strangers' voices telling sad stories in the house."

Not all the stories on the radio were sad, but Martha didn't say anything. She knew Jeremiah and Clare's bishop wouldn't approve of them living in a house with a radio. It was enough that he was allowing them to live with electricity for the time being.

When they reached the farm, Jeremiah went into the house to greet Clare and get something to eat. Martha looked for the PWs, who should have been finishing their lunch break. Sergeant Schwarz came out of the horse barn with Andreas as Dirk came out of the dairy barn.

"They're not in there," Dirk said in German.

Startled, Martha asked, "Who are you looking for?"

"Pavlo and Otis," Sergeant Schwarz said. "They seem to have disappeared."

"For how long?"

"Since before our noon break," Sergeant Schwarz answered.

Martha's heart raced. "Where's Zeke?"

"He was called away right after you left," Dirk said in English, while Andreas stood with his head down.

"We thought Zeke had told them to do something. Fix a fence or something," Sergeant Schwarz took off his hat and ran his hand through his hair. "But we can't find them anywhere. I need to use the telephone and report they're missing."

"You'll have to go to the store. I'll go with you after I tell Jeremiah what's going on. Wait here."

Martha ran to the house, trying not to panic. One of her worst fears had come true. When she entered, Jeremiah sat at the table while Clare dished up a plate for him. She quickly told them what was going on. "Where's Rosene?" Martha asked.

"At the store, helping Mutter," Clare answered. "She put Arden down for a nap and left a few minutes ago."

"Did Zeke tell you why he needed to leave?"

"He had a message that their Mamm's cough is worse. Zeke needed to take her back to the doctor."

"Where's Vater?"

"Resting," Clare answered.

"Don't tell him what's going on." She started to the back door. "I'm going to insist Dirk and Andreas walk with us to the store. I don't want them unattended."

"I'll be right out," Jeremiah said.

Sergeant Schwarz sat at the picnic table, looking a little lost but not very upset.

"Let's go," Martha yelled. "If they're trying to escape, every minute matters." They already had a good head start. "Come on, Dirk and Andreas. You're going with us."

She led the way with Sergeant Schwarz taking up the rear. Her heart raced. What if someone on the farm had helped Pavlo and Otis? What if it had been Mutter? Martha felt ill at the thought.

When they reached the store, Martha held the door and ushered the three in.

Mutter stood at the counter. "What's going on?"

"Pavlo and Otis are missing," Martha said. "Sergeant Schwarz needs to use the telephone."

Mutter seemed genuinely surprised.

Rosene stepped forward with the feather duster in her hand. "How long have they been gone?" She seemed surprised too.

"Since before noon," Martha explained.

Sergeant Schwarz lifted the receiver and dialed the operator. He gave her instructions and then waited. Martha crossed her arms. At last, someone came on the other end of the line, and Sergeant Schwarz explained what had happened. "Yes, at the Simons farm," he said. There was a long pause. "Yes. I'll place a call to the local sheriff." He put the receiver down and then dialed the operator again. It took a few minutes for the call to go through. When it did, he repeated what happened.

After he finished, he said, "The sheriff will be here soon, and someone from the camp is on their way. The sheriff will contact the FBI."

"Why would they try to escape when the war has ended?" Mutter asked.

Martha glanced at Andreas. He'd said he and Pavlo had nothing to return to. He kept his head down.

Dirk stared straight ahead. Martha, Sergeant

344

Schwarz, Dirk, and Andreas headed back to the farm and waited by the picnic table. It wasn't long until the sheriff arrived and then a US Army officer from the camp. They checked the dairy barn and the horse barn. By now, Vater had come out of the house and was answering questions.

A half hour later, two men dressed in black suits who looked like G-men showed up. They showed FBI badges, and then the older one introduced himself as Agent Richard Lewis. He asked if anyone in the family helped the PWs.

"Absolutely not," Vater said.

"Is everyone who lives or works here on the premises?"

Martha explained that Mutter and Rosene were at the store and that Zeke, the farmhand, had gone home to take his mother to the doctor.

"Go get the two at the store," the older FBI man said. "And send word for the farmhand to return as soon as possible." Jeremiah said he'd go to his parents' house, but Martha said he should stay and that she'd drive over and deliver the message.

On her way, she stopped by the store and told Mutter and Rosene to close it and head home. When she reached the Zimmerman home, Martha left instructions for Zeke to come to the farm as soon as he returned. "It's urgent," she said.

When she returned to the farm, the older FBI agent gathered them around the picnic table. "I need everyone in the family to go check to see if anything is missing. Clothes. Hats. Shoes. Food. Anything that could be used as a disguise or for sustenance."

Mutter led the way into the house, followed by the others.

Martha hesitated. It was nearly time to start the milking. Rosene took her arm and said, "Come on. Just look through your things."

As she headed through the back porch, Martha scanned the hats. Her summer straw hat was missing. Perhaps Clare had used it. She went up the back staircase, following Rosene. When she reached her room, nothing seemed out of order. Her dresses were on the pegs on the wall, including her work dresses.

She squinted. One was missing. The green print one that Clare had sewn when she returned from Germany. She opened her bureau drawers. A pair of Vater's overalls that Clare had tailored for her were also missing. She turned toward her row of shoes. An old pair was missing, along with her previous pair of boots that she'd been holding onto in case one of the soles of her current pair became damaged.

She felt ill. There was no way Otis nor Pavlo sneaked into the house. If just her hat was missing, it might be a matter of it being misplaced or someone snatching it off the back porch. But with five items missing? Someone had collected them intentionally.

26

By the time Martha returned to the yard, the others had gathered around the picnic table again. She approached Clare and quietly asked her if she'd worn her gardening hat.

"No," Clare answered.

"Rosene," Martha asked, "have you seen my gardening hat that was on the back porch?"

Rosene shook her head.

Martha turned toward her mother. "Mutter, how about you?"

"No." She wrinkled her nose. "I'd never wear that hat."

True, it wasn't Mutter's style at all. "How about a pair of overalls from my room? And a work dress?"

"No." Mutter turned toward Rosene. "Did you wash Martha's extra overalls and a work dress recently?"

"I haven't done any wash since Monday," Rosene answered. "I'll go check the basement. Maybe I misplaced them." She returned a few minutes later. "They're not down there."

"I need to tell Agent Lewis," Martha said to Mutter, who frowned. She approached Agent Lewis and told him what was missing. He took out a small notebook and jotted down the items. "Who would have access to your room?"

"Anyone in the family."

"Who else was in the house?"

"Zeke eats meals with us in the kitchen and sometimes plays in the living room with Arden—he's my nephew, and Zeke's too—but he never goes upstairs. Sergeant Schwarz and the PWs came into the house to listen to President Truman's speech on Tuesday."

The agent raised his eyebrows.

Martha quickly added, "But none of them left the kitchen."

A car came down the drive and then parked in front of the house. A man in a black suit climbed out—another FBI agent, she assumed. But as he walked toward them, she realized it was the businessman she'd seen with Mutter all those times.

As he approached, he nodded to Mutter and then toward the garden. She stood and walked to meet him, but Martha reached him first, extending her hand. "I'm Martha Zimmerman."

He shook her hand. "Tom Brown."

"And who are you with?"

He cleared his throat. "A federal agency."

"Which one?"

"Those who need to know, know." He took a step toward the garden. "I need to speak with your mother." He brushed past her.

Tom Brown. It sounded like an alias. But he'd

348

arrived at the same time as the FBI, so he most likely wasn't a spy.

Jeremiah approached the older agent and said, "We need to start the milking. Will that be all right?"

"Yes," Agent Lewis said. "But we'll have the PWs stay out here."

As Martha and Jeremiah stepped away from the others, Zeke arrived, out of breath.

"How is Mamm?" Jeremiah asked.

"*Gut.* The doctor increased her medication and said she should rest more."

Martha explained to Zeke what was going on and introduced him to Agent Lewis. Then she and Jeremiah went to do the milking.

A half hour later, Zeke came into the barn.

"What's going on out there?" Martha asked.

"An army guy arrived in a jeep and then the truck. Sergeant Schwarz, Dirk, and Andreas left in it."

"Are the FBI agents still here?"

"Jah, two of them. They're waiting for a crew to arrive to search the area."

"What about the man talking to Mutter?"

"He left," Zeke said, "after speaking gruffly to the FBI agents."

Martha shivered, despite the heat of the afternoon. Something more than Pavlo and Otis escaping was going on.

When they finished the milking, Martha headed

straight to the kitchen. Clare sat at the table, slicing a loaf of bread, while Mutter fried chicken on the stove.

"Who is Tom Brown?" Martha asked Mutter.

Mutter kept her head down. "I can't say."

"Can't or won't?"

Mutter met Martha's gaze. "You need to mind your own business and stop asking questions."

Martha started to protest, but a knock on the front door redirected her attention. She hurried into the living room and opened the door, expecting one of the FBI agents.

But George stood before her, a frantic expression on his face. "I need a translator. Can you help?"

Once they were in the car, George said, "Two POWs escaped today."

"Yes," Martha said. "From our farm."

"Your farm?"

"Yes." She felt ill again.

"They've been found."

Relief swept through her. "Thank God."

"Yes."

"Where?"

George turned onto the highway. "I wasn't told. I had a call from the Red Cross liaison at the camp that I was needed to witness the interrogation."

"Why aren't they questioning them at the sheriff's office?" Martha leaned back against the seat. "Or taking them to the FBI headquarters?"

"I don't know." George gripped the steering wheel. "I've never been involved in anything like this."

"Who is the Red Cross liaison at the camp?"

"Nurse Olson."

"Oh." Martha thought for a moment. "Won't they already have a translator there?"

"Yes. But we want you to verify what their translator is saying."

Their translator. "Nurse Olson doesn't trust their translator?"

He gripped the steering wheel. "I'm not sure."

When they arrived at the camp, Nurse Olson met Martha and George at the mess hall. "We're meeting in the camp superintendent's office," she said.

As she led the way along a trail, George asked, "Where were the PWs caught?"

"About five miles south of here."

"They were headed north?"

"Yes," Nurse Olson answered.

"To Canada?"

"It appears that way."

That didn't make sense. Canada was an ally. If captured, they would have been sent back to the US immediately.

They arrived at a stone building, and George stepped ahead and opened the door. Then Nurse Olson led the way down a hall to a large office.

Two US soldiers waited inside, standing at

attention on either side of a door near the desk. There were two chairs directly in front of and facing the desk and then more chairs to the sides of those, also facing the desk.

Martha and George sat in two chairs near the front. "Are you staying?" George asked Nurse Olson.

"Yes, but I'll sit in the back."

More soldiers filed in and then several men in suits, none of whom Martha recognized. The camp superintendent arrived and sat behind the desk. A few minutes later, Agent Lewis from the FBI entered, and behind him two soldiers escorted Otis and Pavlo, who were both in handcuffs, into the room. To Martha's relief, they were wearing their PW uniforms and not her work dress and overalls. Perhaps Mutter hadn't been involved in the escape after all.

Otis and Pavlo sat in the two chairs in front of George and Martha. Neither acknowledged her.

Agent Lewis began the interview by saying, "We'll be gathering information at this meeting to determine the security of this camp and the use of the POWs as labor in the surrounding areas. The two escapees will be taken to the Indiantown Gap camp and confined there." He turned to the superintendent. "Are we ready to begin?"

"We're waiting for the guard who was in charge of these POWs." The superintendent glanced down at a piece of paper. "A Sergeant Schwarz."

He motioned toward a guard by the door. "Go see what's keeping him."

Fifteen minutes later, the guard returned and spoke quietly to the superintendent. Then the superintendent consulted with Agent Lewis, who looked up and noticed Martha. "What are you doing here?"

"I'm translating for George Hall." Martha motioned toward George. "He's with the Red Cross."

"Come up here," the agent said to Martha. She approached the other two.

"Did Sergeant Schwarz and the other two POWs get on the truck at your farm?"

"Yes," Martha said. "Dirk Neumann and Andreas Witer are the other two POWs."

The superintendent turned to the guard. "Go find those two and bring them here. And find Sergeant Schwarz."

It was another fifteen minutes until the guard returned, but only with Andreas. He came through the side door to the office.

"I couldn't find Dirk Neumann," the guard said.

"Where is Neumann?" the superintendent asked Andreas.

When he didn't respond, the superintendent stood. "We need to get to the bottom of this. Do you need a translator?"

Andreas glanced at Martha and then behind her. Martha turned. Was he looking at Nurse Olson?

Andreas turned back toward the superintendent and then said in English, "I will tell you what I know." Then he turned toward Otis and Pavlo and said in German, "You can tell Dirk whatever you want when you see him again, but I have no allegiance to him. There's no reason not to tell the truth."

Martha could only see Otis and Pavlo's backs. Otis stiffened, but Pavlo nodded, seemingly in agreement with Andreas.

Turning back toward the superintendent, Andreas said, "I have a note from Dirk to Sergeant Schwarz that I found in Dirk's belongings. I have no idea if he ever gave it to Schwarz or not. It's written in German, but I'll translate it as I read. 'The Simons farm is my jurisdiction now. We'll do all we can to bring it down. Machinery, buildings, animals, relationships. And ultimately I will escape, but I'm going to need your help.'"

Martha grasped her seat. Dirk hadn't done as much damage as he'd hoped to. Unless he recruited Mutter to spy. Then he'd done more than she thought.

Andreas lifted his head and said, "I think the escape of Otis and Pavlo was a trick. The true escapees are Dirk and Sergeant Schwarz."

Martha stifled a gasp.

"What makes you think that?" the superintendent asked.

"They came back to camp on the truck this

354

afternoon," Andreas said, "but I haven't seen Dirk since. They were whispering on the truck before we picked up the other POWs and guards." Andreas straightened. "You should know that Dirk Neumann is an alias, one stolen from a dead German soldier—a private. The man who calls himself Dirk Neumann is a Nazi officer. I don't know his real name—"

Otis struggled to his feet and said, "You lie!" Then he lunged at Andreas, his cuffed hands flailing.

A guard stepped forward and grabbed Otis.

Pavlo's shoulders began to shake. "No," he choked. "Andreas speaks truth. Dirk forced Otis and me to leave this morning. We went through the woods. We were to head north. Neither of us wanted to, but Dirk said if we didn't, he'd see that we were hanged when we were sent back to Germany. I believe Schwarz was in on the plan too."

The superintendent turned toward the guard who brought Andreas into the office. "What do you know of Sergeant Schwarz?"

"Yale graduate. Parents are German immigrants. Drafted two years ago. He's been assigned here since January," the guard said. "Parents live nearby—in Hershey. He would go home sometimes on his days off."

The superintendent turned toward Agent Lewis. "What are your thoughts?"

"We don't have enough information to know whether or not another escape has been attempted, but I need to alert the agency immediately that two others are missing. We'll search the area, put out alerts, and send agents to the Schwarz home." He turned toward the guard. "Did Sergeant Schwarz have a car here?"

"Yes, sir. It's still here."

"Find out if anyone is missing a car," Agent Lewis said. "We'll check the train station in Lancaster and put alerts at all the border crossings into Canada."

"They may have civilian clothing with them," Agent Lewis said. "A woman's dress, hat, and shoes, along with a pair of overalls and boots, are missing from the Simons farm."

Martha sunk back in her chair. Mutter hadn't helped Otis and Pavlo escape. She'd helped Dirk. It was all beginning to make sense now.

Except for *why*.

The guards took Andreas, Otis, and Pavlo to Indiantown Gap. Once they were gone, the superintendent told George he'd be alerted if anyone wanted to speak with a Red Cross inspector. "Until then, you may go," he said.

As George and Martha left the room, Nurse Olson followed them. When they reached the mess hall, she asked George, "May I speak to you for a moment? Somewhere private?"

356

"How about in the car?" he asked. "Do you mind if Martha joins us?"

Nurse Olson sighed. "I don't mind. It will probably seem less suspicious if anyone sees us."

They all climbed into the car and closed the doors.

Nurse Olsen said, "I believe Sergeant Schwarz beat Andreas because Andreas had information about Dirk working with a spy. Andreas mentioned a German man who lives near the farm had met with Dirk sometimes in the woods. I wouldn't be surprised if Sergeant Schwarz beat Andreas to keep him from telling me about the man, which Andreas finally did last night. A Mr. Richter. It sounds as if he's a gentleman farmer."

George turned toward me. "Do you know of a man by that name?"

"Yes," Martha answered. "He lives a few miles from our farm on an acreage. He stops in the store from time to time." He was the one who seemed quite fond of Mutter, but Martha didn't say that out loud.

"Thank you for confirming his name," Nurse Olson said. "I'll alert the authorities about him." She opened the car door. "Thank you."

Martha turned in her seat and told Nurse Olson good-bye.

"Andreas said how kind you've been to him and Pavlo," Nurse Olson replied. "How kind your entire family has been. He'd given up on his faith, but he said all of you treated him as Christ would."

Martha swallowed hard and then said, "I hope—and I'll pray—that they'll be safe when they're sent back."

"Thank you," Nurse Olson said. "I'm worried about that too." Her cheeks reddened. "I suppose I'll be judged harshly, but I've fallen in love with Andreas. I won't burden you with the details of that, though."

Martha tried to hide her shock. George didn't seem to be surprised.

On the way home, George drove slowly. As they neared the farm, he said, "I need to speak to you about something else."

"Oh?"

"I received an assignment to Geneva. I need a translator." He turned into the driveway of the farm. "Have you thought more about applying with the Red Cross?" He stopped in front of the house.

It was rare that Martha cried, but she struggled to fight back her tears. A PW from their farm, along with a guard, had escaped, most likely with Mutter's help. Nurse Olson had fallen in love with Andreas. George was going to Europe. He wanted her to go with him.

"I can't," she said. "There's too much . . ." Her voice trailed off.

"Would you think about it more?"

"I've done nothing but think about it for the last month."

"I understand," he said. "I'll pray about it. Perhaps God will provide what your family needs through someone else."

"Perhaps." She turned toward him. "Thank you for including me in this work."

For a moment, she considered telling him she was sure Mutter helped Dirk. But then she decided not to just in case she was wrong. If it were true, he'd find out soon enough. They all would.

27

Brenna

Rosene said, "That's all for now. Treva and Arden will be in soon." She wiped down the counter as she spoke. "Will you stay for supper?"

"Wait, that can't be all. Did your mother help Dirk escape?"

Rosene appeared weary. "What do you think?"

I didn't want to say. What if I was wrong? "I think I'll wait for the rest of the story," I answered.

Her eyes brightened. "Good idea."

"I'd better get back to the apartment," I said. "Johann is going to call."

She smiled a little. "Let me dish up some casserole for you to take. I don't think you eat enough."

She was right. I didn't. "Denki."

After she handed me the container of chicken and broccoli casserole, I gave her a half hug. She wrapped her arms around me and pulled me close. "Tell Johann hello," she said.

"I will." I wondered if perhaps Gran had talked with her about our time in Oregon. "Thank you," I said. "For everything. I'm looking forward to hearing the rest of the story."

"Come back soon."

Twenty minutes later, as I walked into my room, my computer buzzed with a call. I answered as quickly as I could.

"There you are," Johann said.

"I just got back from the farm. How are you?"

"Good. Did you have a good New Year?"

"I had a quiet one," I said. "Just the way I like it." I'd gone to the farm and played Scrabble with Rosene and Treva, then came back to the apartment by nine. "How about you?"

He smiled. "I ended up working. How was your counseling appointment today?"

"Good," I answered. I told him about it, leaving out the part about him. "Rylan has an appointment tomorrow with a VA therapist. He asked me to give him a ride, and I agreed." I paused a moment, expecting Johann to chastise me. He didn't. I added, "I hope therapy will help Rylan."

"I hope so too." Johann paused a moment and then asked, "Have you thought any more about visiting Ukraine?"

"Some."

"And?"

I paused a moment and then said, "I'll keep thinking about it."

As I got ready to leave the apartment the next morning to get Rylan, my message app dinged with a message from Johann.

We know God is close to the brokenhearted. Remember, the only cure for grief, which is actually an outpouring of love, is more love. That love comes from God and from each other. I don't know what the right thing to do is as far as Rylan, but as a soldier, I thank you for caring for him. I'm praying for both of you.

Dyakuyu.

While I sat in the waiting room of the VA office in Lancaster, I watched the veterans come and go. Old ones and young ones, with both visible and invisible injuries.

When Rylan came out, he had a biting expression on his face. He didn't even wait until we reached the van to tell me how much he hated his therapist. "He hasn't even been in the military. He doesn't know what war is like." We'd reached the van. "He has no idea what it's like to—"

He climbed into the passenger seat and slammed the door shut.

I climbed into the driver's seat, hoping this was the last time I'd need to give Rylan a ride. Anywhere.

I started the van.

"Where does your therapist work?" he asked.

"In a clinic on the outskirts of town, south of here. It's designed for Plain people, Amish and Mennonite. It's called Edenville."

He groaned. "So no one there knows anything about war either."

"Maybe not," I said. "But they know about PTSD and grief and loss. And trauma." When he didn't answer, I said, "I had panic attacks and was depressed before our parents were killed, but it got worse after they died. It took a lot of counseling—a lot of therapy—to become functional. I didn't do anything the first year after they died except help Rosene with the housework or help Mammi in the store. It wasn't until after a year of therapy that I was able to get my license and start school. I stopped going to therapy last May, but I've recently realized I need it again. There are some things I can't figure out on my own."

When he didn't answer, I said, "You could call Edenville and see if a therapist has openings. I really think therapy can help—emotionally and spiritually too." When he didn't answer again, I said, "You don't talk about your childhood. I'd love to hear about it—if you want to talk about it."

After a long pause, he said, "I grew up in Cincinnati. I'm the youngest of three boys. Our dad left when I was seven. Mom struggled to pay the rent and keep us fed. My oldest brother moved to California, the next one joined the Marines, and I joined the army right after I graduated from high school. After I left, Mom remarried and moved to Maine. I drove up to see her after I was discharged from the army, but it was really awkward. Then I moved here and joined the Army Reserve. A year after that, I went to Afghanistan." He grimaced.

"What made you decide to move to Lancaster County?"

"A friend from the army. We met in Korea."

"Meg?"

"Yes, Meg."

When he didn't say anything more, I asked, "Is there anything else you want to tell me?"

"I don't think so," he said. "But I appreciate you asking. And I appreciate you being a friend, even though I'm a handful."

I rolled my eyes. "That's an unfair description."

"Oh, I know. A true description would be much worse. But I'd like to go with 'a handful.' My grandmother used to call me that."

"Fine by me," I said, grateful for a moment of levity from him.

"When do classes start?" he asked after a while.

"January fifteenth. Have you preregistered?"

"Yes. Probably the same classes as you," he said. "But lucky for you I'll be able to drive myself."

"You'd better," I said.

"And I'm still going to sue your grandmother."

I shrugged. "Suit yourself."

He began to laugh.

"What?"

"Suit yourself." He laughed some more.

I didn't join in, but I smiled. A little. At his amusement. Not my unintentional pun.

Over the next few weeks, I only saw Rylan in class, but from those brief sightings, he seemed to be doing better. He was limping more than before he broke his leg, but he got around fine. He even smiled some from time to time and always greeted me politely. Then again, I had no idea what he was thinking.

I hadn't heard anything about being deposed by his attorney and hoped that would all go away. But I was probably being as naïve as Gabe was about his unit being deployed in the near future.

When I chatted with Johann, I wanted to ask whether he had a new job or not, but I guessed he had because he wasn't as available as he had been before. Several times when we'd planned to chat, I received a last-minute message saying he couldn't.

In the middle of February, Rylan's truck was in the shop, and he texted me for a ride to class. We had the same two classes together on Mondays and Wednesdays, one in the late morning and one in the midafternoon. He was sullen on the way there. I dropped him off at the building and then went to park. He limped along with his cane.

When I reached the class, I slipped in the

back. He was sitting between Ami and Jessica in the front. After class, I hoped he'd get a ride home with them, but he stood and waved at me. I waved back and nodded toward the hallway. As I waited for him, I checked my phone. I had a message from Gabe, asking if I could make a delivery. He said he couldn't do it since Sharon needed her van all afternoon.

I didn't text Gabe back. I'd have to take Rylan back to the apartment complex first. There was no way I was going to take him by the shop.

My phone rang as we walked down the hall. *Gabe.* I silenced the call. It rang again.

"You should answer it," Rylan said.

I turned the ringer off. "It can wait."

It buzzed again as we reached the van.

"You're avoiding someone," Rylan said. "Because of me?"

I wished I could lie, but alas, I'd never mastered the technique. "It's Gabe."

"Answer it."

When it buzzed again, I did. Without saying hello, I said, "I'll be by in an hour." It would take that long to bring Rylan home and get back to the shop.

"Look," Gabe said. "I really need your help. Priscilla asked me to deliver four chairs yesterday. I said I would and then forgot. The customer needs them today for a meeting at her house. It's a big sale. I don't want to mess this up."

"What time does she need them by?"

"Five."

"Where does she live?"

"Quarryville."

I groaned. That was south of the city of Lancaster. I wouldn't have time to take Rylan home first.

"Fine," I said. "I'm leaving campus now."

As I ended the call, Rylan said, "I can ride along with you. No problem."

28

When we reached the store, Rylan assured me he'd stay in the van.

I opened the door. "Cross your heart?"

"I promise," he said.

Gabe started out of the shop with one of the chairs before my feet hit the ground. But then he froze for a long minute before lifting the fingers of his right hand as it grasped the chair. "Hi, Rylan," he called out.

"Hey."

I jumped down and stepped around to the hatch, lifted it, and then popped the back seat down.

"You'll have to lower the middle seat too," Gabe said.

I stepped around to the sliding door, opened it, and did as he said.

Gabe slid in the first chair and headed back into the shop. I followed him. Once we were in the store, he turned to me. "What are you doing?"

"What do you mean?"

"Why is Rylan in your van?"

"His truck is in the shop. I was going to take him home and then come here, but I couldn't do that and get the chairs to the customer on time."

"You're going to stir up trouble again."

"If you hadn't forgotten to make the delivery yesterday," I whispered, "I wouldn't have had to bring him along."

"Brenna!" Mammi started toward me. "What are you doing here?"

"Picking up these chairs to deliver."

"Oh." She glanced at Gabe. He shrugged.

"You'd better hurry," Mammi said to me.

Gabe gave me a wilting look. I made a face. Mammi didn't seem to notice. We each picked up a chair and started out to the van.

Mammi squinted against the sun. "Who's with you?"

"Rylan."

"Oh."

After we had all the chairs in the van, Gabe went back into the shop for a couple of packing blankets while Mammi stepped around to Rylan's side of the van.

He rolled down the window. "Hello, Priscilla."

She asked, "How are you doing?"

"Better. How are you?"

"*Gut*."

He pointed to the side of the house. "Did you fix the railing?"

She nodded. "Arden did that a few months ago. And the stairs."

I climbed into the driver's seat. Gabe had texted me the address of the customer, and I clicked on it.

"You two should come back for dinner," Mammi said. "Rosene has a pot roast in the oven. Treva would like to have a couple of younger people around."

I suppressed a groan.

"I haven't had pot roast in years," Rylan said. "Not since I was a boy."

I shifted into reverse.

"We'd like to have you join us." Mammi took a step backward.

"I need to get Rylan home after the delivery," I said.

"No," he said. "I don't have any reason not to come back for dinner."

"Oh, and Brenna, we need to talk about this weekend. Gabe needs another weekend off."

"Oh, that's right," Rylan said. "It's a drill weekend."

"Pardon?" Mammi cocked her head.

Gabe, who stood on the porch, now had a confused look on his face. I couldn't tell if he could actually hear Rylan.

"Drill. With our—his—Army Reserve unit."

Mammi turned toward Gabe.

I winced. I thought Gabe had told her after he'd told his mom and Conrad and that she was being discreet by not bringing it up with me.

Rylan was unconscionable, and Gabe was ridiculous.

"Well . . ." Mammi drew the word out. "We'll

see the two of you later. It seems Gabe and I have a discussion ahead of us."

As Mammi headed up the steps to the shop and Gabe held the door open for her, Rylan closed his window. Then he began to laugh. "He's such an idiot."

"Well, he's our idiot. Why would you do that to him?"

"Because I know what a coward he is. I couldn't help myself, not when it was obvious he hadn't told her."

As I backed the van out of the space and headed for the road, he added, "And we're definitely coming back for dinner. I wouldn't miss Rosene's pot roast for the world."

The delivery went smoothly. "I paid half yesterday," the woman said, handing me a check. "Priscilla said to pay the other half upon delivery." That sounded like something Mammi would say.

I took the check and tucked it into my pocket. "Thank you." Now I really did need to go back to the farm. I didn't want to be responsible for the check until I worked on Friday. But I was torn about bringing Rylan.

"I really do want Rosene's pot roast for supper," Rylan said, probably noticing my discomfort. "I've been living off frozen stuff. Corn dogs and tater tots."

"That's gross." Not that my protein bars were

gourmet, but I did try to have an apple a day. And a handful of carrots and celery. "Promise me you'll behave?"

"Ouch," he said. "What are you talking about?" He sounded sincere, but I knew that was part of his act too.

"Just be nice," I said. "Please."

He crossed his arms and looked out the window. He made an odd sound a few minutes later. My GPS was taking a different way back, I guessed to bypass traffic. There were farms on either side of us.

I glanced toward Rylan. "You okay?"

"Yep." He stared out the passenger window. "Why do you ask?"

"You made a funny noise."

He shook his head. "No, I didn't."

"What color is the sky?" I asked.

"Today? Or generally?"

"Either."

"Red." He kept staring out the window.

When we arrived at the farmhouse, Treva came across the driveway from the barn, wearing an old coat. Rylan climbed down, and I came around the side of the van.

"Treva," I said. "This is Rylan."

"Hi." She stopped. "I've heard a lot about you."

"None of it good, I'm sure."

Treva tilted her head and tapped her chin. "I'm sure something was good." Then she grinned.

Rosene stepped out onto the back steps. "Rylan. Brenna. Come on in."

I walked with Rylan past the picnic table. It wasn't the same one where the POWs ate, but it was most likely in the same spot. I thought of Clare on the back steps with Arden in her arms and Rosene working in the garden and Martha in the milking room. Mutter in the store. For a moment, it seemed the generations of our family existed side by side.

Rylan started up the stairs slowly, holding onto the railing with his free arm. Treva stepped to my side and gave me a what-is-he-doing-here look.

1945 faded away and only 2018 remained.

"I need to take a check to Mammi," I said. "I'll be right back."

Rosene held the door for Rylan. "We'll eat in a few minutes."

The sun was low in the sky, but there was still plenty of light to make my way along the fence. As I reached the shop, Mammi and Gabe were coming out the front door as all the clocks chimed five times.

"Wait," I called out. "I have the second check for the chairs for you."

"Wunderbar," Mammi said.

I pulled the check from my pocket and handed it to Mammi.

"You two go ahead," she said, turning back inside. "I'll meet you at the house."

As Gabe and I walked around the corner of the store, I said, "Are you staying for supper too?"

"I guess so. Conrad is going to pick me up in about an hour."

"Have you thought about getting your own car?"

He shrugged. "Someday."

"What did Mammi say about you joining the Army Reserve?"

"Nothing."

That didn't sound like Mammi.

"Are you up for a meal with Rylan?"

"Probably not." Gabe zipped his coat. "We all stopped by and saw him last Saturday, and he blamed Marko for Meg's death."

I opened my mouth but then closed it. Then I asked, "Did you ever find out what exactly happened in Afghanistan?"

"No. I still don't know, but it wasn't Marko's fault. I know that."

It seemed to me that a lot could happen in a war zone and not be anyone's fault. Unless it was friendly fire or something like that. And even that could be a miscommunication or a horrendous mistake.

When we reached the house, Dawdi was washing up on the back porch. We took off our coats and boots and padded into the kitchen. The woodstove was stoked, Treva was setting the table, and Rosene was transferring the pot roast onto a serving platter. Rylan sat at the table with a cup of coffee in his hands. He smiled at Gabe. He appeared at peace. Almost happy.

I thought of Ivy saying that everyone's most basic need was to belong. Rylan looked as if he felt he belonged in Rosene's kitchen. She had a gift for making people feel that way.

Maybe the threat of Rylan suing was over. Maybe me bringing him to the farm today hadn't triggered him. Maybe we could move on and put all that behind us.

29

After we finished eating and Rylan and I thanked Rosene, we headed out to the van. Just as I started the engine, Gabe came out the back door, waving at me.

I rolled down my window.

"Can I get a ride? Conrad can't be here for another hour."

"Where to?"

Gabe cleared his throat and then said, "Marko's parents' house."

Rylan, without missing a beat, said, "It's his birthday."

I widened my eyes at Gabe. What was he thinking?

"Yeah. I'm just going for cake. Then Conrad is going to pick me up."

I sighed. "Text me the address."

Rylan rattled it off. "I'll direct you. Turn south."

I liked it when people used cardinal directions instead of left and right. After a few miles, Rylan said, "Turn west."

We continued toward the city of Lancaster. I turned south again, then west, and then north. We were inside the city limits when Rylan said, "Park. The house is directly north of us." It was a stone two-story Georgian style home.

Rylan opened his door. "I'm going to go in and say hello."

My phone dinged. It was Gabe.

You should come in too. I don't think he'll get weird if you're around.

"You're not very sneaky, Gabe," Rylan said. "You need to work on your stealthiness."

Gabe didn't respond. I opened my door as Rylan slid off the seat. "What are you doing?" he asked me.

"I thought I'd go in and say hello too."

He guffawed. "Likely story."

Gabe led the way up to the house and knocked. Rylan stepped forward and rang the doorbell. A few seconds later, the door flew open. Marko had a smile on his face that quickly dissolved. "Hello," he said. "Gabe. Brenna. Rylan." He gave a quick glance inside the house and then gestured toward the entryway. "Come on in. Mama's just about ready to serve the cake. Everyone's in the dining room."

Gabe led the way through the entryway and living room and into the dining room. A middle-aged woman who wore a navy jumper with a white blouse underneath it and a red cardigan said, "Welcome, Gabe!" She spoke with an accent and wore her brown hair in a bun at the nape of her neck, just like me. "Who do you have with you?"

"This is Brenna."

"Aww, Brenna. I've heard of you. I am Marko's mother—Olena." Her face fell for a half second when she saw who was behind me, but then it shifted into a smile, though forced. "And Rylan. How good to see you."

"Hello, Mrs. Kapinos."

Kapinos. Why had I never thought to ask what Marko's last name was? Viktor's too. I knew their fathers were brothers.

Olena said something in Urkainian that I couldn't understand to a man sitting at the end of the table. He stood and shook Gabe's hand and then Rylan's. Then he turned to me. "I'm Marko's papa—Taras." He gestured toward the man next to him. "This is my brother, Ted."

"Nice to meet you, Taras," I said. "And Ted."

Both shook my hand, and Ted said, "My name is really Fedir—Ted is my American nickname."

"Nice to meet you, Fedir," I said and shook his hand again. Everyone laughed.

Viktor stepped forward and gave me a half hug. Then he motioned toward the closest chair and said to Rylan, "Sit down."

"Thank you." Rylan patted the chair next to him and looked at me. I sat down.

"We'll sing to Marko and then I'll cut the cake," Olena said. She motioned for him to come closer and then she started to sing, "*Mnohaya lita.*" Everyone joined in. It wasn't the "Happy

Birthday" tune, nor words. It was a sort of haunting tune as they sang the phrase "mnohaya lita" over and over. I thought it translated into "many years," but I wasn't sure. When they finished, Olena kissed Marko on the cheek and said, "May God bless you this year, my son." Then she began to cut the cake.

I thought of how worried Olena, Taras, and Fedir must have been when Marko and Viktor went off to Afghanistan to serve.

Olena served the first piece. There were layers of nuts—hazelnuts, I thought—and meringue and jam. The frosting appeared to be chocolate buttercream.

"I remember how good this cake is," Rylan said.

"Jah," Olena said. "It's a Kyiv cake. I make it every year for Marko's birthday. And for Viktor's, Taras's, and Fedir's birthdays too." She smiled. "And for my own."

She handed the first piece to me, then pieces to Rylan and Gabe. Then she served her family, giving Marko the next-to-last piece and the very last one to herself.

Marko took the first bite. After he swallowed, he said, "Dyakuyu, Mama."

We all thanked Olena. The cake was delicious.

Rylan ate his quickly and as soon as he finished, he said, "We should go."

I held up my fork with a bite of cake on it. "Show some manners and give me a minute," I said.

Olena gave me a quick smile, but Rylan kept a solemn expression on his face. No wonder he was jealous of Viktor and Marko and their family.

It took me a long time to fall asleep that night, and I awoke feeling unsettled. I had class in two hours, which gave me plenty of time to get ready and take Rylan to get his pickup at the shop, which was just a few blocks from our apartment complex.

Rylan was as silent on the drive as he had been on the way home the night before. After I dropped him off, I decided to go straight to class. I'd have a half hour to get started on my next reading assignment.

But before I could leave, my phone dinged. Ivy.

You have an important-looking letter here.
It's from an attorney in Lancaster.

Rylan pulled his pickup out in front of me and onto the road. Had he gone ahead with the lawsuit?

I texted Ivy.

I'll stop by and get it.

I followed Rylan onto the highway, and a few minutes later, he continued west while I turned left into the apartment complex. When I arrived at our apartment, out of breath, Ivy handed me an envelope. The return address read Collins & Collins, Attorneys at Law. The office was located on Queen Street in Lancaster. I opened it.

Date: March 6, 2018
Re: Deposition
Rylan Sanders vs. Priscilla Zimmerman

Dear Brenna:
This letter is to advise or confirm that your deposition has been scheduled in the above case for the 23rd day of March 2018 at 3:30 in the office of Collins & Collins, attorneys at law.

> *Sincerely,*
> *Michael Collins*
> *Attorney*

I handed the letter to Ivy, who read it quickly.
"What do I do?" I asked.
She met my eyes. "It looks legitimate."
"I'm sure it is."
Ivy glanced back down at the letter. "Has Mammi been notified about a suit?"
"I'm guessing so."
"Do you think Gabe has?"
"I'll text him." I took my phone from the

pocket of my coat and asked if he'd received a letter like mine.

His reply was quick and terse.

No.

I took the letter from Ivy, put it back in the envelope, and put it in my pocket. "I'll stop by the store and talk with Mammi after class."

"It's not a subpoena," Ivy said. "But I don't think you can blow it off."

"I'm not going to," I said. "Do you think Mammi would?"

"Maybe." Ivy frowned. "Make sure she takes it seriously."

When I reached the college, I didn't see Rylan's truck in the handicap space he usually parked in. I sat in the back of the class, halfway hoping Rylan would come in and sit by me so I could ask him what was going on.

But he didn't show up at all.

I tried to concentrate on the lecture, but my mind kept wandering. During the break, I headed out to the common area to fill my water bottle. Rylan, Ami, and Jessica sat at a table.

Rylan waved. "How's it going?"

"Fine," I answered as I continued to the water fountain.

Ami giggled.

As I headed back to the classroom, Rylan

asked, "Anything you want to ask me about?"

"No." I kept walking.

"She's so odd," Jessica whispered loudly as I passed by.

"Shut up," Rylan said, in one of his quick mood shifts.

I kept walking, fighting back tears. And what had my kindness brought? More losses for my family. We all would be better off if I'd refused to give Rylan a ride to class back in October. Including Rylan.

I decided to skip my afternoon class. Before I started for the farm, I went by the pharmacy to pick up my prescription, by the library to drop off books, and then to buy groceries. When I reached the antique store, Mammi was locking the door. "What's going on?" I asked as I climbed out of the van. It was only three o'clock, two hours before closing.

She turned toward me. "Did you get a letter from an attorney?"

"Yes," I answered. "That's why I stopped by. I wondered if you received one too."

"I did."

"Is that why you're closing the store?"

She shrugged. "Business is slow."

"Are you headed to the house?"

She nodded.

"I'll go with you." As we walked, I asked,

"What are you going to do about the deposition summons?"

"Pray about it. You should too."

"Yes, I will." But God would need to use something or someone to answer our prayers. And I doubted they'd simply show up on the porch of the store. We needed to seek help. But I didn't say that to Mammi.

When we reached the house, Dawdi and Treva sat at the kitchen table. Rosene must have been resting. Treva stood. "Did you get a letter from Rylan's attorney too?"

I nodded.

She asked, "How could Rylan eat dinner with us like he did last night, knowing those letters were on the way?"

"That's the way he is," I answered.

Treva asked, "What's going to happen?" It wasn't like her to worry.

"I have no idea."

Mammi sat down at her place at the table with a thud. She looked old and tired.

"Now, now," Dawdi said. "Let's not overreact. We need to continue to do what we've been doing. Brenna, you keep helping Rylan, and if it works for him to come to dinner again, we'll welcome him." He paused a moment and said, "Do you think he needs a better place to live than the apartment complex? Do you think he'd want to stay in our Dawdi house?"

"Stop, Arden," Mammi said. "Next you'll be offering him the store and the farm too."

"No," Dawdi said. "That's not my intent. I just think he's a hurting young man who needs to be around others."

"It will never be enough," I said.

"The Lord would be enough," Dawdi said.

"That's true. . . ." But it was more complicated than that. Some people were emotionally healed after an encounter with the Lord, but not all. Sometimes healing was a long and slow process.

Mammi placed both her hands palm down on the table. "I need you to take this seriously, Arden."

"I am. Rylan needs—"

She cut him off. "We don't have a child to go live with. We have nothing for our old age without the store and farm. Nothing to leave to the girls."

"The farm isn't in jeopardy," Dawdi said.

"It could be. We have no idea what his intentions are."

"God will provide," Dawdi said.

"We can't lose the farm," Treva said, her voice pitching high. I knew how much she loved the land.

"We've lost so much," Mammi said. "I can't bear to think about losing this property too. You're the one who grew up here, whose family has had the land for generations. And yet you don't seem bothered in the least."

My heart began to race. I blurted out, "Mammi, you and Dawdi can live with me if you need to."

"Denki," Dawdi said, as Mammi said, "In that little apartment?"

She hadn't even seen our apartment.

I added, "Or you could go to Oregon and live with Gran."

"This is our home." She glared at me. "Do you understand that?"

In that moment, I understood a lot. Not only was she frantic about possibly losing everything they had, but she also was blaming me.

My heart skipped a beat and then began to race faster. My tongue started to feel fuzzy. Was I going to have a panic attack? I took a stick of gum from my apron pocket and popped it in my mouth. I concentrated on chewing.

"I'm going to go rest," Mammi said.

"Let's go get started on the milking," Dawdi said to Treva. It was a little early, but he most likely wanted to get out of the house.

"Will you stay for dinner?" Treva asked me. "Rosene made soup from the leftover roast. She's going to make biscuits too."

I nodded, afraid to speak.

As they stepped onto the back porch, I took a deep breath through my nose and held it for five seconds. Then I exhaled through my mouth. It was a technique my therapist had taught me. I inhaled again, reminding myself that whatever was going on—whether panic attack or simply increased anxiety—wouldn't last long. I exhaled again.

"Brenna?" Rosene stood in the hallway. "Are you all right?"

I managed to say, "I think so."

She walked toward me. "What's going on?"

I held up my hand and kept breathing. My heart rate had slowed, and my tongue felt normal again.

Rosene sat down next to me. "Are you having a panic attack?"

I shook my head.

"Is this about the letter from the lawyer to Priscilla? Did you get one too?"

"Yes."

"And did Priscilla's anxiety make you anxious?"

I nodded, took another deep breath, and then concentrated on chewing my gum again.

"Did Priscilla tell you what else she received today?"

I shook my head.

Rosene smiled kindly. "I'm not telling you this to make things worse but to explain Priscilla's anxiety."

"What's going on?"

"She was served the personal injury lawsuit."

"Oh." I forced myself to take a couple of deep breaths. "How much is Rylan suing for?"

"Arden said they didn't want to share that information."

"But it's a lot, right?"

"I think so."

I put my head in my hands.

After a while, Rosene said, "We're going to have to leave the lawsuit and all of that in God's hands for now. Would you like to hear more of the story?"

"Yes, please." My heart had stopped racing, and my breathing was nearly normal. "But I have a question first. Are you sure this isn't a story for Treva? She's strong like Martha. And a good farmer. I'm nothing like Martha."

"No," Rosene said. "This is your story. You'll see."

I wrinkled my nose. "What will you do if Rylan sues and wins?"

"It's too early to think that will happen," she answered. "Besides, it's not the first time we've had to worry about losing our property. . . ."

30

Martha

The next morning Zeke, Jeremiah, and Martha were subdued as they did the milking. The family didn't speak much through breakfast. After Vater led them in devotions, he said, "I'm going to call the camp to see if they'll send a new set of PWs on Monday."

Martha doubted they would but didn't say so.

A half hour later, Vater found Martha in the milk room, sterilizing the vat. He said, "I was told we won't be getting any more PWs. We'll have to make do. I'll go change into my work clothes."

"That's not necessary," Martha said. "Jeremiah is here. The three of us can get everything done today. Rest up for later."

At noon, Martha asked Mutter if the *Intelligencer Journal* mentioned the escape. "Jah," she answered. "There was a small article that two PWs walked away from a local farm—it didn't say which one—but they were apprehended soon after."

"That was all?"

"Jah."

"Nothing about Sergeant Schwarz and Dirk?"

Mutter shook her head.

Perhaps they hadn't gone missing. Perhaps they'd shown up at the camp after George and Martha left.

"Have you seen Mr. Richter lately?" Martha asked Mutter.

"He was in the store the day before yesterday," she answered.

"How is he?"

"Fine." Mutter shrugged. "The same as ever."

Vater shot Mutter a questioning look, but she ignored him.

"Jeremiah," Vater said after he led the opening prayer, "how about if I talk with the Lancaster County CO board and see if we can petition to have you come home on a hardship basis, due to my health? I think they'd be sympathetic considering what happened with our PWs. They might only allow it until we can hire someone else, but I think it would be worth a try."

Jeremiah hesitated a moment and then said, "I'm fine with that."

Rosene seemed unusually quiet throughout the meal, while Mutter was chattier than ever, talking about several customers who'd come into the store.

"Could I ask you something?" Martha asked Clare as Mutter, Rosene, Jeremiah, and Zeke headed out the back door after the meal was over. Vater had already gone to his room to rest.

"Jah." Clare sat back down at the table. "What is it?"

Martha told her about her missing clothes. "I thought someone had taken them for Otis and Pavlo, but now I'm wondering if they were for Dirk."

Clare tilted her head. "Do you think I took them?"

"Of course not." Martha lowered her voice. "But what about Mutter? Who exactly is Tom Brown? And why was she really speaking with Dirk those times? I found a note with 'women's clothes, hat, and shoes' written on it. She said she was considering carrying women's clothes in the store—but what if it was a note from Dirk?"

Clare said, "It wasn't. Mutter told me she was thinking about adding clothing."

"But the note wasn't in Mutter's handwriting."

"That's odd." Clare pushed her chair back. "I keep remembering the pro-German, even pro-Nazi statements Mutter made before we entered the war."

"What if she didn't change her mind? Perhaps she's been loyal to her homeland all along."

"Perhaps." As Clare stood, her hand went to the small of her back. "Mutter's always been hard to understand, but I don't think she'd collaborate with a German spy. Nor a German PW. Do you?"

Martha groaned. "I have no idea. I mean, I

wouldn't put it past her. She's longed for Germany her entire life. I never felt she was happy. Once the war started, she seemed resolved to be here. But . . ." Martha's voice trailed off. She felt horrible saying such things out loud about her own mother, but their Mennonite relatives in Germany *had* collaborated with the Nazis—and Mutter had the same cultural background they did.

"Mutter knows what the Nazis did to Rosene. She knows they killed Dorina." Clare's eyes filled with tears. "Surely she wouldn't still believe in any sort of superior goodness in Germany."

"That's true. But why would she be talking with Tom Brown, or whoever he is?"

"She must have a good reason." Clare crossed her arms over her chest, as if comforting herself. "I know she was distant while we were growing up, but she loved us. Loves us, in her own way."

Now tears filled Martha's eyes. "Thank you for saying that." Perhaps, as a mother herself, Clare had insight that Martha didn't.

Later that afternoon, as Jeremiah, Zeke, and Martha started the milking, she wondered if George could help get Jeremiah home on emergency leave.

"I'll be right back," she said to Jeremiah. "I need to make a phone call."

When she arrived at the store, it seemed to be empty. "Mutter?" she called out. "Rosene?"

"Be right there." It was Mutter's voice.

Martha walked past the phone and toward

the back. Rosene was headed toward her, while Mutter huddled in the very back of the store with Tom Brown. Or whatever his name was.

He nodded toward Martha. "I'm giving your mother an update from Agent Lewis." It seemed he really was a G-man. Perhaps he worked for the FBI too.

Mutter turned toward Martha but didn't smile.

"There's been a sighting of a person who may be Sergeant Schwarz in Kentucky in a car that matches Sergeant Schwarz's parents' vehicle," Tom Brown said. "He's most likely headed to Texas, to the Mexican border."

Martha asked, "What about Dirk?"

"He may be hidden in the car. Or on a plane or bus. There's no way to know at this point. All border crossings, airports, and bus stations have been alerted." Tom Brown spoke with confidence. "We'll catch both of them."

Martha envied his confidence. But if anyone could pull off a successful escape, it would be Dirk. She didn't doubt Sergeant Schwarz would be found, but she wasn't as sure about Dirk.

"Who *is* Dirk?" Martha couldn't ignore the irony of asking a man she didn't believe was really named Tom Brown about a German POW who wasn't who he said he was either.

"We're looking into it," he said. "But Andreas is right. Dirk Neumann was killed in northern Africa in 1943. The PW who worked here on

393

your farm isn't Dirk Neumann. Most likely he is an officer who stole the identity of an enlisted man."

"Dirk told Mutter his father is a high-ranking Nazi officer. Would that information be helpful in figuring out his identity?"

Tom Brown glanced at Mutter. "It could be."

"If what he said is true," Mutter said. "I have no way of knowing whether it is or not."

Perhaps Dirk—or whatever his name was—was simply trying to gain Mutter's sympathy. Martha focused entirely on Tom Brown. "Do you think Dirk had help besides from Sergeant Schwarz?"

Tom Brown asked, "And Otis and Pavlo?"

"Yes."

"We're certain others at the camp helped them, both PWs and perhaps other personnel."

"Besides people at the camp, are you concerned about anyone on the outside?"

Tom Brown cocked his head questioningly.

Martha spoke quietly, "Anyone on our farm?"

"We're still investigating that," he answered.

"What about Mr. Richter?"

Tom Brown asked, "What do you know about Mr. Richter?"

"Nothing," Martha said. "Except he lives nearby and may have met with Dirk a few times in the woods. And he seems to be very fond of Mutter."

"Martha!" Mutter's voice was low and harsh.

Tom Brown ignored Mutter and said, "To be honest, Franz Richter is missing at the moment. As is his car."

"Interesting," Martha said.

Mutter simply shook her head.

Martha excused herself and stepped to the counter to place the call to the Red Cross office. It rang and rang, but no one answered. After she returned the receiver to the cradle, Martha shifted her gaze to Mutter, who had a concerned expression on her face as she listened to Tom Brown.

Martha never should have allowed the PWs on the farm. She should have told Vater no. The risk was too great. What would happen if Mutter had assisted the officer posing as Dirk Neumann? What if she'd been in cahoots with Franz Richter too?

That evening, after supper, Martha helped Rosene do the dishes and then told her she was going into town.

"What for?" Rosene asked.

"I want to ask George to help in getting the board to allow Jeremiah to stay." Martha grabbed the car key from the hook by the back door. "If Mutter or Vater ask where I am, tell them I'll be back soon."

After Martha parked outside of the two-story building George lived in, she stood on the sidewalk and looked up, scanning the windows. Most were open. "George!" she called out.

A woman opened a shade and looked out.

"George!" Martha called out again.

A window on the second floor scraped open more. George stuck his head out. "Martha?"

"Do you have time to talk?"

"Yes," he said. "I'll be right down."

They sat on the stoop while Martha told him they couldn't keep the farm running without Jeremiah. "Vater is determined to help, but I'm afraid it will kill him. We won't be getting any more PWs, and the work is only going to get harder. Could that sway the board to giving him leave from the hospital?"

"Perhaps," George said. "Let's walk down to my office, and I'll give the director a call."

When they reached the office, Martha waited in the meeting room while George went into his office. She looked at the world map George had pinned to the wall with a circle around Lancaster and one around Geneva, where the Red Cross headquarters was. Where George would soon be.

When he came out of the office, he said, "I updated the director. He'll bring it up at the meeting Monday evening."

Once they were on the sidewalk and George had locked the door, he asked, "How about a cup of coffee and a piece of pie? There's a diner a couple of blocks away."

Martha hesitated a moment. Were Mutter and Vater worried about her? They didn't need to be. She was safe.

"I'd like that," she said. She wanted to hear more about his upcoming plans to go to Geneva. She was trying not to think about how dull her life would be when he was gone.

On Sunday, Martha and Rosene went to church, but Mutter stayed home with Vater. That afternoon, Martha gave Jeremiah a ride back to the train station without telling him she'd asked for George's help to get him home for good.

Jeremiah thanked her for the ride and then climbed from the car. He walked into the station slowly, not with his usual bounce in his step.

On Monday evening, George came out to the farm. Martha invited him into the house, introduced him to Mutter, Vater, and Rosene, and offered him a cup of coffee and a piece of German chocolate cake. They sat at the kitchen table as they ate the cake, and George said that the CO board hadn't made a decision yet. "Hopefully they'll decide when they meet Thursday morning."

"Thank you for your help," Martha said.

"How is the farming going?"

"Busy."

"I can help you now for a couple of hours, if you tell me what to do."

"Now?" Martha couldn't hide her surprise.

"Yes."

She glanced at his clothes and then at his shoes and gave him a sassy smile.

"I brought work clothes with me. You'll have to give me detailed instructions, but I really would like to help."

"I was going to muck out the horse barn today and never got to it."

He took the last bite of his cake and then said, "Where can I change?"

George did better than Martha thought he would, and when they'd finished the horse barn, they moved on to the dairy barn, which they finished up by lantern light. When George got ready to leave around ten, Martha said, "Thank you. That was a big help."

"I can't help tomorrow or Wednesday, but I'll come back on Thursday. Hopefully I'll have good news then."

"I'll save you a plate from dinner," Martha said, "so you don't have to worry about eating. Then we can get to work."

Martha worked harder the next few days than she ever had in her life. She and Zeke did all the farming by themselves, except when Rosene could pitch in for an hour or two, or when Vater came out at milking time to help feed the cows. But his presence made Martha anxious, and that wasn't helpful.

When George arrived on Thursday at seven, after everyone else had eaten, Martha felt exhausted. But the sight of him cheered her, and she rallied. As he ate the pork schnitzel Clare and Rosene had made for dinner, he told her the board had approved Jeremiah's emergency leave.

"He'll be on the noon train tomorrow," he said.

Martha leaned back in her chair, absolutely relieved. Then she said, "I'm going to tell Clare. I'll be right back." She excused herself and rushed up the back staircase.

Thirty minutes later, as Martha and George spread a mixture of manure and sawdust around the seedlings in the garden, Martha asked if he'd heard any updates on the PWs.

"Pavlo and Otis are still at the Indiantown Gap camp, but Andreas has been moved back to the local one."

"How is Nurse Olson?"

"Feeling optimistic. There's talk in Congress about a War Brides Act to allow the wives and fiancées of US servicemen in Europe and Asia to immigrate. She's hoping if it passes it might apply to German POWs who are engaged to army nurses."

"Why would an act for US servicemen apply to Nurse Olson?"

George gave Martha a puzzled look.

Martha stated, "She's a woman and a nurse."

George smiled. "She's a US Army nurse."

Martha leaned against the handle of her shovel. "But she wears that white dress all the time. And nurse's cap."

"That's the US Army nurse uniform. She's a lieutenant."

Martha scooped another shovelful of fertilizer. "I had no idea."

"I'm sorry," George said. "I should have explained that."

Martha grimaced. "I'm sure the army frowns on falling in love with the enemy."

"They do," George said. "But it seems Andreas loves her too—at least I certainly hope so. I'll write a letter in support of Andreas being allowed to return to the US, as will others who know both of them at the camp."

Martha shoveled more manure from the wheelbarrow in between the rows of tomato plants. "Any more sightings of Sergeant Schwarz? Any of Dirk?"

"No." George continued to spread the manure with his hoe. "They seem to have completely disappeared."

Martha glanced toward the house. "What about my missing clothes?"

"Your clothes haven't turned up, and even if they had, we don't know what happened." He kept his voice low. "I'm sure there's more to the story than what we know."

Martha didn't say so, but she doubted it. It

appeared Mutter had aided the enemy. After George left at ten and Martha set her alarm for four, she fell into bed in deep despair.

She wouldn't be going anywhere. With Jeremiah home, they might be able to keep the dairy running, harvest the crops, and pay the bills. With Martha gone, they'd never make it. And if Mutter was arrested, Rosene would have to run the store. Martha would probably be working both the farm and helping Clare in the kitchen, especially as her pregnancy advanced, and then even more when she had the baby.

The next day at noon, after picking up a grateful Jeremiah at the train station, Martha drove straight to the stationery story to pick up the printed photos. Jeremiah waited to open the envelope until they were in the car. He flipped through the photos one by one. Then he handed the stack to Martha.

One of the photos was of an emaciated man wearing only underwear. Another was of a woman half-dressed and on a bare mattress covered with feces. Another was of a small person, who looked like a child, curled in a fetal position on the floor. The next one was of a large room with a concrete floor with hundreds of men sitting against the walls or standing, all barely clothed. The next one showed a room of beds with men shackled to the frames. Martha continued through the stack, fighting nausea.

"We've had hundreds of people die—suicides, accidents, medication errors, attacks by other patients," Jeremiah said. "This can't be tolerated. People can't be treated like this. Not anywhere in the world."

Martha handed the photos back to Jeremiah, and he put them in the envelope. "I'll send them to magazines and newspapers with letters about what I've witnessed. A Quaker man also took photos, and he'll send them out too," he said. "God willing, something will be done. And someday I hope I can have a part in helping to create a better system."

31

Brenna

When I left the farm after supper, I couldn't stop thinking about the German officer who had assumed the identity of Dirk Neumann. Martha seemed to think her mother, my great-great-grandmother, had assisted him. But why would she do that? Sure, she was born and raised in Germany, but why would she help a Nazi? What good would that do her or anyone she loved?

I thought of Rosene and how, in just a few years, she'd assimilated into life in the US and seemed to have the utmost loyalty to both her new family and her new country. Perhaps because Mutter treasured her childhood in Germany, she couldn't accept, as Rosene could, how far Germany had fallen because of Hitler and his regime.

When I reached the apartment complex, I parked and then went down the path. As I turned up the steps, I heard music coming from Rylan's apartment. He must have had the kitchen window cracked. I breathed in deeply. Was that Marko's mushroom soup I smelled? I kept going. I didn't want to see Rylan—not tonight. Not after Mammi had been served his lawsuit.

When I reached my apartment, I turned on the living room light and kitchen light. I didn't expect Ivy for a couple more hours. I left the lights on and went straight to my room, dropping my backpack on the floor by my desk. I sat down and stared at my desktop, wishing Johann would call. It was too late for me to call him. Or was it?

I placed the call. It buzzed a few times, and then he picked up.

"Brenna," he said as his face appeared. "How are you?"

"Not good."

"What's wrong?"

I poured out the story about the deposition notice. "It's in two weeks," I said.

"I'm sorry."

"I'm afraid Mammi will lose the store and it'll be my fault."

"I doubt she'll lose her store, and even if she did, it wouldn't be your fault."

I knew that in my head but not in my heart. "I still don't know what happened in Afghanistan, other than that Rylan seems to blame Marko for Meg's death. Do you think knowing what happened would help me understand Rylan more? Perhaps his motivation in suing Mammi?"

"Have you asked Marko what happened?"

"No. It feels intrusive to bring it up."

"Text him," Johann said. "He'll let you know if he doesn't want to talk about it."

"Speaking of Marko . . ." I told him about Marko's birthday. "They sang a song—'Mnohaya Lita' instead of 'Happy Birthday.'"

He smiled. "Lots of people here sing 'Happy Birthday' with Ukrainian words but the American tune. But 'Mnohaya Lita' is more traditional."

"Does it translate to 'many years'?"

"Sort of," he said. "That's the translation, but it means 'many more years,' and hopefully happy ones. It's a blessing. Besides being a birthday song, it's also used like your 'He's a Jolly Good Fellow.'"

"Interesting," I said. "The tune is a little haunting."

"Jah," he said. "It sort of is. Especially compared to the American 'Happy Birthday' tune."

His cell phone rang. "I've got a call," he said. "I need to go."

"Thank you for talking with me."

"Anytime," he said.

After we ended the call, I took out my phone and found Marko in my contacts.

> Could I speak with you about what happened in Afghanistan and what's going on with Rylan now? I'm hoping the information will help me figure out what to do about his pending lawsuit against my grandmother.

He texted back.

I'm leaving Rylan's apartment in a few minutes. Could I stop by your place?

Only if you can without Rylan knowing where you're going.

I think I can do that.

Okay.

I slipped my phone into my skirt pocket. My heart started to race again. I took a deep breath through my nose and then blew it out through my mouth. Ten minutes later, there was a knock on my door.

When I opened it, Marko stood there with his stocking cap in one hand and a box in the other.

"Come in," I said. "Let's sit at the table." I didn't have anything to offer him but water.

He held up the box. "I have leftover banana bread."

I gave him a questioning look. "Ukrainian banana bread?"

He laughed. "No. American banana bread."

I grabbed two plates, napkins, and forks and put them on the table. Then I filled two glasses with water. We sat down across from each other.

"What happened in Afghanistan?" I asked.

"What?" Marko smiled. "No small talk?"

"I don't do small talk."

"I know." He took a bite of banana bread. After he swallowed it, he grew serious. "I think you know that Meg was killed. She and Rylan had been dating on and off for a couple of years. He was crazy about her and hoped they'd get married. I think Rylan was really immature when he and Meg first met—thus the on and off—but he'd been figuring things out and it seemed they were getting serious."

He took another bite and then continued. "Rylan was a good soldier—the best out of all of us. He was fearless. Crazy, at times. Meg was a medic in our platoon, and sometimes she was assigned to our squad." He took another bite of banana bread. And then another. "But Rylan's biggest fault was he didn't trust other people, especially anyone outside of our inner circle. On the day Meg was killed, our translator warned Rylan not to go into the valley to train Afghan soldiers, but Rylan thought he was secretly working for the Taliban and was trying to sabotage our efforts."

Marko sighed. "Obviously the translator wasn't. As we were training the Afghan soldiers, Rylan was hit by a sniper, and Meg rushed to offer aid. Then she was hit. I thought it was too late for Meg, so I rushed forward and put a tourniquet on Rylan's leg—and then took a bullet in the arm. Viktor caught sight of the sniper and took him out. Viktor carried Meg's body out while I dragged Rylan to our Humvee. Rylan never took responsibility for leading us into the valley that day. In fact, he doesn't remember it, and we never brought it up."

He looked down at the table as he said, "However, he did blame me for attending to him instead of Meg. I thought she was dead, but she was still alive. But she'd lost too much blood and died a few hours later at the field hospital. We thought Rylan was going to bleed to death and that we were losing him too, but miraculously they saved him."

Marko paused for a long moment and then said, "After Meg was killed and Rylan lost his leg, it knocked us all flat. He was taken to Germany and then Walter Reed. We only had five weeks left in our tour, so we came home while he was still in the hospital. Viktor and I decided to never tell him he'd gone against the advice of our translator, if he didn't remember it. We also made a pact to take care of Rylan—he's our brother. I had given up, but your pep talk inspired me to give it another try." Marko shrugged. "He seemed better than he has been."

"That's good to hear." I wouldn't tell him about my encounters with Rylan over the last two days. "What was Meg's last name?"

"Evers. Margaret Evers. But everyone called her Meg. Her parents have a farm here. They were apprehensive about Rylan, but Meg slowly won them over. Whenever Rylan got snarky or mean, she'd tell him to knock it off and he would. No one else could make him listen like she could. You've come the closest."

"Do you think in some corner of his mind Rylan blames himself for Meg's death?"

"No," Marko said. "I don't know what Rylan thinks exactly, but he doesn't think he's at fault for any of it. He only remembers that I saved him, not Meg. When we talked to the doctor at Walter Reed, he said that's pretty common with a traumatic event, especially with someone as near death as Rylan was." Marko ran his hand through his hair. "But you know what's really sad?"

"What?"

"I think the reason he had such a hard time trusting anyone was because of how untrust-worthy his family is."

"Wow." His trauma kept on giving—and hurting others. I waited a long moment and then said, "Does Rylan need money?"

"Who doesn't need money?" Marko smiled sadly. "He's getting disability from the army, but he's also scrambling to figure out a career he can do." Marko rubbed the back of his neck and then said, "What he really needs is some kind of community. He's so scrappy, probably because he had to be to survive, but he's always been wounded, long before that sniper blew his leg off. Once anyone gets too close to him, he pushes them away."

"What do you mean?"

"Well, it's different because he didn't know your family until he broke his leg, but I think with both of our families, he wanted to belong, but then once he saw the closeness, he pushed us away."

"Intending to sue my grandmother has definitely been a downer for us, but we've tried to be kind to him, regardless," I said. "How did he push your family away?"

"After a couple of months of us including him in all our family events, he started saying that we didn't really belong in the US. That our food smelled funny and my parents' English wasn't good enough. Things like that. He'd say we just felt sorry for him or that we were only being nice because that's what our religion told us to do."

"What's your religion?"

"Slavic Apostolic."

"Oh. I don't know anything about that."

"My parents were interested in your religion and the way you dress. They've noticed the Amish and Mennonites around here. They were relieved to meet a young woman as sincere as you are."

"Your parents and your uncle seem like good people. All of you belong here." I exhaled and then said, "Rylan only said those things about your family in hopes it would make him feel better about himself."

"I know." Marko frowned. "It makes me sad he feels that way. And even sadder that he pushes the people away who want to help him."

"Me too."

After Marko left, I Googled *Margaret Evers*. An article popped up in the local paper. She was killed October 18, 2012—the five-year anniversary of her death was the day Rylan broke his leg. I took a raggedy breath. We never know what another person is grieving on any given day.

The article said her platoon was on a mission in Khost Province and that two others were injured at the same time. At the end of the article, it said she was survived by her parents, Robert and Margaret Evers of Quarryville, PA.

A second article in the local paper that ran December 30 also mentioned Meg, although it was about the US and NATO formally ending their combat mission in Afghanistan on December 28, 2014, but retaining a reduced force of approximately thirteen thousand troops to continue to support and train Afghan troops.

I Googled *Margaret Evers, Lancaster County, Pennsylvania*. A Margaret and Robert Evers popped up with an address outside of Quarryville. It was south of town—near where Rylan and I had delivered the chairs.

The next day, Rylan was in class, sitting by Ami and Jessica. I wondered if they would be the

411

next group of people he'd look to for belonging, only to eventually push them away too.

After class, I headed south toward the Everses' farm. It was a bright day. Several Amishmen were plowing garden spots and others were working in the fields. Lambs chased one another in pastures and clothes hung on lines, drying in the warming March sun.

I neared the address I'd found for the Everses. It *was* the same farm that Rylan had been staring at. I slowed, not sure if I should pull into the driveway and then knock on the door or not. How would I feel if someone tracked me down to ask me questions about my deceased loved one? I wouldn't want them to.

Would I, though, if it might help someone else?

I pulled into their driveway. There was a warehouse-type building with a sign over the door. *Memories Forevers—Frames, Albums, and Shadow Boxes*. I smiled at the play on their last name, Evers.

I climbed down from the van and, seeing the Open sign on the front window, decided to go to the shop.

A man stood at the counter. Behind him on a desk was a photograph of a young woman in uniform beside a flag in a frame. Next to it was a shadow box with a Purple Heart. "May I help you?" he asked.

"Are you Robert Evers?"

He nodded.

"Was your daughter Meg?"

He lowered his voice. "What is this about?"

"I'm an acquaintance of Rylan Sanders," I said. "I wondered if I could ask you some questions."

"Is he in trouble?"

"He broke his right leg in October at Amish Antiques, a store my grandmother owns, and he had a suicide attempt in December."

Robert grimaced. Perhaps I'd been too blunt. Worse, I was sharing confidential medical information. I hoped Rylan would forgive me.

"I'm concerned about him." I took a deep breath and slowed my breathing. "So are his army friends—Marko and Viktor."

"Marko and Viktor." He smiled a little. "How are they?"

"Good," I said.

"Has Rylan been doing anything constructive, in spite of his setbacks?"

I didn't feel I should explain he got a paralegal degree and was now taking computer classes. "He's enrolled at the community college."

"That's good to hear." He crossed his arms. "I'm sorry about his troubles, but I'm not sure how I can help. In fact, I'm sure I can't."

"I'm not here to ask you to." I hesitated and then said, "I'm hoping for more information is all, about what happened after Rylan came home. Did you have any contact with him?"

"What does it matter?"

I shrugged. "Maybe it doesn't," I said. "He just seems really lost. I'm hoping there's something that can help him. Some piece of information. Some person. Something."

"We decided not to see him. What happened was too painful. . . ." He turned his head for a moment, toward a door behind the counter. "By the time Marko and Viktor came to see us, Meg had been buried for six weeks. They said Rylan would be home soon from Walter Reed. . . ." His voice trailed off. "But we were mourning so deeply, we didn't . . ."

The door opened a crack, and a woman's voice called out, "Robert, who is it?"

"A friend of Rylan's."

"What does she want?"

"She just has a few questions."

The woman sounded angry. "We don't want to talk about any of that." The door closed, firmly.

"It's been hard on my wife," Robert said.

"I'm sorry." I met his gaze. "It's been hard on both of you."

"Yes," he said. "After her four years in the army ended, Meg was going to be done with all of it. We were so relieved. Then Rylan followed her here and joined the Reserves and she did the same. That broke our hearts. Then—well, you can imagine." He turned toward the door and then turned back to me. "Don't tell Rylan you saw us, please."

"I won't."

He exhaled slowly. "What did you say your name is?"

"Brenna. Brenna Zimmerman."

"And you're Mennonite?"

"Yes."

"Well, I'm glad Rylan has friends. His army buddies. You. He needs people. I wish we could help him. . . ."

I stared at Meg's photo. She wore an army beret, and her light brown hair was pulled back from her face. She had a bold smile and dark brown eyes. She looked like someone who would stand up to Rylan.

And Viktor was right. She did look a little like me.

I had my semi-monthly appointment with my therapist the day before the deposition. I took the letter from the attorney and showed it to her.

After she read it, she asked, "Do you have counsel?"

Rylan had used the same term. "What exactly is that?"

"Your own attorney."

"I need an attorney?"

"It would be good to have someone advise you. Perhaps your grandmother's attorney could go with you."

"She doesn't have an attorney either, even

though she's already been served. And the deposition is tomorrow."

"Hmmm," she said. "This is my advice. Just answer the questions. Don't give any more information than you're asked for. Be honest about what you saw but don't speculate. You were a witness, but that doesn't mean you have the whole story."

"Thank you," I said. "That helps."

"Have you talked with Rylan since you got the deposition summons?"

"No—well, just in passing but not about the summons." I told her about going by Meg's parents' place and watched as her face stayed neutral. I wasn't sure how she managed to do that all the time. "I probably shouldn't have done it."

"What were you hoping to gain by seeing them?"

"Insight," I answered. "I hoped it could help me understand Rylan."

"Did it?"

Tears stung my eyes. "No. Except that he almost had the family he longed for, but he lost that too when he lost Meg."

The next day, I stopped by the store and picked up Mammi and drove to the attorney's office downtown. On the way I told her the advice my therapist gave me about answering the attorney's questions. "I Googled *depositions in Pennsylvania,*" I said. "The attorney will be in the room along with a court reporter. We won't be allowed to listen to each other, and the attorney can't question us for more than four hours."

"Goodness," Mammi said. "This might last eight hours?"

"No," I said. "It won't last that long. Not that much happened."

Mammi was questioned first while I sat in the waiting room, reading my assigned chapters for class. When Mammi came out after twenty minutes with a stoic expression on her face, the attorney, Mr. Collins, called me in.

He introduced me to the woman sitting at an odd machine—it looked like a typewriter but with fewer keys and a screen—and said she was a court reporter who would document our conversation and turn it into an accurate transcript of the deposition.

The court reporter stood and said she would administer the oath. She asked if I promised to "tell the truth, the whole truth, and nothing but the truth, so help me God."

I said, "I do."

The questions began with how I knew Rylan and what interaction I had with him the day of the accident. I explained that he was in my class, and I knew who he was but hadn't spoken to him until he asked me for a ride that morning. Mr. Collins asked me to explain what happened. When I got to the part where we arrived at the store, the attorney asked me to describe the building. I said it was built in the early 1900s.

"Was there a railing on the landing of the staircase?"

"Yes," I answered.

"Is there a new railing on it now?"

"Yes."

"When was the new railing installed and by whom?"

"My Dawdi—grandfather—installed it last winter. In December, I think. He'd ordered the lumber before Rylan fell."

"So your grandfather believed the landing was unsafe?"

"Yes," I replied. "That's why there was a rope and a sign blocking off the staircase."

"What happened to the rope and sign?"

"The rope had been untied. I didn't see the sign."

"When did your grandparents realize the landing wasn't safe?"

"I don't know," I answered. "That staircase has been roped off for years, and the sign has been up for years too. The area has never been open to the public. Customers have no business going up the staircase. No one does. I've never even been up the staircase." I felt as if I was saying too much.

"I'll ask again—Did your grandfather know the railing was unsafe?"

I wasn't sure how to answer the question. "I don't think I should speak for Dawdi," I said.

"Tell us about the accident."

I explained that I was in the store with Mammi and Gabe Johnson. I opened the door and saw that Rylan was no longer in my van. I went around the side of the store looking for him and then saw him up on the landing. Then he turned and leaned against the railing, which gave way, and he fell to the ground.

"Would a proper railing have prevented Rylan from falling and breaking his leg?"

"I don't know."

"What is your guess?"

"I don't want to speculate," I answered.

"So, to clarify, the building is over a hundred years old. Your grandfather had ordered new lumber to put up a new railing. There had been a sign to warn people not to go up the staircase, but it wasn't there that day. After Rylan fell and broke his leg, your grandfather installed a new railing? Is that correct?"

None of it sounded good. I nodded.

The attorney said, rather curtly, "Please respond verbally."

"Yes." The court recorder tapped away on the keys on her funky machine.

He asked me to continue with what happened next. I explained that Rylan screamed and then said he broke his leg, and Gabe called 9-1-1.

"Did Rylan seem upset earlier that day? Unsettled in any way?"

"I'd only just met him," I said. "I had no information to make such an assessment. But I've learned since then that it was the anniversary of the death of his girlfriend in Afghanistan and the anniversary of the attack that cost him his leg."

"And you feel that's relevant to the accident that caused him to badly break his remaining leg?"

I stopped myself from saying that it could be coincidental, or it could be relevant. "I don't know."

"What has your relationship been with Rylan since the accident?"

I explained that I visited him in the hospital, gave him rides to class, and helped him with his coursework.

"What was your motivation in doing all of that?"

"To be a good neighbor."

"And to persuade him not to sue your grandmother?"

"No," I said.

"Did anyone encourage you to stay involved in Rylan's life?"

"My family did—my grandparents and older sister. They said it was the right thing to do."

He paused for a long moment and then said, "Because they thought it would keep Rylan from suing?"

When I didn't answer right away, he said, "Remember you're under oath."

"Well, all of us hoped Rylan wouldn't sue, but

we would have done the same thing whether he planned to sue or not. When I visited him in the hospital and helped around his apartment after he was discharged, he'd already threatened to sue, and I still continued to help him. It didn't enter my head that he might sue when the accident first happened."

"Why not?"

"Because he went up a roped-off staircase."

"Do you have evidence he saw it was roped off?"

"No. But my aunt saw it was roped off earlier that day."

"Would that be your great-great-aunt?"

"Yes," I answered.

"Who's ninety-one?"

My face grew warm. "Yes."

"Do you blame Rylan for the accident?"

"No," I said. "It was an accident."

"What is your relationship with Rylan now?"

"I haven't seen him for a few weeks."

"Since you received the summons for this deposition?"

"Yes."

"Thank you," he said. "That's all."

I sat, stunned. The end of the questioning seemed so abrupt. Did he assume I hadn't had contact with Rylan because of the summons? Wait. Wasn't that actually why I hadn't had contact with him?

"Thank you," I said, and then grimaced. Why was I thanking him? I exited the room. As I walked down the hall, I realized I hadn't said that I told Rylan to stay in the van the day of the accident and he said he would. Was that relevant? It might be. I headed back to the room. The door was closed. I knocked and opened it. "I forgot to say some—"

"I said that was all," the attorney said. "Please leave the premises."

"I told Rylan to stay in the van that day." My voice rose a little in volume. "And he said he—"

"That's all, Miss Zimmerman. Thank you."

32

I felt sick to my stomach as Mammi and I walked to the van and then as I navigated my way out of downtown. Once I reached the highway, Mammi said, "I thought my part went well. I'm not worried. How did yours go?"

"I'm not sure," I said. But I was. It went horribly. I'd supported Rylan's case to sue Mammi, and it seemed he really did have a reason to sue. Dawdi and Mammi knew the railing needed to be replaced. A rope and a sign—that was missing—wasn't enough to prevent someone from going up the staircase.

We rode in silence.

When I pulled up by the farmhouse, Mammi asked, "Are you going to come in?"

I took a stick of gum from my stash in the console. "I'm not feeling very well."

"Then all the more reason to come in. You should be with us."

I popped the gum in my mouth and began to chew. *Us.*

I was going to be responsible for losing what kept *Us* all together. The store. Maybe the farm. Maybe the house. Where would we gather? Where would we *be?*

I exhaled, remembering that Johann said even if

Mammi lost the suit, my grandparents most likely wouldn't lose the farm. But what did he know about American law? Other countries didn't seem to have as many lawsuits as the US—or as big of ones. "I'll come in for a few minutes," I said.

Dawdi met us at the door. "How did it go?"

"Wunderbar," Mammi said, as I said, "Horrible."

Rosene was behind him. "Come sit down."

I followed Mammi into the kitchen. Treva stood at the sink, peeling carrots. I remembered the guilt I felt when I thought I'd killed our parents. I couldn't believe my sisters still loved me, still cared for me. It was never an issue of whether they forgave me or not. I could tell they did by how they treated me.

Would they be so gracious when it came to the store and maybe the farm? Impoverishing Mammi and Dawdi and Rosene?

"Treva made chocolate chip cookies," Rosene said. "And I just made a pot of coffee."

I sat down at my usual place and looked around the kitchen.

Treva finished up the carrots and then helped Rosene serve the coffee and cookies. Once they sat down, Mammi told us about her deposition. The attorney asked her about the railing too, and she said Rylan had no business going up the steps. That was all she said.

I shrank inside. Why couldn't I have answered the question that way?

As she relayed more of her questions and answers, shame filled me. I could have done so much better.

"Brenna," Treva said. "Tell us about your questions and answers."

"It was pretty much the same," I said.

Everyone waited for me to say more. Finally, when I didn't, Dawdi said, "I'd like to speak with Rylan in person."

"He's not going to change his mind," I said.

"I don't want him to change his mind," Dawdi said. "I want him to know we care about him. I want to see what he needs."

I groaned. "Besides a lot of money?"

Dawdi ignored what I said. "In fact"—Dawdi was looking at me—"would you give me a ride over to his place now?"

As I stared at Dawdi, I first thought of Dad and his sense of justice and how determined he was to help others. Grief was an expression of love, and so was justice. So was mercy. Then I thought of my great-grandfather Jeremiah and his desire to love others and seek care and justice for them. For the first time, I was aware of the line from Jeremiah to Dawdi to Dad. My great-grandfather, grandfather, and father. All good men. All who shaped me, even though I hadn't known Dawdi most of my life and would never know Jeremiah, except through Rosene's stories.

I didn't think Dawdi speaking with Rylan was a good idea, but what did I know? Maybe Dawdi talking with Rylan was worth a try.

I took one last drink of my coffee and grabbed another cookie. "Let's go."

I led Dawdi down the pathway to Rylan's apartment and then stepped aside so he could knock on the door.

Before he did, he asked, "Will you come in with me?"

"I'd rather not," I answered. "But I will if you want me to."

"I would." He knocked.

Rylan's cane clicked against the entryway tiles. He opened the door and with surprise in his voice said, "Arden? What are you doing here?" He looked past Dawdi to me and broke out in a snarky smile. "I thought maybe Brenna would stop by today. I mean, I thought it could go either way. She's"—yes, he was talking as if I weren't there—"been avoiding me lately, but I guessed my attorney would shake her up."

I'd forgotten how fast he could talk.

"And maybe she'd stop by and try to negotiate. But here you are, Arden. Here both of you are, I assume, wanting to negotiate."

"No," Dawdi said. "We don't want to negotiate. I wanted to see how you're doing and what you need."

"Besides needing to win the lawsuit?"

"In spite of the lawsuit, whether you win or not," Dawdi said.

"Sounds enticing." Rylan stepped backward. "Come on in."

I followed Dawdi. Surprisingly, Rylan motioned for Dawdi to sit in the recliner. He grabbed one of the folding chairs and dragged it to the living room. I grabbed another and followed him.

Dawdi asked, "Has the VA paid for your medical expenses?"

Rylan's face reddened a little as he said, "That hasn't been settled yet."

"How about your living situation? Do you need something less expensive?"

Rylan wrinkled his nose. "I'm not looking for a new place to live."

"Do you need a place with more people around?"

Rylan grinned. "Oh, I get it. Are you proposing I move out to the farm?"

"You spoke favorably of your time on your grandparents' farm."

I winced. His grandparents' fabricated farm.

"I thought you might like to live on the farm. We have a little house you could live in. You could eat meals with us. Help with the milking, if you like. That sort of thing."

My face grew warm. Why would Rylan want to live on the farm?

Rylan asked, "Are you offering this to me out of pity?"

"No," Dawdi said.

"Are you offering me a place to live in hopes of me dropping the lawsuit, rather than have me win the suit and your farm?"

"You aren't suing for the farm," Dawdi said. "You're suing for a set amount of money. And the accident happened at the store. None of this has to do with the farm."

"And yet"—Rylan had that smug expression on his face that I despised—"you'll have to sell your farm to pay the settlement. So, technically, I could then buy the farm."

I balled my hands into fists as I battled my anger toward Rylan. He was snarkier than ever.

Dawdi remained calm. "Why would you want to buy the farm?"

He shrugged.

Dawdi exhaled and wrapped both hands around one knee, lifting it a little as he spoke. "Everyone needs a family, no matter how it's arranged. That's God's plan for us as humans—to live among people who accept and love us. We can trust Him to meet our needs."

Rylan stood and stepped toward the sliding glass door. "You sound like my grandmother. When my father told me right before he left that he was ashamed of me, even though I was only seven, she said to trust God. When I dropped out of high school and got my GED to work to help my mom pay the rent, she said to trust God. When I joined the army, hoping my father would finally have a reason to be proud of me, she said to trust God. When my mom remarried and moved to Maine and stopped answering my phone calls, she said to trust God. When my father died without ever reconciling with me, she said to trust God."

Rylan paced back and forth through the living room, his cane thumping against the floor through the carpet. "Then Grandma died, and I had no one to remind me. But I still trusted God. I *tried* to trust God. Until I realized I never really had trusted Him."

He paced through the little dining room and into the entryway. His voice rose in volume. "I'd trusted that Grandma was praying for me, and maybe God was listening." He paced back toward the living room. "Then, when Meg died, I knew no one was praying for me, and even if someone was, God wasn't listening." He was back at the patio door.

My heart began to race, and I dug in my pocket for a pack of gum. There wasn't one.

The stray cat appeared at the patio door and looked up at Rylan and meowed. He turned his back on her, shuffled back to his chair, and sat down.

I stood and slid the door open. The cat sauntered

in and then jumped up on Rylan's lap. I expected him to push her away but instead he cradled her in his arms.

Dawdi stood. "I'm sorry for your losses, son. I know we can't be your family. We can't replace what you've lost—but we'd like to be your friends."

"Even if I sue your wife?"

He nodded. "Even if you sue my wife." He extended his hand. I thought of the verse: *And as ye would that men should do to you, do ye also to them likewise.*

Rylan held the cat with his left hand and shook Dawdi's hand with his right but didn't say anything.

Dawdi turned toward the door, and Rylan went back to hugging the cat as he shifted his gaze to me. He gave me a slight nod and then lowered his head until his chin rested between the cat's ears.

I drove Dawdi back to the farm and then returned to the apartment complex.

As I turned toward the stairs, I looked over my shoulder at Rylan's apartment. The kitchen window was closed, but the light was on. I couldn't tell if anyone was inside or not.

When I reached the apartment, it was just after four, which meant it was eleven p.m. in Ukraine. Not that late for Johann. He hadn't called for several days. I decided to call him.

He answered immediately. "Brenna," he said. "I was just going to see if you were home."

"I am."

"How did the questioning go?"

He'd remembered. I gave him the details and then told him about Dawdi wanting a ride to Rylan's and our conversation. "It didn't make a difference with Rylan, but it probably made Dawdi feel better to at least try."

"Sounds like your grandfather is a good man."

I agreed. "Even though I'm still annoyed with Rylan, I'm worried about him again. But on the other hand, I'm going to talk with Gran about getting money from our account to hire a lawyer," I said. "The attorney today twisted things around, just like Rylan does. I need to consult with a lawyer and see what we can do."

"That's a good idea," Johann said.

"But I'm also going to try one more time to talk rationally with Rylan."

"Are you sure? It might not be possible."

"I feel as if I should try."

"Fair enough," Johann said. "I have a question for you."

"What's that?"

"What if I came for your graduation and then you flew back with me to Ukraine and spent the summer here?" he asked. "You can stay in our home with Mama, and I can stay with a neighbor, if that would make your grandparents more likely to approve of the trip."

I took a piece of gum from the pack on my desk and unwrapped it. Then I took a deep breath. "If I'm going to go to Ukraine, I think I need to be comfortable traveling by myself."

His face grew serious. "I understand."

"But I would love for you to meet Dawdi and Mammi. And see Rosene, Ivy, Treva, and Conrad again. And Gabe too. And me. Would you still come for my graduation?"

"Of course." He smiled. "I'd love that. I'll book a flight tonight."

33

On Monday, I called to get an appointment with my therapist. She had an opening on Tuesday, so I skipped class. The first topic was to find out how to get an attorney. It might have seemed like an odd question at an Anabaptist facility, but I knew from our conversation the week before that she felt I needed one.

My therapist gave me some ideas on finding one using Google and reading reviews. But then she wrote a name and number on a piece of paper and handed it to me. "This is an attorney I know," she said.

"Denki." I read the information. *Nat Byers* and then a local number. I folded the paper and enclosed it in my fist.

After that, we talked about Johann coming for graduation and me possibly traveling to Ukraine. She asked me lots of questions. I had few answers.

After my appointment, as soon as I reached the van, I called the number of the attorney on the piece of paper and got voicemail. I left a message.

As I drove home, my phone rang. I quickly pulled into the parking lot of a hotel off the highway and answered the call.

"Hi, Brenna. It's Nat Byers," a voice said—a

female voice. "I can see you tomorrow morning at eleven if that works for you."

I'd have to miss class again. "That works," I said.

She rattled off the address. "Hold on a second." I put her on speaker and put the address in my notes app. "I've got it," I said. "I'll see you tomorrow."

Once I reached the apartment, I retreated to my room and started Googling building codes in Pennsylvania. After a few minutes, I came across a government building code site. I couldn't find anything governing the restrictions of access to certain areas of a business, but I did find a site about property with the statement, *You do not have the right to enter private property without the owner's permission.*

I sat back in my chair. What had happened to the *Private! Do Not Enter* sign? It seemed that if the rope and sign were up, Rylan ascended the staircase illegally. If the sign and rope were down when he arrived, then perhaps he did have a case.

I decided to go to the store and do another thorough search for the sign, even though Gabe had looked the day of the accident and hadn't found it. It would be good to look one more time before I met with Nat Byers.

When I reached the store, Gabe was carrying a pie safe out to a customer's car. He gave me a quick smile and said, "There's someone in the store looking for you."

I gave him a questioning look, but he just shrugged.

As I headed up the stairs, Robert Evers opened the door and held it.

A middle-aged woman with short gray hair stepped through. "Oh, there you are. I'm Margaret Evers. I saw you when you stopped by—although I'm not sure you saw me."

"Nice to meet you," I said.

Mammi followed her out, and then Robert Evers closed the door.

Margaret said, "Meg really loved this shop. She stopped by often."

"Really?" I glanced at Mammi. She shrugged.

Margaret nodded. "Meg liked quilts. And clocks. Anything old, really." That made Meg even more interesting to me.

"We've thought about your visit," Robert said. "And we want to get in touch with Rylan."

I hesitated and then said, "Let me check with him."

"Sure," he said. "I'll give you my phone number in case he lost it. It seems he has a new phone, because the number I had for him from five years ago isn't working."

After I put Robert's phone number in my contacts, I said, "It's good to see you both."

Margaret said, "I wasn't very hospitable when you stopped by. I'm sorry about that."

"No need to apologize," I said. "I would have

responded the same way. I blindsided you."

"I think it was what we needed," Robert said. "Would you tell Rylan we'd like to see him? Have him over for dinner. Spend some time with him. That sort of thing."

"Yes," I said. "I'll tell him that. And if he chooses not to contact you, I'll let you know that."

After Robert and Margaret headed to their car, Mammi asked, "What was that all about?"

I explained who they were.

A few minutes later, I was down on my knees under the staircase, searching for the sign and wondering if Meg had any social media accounts that were still up. Would that be creepy for me to look? I wasn't sure.

I found a rusty soda can and an old newspaper under the stairs but no sign. I climbed out from underneath and then stepped over the rope—and the new sign. This one read, *Private Property! Do Not Enter Under Any Circumstance. No Trespassing!* Dawdi wrote it in block letters and then laminated the sign.

I climbed the staircase and stopped on the landing, tugging on the new railing as I did. It seemed solid. I looked to my left, toward a laurel hedge that separated the store property from the field.

There was a piece of paper—or something— caught in the bottom branches. I walked back down the stairs and stepped over the rope and sign again. Then I hurried to the hedge, kneeled, and reached into the bottom branches, pulling out the laminated piece of paper.

I turned it over. It was the missing sign. It wasn't proof that Rylan had seen the sign. Perhaps someone took it down between when Rosene walked by that morning and when Rylan fell. But who would have taken it down?

Or did Rylan undo the rope and take the sign? I turned and looked back up at the landing. If he'd dropped it from the staircase, would it have twirled into the hedge?

I climbed back up to the landing and flung the sign toward the hedge. It didn't land in the exact same spot, but it was close.

Why hadn't Dawdi seen it when he fixed the railing? I wondered how long it had been since my grandfather had his eyes checked. But then I remembered there was snow on the ground when Dawdi repaired the staircase. The sign was probably buried.

I retrieved the sign one more time and then went through the back door of the store. I showed Mammi and said, "I'll see what the attorney I'm meeting with tomorrow says about it."

"Brenna." Mammi put her hands to her chest. "Why are you meeting with an attorney?"

"Because we need advice. We need help."

"We need to trust."

"I am trusting," I said. "But I'm not going to stand by and have you blamed when you've done nothing wrong." I lifted the sign like a flag. "I'm taking full responsibility for this. I'll pay for the attorney." I needed to talk to Gran in case it cost more than I had. "This has nothing to do with you." Not yet, at least.

"You do what you need to do," Mammi said. "But I won't be involved."

"Fair enough." For the first time in months, I felt optimistic. I was taking action. Finally.

I called Gran that evening, and she said that hiring an attorney was a good use of our money—I didn't need to pay out of my own savings. "Use the credit card Ivy has," she said. "I'll text her and tell her to give it to you."

Ivy got home from class at ten and came straight to my room. She walked in without knocking and held out the credit card. "Gran said you needed this, but she didn't say why."

"I'm talking to an attorney tomorrow about Rylan's lawsuit."

"Really?"

I nodded.

"Mammi and Dawdi are cool with that?"

"Mammi said I could do what I wanted. I didn't ask Dawdi."

"Well, you should talk with him after you speak with the attorney, before he—"

"She."

"Nice." Ivy smiled a little. "Before she does anything—whatever it is that she would do. Countersue?"

I winced. I didn't have any idea what she would do. "I'm just going to gather information tomorrow and see what our options are." I turned back to my computer, but before Ivy reached the hall I asked, "Are you still on social media?"

"Some." She stepped toward me. "Why?"

I turned toward her. "I want to see if Meg—Rylan's deceased girlfriend—was on social media."

Ivy wrinkled her nose.

"Is that creepy?"

"Kind of." She sat down on my bed. "Why do you want to see if you can find her on social media?"

"I saw a photo of her at her parents' frame business. Then today they stopped by Amish Antiques—her mom said Meg loved Mammi's store."

"Really?"

I nodded. "I'd like to know more about her. Maybe it would help me figure out Rylan."

"Why don't you ask him if she was on social media. Then it wouldn't be creepy—it wouldn't be like you were stalking her. Or him."

I exhaled. I didn't want to talk with Rylan about Meg.

The next morning, as I came down the stairs, he came out of his apartment. He scowled and said, "What did you do?"

"What do you mean?"

"Gabe said the Everses came by the store yesterday looking for you."

"Yeah," I said. "About that. Robert and Margaret would like to see you. Have you over for dinner." I pulled my phone from my pocket. "I'm texting you his phone number."

"Don't bother. I'm not going to contact him."

I shared the number anyway.

"See you in class," he said.

"I won't be there."

"Oh?"

"I have an appointment."

"What kind of appointment?"

I shrugged and headed toward the parking lot. Rylan's cane clicked behind me.

"Have a good time," he said as I climbed into my van.

"You too," I said out the open door. "Tell Ami and Jessica hello."

He gave me a smug grin as he kept on walking.

"Wait." I climbed out of the van as he turned around. "I'd like to look for Meg on social media. Would that be all right?"

He frowned. "Why are you asking me? You can do whatever you want."

"I don't want to offend you."

"I honestly don't care," he said. "Her mom took control of Meg's socials. Meg's handle disappeared from all the photos I'd tagged her in, so I'm guessing Margaret probably deleted everything."

"Okay. That makes sense. Thanks." I climbed back in the van and started it but allowed him to back out of his space first. After waiting a few minutes, I turned west onto the highway, expecting Rylan to be a ways ahead. But he'd been stopped at a red light, and I soon caught up. I followed him until he turned north toward the community college, and I kept going into town.

Nat Byers's office was close to the hospital. I found a place to park on the street and then opened the door to the office. The waiting area was small, and there was only one interior door.

As I sat down on an old settee, the door opened, and a young woman, maybe in her late twenties, opened it. I hoped she had enough experience to help me. "Brenna?" she asked.

I nodded as I stood.

"I'm Nat—short for Natalini." She motioned toward her office. "Come on in."

She had an old desk with a roller chair. I sat down in the straight-backed chair across from her. She took out a yellow legal pad from a drawer in the desk and then said, "How can I help you?"

After I explained about the personal injury lawsuit, she asked, "Do you know what his medical costs are?"

"The bills are over thirty thousand." I explained that he was a veteran and was one hundred percent disabled. "His army buddies are sure the VA will cover all of them."

"Did he miss work because of the accident?"

"No. He's a student in the same program I am in at the community college. That's how I know him. He asked me for a ride to class that day, and then I had to stop by the store with a delivery. I told him to stay in the van."

"And then he got out?"

"Yes." I explained what happened next as she jotted down more notes.

I continued, "Rylan's attorney, whom he used to work for as a paralegal, is claiming my grandparents were negligent. But there was a sign on a rope blocking off the staircase." I took it out of my backpack and held it up. "My Aenti Rosene saw it there that morning on her walk, but Rylan claimed the rope was down and the sign was nowhere in sight. I found it yesterday in the hedge on the far side of the stairs."

"Interesting." She took more notes. "I need the name of Rylan's attorney and Rylan's last name."

I gave her the information. "What's the next step?"

"I'll let Collins & Collins know I'm representing you, plus I'll get a copy of the lawsuit from the court. Then I'll request copies of both your deposition and your grandmother's." She

442

jotted something else down on her legal pad. "And I'll find an expert witness in the safety field." She looked up at me and smiled.

Her kindness made me start to cry. "I'm sorry," I said. "I feel like this is all my fault."

"This isn't your fault," Nat said. "Either this really was an accident—someone removed the sign and Rylan went up the stairs—or else he removed it and knew he shouldn't have gone up the staircase. You are definitely not at fault." She leaned toward me. "The lawsuit is still in the discovery phase, so you contacted me at the perfect time. I'll do some digging and see what I can find out, and we'll go from there."

"What should I do with the sign?"

"Would you like me to keep it?"

I nodded and handed it across the desk. "It's dirty."

"That's fine. It indicates it's months old and that you didn't just make it." I hadn't thought someone might think I had, but she had a point. I pulled out the credit card. "How much do I owe you?"

"You don't need to pay me now. I promise, I'm very fair about my time. I won't do anything more than I outlined today, which isn't more than an hour or so of work."

"Thank you," I said.

She stood and so did I. "I'll give you a call in a couple of days. Once I have some answers."

I arrived at class the next day two minutes before it started. Rylan sat near the front, with a chair next to him, while Ami and Jessica sat in the middle with a chair on either side of them. All the seats in the back were taken.

Feeling bold, I marched up front and sat next to Rylan. He stared straight ahead and didn't acknowledge me, but the professor gave me a smile. Rylan had a notebook open on the table but didn't take any notes.

When the professor released us for our break, I turned toward Rylan. "How are you doing?"

He grunted. "How's your lawyer?"

"Good. I really like her," I answered. "I think she's going to be helpful."

"I didn't think the Amish hire lawyers."

"I'm not Amish."

He said, "I heard you found the sign."

My face grew warm.

"Gabe," Rylan said. "Gabe told Marko, and Marko told me. Like it was a gotcha moment."

I didn't reply.

He cleared his throat. "Are you ready for our final?"

"Not yet, but I hope I will be. How about you?"

He glanced down at my laptop. "It really helped to study together last time. Any chance we could that again?"

I hesitated. Finally, I said, "Sure. I can do that."

The next day, I worked in the store. On Saturday, Rylan and I studied together for our finals. When he asked if I'd found any of Meg's accounts on social media, I told him I hadn't looked.

"Are you going to?"

"I'm not sure," I answered.

We took our exams on Monday and Tuesday. After the last exam, Rylan asked if I'd go with him to the school coffee shop. He bought me an Americano, and then we headed to the far table. Ami and Jessica stepped into the coffee shop and then stepped out. "What happened with those two?" I asked.

"Nothing." He sighed. "I miss you and Marko and Viktor and Gabe. . . ." As his voice trailed off, I knew he also missed Meg. "Ami and Jessica are fine, but they're—"

"Young?"

He laughed. "They're older than you are."

I smiled. "I'm actually older than you think, if that makes sense."

"It does," he said. "Thank you for helping me study. I think I passed."

"I'm sure you did."

"I need to tell you something."

I tilted my head, hoping to hear he'd dropped the lawsuit.

"I'd been to Amish Antiques several times before Afghanistan. With Meg. It was one of her favorite stores. She bought all sorts of things. Old quilts. A bedstead. A dining room table. That's why I got out of the van that day."

"Meg's mom said she really liked the store." My heart tightened in empathy. "I know it was the anniversary of her death."

His expression grew hard. Was it anger? Grief? I couldn't tell. "How did you know?"

"I Googled it."

He exhaled. "Yes, it was the anniversary. I was trying so hard not to think about it—and then you pulled up in front of your grandmother's store. I couldn't *not* think about it, think of her then."

"I'm sorry."

"It's not your fault."

"I know." I hesitated a moment and then asked, "How are things going with your therapist?"

"I haven't been for a while."

"Do you plan to go back?"

He took a sip of his coffee. "I'll see."

I took a drink of my Americano. "I'm really sorry about Meg. And about your left leg. And about the accident at the store that broke your right leg."

"I know," he said. "And I'm sorry about your parents. And I'm thankful that you have your grandparents and Rosene."

"Thank you." The back of my throat grew thick, and I took another sip of coffee to try to wash away my tears. It didn't work.

"I didn't fall on purpose," he said.

"I know." I didn't expect him to admit he'd taken down the sign and most likely threw it in the hedge. And I could live with that.

Without saying anything, Rylan reached for my hand and squeezed it. And then held it. A single tear escaped my eye. Then another. We sat there a long time, him holding my hand, me crying. He did a better job fighting back his tears.

On my way to work Thursday morning, Nat called. I had my phone in its holder, so I accepted the call—something I never did—and put it on speaker. "Hi, Natalini."

"Hello, Brenna. I wanted to give you an update. I've looked through the depositions, contacted a consultant in the construction business, and talked with Mr. Collins about subpoenaing Rylan Sanders's medical bills. I also told him he doesn't have a case."

"Really?"

"Yes. Mr. Collins, whom Rylan used to work for, is notorious for suing Amish people. He takes advantage of the fact they usually don't obtain legal counsel and often settle to make the lawsuit go away."

I exhaled sharply. "What's the next step?"

"I need to talk with your grandmother. If it goes to court, I believe the judge will throw it out. But I can't be sure. We could settle by offering an amount of money far less than what Mr. Sanders is asking for, but enough for him to feel that his pain and suffering has been acknowledged."

"I'll speak with my grandmother and get back to you." With all the sincerity I had, I said, "Thank you."

I relayed what Natalini had said to Mammi as soon as I arrived at the store.

She simply said, "I'll talk with your Dawdi. We'll think about it."

On Thursday evening, as Johann flew west, I decided to see if I could find Meg Evers on social media. As I understood it, her accounts would have to be public for me to find anything. I didn't expect they would be—but I needed to try. I didn't find anything on the first platform, but I did on the second. *Remembering Meg Evers*. It had been turned into a public memorial account. The photo of Meg was the same one I saw at her parents' business.

The last post was from a few weeks after she died, with the Army photo and the words *Forever in our hearts*. I kept scrolling.

The next photo was of Meg, Rylan, Viktor, and Marko in front of a bus that appeared to be stateside. There were photos of Meg with her parents in front of their house and then of her with a couple of girlfriends. Perhaps one of them was Ami's sister.

I kept scrolling.

Next was a photo of Meg wearing a red, white,

and blue outfit and holding a sparkler, Rylan beside her. Both were grinning. He looked so happy. So carefree.

My jaw dropped at the next photo. It was on the back steps at Amish Antiques. Meg held a gray cat that looked much like the stray that hung out on Rylan's patio and like the multiple gray cats that currently lived on the farm. Rylan sat behind her, on the step above, his hands on her shoulders. Both were grinning. The next photo was taken at a farther distance and included most of the staircase. I enlarged it. There was the sign affixed to the rope at the bottom of the steps: *Do Not Enter*. They'd stepped over it and had climbed halfway up the steps.

Next was the same setting but the photo was a selfie of Meg and Rylan's faces, with a little bit of gray fur under Meg's chin.

I thought of Mammi's story about the couple who'd taken the selfie on the back staircase. There was no way Mammi had taken the photo. They must have found someone else to take it—another customer, maybe? Or someone else who was with them?

Even though they were trespassing, the photo warmed me. They were the audacious young couple Mammi had talked about. I'd heard a story about Rylan and Meg long before I had any idea of who they were.

I took a screenshot of the photo with the *Do*

Not Enter sign, took out Natalini's card with her email address, and sent the photo to her. If the sign had in fact been down the day Rylan fell, which was unlikely, he knew from before that the staircase was off limits. And yet he went up anyway, just as he had with Meg.

I picked Johann up at the Philadelphia airport the next morning. Treva offered to go with me, but I declined. Ivy would have offered, but she had her last final of her master's program that day. I would have declined her offer too. I figured the more time Johann and I could spend together while he was in Lancaster County, the better.

We'd both be staying on the farm, and so would Ivy. Mammi didn't feel comfortable with any other arrangements. She was probably right to worry about Ivy and Conrad—but not Johann and me. However, Johann said he wanted to stay on the farm and see how the Amish lived. He guessed it was much like his Mennonite great-great-grandparents had lived in Ukraine in the 1920s, before Stalin's forced famine and the collectivization of the land cost them their farm.

Johann again had his backpack slung over one shoulder. He wore jeans and a button-up white shirt and looked oh so handsome.

I pulled up to the curb and waved.

He grinned, opened the side door, placed his

backpack on the floor, and then climbed into the passenger seat. "Hello, Brenna Zimmerman." His eyes sparkled.

"Hello, Johann Mazur." He'd told me one time that Ukrainians used first and last names far more often than Americans did.

"How are you?" he asked.

"I'm really happy to have you here," I responded. "How are you?"

"Happy," he said. "Because I'm here."

We talked nonstop as I drove. I told him about my finals, about Natalini's phone call, and about Meg's memorialized social media page.

"Wow. So that pretty much proves Rylan knew not to go up the stairs."

"It seems so, although he could say that he thought he was welcome to go up the stairs since, as he claims, the sign was down."

"What about the back door of the shop? Does it have a sign on it?"

"Yes," I answered. "A *Private* sign."

"Then it sounds as if it's a stretch for Rylan to claim he thought the stairs were part of the store."

I agreed.

"I have something I need to tell you," he said.

"Oh?" It sounded serious.

"I started the new job I told you about in January."

"I thought you had." I stole a glance at him. "How is it?"

"Good. It's with the government—with the army, technically. I'm a soldier again."

I let my surprise settle and then asked, "Doing what?"

"Cybersecurity work. Intelligence. Monitoring—" he paused—"a country that borders ours."

I noticed he said *country,* not *neighbor.*

"Russia," I said grimly.

He nodded. "I can't talk about what I'm doing, but I wanted to let you know I'm back in the military. Things are weird—our President Poroshenko is a corrupt oligarch. Putin and the Russian oligarchs are having a bigger and bigger influence in the world, including through cyberspace and social media."

I thought of the changing geographies of nations and cyberspace—and families. Such different spheres, yet all could shift in an instant. Nothing stayed the same from hour to hour, day to day, or year to year. How we—how I— navigated those changes was what mattered.

Johann continued. "Your president is a billion-aire who doesn't seem to want to adhere entirely to democratic norms." He paused a moment and then said, "I guess what I'm saying is that there's a rise of authoritarian threats in the world right now. I think this new job is the best thing I can do, currently, to fight that."

"Dyakuyu," I said, "for what you're doing. I'll pray for you and your work."

"Thank you." He smiled wryly. "It's very necessary, I can assure you. Both the work and your prayers. I feel privileged to do it. That said, if you ever wanted to come to Ukraine for an extended time, my old company is hiring."

"They wouldn't want to hire me."

"They would," he said. "All of the communication is in English, and your degree qualifies you. I'd be around to help you learn the systems too, if you're interested."

"Thanks," I said. "I'll keep that in mind." But I couldn't see it happening. Not really.

As I continued driving, I thought of how I'd embraced JOMO my entire life. But what if I missed out on my own *life,* on what it could be?

When we reached the farm, Dawdi waved from the porch and then jogged toward where I'd parked by the shed. As I introduced Johann to him, Dawdi extended his hand and said, "Pleased to meet you. Would you like to see how we Amish do our milking?"

I stifled a groan.

"I'd love to." Johann turned to me. "Could I get my bag later?"

"Sure," I said. "I'll leave the van unlocked."

Knowing the milking would take a while, I headed toward the house, hoping Rosene would tell me more of the story in the meantime.

34

Martha

Zeke and Jeremiah's Mamm was on the mend, thanks to the antibiotic her doctor prescribed. Mutter kept quiet about Tom Brown and pretty much everything else. She was mostly running the store by herself since Clare needed Rosene's help more and more in the house. Everyone grew more exhausted and on edge. If Jeremiah hadn't been home, Martha feared they would have all reached their limit.

Martha didn't make it to any Red Cross meetings, but George came out to the farm the first week of June to tell her good-bye. He'd be moving to Geneva in a month but was going home to Chicago first for a visit.

"Have you heard anything more about Franz Richter?" Martha asked.

George shook his head. "How about you?"

"No," Martha said. "But that doesn't mean there's not news. If Mutter knew anything, I doubt she'd tell me."

They sat in the rocking chairs on the porch. George had a briefcase with him, and just before he was ready to go, he opened it and took out a document. "It's a Red Cross application," he explained. "For the translator position in Geneva I told you about." He handed it to her.

Their hands brushed as Martha took it, sending a tingle up her arm. "Thank you."

After he left, Mutter stopped Martha on the porch. With her hands on her hip, she asked, "What are your plans?"

"I have none." She moved the application behind her back.

"I doubt that," Mutter said, "but remember, family must come first."

"Mutter, I'm not going anywhere." Martha started to walk around her to the door, but Mutter stepped in front of it.

"Thank you," she said, "for working so hard for all of us. I can tell you have feelings for George Hall. I'm sorry you can't have more time with him."

Martha shrugged. "He's not Mennonite."

Mutter didn't respond.

"That doesn't bother you?"

"Do you plan to stay Mennonite? You go into town dressed in a skirt and a sweater and a pillbox hat. You haven't courted anyone Mennonite— you haven't courted at all."

Martha's face grew warm.

"Keep in touch with George," Mutter said. "He'll be back someday."

"Thank you." As Mutter stepped past her,

455

Martha turned and asked, "What part did you play in Dirk's escape?"

Mutter's face reddened. "No part," she said. "Please don't keep bringing it up."

"Someone took my clothes."

"You don't know that."

"Mutter, did you take my clothes?"

"Of course not."

Martha pursed her lips together. "Do you wonder what effect the stress of all of that could have had on Vater?"

"He's doing fine. Better now that Jeremiah is home."

Martha shook her head and strode into the house, clasping the application in both hands. She thought of how averse Mutter had been to Clare's interest in Jeremiah. Now she relied on him more than anyone.

The next day, Rosene and Martha were working in the garden as Mutter came down the back steps to return to the store after lunch. A black car drove down the driveway. For a moment, Martha thought it was George. It wasn't. It was Tom Brown. He climbed from the car and called a greeting to Rosene, and then to Martha. "I have some news," he said.

Rosene and Martha stepped out of the garden, kicking the dirt from their boots as Mutter strode toward him. All three of them gathered around him.

"We've had a report from Mexico," he said. "Sergeant Schwarz and Dirk Neumann, who we think is really Heinz König, a major in the German Army, crossed the Mexican border a week ago. König was reported to have been killed in North Africa, but we believe he exchanged his ID with Dirk Neumann, who was a private."

Martha crossed her arms. "Have Dirk—Heinz— and Sergeant Schwarz been captured?"

Tom Brown shook his head. "The German consul in Mexico City helped them on to Argentina. Our contact in Mexico said it seems both plan to stay in Argentina, at least for now."

"Why would Dirk want to stay in Argentina?" Rosene asked.

"We're not sure," Tom Brown said. "But we're working on trying to find out. We don't know if Sergeant Schwarz knew König's identity. At this point, our hope is to force Sergeant Schwarz back to the US and prosecute him for treason." He put his hat back on and tipped it. "That is all the news I have." He started for his car.

Mutter followed him.

He didn't turn to face her until he reached his car. Martha went around to the side of the house, expecting Mutter to say something about the escape or the clothes she'd provided.

Instead, Mutter asked, "Can you get PWs assigned to our farm again through the fall harvest? Losing the help is punishing our family."

Her voice grew louder as she spoke. "In good conscience, can you please intervene? It's the least you can do."

"I'll talk with Agent Lewis," he said. "I'll come back in a few days or call the store."

Martha said a silent prayer as she marched toward the two. "I have something to say."

They both turned.

"I don't know who you really are, Tom Brown, or what you've been saying to Mutter the last couple of months, or where my missing clothes ended up. Whatever you put her up to, you'd better make this right. Or I'll do whatever I can to make it right myself."

Both Mutter and Tom Brown stared at Martha for a long moment, but then Tom Brown tipped his hat again and said, "I'll keep that in mind."

Mutter's request—most likely it wasn't Martha's threat—worked because in the middle of June, six PWs, including Andreas, showed up along with a guard from the camp that Martha recognized from the night Otis and Pavlo were interrogated. It wasn't until the afternoon milking that Martha had a chance to speak with Andreas.

"I owe Pavlo everything," he said. "He took my place."

"When?"

"The day Otis and I were supposed to escape

from here, Pavlo insisted he'd go instead of me. And I let him."

"Because of Nurse Olson?"

"Jah," he said. "I thought if I tried to escape, I'd never have a chance to return to the United States." He looked past Martha. "I doubt I will anyway."

"Where are Pavlo and Otis now?"

"Still at Indiantown Gap."

With the added help of Jeremiah and the PWs, life on the farm grew easier. Martha wasn't needed to help with the milking, let alone the other tasks, and began working with Mutter in the store for a few hours each day.

Martha tried to speak with her a couple of more times about the PWs escaping and her missing clothes and why she'd been chummy with an FBI agent before the PWs escaped, but each time Mutter said, "I won't talk about it with you."

Mutter received a letter from Rosene's sister, Lena, on a particularly hot and sticky day the beginning of August. Mutter read the letter out loud as they all sat around the table after the noon meal.

Dear Tante Monika,

I hope this finds you doing well. Vater and I are doing as well as can be expected. Thankfully, our home was spared in the Allied bombings of Frankfurt, and our health is good, although Vater has aged quite a bit in the last few months as more information has been released about the atrocities committed by the Nazis. We had no idea that was going on and feel ill to know how many were killed in the camps.

I have signed on to work as a translator for the Americans to resettle refugees and will begin my work next month. That will bring a welcome income to our household. Garit is being detained in France with a group of German soldiers who are clearing minefields. It is the best assignment we could have hoped for—far better than being sent to Russia to work. We plan to marry as soon as he is allowed to return to Germany.

I hope this finds all of you well. Please write and let us know how all of you are doing. Vater would like Rosene to return to Germany as soon as possible. He sends his regards to all.

Affectionately,
Lena

No one said anything. To claim that Lena and Onkel Josef didn't know what was going on seemed disingenuous. They did know, at least partly. Martha remembered the conversation from 1937 around the very table where they all sat now, when Vater challenged Onkel Josef about the Nazi policies against the Jews. And Rosene was part of a study performed by Nazi doctors that would have resulted in her imprisonment in a camp and most likely her death if Clare hadn't rescued her and brought her to the US. Lena translated documents for a Nazi officer for years.

Rosene stood and started clearing the table. Martha began to help her. But then, on returning to the table, Rosene collapsed. Zeke rushed to her side, followed by Martha.

"I don't want to go back," Rosene sobbed.

Martha gathered her up in her arms.

"You're not going back." Mutter stood over them as Zeke took a step backward. "You're legally our daughter. Besides, you're nineteen. In his own way, Josef loves you. But you're not beholden to him. You can make your own decisions now."

You can make your own decisions now. Martha was five years older than Rosene. Did she get to make her own decisions too?

Later that afternoon, Martha helped Mutter in the store. The ceiling fan did little to alleviate the heat. Mutter seemed exhausted. Martha fetched her a glass of water, and after Mutter drank it, she said, "I received a letter from my brother, Klaus, from the family farm. I don't want to tell Clare the news until after she has her baby."

"What's happened?"

"My mother was killed in a bombing raid two years ago."

"Oh no." Martha put her hand on her mother's shoulder. "I'm so sorry."

"Danke." Mutter took a deep breath. Then she said, "Your Onkel Klaus, Tante Olga, and Kusine Karl are doing well. They have adequate food. They saved a little Jewish girl, dressing her as a boy through the war and claiming she was Olga's nephew."

"Clare mentioned the child."

"Yes," Mutter said. "That's right. I'm relieved she survived." She crossed her arms. "I never would have dreamed my homeland would fall under the spell of someone like Hitler and would allow such horrors to happen." She shuddered. "I don't blame Rosene for not wanting to go back, but for Josef and Lena's sake, I hope someday that she will." Mutter met Martha's eyes. "If she wants to, will you take her some day?"

"Yes," Martha said.

"I'm sorry for what I said to you, about you staying here. With the PWs back, perhaps you won't have to. I'd like for you to have an adventure while you're still young. Clare never wanted to go to Germany, while I know you wanted to go anywhere—and couldn't. You dedicated yourself to us. I don't know what we would have done without you."

"Danke, Mutter." Martha brushed away a tear.

"I would like to have an adventure, and I'd like to use the German I studied. When the time is right."

She also wanted to know exactly what Mutter did to help Tom Brown—or Dirk. Or both. But if she knew one thing about Mutter, it was that she wouldn't disclose something she was set on keeping a secret.

That evening, Martha sat at the kitchen table and filled out the Red Cross application that George had given her. Then she slipped it into an envelope, addressed it, and readied it for the mail. If she were offered the job and couldn't go, all she'd need to do was decline.

The middle of August, the day after Japan surrendered, Jeremiah had a letter from one of the other orderlies he'd worked with at Byberry. "It's from my friend who is Quaker," he told Martha as they sat at the picnic table. "He also took pictures."

He read the letter silently and then said, "A reporter from *Life* wrote him back. He was shocked by the photographs and said the images reminded him of the concentration camp survivors too. He wants to investigate further." Jeremiah exhaled. "He also wrote that someone, he doesn't know if it was another CO or a journalist, also sent photographs to Eleanor Roosevelt. She's going to meet with a few of the orderlies." Jeremiah met Martha's eyes. "I can't believe it. When I didn't hear back from anyone, I feared no one cared. But people do."

Martha asked, "Do you want to meet with Mrs. Roosevelt?"

"No," Jeremiah said. "I just want someone to stop what's going on and come up with a better plan. That's all I've wanted." He slipped the letter back into the envelope. "I'll write my friend back and ask him to keep me updated on what happens."

Two days later, Clare had her baby. The little girl—named Janice—weighed six pounds wrapped in a baby quilt. But she was strong. Martha took over the store so Mutter could help Rosene care for the baby and Clare.

A month later, Martha received a letter from the Red Cross. She held it to her chest as her family, all seated around the table, stared at her. "What is it?" Rosene finally asked.

"Nothing," Martha answered.

Mutter said, as she held Janice, "Open it. Perhaps it's your acceptance letter."

Martha shot her mother a questioning glance.

"It was obvious George gave you an application the last night he was here." Mutter shifted the baby to her shoulder. "Open it."

Martha wasn't sure why it was so important to Mutter. She wouldn't be returning to the store anytime soon. Janice was still tiny, and Clare needed help. But she did as Mutter said and read the letter. She looked up at her mother. "Jah, that's what it is." She returned the acceptance letter to the envelope and didn't say any more. No one asked what she would do. There was no reason to.

But the next day, Jeremiah approached her in the dairy barn and said, "You should take the Red Cross job. My Mamm is doing much better and can help here some. The PWs are doing well. We'll get the harvest in, and it appears to be a good crop. Zeke will continue working here— indefinitely, it seems. Your Vater's health is stable. I see no reason for you not to go."

"Your mother's health could decline. So could Vater's. There won't be any PWs come spring."

"Nee, but we'll survive. Soldiers and COs will be coming home. We'll be able to hire another hand or two." When Martha didn't answer, Jeremiah said, "Think about it."

She did for the next week, up to the day George wrote her. It wasn't a long letter, but at the end he wrote,

> *I can imagine how hard it would be for you to leave your farm and family. But if you decide to, I hope you'll join me here in Geneva. We could use your help—but I could also use your friendship and your wisdom. I miss you.*

He seemed to appreciate her for who she was. There was no pressure for anything more than a friendship, and yet she couldn't rule out that there might be *something* more for the two of them. That evening, she told Mutter and Vater what Jeremiah had said.

"You should accept the job," Mutter said. "We entrust you to the work the Lord has for you. And we trust you to make the decisions you need to. Make sure to write and visit when you can."

Tears filled Vater's eyes, but he said, "Jah. You should go."

"Perhaps you can go through Frankfurt on the way," Mutter said. "And check in on Josef and Lena. Explain to them why Rosene won't be going back—at least not anytime soon, and never to stay."

"I'll talk to Rosene." Martha felt a new kind of freedom that evening as she wrote to accept the position and then wrote to George. Who knew what the future held? She looked forward to finding out.

The next afternoon, Rosene helped Martha do inventory in the store. Martha told her about accepting the job in Geneva and Mutter's request she go through Frankfurt. "How would you feel about that?"

Rosene shuddered. "It doesn't matter. Just tell them I won't be returning."

"In a few years, if you'd like to go back for a visit, I'll take you," Martha said.

"I won't." Rosene turned away and began counting cans of beans.

Rosene left the store before closing, and when Martha returned to the house later, Rosene and Zeke sat side by side on the picnic table, laughing. Martha stopped and watched the scene, trying to remember every detail.

It was obvious Zeke and Rosene were sweet on each other, but Zeke would be in no position to marry for a few years. He would turn eighteen in the fall. He had no land, and his oldest brother was already farming with their father. She hoped they could come up with a plan. Perhaps the Simons farm could support two Zimmerman families in time.

Martha sighed in relief. Jeremiah was home. The war was over. Vater was still alive. Clare and Janice had survived the pregnancy. They had endured.

Martha had done what she needed to do. It had been a difficult time, but, like all things, it had passed. Now it was her turn to see more of the world than Lancaster County.

35

Brenna

I stood at the kitchen window as Rosene said, "That's Martha's story."

"What? Isn't her story just starting?"

"Well, in one way yes, but in another no. She endured a difficult time, fulfilled her duty to her family, and was finally able to venture off on her own."

"What happened with her and George?"

"That's another story."

"What about Lena and Onkel Josef? Did Martha see them in Frankfurt?"

"She did," Rosene said. "It wasn't a productive visit, but it paved the way for Martha and me to visit later."

My eyebrows shot up. "But you won't tell me about that either, right? That's a story for another time?"

Rosene laughed. "That's right."

"What about you and Zeke?"

Rosene paused. Was that a hint of sadness that flashed across her face? Then she said, "That's definitely a story for another time."

"All right, but what happened as far as the

mental hospital is a story for now, right? Surely you can tell me about that."

"Yes. The story came out in *Life* the following year. It's in the scrapbook." Rosene glanced toward the hallway. "You can read about it later. The article led to reform in mental health hospitals, and Jeremiah's experience, along with other COs in Lancaster County, led to the establishment of Edenville in the early 1950s."

"What? Where I go?"

She nodded. "They recognized the need for mental health care in our Plain communities and wanted a facility that understood our way of life."

A wave of gratitude swept through me. My great-grandfather had, nearly seventy years ago, helped establish an organization that had been life-changing for me.

"Years later, Jeremiah told me some of what he experienced at Byberry. The beatings of patients by other patients. The beatings by staff. The attacks on the staff by patients. It was an atrocious place to work. He also shared how when he was out and about in Philadelphia, such as waiting for the bus to the train station, he would be verbally harassed and called a 'yellowbelly slacker' and that sort of thing. One time a man passing by punched him in the jaw." Rosene sighed. "Those were hard times. But Jeremiah lovingly cared for the patients, even the most difficult, and did his best to make a difference. And he did." Rosene paused a moment and then asked, "Any more questions?"

"Yes. What about your Mutter? Did she help Dirk—I mean, Heinz?"

Rosene's face grew serious. "Martha and I never found out for sure. Mutter took her secret, if there was one, to the grave."

"What? You never investigated to find out what she was doing?"

"No. I never thought to, actually."

"Chances are she was helping Dirk, right? And there was some sort of connection with Franz Ritcher?"

Rosene's eyes grew misty. "Martha and I never spoke of our suspicions about Mutter again. Maybe I didn't want to know." She shrugged. "It was a different time."

"How about now?" I asked. "Do you wish you knew the truth?"

She pursed her lips. "I guess I do. Do you think you can find out?"

"I'll see." I leaned toward her. "What about Sergeant Schwarz? Was he caught?"

"Not that I know of."

"What was his first name?"

Rosene tapped her chin. "I don't know. I'm not sure I ever knew it."

Perhaps I could find information online without his first name. "What happened to Andreas and Nurse Olson?"

"I don't know about them either," Rosene said. "I used to look in phonebooks at the library for an Andreas Witer, and then when the internet arrived, I was sure I'd be able to find them. But I never have, although I've always wondered—and what happened to Pavlo too."

I made a mental note to look into him too.

Rosene gazed deeply into my eyes. "I hope you'll think of Martha as you plan for your own future."

I dropped my head. "If only I was like Martha. I don't serve others the way she did."

"That's not true," she said. "Look what you've done for Rylan all these months. Look what you do for me and Arden and Priscilla too."

"What have I done? Mostly I'm a drag on everyone else. Maybe I helped Rylan, but none of it came easily. I don't have Martha's courage."

"Isn't that what service should be?" Rosene asked. "Doing things we're not comfortable with? We help others not because it's easy for us, but because it's needed."

As I thought about that, Treva opened the back door and stepped into the kitchen. Johann and Dawdi, who was laughing, followed.

Dawdi directed Johann to the downstairs bathroom to wash up while Treva headed up the back steps to her room. Conrad and Ivy arrived for supper, and then Mammi and Gabe. I happily set nine places around the table.

471

Gran arrived the next day, and the days after were a whirlwind of meals, outings, and long conversations.

One morning, I headed to the nearby coffee shop while Johann helped Dawdi mend a fence, and I Googled *Andreas and Betsy Witer*. At first no matches for people with those names who would be in their late nineties came up, but as I kept scrolling, an obituary in the *Seattle Times* popped up for an Andreas Witer who died in 2007 at the age of eighty-five. He'd been born near Medyka, Poland, and was preceded in death by his beloved wife, Betsy, in 1997, and his friend Pavlo Korol, who also lived in Seattle, in 1988.

Goodness. Somehow they'd managed to get Pavlo back to the US too. I thought of Marko and Viktor coming to the US as young boys and serving our country. Andreas and Pavlo had come as young men and were then sent back to Germany, but they'd managed to return to the US, where they felt at home.

I kept reading. Andreas and Betsy had one child, a daughter named Olga Witer Jackson, who lived in Phoenix, Arizona, and would be sixty-nine now. I'd found Andreas. And Betsy. And Pavlo. I bookmarked the page.

I Googled *Heinz König* too but didn't find anything relevant about anyone who could be him, neither in Germany nor in Argentina. I Googled *General König, German Army, World*

War II. I didn't find anything. I tried *Officer König* and then all the different officer ranks I could think of. I couldn't find a match. Perhaps Dirk—*Heinz*—didn't have a high-ranking father in the German Army after all. Perhaps he *had* made that up to garner sympathy from Mutter.

I Googled *Sergeant Schwarz.* A fictional character from a film popped up, and then several real people, but all were from recent listings. Finally, an entry from a book about German POWs appeared, with a mention of US Army Sergeant Fritz P. Schwarz, who was possibly seen in Argentina after, it was assumed, helping a German POW escape. The allegations were never proven, and Schwarz was never found nor prosecuted.

That was a shame.

Next I Googled how to find records on spies, both German and American, during World War II. After going down a bit of a rabbit hole through articles on spy rings and German espionage, I came across an article about a ring of double agents who worked in Washington, DC, during World War II. Documentation about their work was recently declassified and available through the National Archives Military Records.

I Googled the National Archives, searched for Military Records, and then found the Office of Strategic Services Personnel Files from World War II. All I had to do was enter *Monika Simons* and her name popped up. Her entry read: *Monika*

Simons, FBI informant; German spies and German POWs, January 1944–June 1945.

I bookmarked the page and then searched for *Tom Brown*. Twenty-two entries popped up, but none were the Tom Brown I was looking for. I searched *Franz Richter* next. A document popped up about him.

He was fifty-seven years old in 1942 when he was recruited by the Nazis to spy on US politicians and then to work as a liaison with German POWs. He believed he was feeding information to a spy ring in New York, but the spy ring was really FBI agents who were providing false information to the Nazis. There was an agent in Richter's area who went by the code name *Mutter* who helped in his capture.

I nearly choked on my latte. What could be more straightforward than that?

I kept reading. Richter was captured in March 1946 in Los Angeles and served eleven years in jail. It sounded as if he benefited from the government's focus turning toward the Cold War and the Soviet Union. He was released early for good behavior.

I leaned back in my chair. Monika Simons hadn't been a German spy after all. She'd been a patriot.

Johann was spying on the Russians. It was cyber-spying, but spying, nonetheless. He was a patriot too.

I headed back to the apartment and printed out the bookmarked pages.

Rosene's hand flew to her chest as I gave her what I'd found. "What a perfect ending to Martha's story," she said. "If only Martha could have known about Mutter before she left this earth." She smiled. "No doubt she's known for years now, right?"

I nodded, trying not to choke up at the thought of heaven.

"I'm going to write down Andreas and Betsy's daughter's name and see if I can find her address at the library." Rosene met my eyes. "Do you think she'd welcome a letter from me?"

"I certainly think it's worth a try," I answered.

On Tuesday morning, I texted Rylan.

See you tonight at graduation.

He texted back instantly.

I'm not going.

Instead of texting again, I decided to just give him a call. It went to voicemail. The second time I called, he answered. "I don't want to," he said.

"Why not?"

"Why should I?"

"Did you go to your first graduation?"

475

"No."

"Then you really should go to this one."

He didn't answer me.

"Dawdi and I will pick you up at three."

He grunted and hung up the phone.

When Dawdi, Rosene, Johann, and I arrived at the apartment complex, I sent Dawdi to collect Rylan, figuring he'd be more cooperative with Dawdi. It worked. After a ten-minute wait, they reached the van. Johann jumped out of the passenger seat and introduced himself, saying, "Rylan Sanders, we met online. I'm ecstatic to meet you in person."

Ecstatic. I swallowed a laugh. But Johann probably was ecstatic to meet Rylan in person. Sure, he wanted to protect me from Rylan's woundedness, but he had nothing against him.

When I turned west onto the highway, Johann asked Rylan how his right leg had healed. I was hoping Rylan would talk about his time in Afghanistan, but he didn't. Instead, he asked Johann what it was like to fight against the Russians. Johann gave him a few details.

I glanced at Dawdi and Rosene, who sat in the back seat of the van. They both listened intently but kept quiet. I wondered if Rosene was thinking of World War II, both in Germany and in the US. I had no idea what Dawdi might be thinking of. Perhaps the trials represented by the two young men. Perhaps why a faith centered around nonresistance had merit. No matter his thoughts, I knew they were filled with empathy.

The graduation ceremony was well organized and went fairly quick. The graduates sat on folding chairs on the floor, while friends and family sat in the stadium chairs. The president of the college gave a short speech, and then the names were called and we traipsed across the stage. Rylan, with the last name of Sanders, crossed a while before I did. After I received my diploma and heard the cheers of my family, who'd also cheered for Rylan, he was there to meet me on the steps off to the side, and we walked together back to our seats.

We were all quiet on the way home, but when we reached the apartment complex, Rylan said, "Thank you. That was cool."

I smiled. After a pause, I said, "You're invited to a graduation party for Ivy and me on Saturday at five, out at the farm. We'd be really happy if you would be an honored guest."

"I'll think about it." Rylan climbed out of the van and then turned back around. "If I decide to go, would you mind if I invited a couple of people?"

"Of course." I hoped he personally wanted to invite Marko and Viktor. I wouldn't tell him I already had.

The next morning, Ivy's graduation ceremony was short and sweet. Afterward, Gran put her arms around us. "I'm so proud of both of you—for your hard work and perseverance."

I didn't point out that Ivy had just completed her master's degree while I'd only obtained my associate's degree, because I was proud of me too, considering all that had happened over the last four years.

We reached the farm at three in the afternoon and got to work, arranging fruit, vegetables, homemade rolls, and cheese and meat slices on trays. We pulled salads out of the fridge and put out paper plates. We made lemonade and cut the dozens of pies that Rosene and Gran had made over the last few days.

Neighbors took over the milking for Dawdi that afternoon and Gabe closed the store at four to supervise the parking of our guests' buggies and cars. A little before five, people began arriving from our Mennonite church and from Dawdi and Mammi's Amish church. Marko and Viktor arrived a little after five with Olena, Taras, and Fedir.

I immediately found Johann and introduced him to them, and soon they were chatting away in a mixture of Ukrainian and English. Then the conversation grew serious, and I made out the word *viyny*—war. The conversation grew more rapid, full of questions from Marko and Viktor. I greeted a family from our church but caught the word *Afghanistan* coming from Johann. It sounded as if it was embedded in a question.

Ten minutes later, Gabe came into the house, leading Rylan, along with—to my surprise—Robert and Margaret Evers. Marko and Viktor stood, followed by their parents.

Tears stung my eyes. I think Johann must have guessed who the Everses were because he stood too. I greeted Robert and Margaret and then stepped back. Marko and Viktor stepped forward and shook Rylan's hand and then Robert and Margaret's too. Taras and Fedir stepped forward and paid their respects, and then Olena shook Robert's hand, but she kissed Margaret on the cheeks, first her left, then her right, and then her left again, saying, "I pray for you every day."

"Thank you." Margaret gave Olena a hug.

The older people congregated in the living room and kitchen while the *Youngie* moved outside. After we played volleyball, we got pie and sat in a circle of chairs on the lawn as we ate it.

Conrad asked what everyone's plans were for the summer.

I took a bite of strawberry pie, then answered. "Find a job." I wouldn't say where I wanted to find a job. I was beginning to realize that all I had was now. I didn't want life to pass me by.

Treva said, "Go to Haiti."

"What?" I nearly choked.

"I've been talking to Brooke. And Pierre,"

she said. "I want to work in the orphanage for a year. Brooke and Daniel are returning there next month. I'll live with them and help with the garden too."

That sounded perfect for her. And time away from all of us—in a new landscape—might be good for her.

Rylan said, "So, Gabe, any word about being deployed?"

Gabe looked as if he didn't want to talk about it, but he managed to say, "No."

"The last we heard, the army is saying spring 2019," Marko added. "But you know, the army is—"

Rylan interrupted. "Subject to change?"

"Something like that," Marko said.

Rylan sat back in his chair. "I've found a job."

I nearly choked again. "Really?"

He nodded. "With Robert and Margaret's Forevers Frames. They need someone to increase their online business and make it more secure. Plus, they want to add electronic frames. I have some ideas for improving what they have so far."

"That's great," Marko said.

"I'm going to move into an apartment they have in the back of the warehouse. Meg used to live there. And I'll go back to their church with them—Meg and I used to go before Afghanistan." He shrugged. "I'm going to give it all a try, anyway." Then he said, "There's also something else I want to tell you."

"Go ahead," I said. "We're listening."

"I've been seeing a therapist. A good one." Rylan caught my eye and gave me a little nod. Was he going to Edenville? "And I've had a long talk with Meg's parents. I thought they didn't want to see me after I returned from Walter Reed because they never really liked me, but it turns out that wasn't true. They were kind of buried in their own grief and all of the what-ifs . . . mostly what if Meg hadn't joined the Reserves after I did." He glanced from Marko to Viktor. "I acted like I didn't remember anything from that day— but I did. I always knew Meg was killed because of me, because I didn't heed our translator's warning. I just couldn't admit it."

When no one replied, he said, "I wish to God— and I'll never stop wishing this—that I died and Meg had lived, but I don't have control over that. I'm trying to deal with it. But it's hard."

Marko stepped forward and hugged Rylan. "It probably didn't help that none of us talked about what happened that day."

"Yeah." Rylan gazed up into Marko's face. "Why didn't you?"

"We didn't think you remembered. We didn't want to make it worse by rehashing all of it."

"When you guys didn't talk about it, and when Robert and Margaret didn't reach out to me, it made me feel a little crazy. Like I couldn't really mourn Meg because I felt like I'd killed her, but no one wanted to hold me accountable."

Marko whispered, "It wasn't your fault. There was nothing to hold you accountable for."

"I'm the one who made the bad decision and went down in the valley."

"It was war," Johann said. Again, I wondered what Johann hadn't told me about his own war experience.

"No one can make the right decision all the time," Viktor said.

Rylan crossed his arms and leaned back in his chair. "I know."

"We're sorry, Ry," Marko said. "We really are. About everything."

Rylan sighed. "I appreciate it." Then he sighed again and said, "I still can't believe she's gone."

Now Viktor walked over to Rylan, kneeled by his chair, and wrapped his big burly arms around him.

Marko put his arms around both of them. "We're still brothers."

"Yeah," Rylan said. "We always will be." Then he smiled a little and said, "I'll fight for you two to the end, I promise."

I put my arms around my sisters and pulled them close. "Ditto," I said.

Treva squeezed my arm while Ivy leaned her head against my shoulder.

"You didn't say what your plans for the summer are," I whispered to Ivy. "Neither did Conrad."

She smiled and said, "Expect more details soon."

Before Rylan left, he told me he needed to speak with my grandparents. We found them, Gran, and Rosene all sitting at the kitchen table, drinking cups of decaf.

Rylan sat down and said, "I talked with my attorney. He said, after talking to the lawyer Brenna hired, that we don't have a chance with the suit. There was a lot I didn't remember—or perhaps repressed. Like the photo of Meg and me on the staircase. And I probably did take the sign down the day I broke my leg. I wasn't really thinking straight."

That was more than I expected from Rylan.

He continued, "I don't have any medical expenses, like I thought I would. The VA paid the final bills last week."

"What about pain and suffering?" Dawdi asked.

"Yeah. There was pain, and I suffered. But it wasn't your fault." He paused just a minute and then said, "I heard the Amish don't pay taxes. Is that true?"

"Nee," Dawdi said. "We pay property taxes, and state and federal income tax, just like everyone else."

"Well," he said, "then your federal taxes are and have been going toward my support. I appreciate it." A snarky smile lit up his face.

For once, it was nice to see.

The next day after church, I shared a condensed version of Martha's story with Johann while we sat in the yard at the picnic table. When I finished, he asked if I'd looked at the rest of the scrapbook. "No," I said. "Would you like to look with me?"

"Absolutely," he answered.

Rosene had left it on the bookcase in the living room. Johann and I sat side by side on the sofa, and I showed him the photos and memorabilia Rosene had gone through with me and then continued to the pages I hadn't seen.

Tucked in the next page was a printed NPR website article from 2009 about the conscientious objectors in the US during World War II who had alerted the nation to the conditions at Byberry and other mental health hospitals.

The article went into detail about the working conditions and the patients being abused by the regular attendants.

Working in such a brutal and chaotic place tested the men's own ideals of nonviolence. The article described how the conscientious objectors used force but never violence. It then relayed the account of Charlie Lord, a young Quaker man who took photographs inside Byberry. Those were the photographs that were published in *Life Magazine* in 1946. Charlie must have been Dawdi Jeremiah's friend that he mentioned.

On the next page was the *Life* article. The photographs were just as Rosene had described and nearly unbearable to look at. The images were similar to those of the survivors from the concentration camps.

"I'm speechless," Johann said.

So was I. After a moment of silence, I turned to the next page. In a stark transition, the next two pages were filled with postcards from Martha. The first was from Frankfurt. *Lena and Onkel Josef send their love. We had a pleasant but superficial visit.*

I smiled. Martha was honest—like me.

The next was from Geneva. *Enjoying my work with the Red Cross. All administrative translating now. Will go with George to Germany to work directly with refugees next month.*

The postcards continued over the next two years. More from Germany, and then from Belgium and the Netherlands. And then one from Paris in 1947. *George and I married yesterday. I wish all of you were with us, but rest assured I am very happy and confident this is God's plan for both of us.*

I put my hand to my heart and sighed. I flipped the page, but we'd come to the end of the scrapbook. I picked it up and held it against my chest.

"So, what did you learn from Martha's story?" Johann asked.

"That we can't assume we know someone's story, or even who they really are." I put the scrapbook back on the shelf and then sat back down on the sofa. "And we should always live our values but also use our imaginations. I think of the COs taking the photographs in the mental hospital. Their imaginations helped solve a horrible problem. And I think of Martha imagining the possibility of going to Europe to work for the Red Cross, even though she didn't think it could happen."

Johann turned sideways toward me. "You used your imagination with Rylan."

I shook my head. "I really didn't."

"You did. You included him. You encouraged Viktor, Marko, and Gabe to keep investing in his life. You encouraged him to go to therapy and get better—and you modeled that too."

"I'll have to think about that. . . ." I shifted so I faced Johann. "Back to Martha," I said. "She imagined a new landscape for her life. I like the idea of that."

The blue of his eyes deepened as he reached for my hand. "Last night you said you planned to find a job this summer. Do you have any other plans besides that?"

"I think a trip to Ukraine *is* a good idea. Maybe an extended trip," I said. "God—and my mental health—willing." My hand grew warm in Johann's.

"What made you change your mind?" he asked.

"Well, you," I replied. "I decided I don't want to miss out on my life. I need to take more risks. Going to Ukraine"—*and getting to know you better*—"is going to be my first."

He leaned toward me, and our mouths met. For a moment, I felt awkward as he kissed me. But then I closed my eyes and kissed him back. Euphoria wasn't anything I'd ever felt—until now. He let go of my hand and pulled me close as we continued to kiss. For a moment, it felt as if I was nowhere and everywhere all at once. My heart pounded, but not in a panicked way.

Until I heard a noise in the kitchen. I opened my eyes and pulled away. Johann's eyes grew large. I stifled a laugh, and then we laughed together as we headed toward the front door and out of the house.

Rosene had been correct. Martha's story had been right for me. I *was* ready for a new beginning too. I didn't want to let time pass me by.

Before I left, Ivy made me a collage of photos of Mom and Dad to bring along. I was grateful for it, but I didn't need it. Every hill and dale of my life included Mom and Dad, even the ones

I'd traveled since they'd died. My memories were part of who I was—those memories were evidence of my parents' love.

Time had changed me. Johann's care had changed me. God had changed me.

When I arrived in Kyiv, I stepped into Johann's arms. Into an entirely new world. For the time, at least, I was home.

Author Note

We sometimes think of nonresistant Plain communities as being isolated from the world, but they're not. This was especially true during World War II.

One of the main ways communities were impacted by the war was the requirement for young men to register for the draft. Of the 34,506,923 men in the US who registered, 72,354 applied for conscientious objector status. A little over half of those ended up serving with the Civilian Public Service program. According to the NPR article titled "WWII Pacifists Exposed Mental Ward Horrors" (December 30, 2009),

> Ten million men were drafted into the military during World War II. But more than 40,000 refused to go to war. These conscientious objectors came from more than 100 religions. But most were from the traditional peace churches: people from the Church of the Brethren, Mennonites and Quakers. Still, they wanted to serve their country. Many did serve in the military in noncombatant roles. Others did alternative service, like the 3,000 who were assigned to 62 state mental hospitals around the country.

The experiences of Jeremiah Zimmerman are based on conscientious objectors who worked at the Philadelphia State Hospital, known as Byberry. The men, Quakers and Mennonites, took photos of the horrors of the hospital and gave them to journalists, which eventually led to reform in mental hospitals around the United States.

After the war, groups of Plain men also started mental health programs across the country for Plain people. In my story, Brenna receives mental health care at a fictional facility, Edenville, that her great-grandfather Jeremiah helped establish. In real life, Philhaven—a mental health facility with outpatient and community education (now called WellSpan Philhaven)—was established in Lancaster County in 1952 by World War II conscientious objectors to provide high-quality mental health services in a Christian environment.

Besides dealing with the service of their young men and adhering to rationing and other wartime programs, Mennonite farmers in Lancaster County were able to use the labor of Axis POWs from nearby camps. Over 400,000 POWs— mostly German—ended up being incarcerated in the United States from 1943 to 1946. They worked in mills, canneries, factories, and on farms. The treatment of the POWs was mandated by the Geneva Convention, and the Red Cross was used to determine that the captives were treated with dignity and care.

Although rare, over two thousand POWs attempted escapes. Most were quickly found. Even rarer was that US soldiers sympathetic to the Nazis but working in the camps helped POWs escape, but it did happen. Incorporating that scenario into Dirk and Sergeant Schwarz's relationship made the home-front stakes during World War II become more real to me, and I hope it did for readers too.

The common thread in both the historical and contemporary threads, besides the Zimmerman and Simons families, are those who served during wartime in both stories. All are affected in some way by their service, and both good and bad comes from those experiences, which also impacts the Plain families that have connections with the soldiers.

A few of the books that I used in my research for *This Passing Hour* are: *Prisoner of War Camps Across America* by Kathy Kirkpatrick; *Something Like Treason: Disloyal American Soldiers & the Plot to Bring World War II Home* by William Sonn; *Nazi Prisoners of War in America* by Arnold Krammer; *Enemies in Love* by Alexis Clark; *European Mennonites and the Holocaust* by Marko Jantzen and John D. Thiesen; *Nazis of Copley Square: The Forgotten Story of the Christian Front* by Charles R. Gallagher; *Hitler's*

American Friends: The Third Reich's Supporters in the United States by Bradley W. Hart; *The CPS Story: An Illustrated History of Civilian Public Service* by Albert N. Keim; and *Souvenirs from Kyiv* by Chrystyna Lucyk-Berger.

I couldn't write my stories without help! A big thank-you to Marietta Couch for sharing her knowledge about the Plain way of life and for graciously reading my manuscripts for accuracy. (Any mistakes are mine.) I'm also very grateful to my husband, Peter, for his help with military and medical scenes in this story (again, any mistakes are mine). A sweet thank-you to my four grown children, too, for their ongoing support.

I'm also very thankful for my three siblings— Kathy, Kelvin, and Laurie. Their love and support throughout my life has been sustaining and constant and something I don't take for granted, and the fact that they read and share my books and cheer me on is a double blessing.

A big thank-you to my agent, Natasha Kern, for her encouragement, and also to my editors— Jennifer Veilleux and Rochelle Gloege—for their incredible ideas that improve my stories through each step of the process. I'm also indebted to the entire staff at Bethany House, who make my books shine.

Finally, I'm grateful to and for my readers! Thank you for reading and sharing my stories!

Leslie Gould is the #1 bestselling and award-winning author of over forty novels, including the SISTERS OF LANCASTER COUNTY series and the PLAIN PATTERNS series. She holds a bachelor's degree in history and an MFA in creative writing. Leslie enjoys research trips, church history, and hiking, especially in the beautiful state of Oregon, where she lives. She and her husband, Peter, have four adult children and two grandchildren.

Center Point Large Print
600 Brooks Road / PO Box 1
Thorndike, ME 04986-0001 USA

(207) 568-3717

US & Canada:
1 800 929-9108
www.centerpointlargeprint.com